Philip D Whitehead was born in London in 1937, but lived the first two-thirds of his life in the north-west of England, and the most recent third in South Wales.

Changing careers every few years, he has worked in a bank, as a salesman, and in textile engineering. He has been a sailor, a specialist nurse and a tutor in higher education – which he enjoyed best of all.

His interests include politics, travel and walking the Neath Valley and the Samaria Gorge.

He lives in South-West Wales with his wife and his labrador dog. His daughter, son and grandchildren live nearby.

THE
UPRISING

Philip D. Whitehead

The Uprising

Vanguard Press

A CIP catalogue record for this title is
available from the British Library
ISBN 1 843860 05 8

*Vanguard Press is an imprint of
Pegasus Elliot MacKenzie Publishers Ltd.*
www.pegasuspublishers.com

First Published in 2002

**Vanguard Press
Sheraton House Castle Park
Cambridge England**

Printed & Bound in Great Britain

Dedication

In remembrance of

Neil Clements	1944 – 2001
Margaret Battersby	1936 – 2001
Jack Pickford	1942 – 2001

To Judy,

in celebration of
our friendship

Philip Whitehead

Acknowledgements

All direct biblical quotations are taken from The Holy Bible, New International Version, published by Hodder and Stoughton in 1973 et seq.

Several prayers are taken from:
Siddur Avodat Israel, published by Sinai Publishing, Tel Aviv, Israel; Passover Hagadah, published by Hebrew Publishing Company, New York, USA in 1921; The Dead Sea Scrolls, translated by Geza Vermes, published by Allen Lane, The Penguin Press in 1997.

The Celtic verses in chapter 4 are from a translation by Caitlin Matthews.

The Secret Words of Joshua (chapter 23), are taken from The Gospel According to Thomas, part of the library discovered at Nag Hamadi in Upper Egypt in 1945. The 114 'sayings of Jesus' were written Coptic. I have used the translation by A. Guillaumont, H-Ch. Puech, G. Quispel, W. Till, and Yassah 'Abd al Masih, published by Collins in 1959. The publication was rendered into the English of the Authorised Version of the Bible; I have updated the English.

There are no other quotations from any published work.

THE UPRISING

Jerusalem 30 – 31 CE

DRAMATIS PERSONAE

*Denotes historical/biblical character.

ANANIAS*	A Cypriot Jew
ANNAS*	Ex-High Priest of Israel, father-in-law of Caiaphas (q.v.)
AULUS PLAUTIUS*	Tribune in command of the Jerusalem garrison
AVRAM	A young zealot crucified with Joshua (q.v.)
BRANWEN	A British lawyer, slave of Aulus Plautius (q.v.), wife of Mordra (q.v.)
CAIAPHAS*	High Priest of Israel
CLEOPAS*	A Cretan Jew
CORNELIUS*	A centurion
DYDIMOS JUDAH*	A disciple of Joshua (q.v.), also known as Thomas
ETHIOPIAN EUNUCH*	An unnamed official
GALBA	The senior centurion of the Jerusalem garrison
GAMALIEL*	The foremost rabbi, a member of the Sanhedrin
JACOB*	A disciple of Joshua (q.v.), also known as James
JOSEPH	A scribe
JOSEPH*	A Cypriot Jew, also known as Barnabas
JOSHUA BAR ABBAS*	A hill bandit
JOSHUA BEN JOSEPH OF NAZARETH*	A poliltical and religious leader, also known as Jesus
JUDAH BEN EPHRAIM*	A disciple of Joshua (q.v.), a sicariot

	(dagger man), also known as Judas
LUCIUS	A Roman philosopher
MARCUS*	Infant son of Lucius (q.v.)
MARIUS	Legate in command of the Tenth Fretensis Legion
MIRIAM*	An orphan from Magdala, servant of Caiaphas (q.v.), mistress of Aulus (q.v.), also known as Mary Magdalene
MORDRA A	Gaulish historian, slave of Aulus (q.v.), Husband of Branwen (q.v.)
NAHUM	A zealot crucified with Joshua (q.v.)
NIKOLAOS*	A Jew from Tarsus in Cilicia, student of Gamaliel (q.v.)
PAULINA	Wife of Lucius (q.v.)
PONTIUS PILATE*	Procurator of Judaea
SAMUEL	A priest
SAPPHIRA*	Wife of Ananias (q.v.)
SAUL*	A Jew from Tarsus in Cilicia, student of Gamaliel (q.v.), also known as Paul
SIMEON BAR JONAS*	A disciple of Joshua (q.v.), also known as Peter
SIMEON	A Galilean, companion of Cleopas (q.v.)
SIMON 'THE LEPER'*	A priest of Bethany
STEFANOS*	A follower of Joshua, also known as Stephen
TIMOCRATES	A centurion

N.B. Aulus Plautius was Governor of Pannonia, and later conqueror of Britain in 43 CE.
There is no historical evidence to suggest that he was ever in Judaea.
The two men crucified with Joshua/Jesus have been given names.

According to the Gospel of Luke (XXIV – xviii), one of the two men on the road to Emmaus was Cleopas; the other man is not named in the Gospel.

Chapter 1

Aulus was in a foul mood.

As he ran up the steps to the Antonia fortress the afternoon spring sun was hot on his back, adding to his discomfort.

The two soldiers guarding the door snapped off a smart salute, he acknowledged it with a curt nod.

He stomped into the entrance hall of his modest private apartment, hobnails clattering on the heavy paving stones, and flung his crested helmet into a corner.

"Mordra!" he bellowed in his best parade ground voice, and there was no reply.

Aulus was angry.

He was hot and thirsty, grimed with dust and soot. He could still smell the stench of fire, of sweat, and of death.

"Mordra!" he yelled again, removing his sword that was not yet properly cleaned, unlacing his cuirass, and dropping them to the floor. Still no reply.

Discomfort was nothing. Blood and death were a soldier's trade. What annoyed Aulus were the futility, the waste, and the sheer stupidity of the whole exercise. When would the natives learn that the Empire was here to stay and that it was their only hope of stability, peace and prosperity? It was the *Pax Romana* – the Roman peace, and it was the job of Aulus, the soldier, to maintain that peace, by whatever means seemed appropriate to him.

He did not yet know how many men he had lost all together on the three separate sites where battle had raged, perhaps a couple of dozen or so. That was not the point. The point was the pointlessness of a bunch of disorganised terrorists, who usually spent much of their time fighting among themselves, thinking that they could attack the most highly organised and disciplined army the world had ever seen. They should stick to praying to

19

their invisible god, it would do as much, or as little good and be less trouble.

"Mordra," he bellowed once more, "bring me some..."

"Wine, sir?"

The man who entered was tall and muscular with straw blond hair and amused brown eyes. He carried a tray bearing two flagons, one of water the other of rough local wine, and earthenware cups.

"Of course wine," Aulus snarled, "and plenty of it. Why all the cups?"

"Never trust the natives, sir. It would be safer if it were tasted before you drink – and we are expecting a guest."

The thought of the 'guest' irritated Aulus still more. He could handle this affair perfectly well without the help of a civilian tax-gatherer. Neither was he in the mood to show his amusement at his slave's excuse for drinking his master's wine. "Poison is a Roman method, and a patrician one. The natives prefer a knife between the ribs, they lack our subtlety. Never mind, taste it then, but be quick." As Aulus picked up the flagon of water and drained it to slake his burning throat, Mordra poured himself a generous measure of wine and downed it in a single draught. Aulus raised an eyebrow smiling slightly despite himself, "Still alive?"

"I feel all right."

"Never trust a Gaul either. Pour me a cup, if you are sure it's safe."

Mordra dispensed the wine. The soldier drank it down and held out the cup for a refill. He then went to a bowl of water supported on a tripod stand and sluiced his head and arms. Mordra stood by with a towel. Vigorously Aulus rubbed his face, hair, hands and arms. Mordra cleared his throat; "The senior centurion is waiting to report. Do you want to see him now?"

"Yes, send him in."

Aulus picked up his wine and sprawled in a chair. The slave picked up the bowl of dirty water and went to summon the centurion.

Galba came to attention before his commanding officer. He was the *Primus Pilus,* the senior centurion of the first cohort; he

20

had just fought a successful engagement against the bandits, but he looked as if he had strolled off a parade ground. Aulus, despite his rudimentary ablutions, was still conscious of his filth. Galba, he knew, would have washed, carefully dried, and oiled his *gladius* – the short stabbing sword of a Roman soldier, to save it from rust before it was sheathed. As always in the presence of his commanding officer, he had abandoned his vine stick, one of the marks of rank, used to emphasise disciplinary points with the legionaries and auxiliaries. The tribune looked at the veteran soldier from head to toe. Galba had unlaced the cheek pieces of his helmet, which was brilliantly polished. The goose feather crest from earpiece to earpiece, to identify a centurion in battle, was, as ever, immaculate. Over his mail coat were the circes and figured medallions that had been awarded after so many past fights. The sheathed sword was on the left, the dagger on the right; the opposite way about to those carried by the legionaries – all Roman soldiers fought with the short sword, stabbing low, in their right hand. Aulus glanced down to the still bloodied greaves and hobnailed sandals, which would soon come under the attention of a slave and, not for the first time, marvelled at this epitome of a soldier who he was fortunate to have as his second-in-command.

"For the gods' sake, Galba, sit down," was Aulus's response to the military correctness, "take that metal off your head and pour yourself a drink."

The centurion complied gladly, but still with the stiffness of the old soldier.

"Right," Aulus started when they had both taken deep draughts of the too sweet local wine; "Things seemed to be under control before I left you. I think we had them broken before I had to go off to the south-east corner."

Galba refilled the tribune's cup, then his own. "We had no trouble at all, sir. After you left it was only mopping up and killing off their wounded."

"Casualties?"

"Light. Two dead, five serious injuries, one of them is not expected to live. About twenty minor injuries, but all fit for duties."

Aulus glanced at the bloodstained rag around the centurion's

21

upper arm and nodded. "Not much of a butcher's bill, I was not so lucky. But a similar story to yours from the citadel. I went there after the fight at Siloam and had to wade through bandit bodies before I could get to see Timocrates. It cost him only a few men to wipe out all the bandits and catch the ringleader. I also brought the head bandit, only a bit of a boy, from Siloam. Did you manage to pick up the ringleader here?"

Galba smiled and reached for the flagon. The battle, such as it was, had been a simple task. He was pleased with himself for having identified the ringleader in the melee and for detailing a decade of men to take him alive. "There was just one, a real wild man called Joshua, we have him all safe and tightly bound."

"Intact?"

"Reasonably. He'll live – until he dies."

"Well done, Galba. The one that I brought back from the citadel only has a leg wound, and the kid from Siloam is also reasonably intact, just a bit scorched."

"I saw the smoke, used fire did you, sir?"

"Yes, I had to. I gave you the easier job. After I left here we had literally to cut our way through the mob, especially around the temple. Anyway, when we got to the south-east corner we found that they'd taken over that part of the city wall and the tower of Siloam. They were quite well armed and very well prepared. It was obviously intended as their line of retreat. They had a good supply of rocks to throw down on us as well as slings, spears and arrows. As you know it's a bit cramped in that corner, and the natives were in every door, window and alley. Altogether I lost eighteen men, and as many wounded. The wall wasn't too bad, but I had to set a fire at the base of the tower. That brought them out, those who chose not to fry. Unfortunately the tower collapsed with my men at the base of it, that's where we had the most casualties."

Galba refilled Aulus's cup, then his own, "Not a bad day's work then sir."

Aulus took a drink, "Not bad." He paused a moment, then, "Apart from that business in the temple at the start of this week."

"Leave well alone, sir, if I may say so. If the natives want to have a go at each other in their own holy house, let them get on with it I say. Anyway, they were only arguing, and you know

22

how they love doing that, and how noisy they can be about it. Apart from upsetting a few market stalls, there wasn't any actual fighting."

"No," Aulus agreed thoughtfully, "but the temple is much more than just a holy house, and the man who took it over worries me." He roused himself, "What I really want to know is how they could bring what must have been over a thousand men into the city to launch a dawn attack. They were in about cohort strength both here and at Herod's castle, and they were more than a century at Siloam."

"Those who attacked the Antonia came in through the Damascus Gate just before dawn." Galba replied. "I've since discovered that the guards were killed, dagger wounds; it must have been soon after the change of the guard. I would imagine that the bandits assembled in the night on the hills above the city. Judging by their leader, I'm pretty sure that they're hill bandits rather than zealots."

At this point Mordra reappeared, carrying a bowl of fresh water that he placed carefully on the tripod stand. He stood back expectantly. Aulus, mellowing under the influence of the wine, looked up at him, "Yes, Mordra, what is it?"

"The prisoners, sir," the Gaul replied, "The procurator could arrive at any time. Do you want to question them before he gets here?"

Aulus was not pleased to be reminded, again, of the procurator's imminent arrival. He had little regard for civilian administrators, especially in a place like this, especially when they were so obviously his social inferiors.

"Any sign of him yet?"

"Not yet. But we have look outs on the Caesarea road," he glanced at Galba who had placed those look outs, "they'll let us know as soon as he comes into sight."

Aulus was not looking forward to hearing what he knew would be sermons from his prisoners. The natives could not separate religion from politics; their god soon made an appearance in all their pronouncements. But he had to have as much information as possible, by whatever means, which was why he had spared the lives of the ringleaders – for the present. He would have them nailed up as soon as possible but first they had to be interrogated, and he wanted to make a start before the upstart arrived from the provincial capital. "Very good, Mordra, present my compliments to the decurion of the guard and ask him to bring the prisoners to the lower court, I'll see them there."

Tribune and centurion made their way down to the lower court and sat back to take what pleasure they could from their confrontation with those who had dared to attempt an attack upon the invincible power of Rome.

The two soldiers, lounging and filling with wine, were pleased with themselves that they had taken the ringleaders of the abortive attacks. Galba had captured the man who had attacked the Antonia. Aulus had taken the youth who had commanded Siloam, then made his way to the other side of the city to relieve the Greek centurion, Timocrates, of the man who had assaulted Herod's citadel. They were both surprised to see four prisoners brought in under heavy guard.

The natives were a sorry sight. One had sustained burns, which were obviously painful. He and the rest had suffered either in the fight or subsequently, at the hands of the legionaries and auxiliaries. Aulus looked over the rim of his wine cup, "Four? I thought we only had three ringleaders."

Mordra, ever willing, helped out; "The High Priest has sent us another one. It seems that his 'friends' sold him out."

Aulus had to smile at the thought of the High Priest being so co-operative, "Good old Caiaphas. So we can now trust him to sell out his friends."

Mordra was almost indignant; "This one's no friend of the priests. He's the one who attacked their temple." The guard decurion handed his commanding officer a brief scroll. Aulus unrolled it and read. It was a note from the High Priest in his role as president of the Sanhedrin, the supreme civilian court, explaining that this man, Joshua ben Joseph of Nazareth, had been arrested and questioned on a possible charge of blasphemy. Aulus snorted, religious crimes were nothing to do with him. The note went on to say that the charge could not be sustained, but that the man was plainly guilty of other offences under Roman law. The tribune laid the scroll aside, "Is he, by Jove? So the rats are really biting each other. Any sign of the procurator yet?"

"Not yet," the Gaul replied, "I'll let you know as soon as he comes into view."

"Good," Aulus breathed, "I'd like to get this settled before he arrives."

The Gaulish slave padded out. He had replaced the flagon before he left.

Aulus poured more wine into his cup and leaned back in his chair, Galba copied him. The four prisoners glowered at their captors. Aulus took a leisurely drink and looked down his long nose at the terrorists, "Just what did you people think that you could achieve?"

The four returned his gaze, remaining silent. Aulus felt his anger rise, "We have ways of loosening tongues. I don't even mind if we loosen them so far that we rip them out, then your insolence would really be dumb. You must know that, with or without any confessions from you, you're already dead men. I'm going to execute the lot of you, but if you choose to tell me what I want to know you may be the only ones to die. If you stay silent I'll have to look further, perhaps to your friends, your families. How would you like to be nailed up with your mothers and fathers each side of you? Or do any of you have wives or sisters that I could give to my legionaries before they go to their crosses? Now, what was this rubbish all about?"

He surveyed the four bedraggled prisoners. Two were young, one perhaps in his mid twenties, another had probably not yet seen his twentieth birthday. Another, the wildest looking, seemed to be in his thirties. It was the fourth, the one who had attacked the temple and who had been delivered by the Sanhedrin, who captured Aulus's gaze; he found it difficult to look away from him. He may have been about forty years of age. Despite the beating that he had taken, there was an inner calm to the man. Aulus looked at him and felt misgivings. He dragged his gaze away.

Pointing a finger at the youngest prisoner, he said, "You attacked the south-east wall and the tower of Siloam."

The youngest prisoner had been unnerved by Aulus's threat to their families. He raised his scarred head, the hair and sparse beard nearly burned away. Still he was defiant: "I did not attack. I was defending Siloam. You Romans are the invaders, you have

25

attacked our Holy Land."

"Your name?" Galba barked the question.

"Avram."

"Where from?"

"Beth-yerah."

"How long with the bandits?"

"I have always been zealous for the Lord."

Aulus smiled a lupine smile. "So you were brought up to be a bandit?"

Too late, Avram saw the trap, "No! My parents did not approve of my joining the zealots. I had to leave home, I haven't seen my family for two years."

The tribune grinned, "Alright, we'll leave them out of it, for now. Who is your commander in the bandits?"

"I don't know his real name, we use code names."

"Then your name isn't really Avram?"

The youth did not reply. "It doesn't matter," Aulus went on, "We'll put 'Avram' on the tablet that we attach to your cross to publish your crime. Do you know these three men?"

The young man looked at the oldest prisoner who nodded slightly.

"Yes." Avram mumbled.

"And if they won't give me their names then you can do so?"

Again a glance at the older man, again a slight nod. This was going well. The Roman looked at the oldest prisoner, "And I think I now know who is your commander."

"No!" Avram cried, "Joshua is not a member of the zealots." He looked with hope at Joshua who smiled at him, seeming to transmit his strength to the young terrorist. Aulus picked up the scroll and used it to point to the man who was its subject, "So, Joshua ben Joseph of Nazareth, I think this boy's lying. I happen to know that a few days ago you made a triumphal entry into Jerusalem with a ragged band of followers. You went straight to the temple and took it over. You were holding the temple while your comrades attacked the fortress of the Antonia and the citadel, with this child guarding your line of retreat along the watercourse from the pool of Siloam to the spring of Gihon outside the city wall. I would say that you are the commander of

26

this whole bunch of bandits."

The man who had attacked the citadel spoke up; "Joshua took no part in the battle. He has never fought against anyone. Yes he went up to the temple; he visited it on three consecutive days and left it every night. When we launched our assaults he was already in the hands of the judges at the court of the Sanhedrin."

Again Galba barked, "Speak when you are spoken to. What's your name?"

"Nahum of Achzib."

The centurion turned to the prisoner who had attacked the Antonia, "And you?"

"Joshua."

"Another one?" Aulus sneered, "I suppose you're another northerner like the rest of them?" He looked at the prisoner's wild hair and beard, surprisingly fair in colour, his deep scowl and belligerent stance. "I have no home," the man replied, "I am Joshua bar Abbas, originally of Paphos." Aulus nodded, that accounted for the bandit's colouring, he was a Greek from Cyprus. He frowned slightly, "Abbas, what kind of a name is that? I know that Abba means father, whose son are you?"

The man tried to step forward and was restrained by the two soldiers holding him. "Bar Abbas is enough for you, Roman. I am the son of man, the son of my people."

Aulus gave a short laugh, "I bet you don't know which man. I can only assume that your mother was generous to 'your people'."

He turned his attention back to the man who, he had decided was the overall leader; "I can believe this Nahum when he says that you have never done any actual fighting. Generals have other men to do the killing for them. But what was the mob doing the other day, kicking up a fuss and chanting to welcome you into the city? That alone marks you down as their leader. I've met a lot of fanatics since I came to this god-forsaken hole, but you lot must be the worst yet. What made you think that you could make any impression on Roman strongpoints?"

Joshua of Nazareth's eyes bored into the Roman's but he spoke calmly, gently. "Perhaps because your heathen gods have forsaken you, but our God will never forsake his people Israel."

27

Aulus felt his anger and his contempt rising, "More religious clap-trap. And I'll thank you not to call *me* the heathen. Even you must have known that what you were attempting was impossible."

Aulus was surprised when Joshua replied in perfect Greek, "Probable impossibilities are to be preferred to improbable possibilities."

It was not just the switch in language; it was what the man had said. Aulus found himself back in the schoolroom, bored under the Samnian sun, his seemingly ancient tutor droning on about the wisdom of Greece. With an effort he recovered, "What's this, the savage can quote philosophy? Tell me, philosopher, can Aristotle drive enough sense into your thick head to make you accept Rome?"

The man was calm, much too calm; "I'm not talking about your Roman Empire."

"Aren't you?" Aulus struggled to regain control of this exchange. "I think you are. Anyway, it's the only Empire there is." He had a sudden thought. He too switched from the Latin in which he was conducting the interrogation, back to Greek; "Do you also believe that man is by nature a political animal?"

The prisoner smiled, actually smiled. "Living in human society is, in itself, a political act. And we do not recognise the authority of Rome in the Holy Land of Israel."

"I don't care whether you recognise it or not, it's here and here to stay. I hope you know that you have just said enough to guarantee your crucifixion even if you never did kill anyone."

Before Joshua of Nazareth could reply, Mordra came in to tell his master that the procurator was approaching on the Caesarea road.

"Right," Aulus was brisk, "get rid of this scum." He addressed the decurion of the guard, "Bind them together and take them with a strong escort to the praetorium. The auxiliaries can have some fun with them but I want them alive and conscious, I want them to be wide awake when the nails go in. It's getting a bit late in the day now, but I'll have them on their crosses first thing in the morning."

Galba, knowing that tribune and procurator would prefer to talk privately and knowing not to outstay his welcome, stood and announced that he would go with the prisoners and find out how those who had attacked the citadel had entered the city and assembled during the night. Aulus appreciated the centurion's sense of propriety and was ever grateful for his strong support. Despite the relaxation of some of the more rigid social rules here in this remote outpost, both men knew where the line was drawn between them and neither ever stepped over it. The tribune nodded at his second in command. "I want a body count of the terrorist dead. And a maniple to form patrols of a decade each to round up any survivors and keep the natives quiet; let them break a few heads if they want to, but tell them to keep their swords sheathed unless absolutely necessary." Galba's clenched fist thumped into the medallions on his breast in salute and acknowledgement of the order.

Mordra checked that the water in the bowl was still clean, and made to remove the cup that Galba had used. The commander interrupted him, "Pour me some wine." The flagon was at Aulus's elbow, Mordra knew that this was a signal that he was expected to stay. As he refilled the cup Aulus nodded towards the tray, another signal. Mordra poured wine for himself. Aulus said: "I suppose your ears were flapping during all that."

The Gaul's expression did not change. "Perhaps you will need another witness."

Aulus gave a short laugh. "We are dealing with terrorists. I am more than witness enough, we don't need all the niceties of Julian law for this situation."

Mordra waited for his master to get around to the questions that he knew would come. A patrician must not appear to be too dependent upon a slave; on the other hand a military officer must gain information from any and all sources.

In the ten years that Mordra had been in Aulus's service the aristocratic Roman rarely admitted, even to himself, how dependent he was upon his orderly. Occasionally he would realise that the Gaul, who had shaved his moustache and cut his straw-blond hair in the Roman style, did have the talent for making his life smoother and more comfortable than that of some of his fellow officers.

Aulus had come to rely upon Mordra's growing

understanding of the ways of the natives, and the Gaul soon learned that he had been fortunate in that his master gave him considerable freedom to pursue his interests in history and the odd ways of different peoples.

They had now been four years in the province of Judaea. Roman rule began in earnest when the ten-year rule of Archalaus, Ethnarch of Judaea, Samaria and Idumaea, ended with his exile and death. Augustus had appointed Archalaus's brother, Herod Antipas, as Tetrarch of the troublesome regions of Galilea and Peraea, and Herod Philippos as ruler of the northern territories east of the Jordan. He had sent Coponius to Judaea as Procurator – the agent of the Emperor with plenipotentiary powers.

The first three procurators, Coponius, Amvivilus and Rufus, had each served three years in the province. Then, in Rufus's final year, Augustus had died and had been succeeded by his stepson Tiberius. The new Emperor had a different policy regarding his procurators and his first appointment in Judaea, Gratus, had sweated it out in Caesarea, the provincial capital on the coast, for eleven years.

The present procurator, Pontius Pilate, had been in post for four years. Aulus had come to Judaea in the train of Pilate, and had been appointed to command the cohort of 480 legionaries and two centuries of auxiliaries who made up the 640 men of the Jerusalem garrison.

At first Mordra had looked down upon the natives in the same way that his Roman masters did. However his duties brought him into close day to day contact with them and he began to take an interest in their ways. He soon became fluent in Aramaic, the language of their everyday communication, and in Hebrew in which they conducted their religious and legal affairs. He delved into their long history, which covered two thousand years. He studied their unique religion with its single god. He quickly became an authority on native matters, to his own pleasure and making him more valuable to Aulus who frequently consulted his slave on the strange thinking and culture of the often turbulent Jews.

It occurred to neither that Aulus should invite Mordra to sit while he sipped his wine and gave his master the benefit of his local knowledge. The soldier opened by referring to the man who had attempted to attack the Roman headquarters of the Antonia fortress, "What do you make of that 'son of father, son of man, son of people' rubbish?"

This was an easy one to answer; "In Aramaic 'bar Abbas' can mean all three of those. It's probably a political statement meaning either that he represents his people or he represents mankind. You know how the zealots like to pick colourful names for themselves. You will recall that one of their founders called himself Maccabeus – 'the hammer'."

Aulus was not impressed, "I prefer to take it that he doesn't know who his father was."

"If that's the case, he's not really a Jew."

"Why not?"

"Because a bastard can't be a member of their religious congregation. Although theirs is a patriarchal society, a Jew is the son of a Jewish mother; he is not a Jew if only his father is a Jew. However, if a man does not know his father then it is assumed that the mother may have consorted with a Gentile, and they do not accept him."

"Never?"

"Never. They stick to this one, although some of their rules can be flexible, or open to interpretation. A man whose genitals have been damaged can't enter the 'congregation of the lord', but they all have damaged genitals because, as you know, they chop the foreskins off their baby boys."

Aulus laughed, then frowned, "I hope that 'bar Abbas' is a political statement. If he's not a real Jew then he's of less use to us. I prefer to crucify only proper Jews to encourage the rest of them to stop playing idiotic games."

Mordra began to feel that he could afford to indulge himself a little, "They're strange people. As you know, my grandfather fought against Julius. We Gauls had a developed civilisation before the Romans came, and we tried to protect it against what we then saw as a foreign invader. Vercingetorix uttered his cockcrow, and his fighting cocks would rather burn Avaricum than let it fall into Roman hands." He could not resist the temptation to slip in a little of the Gallic version of his people's recent history. "But after the siege of Alesia, even Vercingetorix

31

realised who was master of the world. He prostrated himself before Julius, and laid his arms at the feet of the man who had conquered Gaul. That was more than eighty years ago. What I remember of the Gaul of my childhood" Mordra employed the diplomatic lie, "was the order and the security of the Roman peace, and I knew that it was far better than my grandfather's Gaul where the tribes were forever fighting each other, as the Jewish sects do here. I don't think we'll ever fully understand the Jews. And I'm sure that they will never accept the rule of anyone but their messiah, and they'll almost certainly disagree if he ever comes along, want to examine his credentials – then reject him."

Aulus sighed, "I've heard enough about their messiah. What is it that he's supposed to do? Isn't it that their god will send a deliverer who will solve all their problems and, of course, get rid of the Romans?"

"That's it." Mordra replied, "From what I've read, I think that they've had such people in their past. There was a man called Moses who created their nation out of a rabble of slaves escaping from Egypt. This was a long time ago, well over a thousand years, Moses and his brother Aaron, together with a soldier called Joshua gave them social structure, the rule of law, and this land."

Mordra had always wanted to be a teacher. He was warming to his dissertation. "Then there was a time when they were subjected by the Philistines and a man called Samuel realised that they needed to unite their then divided nation under one king." The Gaul could not but think that this had something in common with the aspirations of Vercingetorix. "Samuel anointed a man called Saul as the first king of Israel. Their kings were priest kings and 'messiah' means 'anointed one'. Saul didn't manage to overcome the Philistines so Samuel anointed his successor, David, and eventually the Philistines were beaten. Then they first became Jews when Nebuchadnezzar… "

Aulus had had enough; "All this is ancient history. So they have these messiahs cropping up from time to time. Do you think that this 'son of my people, son of man' bandit could see himself as the latest one?"

"Possibly. It's an epithet that a messiah, or a pretender to the title, might use."

"Tell me," said Aulus, "The Jews only have one god, but

surely if this messiah is sent by that god for a special purpose then surely they must see him as a god, or at least a demigod?"

"Oh, definitely not! – '*Shema Yisroel, Adonai Elohenu, Adonai Ehad'*."

"Now, I've heard that before, but you know my Aramaic is weak."

"That isn't Aramaic, it's Hebrew. Much too religious for their everyday language. It means, 'Hear, Oh Israel, the Lord is our God, the Lord is One'. Whoever or whatever this messiah may be he cannot be divine. The Jews have only one god, invisible, nameless, all-powerful, totally mysterious, but *one*. He cannot be challenged, or rivalled, or divided. I don't fully understand the concept of the messiah, I only know that he can be no more than a man, although a very special man. Looking at those four sorry objects who you've sent to the praetorium, it's difficult to imagine any of them in such a role."

Without fully knowing why, Aulus felt lightened by his orderly's explanation. He laughed, "There are times when I thank all the gods for your Gallic reason. It helps to keep me down to earth in this place with its invisible gods and divine deliverers who aren't divine, and which is a seething political cauldron where all the natives fight among themselves and only agree on a single point – their inability to accept Rome."

Then the Procurator arrived.

Chapter 2

Pontius Pilate was an impatient man, although four years in Judaea and the prospect of as long again, or twice as long, to remain in the province had taught him to move more slowly, for himself as well as for the Emperor.

Tall, bald, thin and gaunt, his high cheekbones and occasional humourless smile gave him a cadaverous appearance. His deep-set eyes either darted about or could fix the person at whom he was talking with a penetrating stare.

His impatience with, and intolerance of, any opinion different from his own arose from his absolute certainty that the Roman Empire was the most civilising influence the world had ever known (although he knew nothing of the history of the world), and that any Roman was inherently superior to anyone else. He also believed that the force that kept the Empire going was its organisation in the hands of professional administrators, and that all other aspects of society – the army, the world-wide trading network, the very social structure only helped to maintain the order that was Rome.

The forty one-year rule of Augustus had seen massive reorganisation in metropolitan Rome and throughout the Empire. One of the many reforms of Augustus (who had now been dead for sixteen years) was to take the financing of the army away from the *aerarium,* the public treasury and set up a separate *fiscus* or fund, which became the *aerarium militare.*

Pontius Pilate had begun his career in the aerarium militare and so had intimate knowledge of the costs of maintaining each of the twenty-eight legions, and almost as many auxiliaries that made up the army of Rome. Much of the income was derived from sales taxes, and from time to time the army's coffers would receive a major boost from prizes of war. The expenditure was massive. Pay and occasional donatives for up to a quarter of a million men, retirement bonuses for every legionary who survived his twenty-year term, each auxiliary after twenty-five years, as well as marines after twenty-eight years and praetorians at the end of their sixteen-year service. This was before the cost of equipping and supporting the worldwide army. As a young man Pilate had attempted to reform the way in which the sharing of booty was organised. He wanted proper accounting and sharing, with a substantial proportion returning to the aerarium militare. The fact that he made absolutely no headway with this plan was because he had never seen soldiers sacking a conquered town, or stripping a countryside, or searching the clothing of the dead on a battlefield. Each century of eighty men tended to share much of the loot among those that survived, but the chaos of war was far from Pilate's well-ordered life as an accountant. Despite the failure of his scheme, Pilate's work was recognised and he was promoted to the post of assistant procurator – revenue official.

Because of the recalcitrant problems of raising revenue in Judaea, and the reluctance of the Jews to pay Roman taxes, he had been sent as procurator of the province four years earlier. A procurator was nominally in charge of the army in his area of influence and this sat badly with Marius, the experienced Legate of the Tenth Fretensis Legion. The professional officers of the legion not only resented his attempts at interfering in military matters; they despised his lowly origins. Although he was now an *equus,* a knight, and was entitled to be addressed as *Praefectus* by virtue of the post that he occupied, he was lacking in pedigree and the aristocratic officers wished that he would keep in his place and let them get on with what they knew best – maintaining order in this hell-hole.

The last place that Pilate wanted to be during a Jewish festival was Jerusalem. Had he been able to remain in Caesarea he could have continued to enjoy the gentle sea breezes in a more sophisticated setting, and would have been far way from the stink of this overcrowded city and the din of Jewish religious fanaticism.

Now the natives had been causing trouble again, and he could not trust the garrison commander not to take all the credit.

Records had to be kept, reports had to be written, and the procurator was determined that it would be his version of the events, from one with overall control of the province, that would reach the Emperor on Capri and those who held the power in Rome. Such people would prefer the version of one of their own class to that of a hard working public servant and so he must take control of this situation, now.

He had been forced to undertake the dusty journey from the relatively pleasant coastal plain, climbing high into the Judaean hills. To make matters worse he had been burdened with the company of a wandering upper-class scholar, Marcus Lucius, whose head was permanently in the clouds and with whom he had absolutely nothing in common. This young man had been a week in Caesarea, serving no useful purpose as far as Pilate could see. Upon hearing of the trouble in Jerusalem he had intimated that the city was his destination and he more-or-less insisted that he go along. Pilate dearly wanted to refuse the request, but he knew that Lucius was well connected in the upper strata of Roman society.

The procurator stamped into the lower court without ceremony, Lucius trailing behind him. He was not surprised to see the garrison commander lounging in a chair, cup of wine in hand, deep in conversation with that damned Gaulish slave who seemed never to be out of his master's sight.

Aulus took in the fact that Pilate had donned military uniform, to which, from a soldier's point of view, he was not entitled, and rose, a little too slowly from his chair, "*Ave*, Hail, Praefectus."

"Ave, Aulus. Wine first, then a bath. This country gets dustier every day. Then you can tell me about this latest mess. I think you know young Lucius here."

Genuine delight lit up Aulus's face at the sight of the scholar. "Lucius! What brings you to this wilderness?"

Mordra quickly poured wine, which was quickly drunk, while the two patricians greeted each other like long-lost brothers. Although they were only distantly related, theirs was an almost brotherly relationship, and had been all their lives. As they grew to manhood they had followed very different paths but had maintained contact by the occasional letter and even rarer meeting. "You're not tired of your wife already are you?"

Lucius smiled, "No. It will be a long time before I tire of Paulina, but she does have another man in her life now."

"What?"

Lucius's smile broadened, "We have a son, Marcus."

"A son! That's marvellous. You didn't waste any time, I've only recently had news of your wedding."

"We were married long enough, just."

They laughed, embraced, and clapped each other on the back. Pilate champed, "If I could break up this old boy's reunion, my bath?"

Aulus glanced casually at the procurator, "I'm sorry, chief. Mordra, get a decade to escort the procurator to the hippodrome baths."

As the Gaul led Pilate out with studied ceremony, Lucius raised a quizzical eyebrow to his friend. Aulus chose to interpret it as a response to the fact that the procurator had to leave the security of the fortress in order to have a bath, although he knew that Lucius could not have missed the way in which he behaved towards the provincial governor. "I'm afraid we're a bit primitive here," he explained, "No proper baths in the Antonia, only a lavatorium. Do you want to bathe now, or will you wait till later?"

Lucius went to the bowl of water, "This will do fine for now. It's my throat that's the dustiest."

Aulus handed over the flagon, "You must think that I've forgotten all my manners, living among these savages."

Lucius took a deep draught, and did not look impressed with the vintage. "I'm afraid its only the local stuff," Aulus apologised, "tonight, when we've got rid of Pilate, I'll broach my secret stock of Italian wine. This stuff is good enough for him, and for laying the dust."

Again there was open contempt for the procurator of Judaea. Was it the man or the position, or both that Aulus objected to? Despite his background in the study of philosophy, notorious for its convoluted thinking, Lucius always believed the direct question to be the best, "What do you think of Pilate?"

A cloud of suspicion crossed Aulus's face but he kept the tone of his voice light, "Is that just curiosity, or are you on

37

somebody's errand?"

Lucius had seen the fleeting shadow, his laugh was a little uneasy, "Pure curiosity, I promise you. My reasons for being here are nothing but scholarly, my old obsessions with philosophy and religion I'm afraid."

Aulus was glad to get off the subject of the procurator, "I seem to remember you telling me that Pythagorus tried to reconcile religion and philosophy six hundred years ago, and that it ended in war between to two, and his death."

"That's true, but 'much learning does not teach sense' – that was said about Pythagorus."

"So you're still chasing lost gods and obscure ideas?"

"I am, but the more gods I find the more they all begin to look alike."

"I could have told you that. I suppose the Jewish god's a bit different but they're weird people."

"Oh, I prefer reason and rationality, argument and evidence to all the supernatural mysteries that people invent to surround and support their gods. But you are right, the Jews do have a rather interesting god and they use him as a direct inspiration and motivation for their laws and legal system. I want to explore the link between religion, which is superstition, and law, which is rational. I was starting to make some overtures to the Jews in Rome, but the Emperor has recently expelled them all. That's what I'm doing in Judaea. The fact that it gave me a chance to visit you is a bonus."

"Why did Tiberius throw the Jews out, not that I blame him, but Augustus gave them a lot of freedom, too much in my opinion?"

Lucius was pleased that he could relate some of the latest gossip, "It's not just the Jews, he's clamped down on all oriental cults. Now that a lot of people are losing faith in the gods they are searching around for something else to believe in, and two of those that they have chosen are the cult of Isis, picked up from Egyptian traders, and Judaism. Isis is very popular with the ladies; they love the romanticism of her searching for her lost husband Osiris. And I've heard of some interesting sexual practices, but that may be just rumour. You probably know Senator Saturnius."

Aulus nodded.

"And another senator, Decius Mundus."

Again the tribune nodded. Lucius went on, "Well, Saturnius's wife, Paulina (nothing to do with my Paulina, she has more sense), but the other Paulina joined the followers of Isis. Decius Mundus saw his chance and he came to her by night pretending to be Osiris, at least that's what Paulina claimed when their affair was discovered. Mundus took himself off to his country estate, nobody's seen Paulina, and Saturnius hasn't set foot in the senate since the scandal broke."

The two friends roared with laughter at his juicy bit of gossip. Wiping his eyes, Aulus said, "Well that takes care of the Egyptians. What about the Jews, have they been seducing senators' wives?"

"Oh, no," Lucius replied, "what they did was even worse because their victim was the Lady Fulvia of the imperial family."

"Not old Aunt Fulvia, who could fancy her?"

Lucius laughed again, "It wasn't sex, it was money. The old girl decided to start following the Jewish god. The Jews of Rome welcomed her with open arms – and promptly defrauded her of large quantities of gold and purple."

Again Aulus joined in the laughter; "Tiberius wouldn't like that. She must have one foot in the grave and her fortune should have come to him."

"That's right. He decided to rid Rome of all eastern cults before any more of his relatives were robbed. And before any more supposedly virtuous matrons were led astray."

Aulus was keenly aware that this was the first time in four years that he had been able to enjoy an easy conversation with a social equal. His only diversion was his mistress, Miriam, and he believed that to be a close secret. Forced to concentrate upon military and administrative matters, far from the hub of the world, the only person with whom he could have a half-decent conversation was his slave.

"You'll have to talk to my orderly, Mordra. He's made quite a study of the Jews, their history and religion; he has quite a few contacts among the natives. I suppose if I were to be looking for a religion, which I'm not, I could do worse than join my legionaries in their worship of Mithras. You know how they enjoy their mysteries and the whole secret society. It is also very useful for the army to have its own god, it fosters comradeship."

"I agree." said Lucius, "You know, the beauty of worshipping any of the Magi is that you can make them whatever you want, build your own religion to suit yourself. That and the secret ceremonies must make Mithraism very attractive."

For a hundred years the Persian Magus, Mithras had been a popular god with the Roman army, merchants, and those hoping for immorality. The Magi were anything from wise men, up through prophets, to minor deities.

Although Zoroastrianism claimed to be a monotheistic religion, the single god was in the form of twins, one representing truth and light, the other untruth and darkness. From this a number of demigods arose, among them was the sun god Mithras, whose titles included 'Saviour from Death', 'Victorious' and 'Warrior'. He had killed a cosmic bull, whose blood was the source of all animals and plants, symbolising the regeneration of life. Those initiated into the mysteries were baptised in a bath of sacrificial bull's blood and assured of eternal life.

Mithras had been born as a result of a union between heaven and earth. Lightning struck a rock and Mithras came forth in a cave, the miraculous birth being witnessed by shepherds.

Gathering a small group of disciples around him, he preached justice, goodness, immortality, and his own divinity. His teachings led him into conflict with the Persian authorities and, after partaking of a symbolic, thanksgiving meal of bread and wine, Mithras was arrested, tried, and executed by archers. Three days after his death he was restored to life, and ascended into heaven where he carried the sun on its daily journey across the sky.

Lucius and Aulus could laugh at such primitive beliefs. Even Aulus knew that many elements of the Mithraic legend could be found in the tales of other, older gods such as the Egyptian sun god Re and the Greek Apollo.

Lucius, who had studied on the island that is supposed to be the home of Apollo, preferred to give that deity his older name of Ilios.

Aulus had served in Germania where their sun god, Odin,

40

had also been impaled, in his case by being nailed to a tree at the year's lowest point of the turn of the *Yule,* the wheel of the seasons. After three days he had, miraculously, descended. The soldier had stood in the northern forests and seen the dying winter sun apparently impaled upon the bare branches of a tree. Both men could understand how simple minds created such myths.

Aulus thought that his friend might be amused to hear what he himself had recently heard. "Today I've been treated to a snatch of Greek philosophy, in this place oddly enough. After this bit of a disturbance we've had we rounded up the ringleaders. One of them was quoting Aristotle just before you arrived."

"What did he say?"

"Oh, that thing about possibilities and impossibilities. I can vaguely remember it from school, but you're the one who went to the academy."

"'Probable impossibilities are to be preferred to improbable possibilities' was that it?"

"Word for word. Then, and you'll be proud of me here, I countered with a bit more Aristotle. I asked him if he believed that man was, by nature, a political animal."

"And?"

"He gave me a very reasonable reply, as far as I can remember it sounded like Aristotelian sophism, and all in passable Greek."

Lucius was surprised to hear of such scholarship, superficial though it may be, in such a remote and backward place. He had assumed that the Jews were uninterested in any culture but their own. "You must have a higher class of terrorist here."

Aulus snorted, "A terrorist is a terrorist, even if he can quote a bit of Aristotle."

The commander began to feel guilty that he had doubted his oldest friend. He returned to an earlier question, "You wanted to know what I thought of the procurator."

Now Lucius was cautious, "He seems a bit dull to me. I haven't been long in Caesarea, but long enough to discover that he isn't the most scintillating company. The journey here was

41

unrelieved boredom, he has no sense of humour."

"What do you think of Caesarea?"

"I was pleasantly surprised. The place is really quite civilised." Lucius had known before he arrived that there were, in this region, ten cities built by the Greeks following the Alexandrian conquest, which were all in the classic pattern. He had not known that Caesarea had been constructed on similar, although Roman, lines. There were temples to Jupiter, Minerva, Diana and Mars, a theatre, a forum, stadium, gymnasium, and baths, and, as he intimated to his friend, quite a good social life.

"If it's a social life you're looking for then you've come to the wrong place," Aulus told him. "There's a forum here, and a theatre, a hippodrome and, of course, baths. The Jews will deign to walk in our forum but they won't set foot in the other places, especially the baths. They have their own baths that they call *mikveh* and, being Jewish baths, they are, of course, holy. We have a garrison of six hundred or so, and a few assorted Greek, Egyptian and Syrian civilians for our underused facilities. There are fifty thousand Jews resident in this city, and at the moment it's twice or three times that number because it's one of their festivals. You're right, Caesarea isn't at all bad, but Jerusalem has to be the most miserable city in the world."

Aulus wanted to get back to what he saw as the main topic. He had to talk to someone; it had been four years. Who better than the man with whom he had shared his boyhood? "You must have realised that our procurator is hardly patrician. Neither is he the brightest of men, he's a plodder. He has no imagination whatsoever, he's totally lacking in humour, he's utterly convinced that he's always right, there isn't a merciful bone in his body, and he detests the Jews even more than I do. In short, he's as near perfect as procurator of Judaea as it's possible to be. Four years ago Tiberius pointed him in this direction, set him in motion, and he's been busy ever since."

The vehemence made Lucius pause to think quickly. "So he could be a victim of his own success."

"How?"

"Well, he detests the Jews, he obviously hates the place, but if he's good at his job Tiberius won't be in a hurry to replace him."

Aulus looked at the scholar and shook his head. "My dear Lucius, if you spent less time on the slopes of Parnassus and came down to the real world more often you'd see how wrong you are there. Pontius will one day retire to a villa with that plain wife of his, but he will be here for a long time yet, and happy to remain. That fly hasn't grown fat enough yet. Have you ever wondered why Tiberius is so slow to replace his provincial administrators?"

Lucius sensed that they were now moving onto dangerous ground, but he trusted Aulus and he thirsted to know more about everything. "I always thought it was his natural indolence. He seems happy to let the senate run things, especially now that he's got Sejanus to rule Rome while he pursues his Athenian pleasures on Capri."

"Don't forget that Sejanus might once have been one of those Athenian pleasures." Aulus suspected, as did many who were close to the seat of power, that the emperor was, at least, bisexual and that Lucius Aelius Sejanus, prefect of the elite Praetorian Guard, had submitted to his Emperor's unnatural desires, but only to further his huge ambition. The man who was Tiberius's indispensable lieutenant had tried to marry Livilla, widow of Tiberius's only son Drusus who had died in mysterious circumstances. After permission for the marriage was refused, Sejanus imprisoned all rival candidates for the throne. He assumed the airs of an autocrat and had the audacity to ask for tribunician power as though he had been the heir designate. Although something of what was going on must have filtered through to him, Tiberius never made a sign. Aulus was confident that this state of affairs would not last long, "He's only waiting" he told Lucius, "Until the political moment is fully ripe, then Sejanus's life will be worth nothing. We're all sure that he killed Drusus, and Tiberius probably has proof. The way in which Tiberius deals with those he would destroy is slowly, ruthlessly, and thoroughly."

But this did not help Lucius to understand why a provincial governor should remain a long time in his post when the previous term, under the rule of Augustus, had been a mere three years. Aulus attempted to explain some of the intricacies of provincial government to his friend. "Our Divine Emperor seems to have found a simple political system that works very well. Everyone knows that all of these people are corrupt. Paying salaries is no safeguard against that, if a man is determined to dip his hand into the pot he will do so, and plebs like Pilate came from nothing and have no financial reserves to support them. They are out to make a fortune before they retire. Tiberius gives his procurators a good long spell in their province. That way they have plenty of time to line their purses. If he changed them more frequently they'd have less time to get rich, be greedier, and upset the natives. Result, civil unrest."

Aulus's sweeping generalisation was unfair. Another of the reforms of Augustus was to pay provincial procurators a salary, and this greatly reduced the amount of corruption. Neither did Aulus have any firm evidence that Pontius Pilate was helping himself to imperial funds. But he went on, "That's what I mean about the fly getting fat. Tiberius himself has a parable about a man who was attacked by thieves and left wounded and covered in flies at the roadside. A kind-hearted passer-by went to brush them off, as they were an obvious cause of discomfort. The wounded man told his would-be helper to leave the flies where they were. He said that if the already full flies were brushed away new, hungry flies would take their place and his suffering would be that much worse, it could even cause his death. So it is with a provincial procurator. Let him know that he will sit on his little dung heap for a long time and he will feed slowly, but still come away a wealthy man."

"So Tiberius rules by doing nothing?"

"By *appearing* to do nothing. He usually does something, but slowly. Do you know why the process of justice can be so slow in capital cases if the accused is a patrician or a scholar?"

Lucius knew something of the law, but he had to admit that he knew little of the ways in which it was administered. "I'd always assumed it was to ensure a just verdict."

"Ha! Don't you believe it. I'll tell you something, sitting out here on the edge of nowhere for the last four years has given me lots of time to think and to see things from a distance, it gives you a new perspective. Out here we tend to go for swift justice, it's what the natives understand best; those four I have prisoners in the praetorium will be dead tomorrow, or the day after, depending on how long they last on their crosses. But in Rome it can take ages, it drags out the agony. If the accused knows that he's guilty, or has reason to believe that he'll be found guilty even if he isn't, the longer he has to wait for a verdict the worse it is. Then, after a guilty verdict, he often has to wait again for execution, no quick release. Of course it doesn't work with plebeians, but to a thinking man it must mean dying a thousand times. I think that Tiberius is naturally lazy. He prefers a life of idleness on Capri, but he has turned his indolence into a political tool. Never underestimate Tiberius, never underestimate any Emperor. You and I know that they aren't really gods, and they know it too. It's only the lower orders that fall for that kind of mumbo-jumbo, they need it, it helps maintain the natural order so it's good for them to…"

"No," Lucius interrupted, "Of course they aren't really gods, there aren't any. But if people believe them to be gods then, through that corporate belief, they become divine. My studies have shown me that gods only exist in the belief of those who follow them. They reflect the particular society that they serve; men make their gods in their own image. The Roman gods are the gods of Roman society, and they serve the needs of Romans, it was the same with the Greeks. And don't forget that, apart from a few primitive Etruscan idols, we have no gods of our own. We took the Greek gods, changed their names, and adapted them to our society and its needs. At the moment the gods seem to be dying, we live in interesting times, that's why people are searching for something else and turning to Isis, and the Jewish god, and others. Sooner or later they'll invent one that answers their perceived needs and a new religion will be born. According to Julius the gods of Gaul were essentially Gaulish in their nature, but he tells us that you can see a transition from their old ideas and their native gods are merging with the Roman gods as civilisation reaches out to them. That's why I want to visit Ynys Prydain sometime. You've read *Gallic Wars*?"

Aulus nodded, Julius Caesar's self-congratulatory work was required reading for Roman officers. "I didn't know that you spoke British."

"I don't. All right, the Isle of Britain then if you prefer it, but they still call it Ynys Prydain. Anyway, Julius says that anyone who wants to make a study of European religion and the way that the Druids not only administer and guide religious life, but also maintain the theory and practice of the law should go to Britain to do so. I'd love to see a religion surviving in its pure form, everywhere else they are all getting mixed with each other."

Aulus was enjoying this; "I know nothing of Britain, only what I've read, and don't forget that Julius only really met one tribe, the Cantiaci, on his first punitive expedition. And a couple more tribes the second time he went – before he had to dash back to Gaul to deal with the uprisings there. But I don't think that you can talk about a European religion as a homogenous mass. They are not one people but many with a common culture; they share most of their gods and the Druids are the priests, scholars, and teachers, but each tribe has its own version of their religion. When I was in my first posting at Lutetia I was on the river that forms the border between the lands of the Lugdunensic Gauls, and the Belgae, two very different peoples. The Belgae are terrific fighters and we have a lot of them in the legions. All the Gauls can fight like madmen, don't forget that they sacked Rome four hundred years ago, but today, just like the Jews, they do most of their quarrelling among themselves. The Gauls also produce some scholars, that's why you've got to talk to Mordra. I picked him up in Lutetia and he didn't cost me a single denarius."

"So your slave's a scholar?"

"In at least five languages. The clever brute's the best bargain I ever found. But going back to your European gods, Mordra tells me that his people were originally Greeks who migrated westward and brought their gods with them."

"Yes," Lucius agreed, "According to their legends they do claim Greek, or pre-Hellenic origin. Julius Caesar claimed that the Gauls worshipped Mercury, Apollo, Mars, Jupiter and Minerva, which are only our names for the Greek deities Hermes, Ilios, Aries, Zeus and Athena. I think that Caesar was probably right, but that the Gauls and the British have their own names for their gods that have the same functions as those whose names are more familiar to us, and that the probable Greek origins are lost in time. What matters now is that their gods, and the practice of their religion, are essentially Gallic and British. They belong to those lands and the people of those lands. That's

46

why I want to go to Ynys – to Britain, to study a pure culture in a place that, apart from trade, we have not yet touched."

Aulus took a deep draught of his wine and leaned back in his chair, "The only reason why I would want to go to Britain (I hear that it's a miserable place with a bad climate) would be to bring it into the Empire. It's about the only place of any value that we haven't taken over yet. Perhaps we can go together some day, me as the conquering general, and you to pursue your studies – and to record my gallant deeds. And if I ever get there I want at least one auxiliary of Belgae with me." It did not occur to Aulus that such a plan would ruin the idea of studying a people as yet virtually untouched by Rome. "A lot of what you say is a bit deep for me. I can see that your time on Rhodos wasn't wasted. But I think I can see what you mean, the fact that the people believe a god to be real makes it real because it satisfies their needs. Without that belief the god is no more than the carved idol that it actually is. I see your argument about the Gauls adapting their native versions of the Greek gods to make them more Roman. I don't know, I'm only an ignorant soldier with too much time to think."

Lucius laughed, "You do yourself an injustice. Your thinking must be right because you've reached the same conclusion that I have."

Aulus lowered his voice, "Has it ever occurred to you what might happen if the Emperor ever started to believe that he really was a god?"

Lucius stopped laughing, "I suppose it could happen."

"It could. There's a strain of madness running through that family, and they're all totally ruthless. I sometimes wish that the senate would look beyond the Caesars for our leaders. Emperor of the World is more than enough for any man. If ever one of them becomes convinced that he really is divine – I just hope that I'm not around to see it."

"That sounds almost like republicanism."

"Take it as you wish; despite my soldier's annual oath of allegiance. You see I do trust you when you say that you are here on your own account and nobody's spy. If our old friendship doesn't hold as good as it once did, I've just talked myself into a lot of trouble."

Lucius was not offended by the implication that he could betray his oldest friend. Intrigue was a way of life, and no one ever knew whom he could really trust.

"Aulus!" he exclaimed, "You need not doubt me. If we two can't trust each other then there's no honour left anywhere. You've known of my republican leanings for a long time, and your knowing has never done me any harm. Our friendship is your guarantee that, no matter what either of us says to each other, privately, about our leaders it will not lead to betrayal. After all, we both agree that they are only men."

At that point, Pontius Pilate returned.

Chapter 3

Fortunately the procurator had only caught the last snatch of conversation. "They're not even real men. Subhuman."

Aulus started, "Praefectus?"

"I would hardly describe the Jews as men. They have no attributes that I would describe as manly, or even human."

The two old friends had been holding their breath when they thought that the procurator might have overheard their treasonable remarks. They breathed again when they realised that he was preoccupied with his own thoughts. "The baths are inadequate. It's time we had some baths in this city that are fit for a Roman."

"I entirely agree," said Aulus who had to spend far more time in Jerusalem than the flying visits that Pilate made. "But space is at a premium, and I doubt that the water supply would stand it."

Pilate was not satisfied; "You must be better supplied now, after the winter rains."

"We are, but it will soon start to go down again." He turned to Lucius, "The Antonia is supplied by two cisterns, one right under our feet and the other beneath the outer court. Most of the major buildings have such cisterns. The city gets its water from several springs or by watercourses that carry seasonal rains, and the two main wells are the Bethesda pool between here and the Hippodrome and the pool of Siloam at the southeast corner. Herod built an aqueduct across the city to supply his citadel and the temple. The temple's ritual baths, the mikveh, use nothing but rainwater, which is stored in separate, 'holy', cisterns. The elevation is the problem, water won't flow uphill."

In ancient days a shaft had been sunk within the city wall at Siloam and a tunnel carried the water from the Gihon spring outside the city's walls. It was through this tunnel that Joab, King

David's general, had entered the city to capture it a thousand years ago. Two hundred years later King Hezekiah had deepened the tunnel. This was why the zealots had guarded that corner as a line of retreat after their twin attacks upon the Romans.

Pontius Pilate was on one of his hobbyhorses. He wanted to leave behind some tangible reminder of his tenure. In Caesarea he was building a temple in honour of the emperor, he would ensure that his name as well as that of Tiberius would be inscribed upon it. In Jerusalem his thoughts had turned to something more practical. "We need an aqueduct from further north. We should tap water from the River Jordan, at the moment it just runs away and evaporates in the Dead Sea."

Aulus had heard all this before, "A worthwhile scheme, but think of the cost."

Pilate had already thought of that and he had his plans. "I have a few ideas for getting the money. It would benefit the Jews as well and they have their resources, the temple is stuffed with money."

Aulus's heart sank to think of the trouble that would arise if Pilate raided the temple treasury, or if he tried to tax the Jews further to pay for an unwanted memorial to a Roman official. The water supply was adequate, even though the natives used a lot of it in their ritual washing and bathing.

Lucius was amazed that they had travelled all this way in response to an armed uprising, just to discuss water. But Pilate was wasting time until he was ready. "I have summoned the Primus Pilus and the centurion who commanded the citadel. When they arrive I will have a full report, and I want it in writing by tomorrow."

"In that case," Aulus replied, "I must have Mordra here so that he can make notes."

"If you must." Pilate murmured.

Jerusalem was not a big city, about a mile each way but irregular in shape. It was a natural fortress that had been strengthened by the hand of man since ancient times. The Kidron valley, overhung by the mighty edifice of the temple, bound it to the east. To the south and west lay the Hinmon Valley, and the Central Valley cut to its heart. The whole was surrounded by a complex series of walls.

Primus Pilus Galba walked, alone, down the steps of the Antonia and across the outer courtyard where auxiliaries were counting and stacking the Jewish dead. The streets were silent but for the hobnailed tread of the sixteen patrols. The centurion walked down a broad street and turned left towards the forum, which crowned the highest point, the upper city, then right into a maze of narrow alleys. He was conscious of a hundred eyes watching him through the slats of closed shutters.

More men were working in the charnel house before the citadel where the slaughter seemed to have been even greater than at the Antonia.

Herod the Great, who had now been dead for thirty-four years, had built his citadel inside the western city wall. It contained not only Herod's palace, but also barracks, workshops, storerooms, everything needed for the protection of a hated ruler. It now housed the Jerusalem cohort of the Tenth Legion.

Galba strolled through the main gate, glancing at the array of pili racked and gleaming. A slender metal neck attached the sharp head of each weapon to the long wooden haft. When thrown the metal either bent or broke off, whether it had struck its target or not, and could not be reused by those at whom it had been aimed. Galba noted that the weapons were clean, sharp and lightly oiled. He asked a legionary where he could find the commanding centurion. "In his quarters, Primus," was the reply, "He's questioning one of the prisoners." Walking through the barracks he glanced in at the living quarters of the men. Each room, holding four bunk beds and a small table, was home to eight soldiers and each bore the marks of their individuality as well as the aura of their common bond. All had cleaned and sharpened their swords and daggers and had lovingly wiped them with a fine coating of olive oil before they were sheathed and hung upon the bedposts. Some were still polishing their metal helmets and the leaves of their armour. A few had washed their dark red tunics and wore only a breechcloth. This was Galba's world and he loved it.

Timocrates had been expecting the visit and had been looking forward to a talk with Galba. The two were old friends and had fought together more times than either could remember.

In battle they knew that each could count upon the unstinting support of the other. They often shared their leisure time, reminiscence, drink, and women. They were among the finest products of the training and experience that made the Roman army what it was, and made centurions the strong backbone of that army. Of the prisoner there was no sign and Timocrates told his friend all the information that he had gained about how the zealots had managed to enter the city and position themselves for the dawn attack. Galba was satisfied. The two fell into easy conversation until they heard off-key singing coming from somewhere nearby. Galba looked up, "What's he been drinking?"

A look of irritation crossed the Greek's face, "Something strong by the sound of it." The two men rose and followed the dreadful sound. It was coming from a latrine and Timocrates pushed open the half door. They entered a noisome corridor; a wide board with eight holes in it stretched along the left-hand wall, and a similar one to the right. Water trickled in a shallow trough that ran beneath the board, and in a stepped channel down the centre of the room. There was a bucket containing vinegar, sticks poking out of it, and another bucket held dirty water. A naked man sat over one of the holes singing a bawdy song at the top of his voice and trying to keep time by waving one of the sticks that had a small sponge on the end of it. Timocrates roared and two legionaries came running. The centurion was also in fine voice, "Take this thing off to its bed, I'll see it in the morning. And bring me the bottle, he's had more than enough."

As the drunken man was hauled to his feet he struggled to sponge between his buttocks, sluiced the sponge in the bucket of dirty water, then tried to return it to its bucket of vinegar – and missed. He was dragged away by his two comrades, who were having great difficulty in keeping straight faces. The centurions returned to Timocrates's room and closed the door before they allowed their laughter to burst out. Soon one of the legionaries knocked upon the door and handed over a bottle. Timocrates shook it, it seemed to be half full, then sniffed at the neck. "Phew! No wonder he's in that state." He reached for two cups and poured the clear liquid. The old soldiers raised their cups to each other in silent salute, and downed the fierce spirit with practised ease. After another cup Galba announced his regret that

52

they must both return to the Antonia with their reports.

The great spring festival of the Jews was under way. The Passover, commemorating the time when their forefathers had escaped from Egypt before going on to found the nation of Israel, was an eight-day period when religious and nationalistic fervour would often boil over. People had been flocking into Jerusalem for days, until well over a hundred thousand Jews were cramped into the limited space, overflowed into the nearby villages, or camped out in the surrounding countryside. It was now all too apparent that the zealots had grasped the golden opportunity to smuggle a substantial force into the city. And Aulus had just 640 men.

The tribune reminded Pilate that he had despatched a message to Caesarea five days earlier when he had had the first intimation that this year, there could be more trouble than the usual noisy celebrations, and had asked for reinforcements, which had not arrived. The procurator had the message with him and glanced through it. Looking up at Aulus he said, "You say here that a Jew with a very small band of followers entered the city last Sunday and that a mob, you think mainly Galileans, made a lot of noise when welcoming him. He then disappeared into the temple, then left it and was not seen again until the following day when he returned and overturned the stalls of the traders. You did not make it clear that there was a very real threat of military action. From your report I quite reasonably assumed that this was no more than part of the excitement stirred up by their festival."

Aulus remained silent. Pilate always tried to shift the blame when things went wrong, but was ever ready to take any credit even when not entitled to it. The procurator went on, "I am amazed that you were so concerned about one man and his handful of followers, yet you completely missed the presence of a substantial army of bandits within the city."

Aulus had had enough, "With respect, Praefectus, the garrison can control the fifty thousand residents of Jerusalem with little difficulty. But I would remind you that I have suggested several times that we reinforce at this time of year when the population can double or treble. They are not only

53

celebrating the birth of their nation; they are anticipating its rebirth. Mordra, what is that they say about slaves and free men?"

Mordra had cultivated his Jewish contacts, and enjoyed their company. This year was the third time that he had been invited to a *Seder,* the Passover ritual feast held in every Jewish home whether in Judaea, the Galilee or anywhere in the world where Jews had settled. He alone in that company could see the irony of a Gallic slave telling his Roman masters what Jews throughout the world had prayed on the previous evening, the first day of Passover. Keeping a perfectly straight face, the Gaul said, "It's quite a long ceremony, it takes up the first half of the evening. As far as I know they have been carrying out this celebration ever since they escaped from Egypt many centuries ago. Since Alexandros conquered this land about three hundred and sixty years ago, and the Greeks started to impose their religion and culture, the Jews have said: 'This year our brothers are slaves, but next year we all hope to be free men in the land of Israel'."

"There." Aulus was triumphant. "Passover isn't only looking at their legendary past. Passover is the most likely time of the year for them to revolt." The tribune smirked; knowing that he had a lot to teach Pilate about military matters. "Do you know the best time of year to start a military campaign?"

The procurator said nothing. Aulus went on, "In the spring. Winter rains fill watercourses and make them difficult to cross, turn fields into quagmires that bog down cavalry. They deprive men of rest because they are too wet and cold. Up here it often snows in winter. No, the time to begin a campaign is in the spring, and Passover is a spring festival."

"Then you should have been ready for it."

"I was, as far as my limited resources allowed."

Pilate knew that he was on the defensive, "When I left Caesarea I ordered two cohorts to force march to Jerusalem. They will be here later tonight or early in the morning. I would imagine that you will be able to control the city with almost two thousand men."

"Two cohorts would have been very useful," Aulus replied, "Had they been here yesterday. We no longer need them. We've already killed the enemy, with my little force. I have two centuries out on patrol within the square mile, with orders to round up any suspicious characters, or kill them if they resist. I'm sorry, Praefectus, but it's too late for this year. Next year, and in all years, I want at least three cohorts in Jerusalem before Passover starts."

It was perhaps fortunate that the two centurions arrived before the mutual recriminations could go further. Both of the old soldiers had divested themselves of their full uniforms as soon as they had entered the Antonia and appeared in undress red tunics. Aulus had to suppress a smile; he too was similarly dressed, while Pontius Pilate had removed the uncomfortable armour that had never been splashed by the smallest drop of blood, and wore a toga. Pilate looked directly at Mordra for the first time, "Slave, are you ready to take notes?" The Gaul indicated his wax tablets and stylus and, without being bidden, sat down so that he could write. Aulus knew that the procurator's Greek was execrable, "Shall we keep the record in Latin?"

"Of course," Pilate replied, "It is the language of Rome."

Again the tribune had to suppress a smile. From the Emperor down, all patricians and learned Romans conversed in Greek. Latin was now the language of the army – and of plebeians.

Pontius Pilate took control, "Tribune, I will hear your report first, then the Primus Pilus, then this other centurion."

Aulus leaned back in his chair. "As far as I'm concerned, Praefectus, the trouble started last Sunday when a Galilean Jew who has since been identified as Joshua ben Joseph of Nazareth and who is in my custody, came into the city. He entered, riding on a donkey, through the Lion Gate, just north of the temple. He was surrounded by a handful of followers but they seem to have picked up a few hundred Galileans on the way and they all chanted a welcome. Mordra, what was it they were chanting?"

"It was a quotation from one of their psalms," the Gaul replied, "They were waving palm branches in greeting and laying them, and some of their clothing, beneath the donkey's hooves, and they were saying; 'Hallelujah! Praise the Lord from the heavens; praise him in the heights. Blessed is he who comes in the name of the Lord; we bless you in the House of the Lord. The

Lord is God and he has given us light; order the festival procession with boughs, even to the horns of the altar.'"

Pilate frowned, "That's more than just Passover rubbish. They were greeting a leader of some importance to them. It could even be that they think that their messiah has raised his ugly head."

Aulus shook his head, "A leader among the Galileans, probably. But he was hardly of regal aspect; he and his little gang were dressed like beggars. If you want a pretender to the title of messiah, I'd put my money on the man who attacked the Antonia." He preferred not to think too much about the man from Nazareth.

"Why?"

"Because he calls himself 'bar Abbas', which means 'son of the father', 'son of man' or 'son of the people'. You might expect a so-called messiah to choose such a name. But what was that other thing they were saying, Mordra?"

The slave was solemn, "They had chanted the psalm in Hebrew, but they repeatedly cried, in Aramaic, 'Ossanna Baram' – save us, son of David."

The procurator sneered, "And you still think that this bar Abbas terrorist hopes to be their priest king? Their saviour is expected to be a direct descendant of David."

Aulus was tired of all this. "I beg your pardon, Praefectus, but even with the Jews' love of record keeping no-one can know who is or is not descended from a king of a thousand years ago. This place has been invaded and fought over so many times, their first temple was totally destroyed by Nebuchadnezzar, and all ancient records must be lost. Besides, David was a Benjaminite from Bethlehem in Judaea, but he did away with the old tribal divisions, and Joshua ben Joseph is a Galilean from Nazareth. Not that it makes any difference; both of the Joshuas have seen their last sunset so if either of them wanted to be the messiah, he didn't make it."

Pilate nodded, and turned to Mordra, "I take it that you witnessed this little triumph, slave. What did he do next?"

"He dismounted and he and his small group went into the ritual baths in the northern wall of the temple. I waited until he came out. He went back to the eastern side and entered the

56

temple precincts through the Golden Gate."

"And you followed him?"

"I went in through the Northern Gate, under the building works. I was in time to see him go into the inner part where only Jews may enter. He was not there long and I could hear nothing of what went on. When he came back to the outer court he left by the Golden Gate and made off over the Mount of Olives. I came back here and reported to the tribune. He sent me back there the following day."

Pilate turned to Aulus. "And it was after your slave's first visit to the temple that you sent your message to Caesarea?"

The soldier nodded. Pilate was thoughtful, "I think that this was more than the usual nonsense that we get at this time of year. But I still fail to see how you missed the presence of a thousand armed and dangerous terrorists."

Aulus was managing to control his temper, "We are now sure that those who attacked the Antonia were not in the city until immediately before their onslaught. They may have assembled in the hills to the north. We now know that they must have come in through the Damascus Gate because their sicarii murdered the morning guard." He looked at the Greek centurion, "Timocrates, did you find out how your lot got in?"

"Yes, tribune. I questioned their leader just before I came here. They had entered in dribs and drabs throughout the past few days and hidden in various parts of the city. They must have been supported and sheltered by a number of Jerusalemites. Some came in through the Joppa Gate before dawn; they also murdered the guard. It seems that they assembled in the warren of houses opposite the citadel, either with the support of their owners or because of threats to them."

Pilate was satisfied, "Thank you, Centurion. Now all that we need to know is how they could establish themselves so well at Siloam. Tribune, tell me of the attack on the Antonia."

Before Aulus could answer, a decurion, besmirched in blood, entered and came to attention before his commanding officer, "Tribune, we have 624 dead from the Antonia and the citadel. We're still digging them out at Siloam, about forty so far. It should be about seven hundred by the time we've finished."

"Excellent, Decurion. I think we can say that we've

completely destroyed their terrorist army, more than half dead and we have the leaders. Get a message to the house of Caiaphas, tell them to claim the bodies and get them buried."

The decurion saluted and left on his errand. Aulus began his brief narrative, "It was a frontal attack, they stormed into the outer court just as the sun was rising. The fools should have known that they'd have the sun in their eyes once it got over the Mount of Olives. And, of course, they had to come in through the six narrow gates so their charge wasn't much. I had two centuries here and was able to concentrate on the front, with strong lookouts on the eastern and southern sides in case they came at us from the temple. I received a heliograph from Timocrates to tell me of the attack on the citadel. There was nothing that I could do to help him, but he had the main force of about four hundred men so I knew that he could deal with the problem. It didn't take too long here. I'd just sent three decades to stand outside the outer portico to cut off their retreat when a wounded man from one of the standing patrols managed to get in through the temple's outer court, over the builders' scaffolding, to tell of the attack on Siloam. I left Galba in command here and took a century to the south east corner."

"Half your force, was that wise?" Pilate interrupted.

"The decision of a commander in the field, Praefectus, and the right one as it turned out. We had to cut our way through the mob and found that the bandits had taken over the tower and adjoining wall. It was obviously intended as their line of withdrawal through Hezekiah's tunnel. We cleared the wall and raided the nearby houses for wood and oil so that I could smoke them out of the tower."

"And the tower collapsed, with your men under it?" Pilate raised an eyebrow.

"Yes, Praefectus. I lost eighteen men, most under the tower. Those bandits who ran out were killed on the spot, except for the one I judged, correctly, to be their leader. I brought him back to the Antonia and he's now with the other three in the praetorium."

Aulus had cursed himself when, as he was wiping his sword on the clothing of a dead Jew, the tower had cracked open and fallen outwards onto his men.

The Procurator turned his attention to Galba. "So, Primus,

58

with only a century left you managed to rout out the bandits?"

Although he was seated, Galba stiffened to attention. "They were already beaten when the tribune left. All that we had to do was make a sortie into the outer court and trap them against the already defended portico. We only had to chop them down and kill off their wounded. We'd identified their leader and I detailed a decade to take him."

Timocrates told a similar story. It had been a frontal assault with some harassing missiles over the southern wall. His four hundred men had easily halted the Jews and his main concern had been that too many would escape. He had kept one century in reserve and to defend the citadel, and sent his main force out to encircle and slaughter the attackers.

During Timocrates's report a legionary came in and spoke quietly to his commanding officer. When the story of the attack upon the citadel was over, Aulus looked at Pilate with a look of satisfaction on his face. "I think that we are about to hear something of interest. I've just been told that one of their priests is outside and wants to speak to us urgently."

Pilate groaned, "I could well do without their god coming into all of this."

Aulus gave a short laugh, "Don't worry. They've sent a man I know called Samuel. He's the one the rest of the priests never refer to by name because he's an atheist."

Lucius began to think that he had entered a madhouse, "An atheist priest?"

"Why not?" Aulus grinned, "You're preoccupied with religion, but you don't believe it either. You've a lot to learn about the Jews, Samuel's one of those who seem to believe that there's more to religion than gods."

Pilate frowned, "Before we see him, is the temple back under control?"

"All quiet again, or as quiet as it ever is."

"Intact?"

"Nothing missing."

The procurator turned to the legionary, "Right, bring the holy gentleman in."

Lucius, who had gained the impression that religion was dominant in Judaea over all other considerations, and that religious matters were conducted always with high emotion, did not know what to expect of a priest who was also an atheist. Despite the gentle ribbing from Aulus, all who knew Lucius, knew that his interest in religion was purely academic. He could not visualise Zeus sitting upon his throne with a bowl of fortunes at each side of him, arbitrarily dishing out good fortune to this man and ill fortune to that one. He believed that men were in control of their own destiny. Although he could appreciate that there were those who gained security from their belief in the supernatural, he decried the certainty that religions gave to their followers. He preferred doubt, uncertainty and argument to the dangerous attitude of the religious – that they were the sole custodians of a divinely inspired truth and therefore everyone who did not agree with them was wrong. That way lay intolerance and bloodshed.

When Samuel entered, the Roman scholar regarded him as an interesting specimen. The priest was a small, portly figure in his mid-fifties. He wore an ankle-length, seamless tunic of white linen, bound at the waist by a long girdle with the ends reaching to the hem of his tunic. On his head was a high, white linen hat, which he did not remove. His full, luxuriant beard was grizzled with his years.

The procurator greeted him civilly, "Welcome, Samuel, do take a seat. Some wine?"

The priest hesitated just a moment, "A little wine, with water please."

As Mordra, knowing Jewish customs, poured the smallest drop of wine and filled the cup with water, Lucius was mildly surprised to see Samuel go and hold his hands out over the bowl on the tripod stand. Without a word, Mordra poured water over the priest's hands so that he could wash them. When he had finished, Mordra handed him a towel, then his wine and removed the bowl, returning a few minutes later with clean water. Pilate waited until his guest had settled in his chair and placed his untouched drink upon a low table. Then, "A sad business this."

"Indeed, Praefectus, indeed." Samuel looked as if he had all the troubles of the world on his shoulders. "We must be thankful that it was so quickly resolved, for that we owe a debt to Aulus Plautius here. We must be sure that such a sorry state of affairs is not allowed to happen again."

Pilate's sarcasm was just below the surface, "We must. Do you have any suggestions?"

"Not suggestions exactly, but I may be able to give you some information which could clarify the situation and guide us in what to look out for in order to prevent such a thing happening again in the future."

The procurator wanted to be sure of his ground, "Are you here on your own account, or has Caiaphas sent you?"

"Forgive me, Praefectus, I am here on behalf of the assembled Sanhedrin."

Pilate showed his surprise, "All of you?"

The priest smiled slightly, "As many as we could assemble in a time of crisis."

The Sanhedrin was the highest court of justice of the Jews. It comprised seventy-one members, priests and important landowners. In such a gathering there were bound to be internal tensions and disagreements. Pilate could well imagine that the High Priest, Caiaphas, had assembled only those members who would agree with him.

Caiaphas had been appointed to his position by Pilate's predecessor, Gratus, succeeding his father-in-law, Annas who continued as a member of the Sanhedrin and still wielded enormous power.

Pilate trusted none of them. They were mostly of the sect of the Sadducees, the nearest thing that the Jews had to an aristocracy, who were advised by the scholars of the sect known as the Scribes. Their scholars, the Rabbis, advised the more liberal Pharisee minority. For the most part the Sadducees, realising that they benefited from Roman order, co-operated with the occupying power. This obviously suited the Romans, but most of them were contemptuous of Jews who would side with Rome, often against their own people. It was only on sticky questions of Jewish religion and Jewish law that the Sanhedrin showed any stubbornness and Rome preferred to leave such matters to them and not to interfere. Rome even compromised to the point where they did not take the imperial standard of the legion into the Jews' 'holy city', and excused them from making sacrifice to the Divine Emperor in their temple, instead they sacrificed to their god on behalf of Tiberius.

"When you return to the Sanhedrin I want you to inform them that I am to try these four bandits tomorrow morning." Pilate did not see Aulus's look of shock and dismay. A trial? These men needed no trial; they were guilty, all they needed was execution. "Arrange for a representative group to be here, not all of you. Now, what message does the Sanhedrin have for us?"

"As I say, Praefectus, I have information which, most of us feel, you should have."

"*Most* of you?"

Samuel shrugged, "There are always dissenters. Perhaps I should have said an overwhelming majority of us."

Pilate nodded, "Go on."

Samuel knew that what he had to tell the procurator would defuse some of the animosity between them: "Just before all this trouble began, one of the zealots entered Jerusalem riding on a donkey…"

"I already know that, and about the mob laying palm branches in his path. And I know what it implies. The donkey is the traditional regal mount of your people isn't it?"

"It is, Praefectus."

"I also know that he took over the temple for a few days. It was your people who sent him to me. And I appreciate the gift. Now, I want every detail, including how your temple guard allowed it to happen."

"The guard was overwhelmed by weight of numbers, and they cannot shed human blood within the temple precincts."

"So, this Galilean rode his donkey in triumph into Jerusalem, and the mob laid palm branches in his path."

Samuel nodded. "Shouting his praises at the tops of their voices."

"Then, with this sweaty mob behind him, he stormed your temple."

"Not stormed, exactly, but he did take it over. He also caused some damage and injury."

Aulus laughed, "I am told that he upset the stalls of the money changers and sellers of sacrifice."

"These men are ruined, Tribune, they have lost everything."

Lucius butted in; "Who are these money changers?"

Aulus put him in the picture: "The Jews are not allowed to take Roman coinage into the temple because it bears the head of the Emperor, and they regard that as, what do you call it?"

Samuel helped him, "An engraved image, which is contrary to our second law."

"Something quaint like that. These money changers exchange Roman coins for Jewish coins so that the worshippers can make cash offerings and buy sacrificial animals from the approved suppliers in the outer court."

Pilate saw no reason why they should waste time explaining such things to Lucius. "Yes, yes. Go on, Samuel."

"The mob scooped up the coins, regardless of type, and the money changers lost everything. The same applies to the suppliers of sacrifice, all the birds were released and the animals escaped. These men are ruined."

The procurator was less than interested in the problems of a few Jewish tradesmen. "What were your people doing about this?"

Samuel was concerned with the welfare of those who, through no fault of their own, had lost so much. "A group of my colleagues remonstrated with Joshua, and asked him by what authority he was taking over the Temple."

Aulus could only think of zealous bandits, "I bet I know the answer to that one."

Samuel was trying not to be patronising to the ignorant Roman. "I'm afraid it wasn't that simple, Aulus Plautius. He answered their question with a question did they think that his authority came from the Lord or from his followers?"

"Typical," said Aulus, who had little time for the labyrinthine workings of the Jewish mind.

But Lucius could appreciate such a response; he butted in again. "I can see that he presented you with a dilemma. However that question is answered, it is equally right or equally wrong. In the light of your religious beliefs on the one hand, and under the implicit threat of a mob on the other hand, it is unanswerable."

Samuel was encouraged to think that here was a Roman who had at least some idea of the complexities of thought and argument. "Exactly, sir. Had they said that his authority came from the Lord then he could have asked why they, as priests, had

63

to question him. If they had said that it came from his followers, or from the zealots then the priests would have recognised them, which they cannot do. And, as you say, such a mob did present a very real threat. After some discussion, my colleagues could only say that they did not know the source of his authority."

"Bravo!" said Lucius, "Let the questioner answer his own question." He turned to Aulus. "These people certainly know the rules of philosophical argument." He turned back to Samuel. "What did he say?"

"That if they did not know he would not tell them."

Lucius was crestfallen, he had expected more. Pilate was uninterested. "I'm sure that this is all very interesting to Greek philosophers and Jewish mental gymnasts, but I want to deal in facts. After ruining the livelihood of your temple tradesmen, what did he *do*?"

The priest, ever urbane, sighed. "Talked, and talked, and talked."

"He is a Jew," muttered Aulus.

Samuel ignored the remark. "Some of it was quite interesting. He told a parable about the son of the owner of a vineyard who was murdered by the tenants. I take it that he sees himself the rightful owner of the vineyard, which is the land of Israel, and the tenants, the interlopers, are the Romans. A lot of what he said was his interpretation of our Holy Law, helped with quotations from our prophets, particularly Isaiah. But we think that he did actually claim to be descended from David."

Pilate sat forward. "Your ancient king? Did he say anything to support his claim?"

"I'm afraid there was nothing too specific, he's a master of ambiguity. He did quote Isaiah that a branch shall grow from the stock of Jesse, the father of King David."

Aulus knew how carefully the Jews recorded everything, and asked Samuel just what the records had to say about the Galilean Joshua ben Joseph. In return, Samuel asked him how much he knew about the brotherhood, the ruling body of the zealots. Now the Roman was really interested. Of course he knew of the existence of the brotherhood, but he could never know too much. "You tell me, Samuel."

"You must know, Tribune, that the zealots are not a single

64

group but a loose alliance of those who would restore a fully independent Israel. Together they call themselves the *Kanaa'im*, the Canaanites, because Canaan was the name of the entire area between the Jordan and the Mare Internum when it was conquered by Joshua twelve or thirteen hundred years ago. During the reign of Solomon, about a thousand years ago, the territory was extended, and it is the aim of some of the zealots to reclaim Solomon's kingdom, while others would be content with the area of Joshua's conquest. By the way, according to them, it would not be a kingdom but a republic because we tend to be a republican people. Our experience of kings, especially recently, has not been good. But all zealots agree in their aim for a purely Jewish state. They are drawn almost entirely from the Pharisees, although we never know what the Essenes are up to out in the desert and we think that they act as a breeding ground. The Galilee is the centre of zealotism. As you know, the Pharisees are stronger up there than here in Judaea. There are also Greek zealots, and the idea of the Hellenic Jews taking their terrorist tactics out of the land of Israel and to other parts of the Empire is very worrying. You must be aware that they have an extreme group of assassins known as the sicarii because they all carry a sicar, a curved dagger and are experts at using it. Now, most of the time all the different zealot factions fight independently of the others, but they all have representatives on an *ad hoc* central council known as the brotherhood, about a hundred or so in all."

Both Pilate and Aulus knew much of this, but it was useful to have it presented so succinctly by a Jew. Aulus wanted to know which party of the zealots Joshua of Nazareth belonged to.

"None of them, Tribune," Samuel replied, "he is the leader of the non-belligerent wing."

"I didn't know that there was a non-belligerent terrorist," said Pilate.

Although he did not show it, Samuel was enjoying instructing a Roman administrator and a Roman soldier on the realities of the situation, and at the same time knowing that he was removing a threat to the established Jewish rule. "These men are the most dangerous, Praefectus. Their weapons are ideas and visions of the future. No army, not even that of Rome, can fight an idea."

65

"Perhaps not," said Aulus, "but if we kill the man the idea dies with him."

"No, Tribune, ideas do not die so easily. Herod Antipas beheaded Joshua's predecessor, but before his head had left his shoulders, Joshua was already carrying on with the idea. When Joshua dies there will be others to follow him. The only way to destroy an idea is to discredit it, and to do that we must work together."

There was a brooding silence as procurator, priest and soldier considered the unattractive prospect of Jews and Romans working together. Given Jewish stubbornness, the Romans were of the opinion that only stern rule would work. No Jew, including all the members of the Sanhedrin, could be happy under alien rule in the Holy Land. Samuel went on, "You may know something of the sect of the Nazarites." No one replied and he continued, "They are a highly respected group because they are prepared to give up everything for their god. They give up their homes, their families, their everyday work, and their possessions. They travel all the time, with nothing but the simple clothes upon their backs. Some even go barefoot. They do not even have a bag in which to put their belongings because they have none. They go only to Jewish homes and beg for food and perhaps shelter. If they do not receive them they never go there again. Because they have no homes there is a court within the temple where they may rest and meet with their own kind."

Lucius was fascinated. "And Joshua ben Joseph is one of these Nazarites?"

"Yes, but different to most of them. Oh, he lives the ascetic life; he wears his hair long, abstains from wine and will not approach a dead body, all this and more that is the Nazarite way. The difference is the message that he preaches. The Nazarite message is purity in life and absolute obedience to Holy Law. Joshua does this, but he also preaches the coming of the kingdom of the Lord."

"Kingdom?" Pilate queried.

"The kingdom of the Lord," Samuel stressed, "the sovereign state of Israel. A zealot message. That, as a part of the usual Nazarite vision is the dangerous idea. He is a rabbi who had his Bet Knesset in Nazareth for quite a number of years. At that time he earned his living in his family's trade as a carpenter…"

Lucius interrupted, asking for explanation. Samuel told him that rabbis, the Pharisaic scholars and teachers, especially of the law, were not paid and supported themselves in other ways. He went on to say that the Pharisees believed that this kept their rabbis in touch with the ordinary lives of the people, that many rabbis had a *Bet Knesset,* a house of meeting, which was a communal house of prayer and study, and a community centre. "About five years ago he suddenly abandoned his Bet Knesset and simply disappeared into the desert. He can only have gone to Qumran to join the Essenes. Of course, this turned the Pharisee leaders, and most of the people of Nazareth, against him, and from what he has said since his reappearance, he seems to have turned against his Pharisaic upbringing. Then, just over two years ago, he was seen to be associating with Johannan ben Zechariah, an Essene who was stirring up trouble in the north. We have since suspected that this Johannan was the then leader of the political wing of the zealots. Such a loose alliance as the zealots needs a political core. They claim that they only kill as a means to an end, although some of them, especially the sicarii, seem to enjoy it. The end is, of course, political, so they need a group who keep away from the killing, even though they condone and may even control it. If they were ever to achieve their aim, this political group would form the government of the newly independent state. They would restore the Knesset, our ancient parliament and it would be a black day for us all if such extremists took over – for Jew and Roman. Of course such a thing can never come to pass, but we must strive to stop them trying.

"Joshua is a more dangerous man than Johannan was, because he appears to be more reasonable and he is much more persuasive. Johannan was very extreme, he went far beyond the strict rules of the Nazarites. They let their hair grow long, but his, along with his beard, was like a wild bird's nest covered with a simple veil to protect him from the sun. He wore a simple shepherd's tunic, tied with a broad leather belt. He did not beg for his food, but lived on what he could find, such things as wild honey, the pods of the carob tree, and milk from wild goats. He was always covered in bee stings. He made the mistake of criticising Herod Antipas for his somewhat unorthodox marital and other domestic arrangements and the tetrarch had him arrested and thrown into Machaera. Later he chopped his head off. It seems that Joshua, very wisely, went off into the desert again at this time. His next appearance was at Capernaeum; this was when the Jewish authorities began to take an interest in him. Since then he has been wandering about trying to stir up the rabble."

"What do we know of his family background?" Pilate wanted to know. It was always useful to have such information.

"He was born in the late summer forty two years ago. His father, Joseph ben Jacob a carpenter, was a prominent Pharisee and a leader of his small community. He has five brothers and some sisters, all still in Nazareth. Oddly, we have no record of a wife or children, although this does not mean that he does not have any. Rabbis are expected to be married men. But, as a Nazarite he may well have abandoned them to live a celibate life as some of them do. One thing that is remembered from thirty years ago is that when he entered the congregation, here at the temple, his dissertation so impressed the priests and the rabbis that one of them, Gamaliel, can still recall it."

This was not what Aulus wanted to know. "I can believe that he's clever, he can even speak Greek and quote the philosophers. But if that is a crime then my friend Lucius here would have been executed years ago. He's a Galilean troublemaker who has been active with the zealots for at least two years. Your people have been watching him, you let him take over your temple, he was involved in the uprising, probably even planned it. Yet he has been allowed to travel about freely, preaching his poison. Has he led a charmed life?"

"Until now," Pilate said, solemnly. "This has been quite useful, Samuel, and I thank you." But the priest had not finished. All that he had said was no more than the introduction to the two pieces of information that would crush Joshua and rid the Jewish authorities of the threat that he posed to the peace and stability of the Roman province of Judaea. "And then," he said, almost casually, "There was his direct incitement not to pay Roman taxes."

"What?" Pilate started forward.

Even before Judaea had come under the direct rule of Rome, taxation had been a major issue. Before he began his thirty three-year reign, the Idumean Herod the Great had been exempted from Roman taxes. But ten years after the death of Herod, his successor in Judaea, Archalaus the client ruler, had made a fatal mistake. The Emperor Augustus decided to introduce the *lustrum,* the five-yearly census for the purpose of taxation and military service, into Judaea. The Jews were incensed. They believed that the land and all its produce was the exclusive property of their god, with themselves as the only rightful tenants, and that to pay foreign taxes was to support a heathen regime. They also objected to the lustral sacrifice as this usually involved a boar – an animal not permitted within their land. The zealots, who had been growing in strength since the death of Herod, used this to stir up the people and urge them not to co-operate in the census. In Bethlehem, the traditional birthplace of King David, not a single family registered. Archalaus decided to make an example of this town and he imposed a dreadful sanction. The idea came to him from the Passover ceremony and the retelling of how the god of Israel had sent an angel of death to kill off all the firstborn of Egypt. Archalaus sent soldiers to Bethlehem where they killed the firstborn sons. About 25 infant boys died. Augustus was horrified by this action because he could see that it would make the Jews much more difficult to rule. Archalaus was banished to Gaul and later killed. Coponius was appointed first procurator, and Judaea came under the direct rule of Rome.

Foreign taxation would always be a rallying point for the Jews. They had their own system of taxes, known as 'the Temple tax', which involved the periodic payment of one tenth of the value of their possessions. In fact this was not the only support for the temple which gained its income from fees for sacrifice. Rents on the stalls of the money changers and sellers of sacrifice, and voluntary donations placed into the thirteen rams' horns in the Court of Women. But the temple and the Jewish civil administration employed 17,000 men, priests, Levites – the temple attendants, and scribes. The Sanhedrin had 71 paid members and a substantial support staff. One third of the population of Jerusalem was employed in the temple and in administration. Apart from the religious objection to Roman taxes, their own leadership already taxed the Jews enough.

Now Samuel was saying that the leader of the political wing of the zealots was using this issue as a rallying cry. The procurator's first responsibility was financial, he wanted to know more and Samuel was willing to tell him. "I don't know who asked him the question, it may have been another Galilean." Samuel knew well enough who had asked, it had been thought out by the priests and posed by a scribe. They had led Joshua into a trap. " A man said to him, 'Rabbi, we know you are a man of integrity. Men don't sway you, because you pay no attention to who they are; but you teach the ways of the Lord. Is it right to pay taxes to the Emperor or not? Should we pay or shouldn't we?' For once Joshua gave a clear and direct answer; 'Bring me a denarius and let me look at it.' He had specified a Roman coin, which is not allowed in the Court of Women where he stood, but there were people who had collected coins when he had attacked the moneychangers, and someone produced the denarius. He held the coin in his hand, looked at it, then held it up. 'Whose portrait is this? And whose inscription?'

'Tiberius,' they replied. He then flung the coin from him and said, 'Then give to Tiberius that which is his. But give only to the Lord that which is the Lord's.' Given the generally held belief that this land and all its produce are the property of the god of Israel, this was the clearest injunction not to pay imperial taxes."

Pilate was satisfied. There was now no doubt that this man was far more dangerous than the three who had attempted a military coup. His pathetic attempts to take over the temple were enough to seal his fate, but tribute was the central issue. The empire had to be paid for. All who lived under the protection of Rome and who were given the advantages of Roman civilisation had to pay. The procurator now had the clearest evidence that this northern rabbi had, without recourse to arms, posed the gravest threat to the empire. "Samuel, I thank you again. This has been most helpful to us. I am grateful to you and to the rest of the Sanhedrin."

"Thank you, Praefectus, but there is yet more."

"Go on."

"Among his close followers there is a man called Simon

70

who is known as the Canaanean, an obvious zealot epithet. There are two more, possibly brothers, known as *Boanerges,* a difficult word to render from the Aramaic, but it refers to the storm and is used by the zealots. Yet another is a known *sicariot,* a dagger man. It seems that Joshua ordered his inner circle of followers to arm themselves, breaking out of his non-violent political mould. He even told them that if they did not have a sword they must sell their cloaks to buy one."

Pilate liked this information, but; "You seem surprisingly well informed about the secret discussions of these people. How can you know all this?"

Samuel was ready for this question, secretly he welcomed it. "Fortunately one of his close followers, actually it was the dagger man, came to Annas and Caiaphas and offered his master to us. Naturally Caiaphas brought him before the Sanhedrin. We questioned him and he told us a great deal. Later the dagger man led us to him and the temple guard was able to arrest him, though not without losing some blood in the struggle. Some of my people never want to hear his name again."

Aulus was not surprised to hear of such treachery among Jewish vermin. "Not much honour among your thieves, or your bandits if they sell each other out so easily. How much did you pay him?"

"A lot."

"How much?"

"Fortunately there is a precedent in Scripture."

"For blood money?"

"I would not express it quite that way. When the Persian Darius was King of Kings, the prophet Zechariah was charged with tending the sheep that were destined for slaughter. The healthy sheep he fed well and they grew fat, but he did not feed the sickly sheep and he allowed them to die. In this way his master made a good profit and Zechariah was able to demand a full year's wages for a season's work. The treasurer weighed out for him thirty shekels of silver. Our informant felt that this was a fitting sum for a sacrificial lamb."

This only confirmed Aulus's low opinion of the natives. "You can afford it."

"Perhaps," Samuel replied, "but we are more interested in

71

our informant's motivation. He had been a loyal follower for over a year. Joshua performed a deed that was abhorrent to the dagger man. Now, he could have employed the usual solution that he always carried under his cloak, but we think that he may have been trying to redeem Joshua and return him to the path that this man, Judah is his name, thought that they were following, and not the one upon which Joshua had now set his feet."

Pilate licked his lips. "What path is that, and what did Joshua do that caused such deep offence?"

"Praefectus, we must go back to the beginning of Joshua's activities about two years ago. He gathered around him a group of followers. You could call them a bodyguard, but Judah has told us that they were each given specific political responsibilities. They were being prepared to form a government. He entered Jerusalem in triumph, riding on the royal beast. He went to the temple and grasped the horns of the altar where he uttered a prayer called the *Hallel,* which is a prayer of praise and dedication. Herod built the Temple as a fortress as well as the spiritual centre of our people. Joshua demonstrated that he could take it over and control it, which he did for three days. He even had the confidence to leave it each night and return the following morning. So he did not make one entry into the Temple, through the Golden Gate which is to be the path of the Messiah, he came that way three times."

Pilate was still not impressed. "So he was trying to set himself up as your messiah-king. He's now locked up in the praetorium and he will die tomorrow. Much good it's done him."

"Praefectus," Samuel was grave, "he *is* our king."

"Impossible!"

"No, not impossible. What I have just told you about his actions over the past two years are all but one of the requirements of a king of Israel. Our kings were all priest kings. On the night before Passover, in Bethany, a renegade priest, but still a bona fide priest, named Simon, anointed Joshua as priest king of Israel. This was what was so shocking to the egalitarian republican Judah the sicariot. According to Jewish law he is at this moment the *de jure* and *de facto* king of Israel."

"Not for much longer," Pilate said. "Aulus, this priest in Bethany, I want him dead. And I want every one of Joshua's band of followers."

"It will be a pleasure, Praefectus. I have men out now looking for any zealots, I'm sure they'll round up Joshua's group with them." He turned to Samuel. "Just how many are there in this inner circle?"

"In many places he has visited he has attracted large audiences, mainly out of curiosity I would imagine. When he entered Jerusalem a few hundred greeted him, but they were mainly Galileans, and at this time of year people are more susceptible to such things. As far as his close circle is concerned, including our informer, there are twelve."

Lucius had been expecting a mighty hoard of bandits. "Is that all?"

The priest smiled slightly. "It is enough, more than enough."

The philosopher's mind went off on its usual track. "Why? Is twelve some mystic number?"

"Not mystic, sir, but highly significant."

Now Pilate was interested. "Why?"

"Praefectus, gentlemen, let us see where we are with Joshua and the zealots. The father of our people, in ancient days, was Jacob who was called Israel. He had twelve sons. Many years later the descendants of Jacob were enslaved in Egypt and Moses, our teacher and lawgiver, led his people out of the land of Egypt, out of the house of slavery. It is that deliverance that we are celebrating at the moment, Passover, when the angel of death visited the first-born of Egypt and passed over the houses of the Israelites so that they could be freed and cross the Red Sea, ultimately to enter and possess the land of Canaan. Not all of those who escaped from Egypt were the children of Israel; there were many other slaves of different origins. The Egyptians called them the *Habiru,* people from the other side, meaning aliens. It was Moses's task to mould the Habiru, including the Israelites, into a coherent nation. He did this in two ways: he gave his people the rule of law under which all civilised societies must live, and he gave them social structure by dividing them into twelve administrative groups, some with special functions, who he called 'tribes', and he identified the 'tribes' by the names of the twelve sons of Jacob. Many years later, after we had taken possession of the land of Canaan to be the Land of Israel, and the 'tribes' had settled in various parts of this land, the Philistines subjected us. A great prophet, our first prophet whose name I bear, realised that the Philistines could only be overcome if the twelve 'tribes' were united under one leader. Thus Samuel anointed Saul as the first king of Israel. The great King David followed him, also anointed by Samuel, and, after a very long war, the Philistines were beaten. King Solomon followed David and brought prosperity to this land. He also built the first temple here in Jerusalem.

"Traditionally Israel has twelve tribal leaders under a king anointed in the unknown name of the God of Israel. Joshua ben Joseph of Nazareth has entered Jerusalem mounted on the royal beast with palm fronds laid beneath its hooves. He and his *twelve* close followers occupied the very heart of David's city, the temple, where Joshua went to the altar to claim his kingdom. He and his *twelve* close followers have told the people that the world may belong to the Emperor, but that the Holy Land of Israel, all that is in it and all that it produces, is the exclusive property of the Eternal God, King of the Universe."

Lucius's scholarly detachment deserted him. "And he is, at this moment the rightful Jewish ruler of Judaea in the eyes of the Jews and according to their law."

Aulus was concerned with the immediate problems of public order. "And, even without the zealots, he has a large popular following, right now when the Jews are celebrating the festival that is supposed to mark the birth of their nation."

Pontius Pilate had unswerving faith in Rome. "Then we must give him his coronation. I will present 'King Joshua' to his people in a way that they will never forget. I look forward to crucifying the King of the Jews."

74

Chapter 4

Mordra conducted Samuel out of the Antonia. The Gaul had understood more of what Samuel had said than had his Roman masters. The priest turned to the slave.

"Thank you, Mordra, you know our ways." Mordra remained silent, the priest went on, "And we have welcomed you among us because you are not a Roman, and you have accepted our hospitality without abusing it. Which side are you on?"

Mordra chose to ignore the question. Instead, "As you accepted Roman hospitality – without using it."

Samuel smiled. "The wine? I think you know that I cannot eat or drink in a pagan setting."

"Yet you accepted it, although you did not drink."

"It would have been impolite to refuse."

They came through the doors of the Antonia and paused at the head of the steps. The stink of blood rose up from the outer court where weeping women searched among the stacks of Jewish dead, throwing themselves upon the corpses as they were identified. Men carried the bodies away to burial. Jew and Gaul looked in horror at the scene. Mordra turned to the priest, "I'm a slave, I am not entitled to take sides."

"Not even when you look upon a sight such as this?"

"Especially then. I am the property of a Roman, a chattel."

"But you're a clever man. Had you been a Jew you would have been a scholar."

Mordra frowned. "Had I remained in Gaul I would probably have become a Druid."

"Is that a priest?"

"No."

"Then what would you have been?"

"Mordra sighed. "My interest is history."

Samuel paused, looking at the destruction and the grief that lay beneath them. A dog was kicked as it ran off with a length of human intestine; there was no dignity in the deaths of those who had fallen under the brutal swords of the Romans. "And did you Gauls ever suffer as we do under Rome?"

"This, and worse," Mordra replied. "Caesar wiped out whole towns, whole tribes. He set about the systematic destruction of our intellectual class," the Gaul smiled grimly, "especially historians and priests. And, unlike you, we did not have a messiah to look forward to. Oh, my people thought that they had found a deliverer in a man called Vercingetorix, but he was defeated and laid his arms at the feet of Caesar. He was taken to Rome in chains, imprisoned in a stinking pit for three years, then dragged through the streets behind a chariot, and ritually strangled. That was done by the people who call us, and you, savages."

The priest shook his head, "I don't even know how we would recognise the messiah if ever he came; there have been pretenders, perhaps even among those who arose this morning, but we have no test of his authenticity."

"That's odd," said Mordra, "because although we have no hope of a messiah, we do have what may pass for a test for such a man."

"What is that?"

Mordra's mind went back to the fruits of the years of study that he had enjoyed in the Druidic schools, and the seemingly endless verses of Druidic lore that he had committed to memory:

"'Let him magnify the truth, it will magnify him.
Let him strengthen the truth, it will strengthen him.
Let him guard the truth, it will guard him.
Let him exalt the truth, it will exalt him.
For so long as he guards the truth, good shall not fail him and his rule shall not perish
For it is through the ruler's truth that great tribes are governed.
Through the ruler's truth massive mortalities are averted from men.
Through the ruler's truth mighty armies of invaders are drawn back into enemy territory.

Through the ruler's truth every law is glorious and every vessel full in his lands.
Through the ruler's truth all the land is fruitful and every child is born worthy.
Through the ruler's truth there is abundance of tall corn.'"

Samuel was surprised that the Gaul had spoken of such matters in Greek. Mordra explained that the Gauls compiled their scholarly books in their own language but wrote in the Greek alphabet, and since the Roman conquest some were now written in the Latin alphabet. And that all of their scholars had both Greek and Latin. The priest thought on the words that Mordra had uttered. "It is strange that we have no equivalent to that. It is the best definition of a messiah that I have yet heard. But, tell me Mordra, what is truth? And why do you not write it in the language that you speak?"

"I think that different peoples have their own, different, truths, and that truth can change as circumstances change. This is a departure from what I was taught. But I was brought up to believe that Truth is the Word and the Word is sacred and divine and not to be profaned. The Word has magic power. Truth is the foundation of speech and all Words are founded upon Truth. That is why Druids do not commit our deepest philosophies to writing, we learn such things orally. That is why those who follow the many disciplines of scholarship write in other alphabets."

Samuel gazed out over the outer court. "And when you write the history of today's events, how will you portray it? Which side will you be on?"

Mordra paused to think. "I will try to be on the side of truth. It's no use asking me if I will approach these things from the point of view of the Sanhedrin; but I cannot approach it from the Roman side either. Yesterday evening you all prayed that next year you hoped to be free men in the Land of Israel, and, as a guest, I joined that prayer. I want nothing more than to be a free man in Judaea, in Gaul, anywhere. But you and I know that prayers are not answered. These men," he indicated the piles of dead before them, "were hill bandits. I cannot support them. I do have some sympathy with the zealots because they are

77

attempting what my grandfather attempted when he fought against the Romans more than eighty years ago. But, as he learned, such a fight is useless; Rome is too powerful. You ask which side I'm on; a slave cannot take sides. I am on the side of Mordra the Gaul."

Samuel wished him good night and picked his way through the outer court. Mordra watched the priest as he stepped amid the carnage. "Men and women make their own history," the Gaul murmured to himself, "but they do not make in circumstances chosen by them."

Hurrying towards the Court of the Sanhedrin, the priest passed under the shadow of the western wall of the temple platform. Solomon had built the first temple a thousand years ago, two centuries before the foundation of Rome, and it had been destroyed by the Babylonians. In recent times, the tyrant Idumean Herod had built his palace within the citadel, and the Antonia, here in Jerusalem. He had built other palaces, and the desert fortresses of Machaera and Masada, and he had rebuilt the temple, although work still continued upon it.

It was in the desert that they who called themselves the 'sons of light', those who scorned the temple and all who toiled within it, who turned their backs upon Jerusalem when they prayed, had their secretive settlement. The Essenes were a breeding ground and a refuge for the zealots, and the zealots could bring upon the Jews the great catastrophe that many feared.

More than two hundred years ago the family of the priest Mattathias had raised an army of Israel against the Greeks who then ruled the world. The leader of the Jewish army, Judah who was called Maccabeus, had much success against his enemies, although the Greeks twice attempted, and came close to achieving, the complete destruction of the Jewish people. There were years of bloodshed, huge loss of life, and all that happened was that the Romans took over from the Greeks and the descendants of the original zealots degenerated into a corrupt regime. The present generation of zealots arose immediately after the death of Herod, but they had only started to become an organised force at the time of the census ten years after Herod had died. The Maccabeans had failed, Samuel's party believed, because they had failed to accept that there are times when it was necessary to drift with the current, to accept what was happening, knowing that it would pass. The Sadducees reluctantly accepted heathen ways for the sake of peace and public order. They knew that all things pass and that true worship of the Lord would return in the fullness of time.

As a Jew, Samuel accepted without question the manifold divisions among his people. Dissent was not only tolerated, it was encouraged – men must think for themselves.

There were the *Chassidim,* the 'pious ones', sound men but not really in touch with the practicalities of life. With the decline of the Maccabeans, the Chassidim had fragmented. First to break off were the *Pharisees,* the 'separated ones'. Samuel had to admit to himself that he had a great deal of respect for the Pharisees. They were progressive in their views and liberal in their dealings with other Jews. The Pharisee movement remained lay and unofficial, but it served as a focus for Jewish hopes and aspirations. The leaders of the movement often championed the cause of the poor and oppressed. In many ways their tendency to puritanical formalism made them the guardians of the Jewish way of life. The father of Joshua, Joseph ben Jacob of Nazareth, epitomised the Pharisee leadership. A scholar, devout in his observances, he was a prosperous self-employed carpenter and recognised as a leader of his community.

The strength of the Pharisees lay in the Bets Knesset that were to be found in every town and village in the land. These many focal points of religious life were also academic centres where Scripture was carefully studied and expounded and fervent prayers were offered for the restoration of the nation. And they were independent of the Sadducee dominated temple.

Then there were the Nazarites who lived an ascetic life, forsaking family and all earthly possessions, wandering from town to town and begging for their subsistence.

It was the uncompromising nationalism of the Chassidic groups that Samuel, and most of the Sanhedrin, found hard to take. All things passed in time. Rome would depart and Israel would be a free and independent nation once again, it was simply a matter of waiting.

The Chassidim were impatient. Their claim that the very soil of the land of Israel was sacred was well founded in scriptural teaching, but it was unrealistic. Surely it was more sensible to guard Holy Law, to interpret and update it, to build a protective hedge around it to protect the Jews under Roman occupation, and in readiness for the day of liberation that would surely come.

Then there was the problem of the Samaritans. Their land lay between Sadducee, dominated Judaea and Pharisee, dominated Galilee. The split between them and mainstream Jews dated back to the time of Solomon, whose death heralded the division of the land between the rival states of Israel, in the Galilee, and Judah in Judaea. The Sadducees could agree with the Samaritans that only the five books of Moses could be regarded as divinely inspired Holy Writ, unlike the Pharisees who accepted the prophets, the songs, and the histories as sacred books. But the Sadducees knew that Mount Zion was the centre of the Jewish world, not Mount Gerizim, in Samaria, as the Samaritans claimed.

But now there was another branch of the Jewish tree that was becoming more influential and more dangerous. The Diaspora was long established; for many centuries Jews had established themselves throughout the basin of the Great Sea. These people were more Greek than Jewish, they had a different agenda. The Jews of Alexandria had translated Holy Scripture and the prophets, songs and histories into Greek to make them more accessible to the Greek Jews. Profound ideas do not translate. A language is the product of the experience of the people who use that language. Scripture can only be fully understood in Hebrew. They even used the Greek word *Synagogue* for 'house of assembly' instead of the Hebrew Bet Knesset that meant the same thing.

Samuel was deeply immured in the history, the lore, the total culture of his people, but he could no longer accept their god. When he had become an adult and entered the congregation, forty-two years ago, from mid summer to early autumn a brilliant star with a hairy tail could be seen in the night sky. There were many who were prepared to believe that this celestial phenomenon was the harbinger of momentous events, the

80

coming of the Messiah, the end of the world, the Lord's vengeance upon the Greeks and Romans. These and many others were the guesses that were made. But the star faded and disappeared and none of these wild prophecies were fulfilled.

When Samuel was a nineteen-year-old trainee priest and already beginning to question some of the, to him, less rational tenets of Judaism, Herod had died and the new zealots had started to arise.

When Samuel was a thirty-year-old priest, Augustus had reintroduced the census into Judaea. The Bethlehemites had refused to register and Archalaus exacted the terrible revenge of murdering the infant boys of the town.

That was the price paid for open resistance to Rome.

The dreadful massacre was the final turning point in Samuel's conversion to rationalism. The Sadducees prided themselves on the down-to-earth and practical nature of their beliefs. Let Chassidic fanatics waste their time worrying about the nature and purpose of the Lord; Sadducees preferred to follow main line thinking. The arena of spirituality was here on earth. The concept of the Jewish god was so vast that it could never be understood, so there was no point in trying to understand it. If the Lord was a being who had singled out the Jews for a special purpose that even they did not understand or question, then surely that being would protect his 'Chosen People'. How could such a god allow the destruction of so many innocent young Jewish lives?

Samuel had abandoned the god of Israel, but he still believed in Holy Law and that the Jews had a destiny that was yet unknown. He was deeply involved in the continuing school of scholars that examined and debated upon the Law. The preservation of Israel through Holy Law and rationality became all important to this priest. He was listened to with respect during all the long and minutely detailed debates, but because of his atheism, his name was never recorded in the written record of those debates. His views were recorded, but always anonymously.

If the zealots were allowed to follow their path, it could lead to the final destruction of Israel. It was written in the Book of Genesis that the Lord had destroyed the evil cities of the plain with fire from heaven and that only the righteous ancestors of the

Jews had survived. It was written in the book of the prophet Amos: "You have not returned to me," said the Lord. "I have overthrown some of you, as God overthrew Sodom and Gomorrah, and you were as a firebrand plucked from the burning. Yet you have not returned to me," said the Lord.

There was an opinion that there could be a great *shoah,* a catastrophe, a great destruction of the Jews. From this, there were those who had arrived at the belief that there would arise a tyrant more terrible than the world had ever known. That he would have at his disposal the men and the technical ability to put an entire nation into the fire. That his hatred of the Jews would be so profound that he would destroy them by their thousands and by their tens of thousands, whatever it might cost him to do so. The Greek Jews shared this fear, but in their translation of Scripture they used the Greek word for 'great burning' – *holocaust.*

The Jews looked at Rome and they saw the tyranny of the Emperor. They saw the technical brilliance of Roman civil and military engineering. They knew that Rome had the ability to bring about the final conflagration. The Sadducees saw it as their responsibility to their people to give Rome less cause to hate the Jews so deeply that they would put them to the flame. That was why the Jewish authorities were prepared to meet and hold discussions with the political wing of the zealots. They had to be persuaded to stop their futile and dangerous campaign. The Sanhedrin was prepared to make a few concessions, to pretend to hold out some hope to these people. And now the political leader of the terrorist movement had ordered his small band to join the armed struggle, he had revealed his true intention by making himself King of Israel. He had to die.

Mordra was no peasant from a remote village. He was of the tribe of the Parisii, born in the now very Roman city of Lutetia. The centre of the city was an *oppidum,* a fortification, secure on its island site in the river that was named for the goddess Sequana. Bridges connected the oppidum to both banks, and Roman Lutetia sprawled many miles from the central stronghold.

Mordra was deeply aware of his Gaulish heritage. At the age of three he had begun his elementary education. After three years of basic learning he had gone on to study for the first degree of *fochluc,* because 'his art is slender as his youth', like a sprig of the lime tree. He had then gone on to be set to learn the art of the scholar. Next he qualified as a *dos,* a 'young tree'. He then reached the degrees of *cana,* and on to *cli,* a 'pillar of the house'. After eight years of secondary education, Mordra qualified as *anruth,* 'noble stream'. At the end of eighteen and a half years of formal education, at the age of twenty-one, he would have spent a final year on original work in his chosen discipline of history and would have achieved the highest degree of *ollamh,* or professor. As he had progressed he had been awarded metal wands to signify his academic achievements. As a cli he had been given a bronze wand. When he became an anruth he was awarded a wand of silver. He had looked forward to holding the golden wand of the ollamh.

Mordra was a scholar, but he had never become a Druid. Before he could sit upon the *gorsedd,* the throne that would signify his entry into the assembly of Druids, his family circumstances had changed to cast him upon another stream of life.

His love of history was older than his formal education. Eighty years ago his grandfather had taken part in the fierce resistance to the Roman invasion. As a young boy Mordra had listened fascinated to the old man's tales of how he had stood with the great Vercingetorix against the Roman hordes.

It was now eighty-eight years since Julius Caesar had used a paltry excuse to advance from Roman held Gallia Narbonesis in that southern area that the Romans simply called 'The Province' and move north to subdue Gaul. Within three years, Caesar defeated most of the Gaulish leaders and was able to take an invasion force to land on the south eastern shore of Ynys Prydain, defeating the tribe of the Cantiaci on that inhospitable island, but the Proconsul had to return to Gaul to put down an uprising by the Treveri. The following year he tried to force the Treverian leader, Dumnorix, to accompany him on another expedition to the offshore island. Dumnorix had declared that he was a free man of a free people and would not follow Roman demands. Caesar's legionaries immediately cut him down. Caesar had made further inroads on Ynys Prydain but again was forced to return to Gaul, this time to put down an even greater uprising.

'Gallus' means cockerel, and a new leader, Vercingetorix, whose name meant 'king of warriors', chose this bird as his national emblem and issued his cockcrow to unite the Gallic tribes against the invader. Mordra's grandfather had answered the call and had been at Avaricum when it had been torched so that the Romans only gained an empty oppidum. He had been at Gergovia when Caesar attacked. The old man chuckled when he told how the women of the town had appeared bare-breasted on the walls to plead with the Romans not to attack, and how the Gauls had unleashed their forces upon the distracted Romans, tied down in mountainous terrain. In that one day Caesar lost thirty-six centurions and seven hundred legionaries.

Mordra's grandfather had grown melancholy when he spoke of the siege of Alesia and the final defeat of his great leader.

The old man had brought life to these old tales. Although he could not remember what he had eaten for his most recent meal, his memory of those days was crystal clear. He was almost ninety when he died, having by then forgotten even Vercingetorix, and the battles of his youth. The Druidic teachers told the same tale as Mordra's grandfather, but the young man was becoming increasingly aware that there was a different version of the story: that the Proconsul had brought to Gaul all the benefits of Roman civilisation and the Roman peace. That Caesar was, at least, the greatest general since Alexandros, and probably the greatest general ever, and that he had out-manoeuvred and out-fought the Gauls. Mordra came to the sad realisation that the winners write history.

A few days after his twentieth birthday, he had raced home wanting to tell his family about something that he had discovered when studying the development of the mother goddess Danu and the father god Nudd, something that had a bearing upon the very origin of their people. As he approached the house he saw that the shutters were closed and a bowl of water stood upon the step. With dread in his heart, he knew that he must wash his hands before he entered, and as he did so he could hear the wailing of his mother and his sisters. His beloved father lay dead.

Mordra's father, Abaris, had been a trader in precious and semi-precious gemstones and the family had enjoyed a good life in the belief that the trade had prospered. It was only after the death of Abaris they learned that the Romans, who were now the only ones who could afford to buy his wares, had owed him huge amounts of money that they did not intend to pay. The family was not impoverished because the eldest, a twenty-two year old girl called Faenche, was just beginning her career as a physician. The family mourned their loss of Abaris, yet rejoiced at his birth in the Otherworld. Widows and orphans did not starve in Gaul. In a society that had no private property all those in need were provided for. Nevertheless, the young man began to feel that he was a burden, and his future was uncertain. He did not yet know it but his destiny was ultimately to give him the undreamed of opportunity to pursue his scholarly interests. In the days following the death of Abaris, he sat with his mother and two sisters to consider his future. He shocked them by saying, "I have decided that I will not yet join the assembly of Druids. You are safe, Faenche, there will always be a need for physicians and illness knows no ethnic boundaries. But the Romans will never want a Gallic historian, they prefer their own version. I do not think that I would live long after I had been enthroned upon the gorsedd."

The three women had no choice but to agree with him.

"What will you do?" his mother asked.

"I don't know. What does a redundant scholar who has not yet started his career do?"

Faenche looked pained. "Will you go to Prydain as many others have? It's still a free land."

"For how long?" her brother replied, "Caesar would have conquered it, twice over, more than seventy years ago if he hadn't had to come back to deal first with first Dumnorix then again with Vercingetorix. It's only a matter of time before they make another attempt, and they'll almost certainly succeed the next time."

Wandering through the forum a few weeks after his father's funeral rites had been completed, Mordra was accosted by a haughty Roman, of about his own age, in new and too shiny armour. In the simple Latin used by some of the occupiers when addressing the natives, the young soldier had asked the way to the baths. Mordra replied, in perfect and sophisticated Latin,

"There are three nearby, sir. Which would you like, those halfway between here and the oppidum, the small baths down that street there, or the ones right here in the forum?"

The Roman was not sure whether the Gaul was being insolent, but he had been addressed as 'sir', which made him think that the young man whose hair was long in the Gallic style, and who wore a flowing moustache, had the right sense of deference. Neither was he sure which baths he wanted. The Gaul saved him by offering to be his guide. So it was that Mordra, the frustrated scholar, entered the service of Aulus Plautius, newly commissioned officer in the great army of Rome.

The ten years that had passed since then had been kind to the Gaul. There had been danger when his new master decided to sharpen his military skills by volunteering for expeditions deep in the hostile forests of Germania among the alien tribesmen who were the enemies of Mordra's blood. But Aulus had proved to be an instinctive tactician and quickly learned how best to conserve his men, for the legionaries were the tools with which he conducted his trade of war.

The young Roman had wanted to know as much as possible about Gaul, particularly about the conquest by Julius Caesar. Mordra was happy to oblige, but always diplomatic in how he presented the story. In Germania the slave sought out as much information as he could about the uncivilised tribesmen and their ways, mainly to satisfy his own curiosity, but Aulus soon discovered that Mordra's enquiring mind and his gift for picking up languages were invaluable assets.

In the four years that they had been in Judaea, Mordra had delved deeply into the rich seam of Jewish history and religion. It never ceased to fascinate him, and he could feel some sympathy with the zealots in their attempts to overthrow Rome, but he knew from the story of his own people that such a fight was hopeless.

Although he admired the Roman gifts for organisation and administration, their technical brilliance and military power, he had little regard for their intellectual qualities. As a Gaul he knew that he was of a people older than the Romans, a people who had spread their culture across Europe from Galatia in the east, through the long basin of the river named after the mother goddess Danu, and on as far as Iberia in the west, and north to Gaul and Prydain. As a scholar he knew the history and the lore of the highly developed culture of which he was a part. He had been brought up in the belief that his people were descended from the pre-Hellenic Greeks, although he now doubted that. He now believed that his people had not originated in Greece, but around the headwaters of the river of the goddess Danu, and had spread from there both east and west. But he admired the culture of Greece. He could appreciate the clarity of Greek reason and rationality. Although he did not follow them, the anthropomorphic gods of the Gauls and of the Greeks were so very human that they made some sense. The Roman gods were no more than pale imitations. To Mordra, the Romans were unimaginative. Even Roman scholars and artists were limited in their outlook. He believed that he knew the reason for this; the Romans had never learned to doubt themselves or to laugh at themselves. They had an unswerving and unquestioning belief that theirs was the best, the only, way. Wherever they spread their empire they assumed that it was in the interest of the conquered people to adopt Roman ways and to abandon what was often an older and a more sophisticated culture. Tonight, for the first time, he had met a Roman scholar who came close to his ideal. Marcus Lucius was the first Roman that Mordra had ever met who appeared to express uncertainty.

When Mordra was more than half way through his secondary education, and when Aulus was still dreaming of distant conquests, Lucius had begun his study of philosophy on the beautiful island of Rhodos.

In their childhood together, and at school, the friendship between Lucius and Aulus was based upon the attraction of opposites. The two distant cousins complemented each other, the man of action and the thinker. Together they made a formidable team for each was able to give to the other what he lacked, and restrain the potential excesses of either the budding man of action or the dreamer. Aulus kept Lucius down to earth and Lucius could persuade Aulus to hesitate and think before taking on all comers. Now, Lucius's theories were based upon practicality and he could see practical application for his philosophy. Aulus could pause, observe, and plan before taking action. Each had contributed to the successful career of the other.

Whilst Aulus was learning the ways of the soldier, and Mordra was earning the precious metal wands of a scholar, Lucius was sitting beneath the pines, on the marble benches of the *odion* – the small amphitheatre where lectures were delivered. He learned how Thales of Miletus, said to be the father of philosophy, had accurately predicted an eclipse of the sun by studying past records almost seven hundred years ago. From this Thales deduced that celestial phenomena were not the result of the whim of the gods, but could be understood by men. This was the beginning of natural philosophy, and from this there developed the belief that men have free will and are masters of their own destiny. Others concerned themselves with how men should live together in harmonious society; this was the birth of moral philosophy and the rule of law based upon common consent. Lucius would later realise that, unlike Athena who had supposedly sprung fully armed from the head of Zeus, the mind of Thales had been prepared by his own life experience and by unknown thinkers who had gone before him. He would also learn that there would always be those who opposed the philosophical approach. Aristotle had said, "All men by nature desire to know." But this was not necessarily true. Philosophers had such a desire, but there would always be those who preferred to be told rather than thinking it out for themselves. The ones who continued to believe that the gods govern all human actions, that man has no free will, and cannot control his own destiny.

Sitting in the shadow of the temple of Ilios Pythios high up on the acropolis, Lucius had begun to absorb the accumulated wisdom of the centuries of learning. On Rhodos he felt his vision of the world broadening, shaking off the narrow constraints of Roman certainty. After morning lectures he was able to exercise in the stadium adjoining the odion, then relax in the baths before descending to the bustling lower town where, like Socrates and Plato, he would stroll in the *agora,* the market place, to talk with fellow students, ignoring the taunts of those who made fun of their distinctive caps and gowns, knowing that in this exchange of ideas there lay the true seeds of knowledge.

He saw the shattered remains of the colossal statue of Ilios that had been set up by Chares of Lindos beside the harbour to commemorate the raising of the siege of Rhodos conducted by Demetrios Poliorketes, the son of a general of Alexandros more than three hundred years before. The statue had stood for only eighty years before crashing down in an earthquake – so much for the power of the gods.

Now in this strange, distant outpost, Lucius had found a kindred spirit. Mordra's quick mind, the product of Druidic schools, was the perfect foil for the more formalised education that Lucius had been privileged to receive.

Dinner had been a hurried, spartan, ill-cooked meal. Pilate, Aulus and Lucius had reclined upon couches, but none of them were relaxed as the silent Mordra served their food. Procurator and soldier were preoccupied with their own thoughts. Pilate did not feel the need to ask any more questions. Aulus was only prepared to give the procurator the information he asked for; this was a military matter. Lucius could feel the tension in the air and spoke only when spoken to, which was not often.

After the uncomfortable meal Pilate had retired to his apartment. Aulus had gone off on his own business, but first he had kept his promise to his old friend. Mordra had been despatched to the lower depths of the Antonia and had returned with Italian wine. Left alone, Lucius invited Mordra to sit, and soon the Gaul was reclining as they talked, and talked, and talked some more. It was remarkable how quickly they arrived at the point where people of like mind can understand each other so well that they can leave much unsaid, confident that it need not be said. At first Lucius wanted information about the Jews, their religion and their laws. Mordra opened up and they discussed these peculiar natives, the like of which neither had met anywhere outside Judaea. They agreed that the Jews of the Diaspora were different to those in their own land. They could both see parallels with other people in other times and places. (Lucius thought like one of the conquerors, Mordra like one of the conquered), but they agreed there were things about the current situation in Judaea that seemed to be unique.

Soon the talk turned to other things. Lucius expounded his opinions upon the differences between philosophy and religion, and those who follow them, opinions that he had formed on Rhodos. Mordra had held the same beliefs all his life. From the cradle, his people learned that men have free will and are not the puppets of supernatural beings. Lucius was surprised at the breadth and depth of Mordra's learning.

"You must have a brilliant mind to have learned so much in ten years."

Now Mordra was puzzled, "It's taken longer than that. I've been in continuous study for twenty seven of my thirty years."

"But how?"

"From the age of three to the age of eight at primary school, then twelve years in higher education. In the past ten years I've been building upon what I learned in Gaul."

"You have schools in Gaul? I thought your people were illiterate."

Mordra laughed aloud, "You've been reading Julius Caesar. And I recall that Poseidonios was head of one of the schools of philosophy at the Rhodian academy."

Lucius began to think that he could learn much from this man. "The works of Poseidonios are highly regarded on Rhodos, and he did travel among the Gauls, didn't he?"

"Oh, he visited Gaul. And you will recall that he was not entirely critical of my people. But his fifty-two books were a continuation of the works of Polybius, two Greeks charting the rise of the power of Rome. He wrote from the point of view of one totally committed to the Empire, and much of what he saw was so alien to his experience that he simply did not understand it, and I doubt that our scholars would willingly share their knowledge with him. Caesar had his own agenda. He had to justify his invasion of Gaul. What better way than to claim that he was bringing the benefits of civilisation to a nation of savages? He set about the total destruction of our intellectual class, the Druids, in order to wipe out our culture and replace it with the Pax Romana."

Lucius was floundering. "But I thought that the Druids were evil priests who practised wholesale human sacrifice."

"According to Caesar." Mordra nodded. "In fact only a small minority of Druids are priests. Religion sits lightly upon my people, and human sacrifice has had no part in it for a very

90

long time. Even then my ancestors only sacrificed criminals and prisoners of war. Anyone would have killed them, but my people used their deaths for what they then believed were a useful purpose. We have no less than 33 gods and goddesses common to all the peoples across temperate Europe, and some of them are in the form of three gods in one. Then each nation has its own gods, and every tribe, you could say every village. There's a god or goddess in every stream and hill, every cave, every well, everywhere. My people believe that we are descended from parent gods, but our hundreds of deities are more servants than they are masters. With so many gods, do you think that I can take any of them seriously? The Jews have a better idea. A Druid is a scholar, he may be a judge, a teacher, historian, physician, astronomer, poet, musician, priest or seer; all are philosophers."

"Are you a Druid?"

"No." Mordra was solemn. "I almost completed my formal education up to the highest level. But before I could enter the circle of the Druids my father died and I entered the service of Aulus Plautius, which is probably as well because Druids don't live long under Roman rule. I overheard you telling the tribune that you wanted to visit Ynys Prydain. One true thing that Caesar said was that it was there that one could best study our culture."

"Then I am more determined than ever to go there. Would you come with me?"

Mordra sadness increased. "I'm a slave, I can only go where Aulus Plautius takes me."

Thoughtfully, Lucius again reached for the flagon. Mordra was careful to sip his wine. Lucius whose mind and tongue were both working quickly, and who wanted to rid his palate of the too sweet local wine, found, not for the first time, that the more he drank the thirstier he became, and so he drank some more. He still had control over his mental processes and he realised that his treasonable discussion with his old friend had been overheard. It was as if Mordra read his thoughts. "A slave may have opinions, but he dare not express them. A slave may hear things, but who would believe him if he told the wrong people? Tonight I have expressed opinions, told you things about the relationship between my people and yours that could at least have me flogged."

91

Lucius relaxed, poured more wine into his cup, and they returned to their consideration of the Jews. Much later Mordra shocked him by saying, "You know, I think we are making a basic mistake. We keep comparing one historical situation, and this current situation, with other historical situations. The Jews are not Gauls, or Greeks, or Egyptians. They are a different people, the product of a different history – as are all peoples. I think that we are mistaken when we suggest that what is happening here is the same as what happened in Gaul, or has happened to other people in other places and at other times. Surely each human situation is new and unique. Human society is dynamic, it is in a constant state of change, it can move forwards but it can also go back, it never stands still. I think that what I am suggesting is that the first lesson of history, no matter how similar situations may appear to be, is that there are enough differences between peoples and times to say that history does not repeat itself."

Then Mordra saying, "We are too ready to equate civilisation with empire, and empire with civilisation," suddenly roused Lucius, whose concentration had been rapidly slipping away and who was becoming desperate for sleep. The Gaul went on, "An empire may bring some material benefits, but you and I know that civilisation resides in the collective intellect and in the achievements of thinkers, scientists and artists. Civilisation is men, and women, living together by common consent and for the common good. Not the imposition of alien rule."

Dangerous ideas, thought Lucius as he staggered off to his bed. Just before sleep overtook him, he recalled something else that Mordra had said when talking about Jewish kings. He had gone on about consecrated oil and anointing. He had talked about the Jewish Messiah, the 'anointed one'. They had been conversing in Greek and so the Gaul had used the Greek word for 'anointed one' – *Christos.*

After a hurried evening wash, Mordra made his way to the kitchens in the cellar of the fortress. A beautiful, slender, brown-eyed woman with braided dark hair was waiting for him. She rose and they embraced. Seeing his fatigue, she stroked his face and said, "I hope you don't have many days like this."

92

Mordra sat heavily, and she poured him a cup of milk. "I'm afraid that all our days will be like this. The morning certainly promises to be worse," he sighed. She kissed him gently, her heart going out to this man who was the centre of her life, as she was the centre of his. Mordra smiled. "It ended quite well. The man who came from Caesarea with Pilate is an unusual Roman scholar."

The girl frowned. "Unusual?"

"Yes," he replied. "He isn't stuffed with certainties, he's prepared to doubt, to question, and he's prepared to listen."

"Even to one of us?"

"Especially to one of us. He has an interest in our culture, even though he studied at the academy of Rhodos."

She pulled a sour face. "The home of Poseidonios."

This was not a new discussion between them. The writing of those, such as Poseidonios and Caesar, who, for their own ends, portrayed their people as savages, stung both of them.

Branwen was not a Gaul, she was a Silurian from the island that the Romans called Britain. Her father was a skilled craftsman in the busy ironworks in the industrial complex that the community owned on the banks of the river that was named for the god Nudd. As a girl, the iron trade was not for her and she had embarked upon a life of study in the expectation of becoming a Druid. In British and in Gallic society, women had equal rights and opportunities with men, unlike the Greeks and Romans who saw women as no more than the chattels of their fathers and later, their husbands. Branwen had studied law and it was her ambition to become a judge, making decisions not only between her own people, but also between the people of different tribes and nations. The third of the five children of Efan and Rhiannon, she was the one chosen by her parents to be head of the family after they had departed to the Otherworld.

A little over four years ago Branwen, then aged nineteen, had accompanied one of her brothers, Gruffydd and a young man called Owain on a voyage to the land of the Bituriges in south-west Gaul with a cargo of fine iron-ware. Having received a good price for their cargo, the two young men had got drunk in a taverna and picked a fight with a group of legionaries. The spirited young woman, who had been asleep upstairs, heard the commotion and tried to go to their aid. Acting instinctively, she had stepped between the opposing belligerents, arms spread wide. In her law, a judge could prevent conflict by this action. Even mighty armies would stand and call off their battle when a Druid judge stepped between them. Even had Branwen been a fully qualified judge, the Romans knew nothing and cared less about the laws of Siluria, and she was cruelly thrust aside. The young men had been killed, Branwen had been raped repeatedly, and then taken by the soldier who had claimed her, to the southern port of Massalia. As Aulus and Mordra were passing through that port to depart from Gaul, the Roman officer had been looking for a cook and had bought Branwen from the legionary who owed too many gambling debts. At first Aulus had been reluctant to buy the girl who was pale, listless and withdrawn. Mordra was driven to rescue someone who spoke a language very similar to his own, and managed to persuade his master.

The sea air on the journey from Massalia to Ostia brought back a little colour to the girl's cheeks. Aulus ignored her and Mordra was solicitous but kept his distance.

The ship was in the strait between Corsica and Sardinia when the emasculated and decapitated body of the legionary was discovered in a dark gully on the edge of Massilia. The head was never found.

They proceeded to Rome where the soldier received his new orders, then on to the estate of the Plautii. Mordra made no demands and Branwen started to trust him, the first man she had trusted since arriving in Gaul. In short segments at first, then more fully, she told him of her life and her family in Nudd. He told her of his life in Lutetia. They learned that they had much in common in their academic backgrounds. One night she confided what he had already guessed, that her condition when they had first met was due to the steps that she had taken to, as she put it bitterly, "Rid my womb of the Roman filth that lay there." Gently, without desire, he took her in his arms and held her as the tears flowed from her sad brown eyes.

It was not only that they were both of the same culture and were both slaves. Both knew that they would have loved each other as deeply even if they had met in Gaul, or in free Prydain.

Like the legionaries of Rome, they were not allowed to marry. But what the Romans did not know, for they did not have knowledge of the ancient lore, was that Mordra and Branwen could exchange vows before witnesses and become husband and wife. In their own lands they would have clasped hands through a hole in a *menhir*, a standing stone, but there were none of these in Judaea. Mordra had invited two Jews, a man and wife with whom he had become acquainted. To their surprise, the Gaul had washed their feet in a bowl of water containing a silver shekel.

Before the bewildered Jews, they held each other's hands and, in their own tongue, declared that they were man and wife.

After this brief ceremony, Branwen had taken the silver coin from the bowl and handed it to the woman who was witness to her marriage. "Have you a daughter?" She asked the Jewish woman through Mordra's interpretation.

"Yes," the woman replied.

Branwen handed her the shekel. "Give this coin to her and she will soon find a loving husband."

Aulus always referred to his cook as 'Mordra's woman' and it was to be fifteen years before he knew that they were married according to their own law and custom.

As they made their way to their sparse room, Branwen, who had no love for any Roman, wanted to know how Lucius intended to pursue his interest. "Is he to lay us out on a table and dissect us?"

Mordra hesitated. Then, "He wants to go to Prydain."

His wife stopped and looked hard at him. "There's more, what are you not telling me?"

"He said that he would like me to go with him."

"And what did you say to that?"

"That I could only go where Aulus took me."

In their room, they sat upon the bed and Branwen took her husband's hand. "You must foster this man's interest in our people. Do anything, even tell him some of our secret verses. Think what Ogma would do." She had deliberately invoked the name of the god of eloquence and learning, the patron god of the Druids.

Mordra shook his head. "What good will that do?"

"It will make him want to buy us."

Mordra was astounded. "Aulus will never let us go."

"Aulus can find other slaves. After today's events he could probably get some Jews for next-to-nothing. If we can get to Prydain with this Lucius, he will be just one puny Roman in a land where there is no slavery, my land, among my people."

Mordra put his arms around her shoulders and smiled at his lovely wife. "I thought it was only Gauls who were cunning."

Branwen kissed him. "You wait until I get you to Siluria, the Cymreig will tie you in knots."

For too long Branwen had not dared to allow herself to think of the green rolling hills, the wooded valleys, the rushing streams and waterfalls of Nudd. Later that night her sobbing awakened Mordra. Gently, he took her in his arms and comforted her.

Chapter 5

The garrison commander did not want to think that his prominent
social standing would ease his advancement in the army. He
preferred to believe that he would succeed on nothing but merit.
His family, the Plautii was of the ancient aristocracy and their
extensive lands in the foothills of the Apennines were the basis
of considerable wealth. The battle of Sentinum, the final defeat
of the Etruscans and Gauls in Italy, was more than three hundred
years in the past, and it was as a result of that victory that the
Plautii had gained their lands in Samnium. They had been close
to the centre of political influence ever since. Often they drifted
with the prevailing wind, only making a public declaration when
it suited their purpose, at other times sharpening the arrows for
others to shoot. Always more than surviving – coming out on the
side of the winners.

Aulus's first posting had been to the largely pacified
province of Gaul, but even there, he sought out the action. He
had travelled deep into the German forests and there had learned
the rudiments of warfare. So thoroughly did he learn to adapt his
tactics to the terrain, that he gained the epithet *Silvanus,* 'lord of
the forests'. He refined the arts of countering the thrusts of those
who fought in their native woodlands, taking the fight to them
and winning.

Although he was privately deprecatory about the writings of
Julius Caesar, he read them avidly and gleaned what he could
from the account of the conquest of Gaul. He had read Homer's
account of the distant Trojan wars, and of the deeds of
Alexandros.

Thucydides's "History of the Peloponnesian War" was one
that he had re-read, mainly for the political detail. Since arriving
in this land, Mordra introduced him to the history of the early
zealots under the command of Judah Maccabeus. The Gaul had

97

written a summary of the Hebrew history of the Maccabeans. By putting this knowledge and his experience into practice against the new zealots, and against the hill bandits, Aulus had not yet tasted defeat.

He knew that he was a brilliant field commander, but he knew that he was capable of more than that. When he studied the strategies of the old generals he could see where they had gone wrong, and he knew that he could do better. He wanted his own legion, to be a legate with ten times the men under his command than the single cohort of the Jerusalem garrison. Since coming to Judaea he had learned to play the political game that was in his blood. He was convinced that any province, especially such a troublesome province as this one, should be under the overall control of the army, not a civilian administrator. He would dearly love to prove himself as a provincial governor. If he could only get rid of Pilate he could show what a soldier could do to keep order. Perhaps this was the opportunity to manoeuvre himself into the right position to show up the procurator as an incompetent with an incomplete grasp of the situation. Aulus Plautius, stuck in a corner of a backwater of a province, did not waste his time. There was no reason why, given time, good fortune and perhaps the influence of his family, he should not rise to the highest rank.

Now, without helmet or armour, muffled in a coloured, checked cloak of finest British wool that he had brought back from Gaul, he moved through the dark streets of the city. He followed close to the path recently trodden by the priest Samuel. He was heading for the house of Caiaphas.

She was waiting for him, looking out from a small side window to the alley where he had appeared so often. Miriam knew that she was lost. She knew that the man she loved, beyond all that she had been born and brought up to respect, would one day leave Jerusalem and he would not take her with him. She had no hope for the future and could do nothing but grab what joy she could from the stolen moments with her lover. She was now eighteen years of age. An orphan from Magdala, she had been taken into the house of he High Priest as a servant three years earlier. She was no longer a virgin, for almost two years she had been the secret mistress of the commander of the Jerusalem garrison. No Jewish man would ever marry her, and if it were discovered that she had given herself to a heathen, she would be forever outcast. She may not even live.

Still she waited for him, knowing that tonight he would only want her for the help that she could give to him by spying, once more, upon her own people.

Aulus appeared in the alley. Miriam's heart leapt and she flew down the curving staircase to let him in through a narrow door. They embraced passionately. As the girl covered his face with kisses she could feel the sword beneath his heavy cloak. Taking the Roman by the hand, she led him, once more, up the staircase and into her small, dimly lighted room. There was no chair, she sat upon the bed. Aulus remained standing.

"I knew that you would come here tonight." She smiled slightly and spoke softly, afraid of being overheard.

Aulus loved Miriam. He enjoyed her lively wit, her tenderness, and her intelligence as much as he enjoyed her smooth skin and long, perfumed hair. It was possible, and he had considered the possibility, for a patrician to marry a plebeian woman by invoking *lex cannulaea* – the law of passage, and making her a social equal by taking her as his wife. It was common enough for such a Roman to take a foreign wife, provided that she was of high enough social standing in her own land. It was not possible for a man like Aulus to marry someone who was both foreign and of low birth. If he returned with a Jewish servant girl he would no longer be recognised by his own family. He would be ostracised from society, and his military career would be blighted.

They both knew that they were the victims of rigid rules. He was subject to the social mores of Rome. The ancient and uncompromising Holy Law of Israel bound her.

Aulus gazed sadly at the lovely girl. He wanted to take her in his arms and together forget, for what was left of the night, that they were both subject to forces that they could not control or overcome. Miriam knew what he was thinking, and that he was here tonight on a different errand. "You want to know about Joshua of Nazareth." It was a statement, not a question.

The soldier nodded. "Him and his followers. Samuel came to see me and gave what must have been an edited version of events. I need to know what the Sanhedrin really said."

"Sit beside me, Aulus. At least you can hold my hand while I tell you what I know. And you tell me what else you want me to do." Dark secrets gathered over Miriam's head like a black cloud. Her secret affair with a hated Roman, her secret activities, spying upon the priests, and another secret that she dare not share with Aulus.

They sat together on the narrow bed.

"What did Samuel tell you?"

Aulus frowned. "A lot of it I already knew. Mordra witnessed Joshua's entry into the city and the temple, he saw him attack the money changers and sellers of sacrifice. But, of course, Mordra could not follow him into the inner part of the temple. Samuel told us some of his arguments with the temple people, and his incitement not to pay taxes. He said that Joshua is a leader of the zealots and, most important, that he is, according to your laws, the king of Israel."

The girl was grim. "Samuel certainly told you what the Sanhedrin wishes you to know, and it's all perfectly true. His kingship, which is real, that and what he said about Roman taxes would give you no choice but to execute him. They were hoping to find him guilty of blasphemy so that, with your approval, he could be strangled to death under Holy Law."

"He'll be dead tomorrow, under our law," Aulus replied. "Do you know anything of his family?"

"Yes. He comes from a good Pharisee family in Nazareth and he's a rabbi. The Jewish authorities have been watching him for about two years, and are satisfied that he's the leader of the political wing of the Kaana'im. He's the eldest of five or six brothers and there are also some sisters. The brothers are Jacob, Judah, Simeon, and there's one called Joses who must have been named for his father to keep the name alive. There may also be one called Didymos who must be a twin because that's what the name means. Whether the other twin is one of the living brothers or is dead I don't know. His father is dead but his mother, who has the same name as me, still lives and may be here in Jerusalem at the moment. One of his twelve followers may be his brother Jacob, and another is called Didymos. If that's his brother then there may be two members of the family involved with the zealots, and heirs by blood to his kingship.

"One of his close followers, Judah a sicariot, came here from Bethany during the night before Passover. He was hammering and kicking at the door and when I opened it a crack, he burst in and demanded to see Caiaphas. He was the one who told them that Joshua had fulfilled all the legal requirements to become King of Israel."

Aulus was solemn. "Within the Empire a king can only be a client king, like the Herods, appointed by Rome. We have this Joshua and he can do no more, but his followers will probably pick another leader, especially if some of them are his brothers. I must have these men. I believe that they are all of the sect of the Nazarites and they are probably all Galileans, so they should be easy to pick out."

Miriam nodded. "What do you want me to do?"

The Roman soldier and the Jewish girl were lovers before she became his agent. She betrayed her people out of her love for him, and because she knew what they would do to her if their love was to be discovered. Aulus hated using Miriam in this way, but his duty demanded that he did so, and she was very effective in gathering information in the house of the High Priest. He was every inch the tribune when he said, "I have doubled the guard on all the gates and I have patrols out in strength in the streets. These people must still be in the city, hiding among the crowds. I want you to go out now to wherever people are gathered, in alleys or courtyards, anywhere. I doubt that they have been given shelter in houses, they are probably out in the open somewhere. Look out for the long hair and the Nazarite beggars' white clothing. Listen for the accent of the Galilee. Watch for any northern Nazarites who seem to be avoiding other people. See if you can find them, and let me know."

Miriam stood up. Taking Aulus by both hands, she gently drew him to her. They kissed tenderly; this was not a time for passion. "You go now," she said, "I will follow you out in a little while and see what I can find."

Aulus did not want to leave her. "Even if you don't find them, I must see you soon. When can I come again, or when can you come to the Antonia?"

Miriam hesitated, just a little too long, then, "Soon. Go now."

Galba, the senior centurion of the legion, was an Italian from Campania. Born in Herculaneum at the time when the Empire was expanding as far as the river Albis, he had grown up to enjoy the fleshpots of the sophisticated city of his birth. At the age of twenty, two years before the death of the Emperor Augustus, Galba had spent a riotous night in the House of Neptune, enjoying the wine and the women. Awaking at mid morning with a thick head and a mouth like a cesspit, he had looked at the naked girl snoring by his side and suddenly wondered how much longer he could live like this. His life had no purpose, no joy. Galba had gone out and joined the army.

Rome's standing army was unequalled in the world. The Romans believed that he who desires peace should prepare for war, and the legions were ever prepared. Galba had learned the manifold skills of the fighting man with double-edged sword, dagger and pilus. Dressed in a tunic of red wool, leather surcoat protected by metal bands, greaves and hob nailed sandals, he marched long miles with weapons and shield, his polished helmet slung on his chest, his rolled square cloak, which also served as a blanket, was on his pack which contained three days' rations. He also carried a saw, basket, axe and pick, as well as strap and reaphook. Legionaries were not only fighting men, they could build a fortified camp with accommodation for the whole legion and pack animals, bread ovens, cook houses, orderly rooms, latrines and washrooms in a few short hours. Such a camp was laid out to a rectangular plan with towers at each corner and a gate in each of the four walls. Between the towers artillery pieces were sited.

Galba drilled with his comrades. The drills were bloodless battles, and he was soon to learn that Rome's battles were bloody drills as the disciplined force demonstrated its invincibility.

The army was a state within a state. Patently it had its own structure which had been developed over the years and brought to its present form by Marius, more than a hundred years before Galba had enlisted. Each legion was now led by a professional legate instead of being the private army of a rich man who may or may not have had any military experience. The administrative reforms of Augustus ensured that the payment of the soldiers came from state coffers rather than from the pocket of the commanding officer.

The army also had its own culture, often removed from that of Rome or from the polyglot, worldwide empire. When the upper classes of metropolitan Rome abandoned Latin and addressed each other in Greek, the legions stuck to vulgar Latin, salted with the jargon of those whose trade is war. Rome stayed, for the most part, with the traditional gods and goddesses, Jupiter, Minerva and the rest. The common people tended to have real devotion (although those of the countryside often identified them with earlier Etruscan deities). The patricians increasingly worshipped their gods with their tongues stuck firmly in their cheeks. The legions gave their allegiance to Mithras, the army had is own religion.

In addition to those who served twenty years in the 28 legions, there was a variable number of auxiliary troops; Gallic and Numidian light infantry, Cretan archers, slingers from the Balearic Isles, and squadrons of Germanic cavalry and light infantry. Those auxiliaries who stayed with the army and survived twenty-five years were awarded Roman citizenship and a pension.

Galba had first been posted to Avaricum in Gaul, once the site of fierce resistance to Rome. The young legionary had been disappointed to find himself in a pacified region, but soon his warlike ambitions were to be more than satisfied. By extending to the Albis, the empire had been over stretched. There was a huge revolt in Pannonia, and the total destruction of the forces led by Varus. As a quick stopgap, many ex-slaves had been drafted in as auxiliaries, and this had a destabilising effect. There were simultaneous revolts on the Danubis and the Rhine with demands for better conditions, shorter service, less bullying, and more pay. The mutiny in Pannonia was crushed by Drusus, the son of the new emperor Tiberius, who used a convenient eclipse of the moon to work on the superstitions of the rebels. The Rhine frontier was the responsibility of Germanicus who was governor of the three Gauls and commander of the armies on the Rhine.

Galba went to war in the forests of Lower Germania and became a decurion.

Germanicus, the son of Tiberius's popular brother Drusus,

was himself well liked. Young and handsome (he was twenty-eight at the time), he was accompanied by his wife Agrippina and his infant son Gaius. The soldiers adopted the child as one of their own. His mother dressed him in full military uniform and the legionaries were delighted to see the toddler strutting and attempting to issue imperious orders. They named him 'little boots' – *Caligula*.

Galba was in the thick of the fighting when Germanicus, without imperial permission, crossed the Rhine and conquered the vast territory to return Rome to the Albis. The army advanced from Vetera along the Lippe against a Germanic tribe called the Marsi. They then went on from Moguntiacum against the Chatti, rescued the pro-Roman chieftain Segestes from his hostile son-in-law Arminius, and executed a converging move to the Amisia, where Germanicus brought four legions by sea. He then visited the Teuoburgian Forest and buried the remains of Varus's troops, but as he withdrew for the winter he suffered losses of men and stores from flood tides in the northern sea.

Galba had just been promoted to centurion when he took a spear to the upper chest in a minor skirmish as the army drew back to the mouth of the Rhine. More dead than alive he was dragged into the ship that was trying to run ahead of the flood. Finding haven at the mouth of the Sequana, the half-drowned army disembarked and a now feverish Galba was slowly nursed back to health.

It may have been fortunate that the newly promoted centurion did not take part in the unjustified fall of Germanicus. Despite his attempts to overcome transport difficulties, Germanicus had in three campaigns advanced then retreated. He had failed to create conditions that would have allowed him to remain in the vast hinterland of Germania between the Rhine and the Albis throughout the year. Tiberius recalled him to Rome.

The Tenth Fretensis Legion had been among the mighty force that Caesar had employed in the conquest of Gaul. After the downfall of Archalaus, it had been decided that the tenth would be sent to garrison Judaea. It was a crude irony that the standard of the legion was a wild boar – an animal that was an anathema to the Jews. Having recovered from his wounds, Galba was sent to Judaea and had now spent twelve years in the province. He had progressed to become the first centurion of the first cohort, the Primus Pilus, and Pontius Pilate's predecessor had, sensibly, drafted him to Jerusalem.

A rigid disciplinarian, his vast experience had tempered his authority with an amused humanity. He was lucky in that he was answerable to one who was, in his opinion, a 'good officer', and in Aulus's presence he allowed himself, and was allowed, to relax the formality that, closer to the seven hills of Rome, would have been natural to both of them.

Galba had another three years to serve. He had already looked over the piece of land that would be his as part of his gratuity for his years of service. He was not yet forty and vigorous enough to contemplate farming the lower slopes of the brooding Vesuvius, finding himself a wife and looking forward to establishing a modest dynasty to till the volcanic soil and, who knows, to follow the wild boar standard of the Tenth Legion. All that he wanted was a quiet life until his pension, and today the natives had done their best to deny him that.

Before retiring, the senior centurion did his rounds. In the Antonia he spoke to each sentry. Most of them were experienced soldiers, a few were boys who had had their first taste of battle that day. He then crossed the city to the praetorium and went to see the wounded; he learned that one had died. He spoke, briefly, to Timocrates then went, with his friend, to check on the prisoners and to ensure that they would be in a fit state to withstand their trial and to appreciate their punishment.

The sight that greeted the two centurions caused them to burst into laughter. Three of the terrorists were sitting on the cold stones, their backs to the wall. All, knowing what the morning would bring, were subdued but still trying to appear heroic. The one who had attacked the Antonia was glowering. The man who had attacked the citadel was stiff against the untreated wound in his leg. The burned youth who had been at Siloam was obviously in pain and exhausted, clenching his jaw against his fear.

What amused Galba and Timocrates was what the guards were doing to the older prisoner. They had seated him upon a rough bench. A cloth was draped around his shoulders, bloodstained from the whipping that he had received. A bunch of

105

soldiers pranced around the tormented man. One had a stick, and every time that he passed behind Joshua he would beat him on the head shouting: "I salute you, great king of the Jews." Others would kneel before him, fling out their arms and cry: "Oh, save us, great king." A Syrian paused before him and spat full in his face.

The centurions paused, enjoying the horseplay, then they descended. The soldiers left off their game.

"Carry on," said Galba, "Why have you got him dressed up like that?"

An Egyptian auxiliary told him, "Well, Primus, he wanted to be a king, so we're making him one."

"And what has he got on his head?"

"A king has to have a crown, so we made him one out of twigs, it was all we could find."

"I'm sure it was," said Galba, "And only from a thorn bush."

Chuckling together, Galba and Timocrates turned to leave their men to their fun. Galba knew that he would miss this when he retired from the army, the boisterous humour of honest soldiers.

Half way up the steps he paused, turned, and looked again at the man who was crowned with thorns. He looked into the eyes of Joshua ben Joseph of Nazareth and his blood was cold. The Jew should have been protesting, or weeping, or crying out in pain. Joshua did none of this. Galba could not avoid the feeling that he was, indeed, looking into the eyes of a king.

Chapter 6

The Earth rolled slowly towards the light.

Few slept in David's Holy City that night. Many prayed, and their prayers rose up to a god who, too often, seemed to be indifferent to the sufferings of his chosen people.

There were those who nursed their wounds, and those who lay in fear of capture.

There were those, and they were many, who mourned their dead.

In the hopeless hopefulness that is the blessing and the curse of their nation, Jews prayed:

Magnified and sanctified be his great name in the world, which he has created according to his will. May he establish his kingdom during your life and during your days, and during the life of all the house of Israel, even speedily and at a near time, and say you, Amen.

Let his great name be blessed forever and to all eternity.

Blessed, praised and glorified, exalted, extolled and honoured, magnified and lauded be the name of the Holy One, blessed be he; though he be high above all the blessings and hymns, praises and consolations, which are uttered in the world; and say you, Amen.

May there be abundant peace from heaven, and life for us and for all Israel; and say you, Amen.

He who makes peace in his high places, may he make peace for us and for all Israel; and say you, Amen.

This was the *Kaddish,* the Jewish prayer for the dead.

Now, as on that first Passover, thirteen centuries ago, doors were closed against the angel of death, which stalked the streets, this time in the form of heathen soldiers whose hobnailed tramp could be heard throughout the city.

Not one only has risen up against us, but in every generation there are some who rise up against us, to annihilate us; but the Most Holy, blessed be he, has delivered us out of their hand. And the Egyptians ill-treated us, afflicted us, and laid heavy bondage upon us. And we cried out to the Lord, the god of our ancestors; the Lord heard our voice, and observed our affliction, our labour and our oppression.

And the Lord brought us forth from Egypt, with a strong hand and with an outstretched arm; with terror and with signs of wonders.

How much more then are we indebted for the manifold favours the all-present conferred upon us? He brought us forth from Egypt; executed judgement on the Egyptians and on their gods; slew their first-born; gave us their wealth; divided the sea for us; caused us to pass through on dry land; plunged our oppressors in the midst thereof; supplied us with necessaries in the wilderness for forty years; gave us manna to eat; gave us the Sabbath; brought us near to Mount Sinai; gave us the law; brought us into the land of Israel; and built the chosen house for us, to make atonement for all our sins.

The Passover prayers could give little comfort now.

Those who had no shelter on this night huddled in alleys, in corners and in courtyards, hunched and muffled in their cloaks. Some gathered around guttering fires. They protected themselves as best they could against the cold and against the prying eyes of their oppressors. All awaited the return of the sun.

Let us this day, as on all others, find grace, favour, and mercy in your eyes, as in the eyes of all who see us; and requite us with acts of loving kindness. Blessed are you, O eternal! Who bestows loving kindness upon his people, Israel.

Despite their hopes and their prayers, the Jews waited in despair, in dread.

Caiaphas, High Priest of Israel and president of the Sanhedrin, did not sleep that night. He stood at an upper window, gazing across the rooftops to the dark bulk of the temple.

Caiaphas prayed:

Blessed are you, the Eternal, our god, King of the Universe, who has hallowed us with the holiness of Aaron, and commanded us in love to bless his people Israel.

He wore the breastplate of Aaron, the first High Priest. It was his sacred duty to continue to bring the blessings of the Lord to Israel. To serve, and protect them – even against themselves.

The Eternal shall bless you from Zion, the maker of heaven and earth.

Eternal, our Lord! How mighty is your name throughout the earth.

The might of the Lord was greater than that of any of Earth's proud empires. Trust in the Lord for he will prevail.

Preserve me, O Lord! For in you I trust.

Lord be gracious unto us, and bless us. O may he cause his countenance to shine upon us.

The Eternal, the Eternal, is a god compassionate and gracious, long-suffering and abounding in kindness and truth.

O turn your face unto me and be gracious unto me, for I am solitary and afflicted.

Unto you, O Eternal! Do I lift up my soul.

Lo! As the eyes of servants unto the hands of their masters, as the eyes of the maid to the hand of her mistress, even are our eyes directed unto the Eternal our god, until he is gracious unto us.

May he receive a blessing from the Eternal, and just recompense from the god of his salvation; and find grace and understanding in the sight of the Lord and of man.

The Priest was sure that he was right in what he was doing. He needed the reassurance of this prayer of benediction of the priesthood to find the grace and understanding that he craved.

O Eternal! Be gracious unto us, unto you we hope. Be their aid every morning, and our salvation in the time of trouble.

There could be no salvation for Israel but trust in the Lord. Those who risked not only their own lives, but also the threat of the shoah, were wrong to bring down upon the Jews the vengeance of Rome.

O do not hide your face from me, in this day when I am troubled, incline your ear unto me; on the day when I invoke you, quickly answer me.

More Jews would die on this day. They would suffer the cruel, lingering death by crucifixion at the hands of Rome.

Caiaphas had to pray for these men for they were his responsibility. But they had to die for the survival of the majority.

In distant days the Canaanites had sacrificed their sons on the altars of their gods. Now Israel was to do the same. Yet the Jews had always sacrificed their sons by dedicating them, on the eighth day of their lives, to the Lord by giving them the indelible mark of circumcision. A Jew could never escape from being a Jew.

Unto you do I lift up my eyes, O you who dwells in the heavens!

And they shall put my name upon the children of Israel, and I will bless them.

Unto you, O Eternal! Is greatness and might, glory, victory, and majesty; for over all that is in heaven and on earth is the sovereignty yours, and you are exalted head of all.

Israel had no friends but the Lord. The Jews were the chosen people of the Lord, but the price that they paid was high, sometimes almost unbearable.

Caiaphas knew that the Jews would always be an outcast people, no one would ever come to their aid in times of need. When they were oppressed they could only rely upon the Lord – and upon themselves.

Peace! Peace to him that is afar and to him that is near, says the eternal; and I will heal him.

The High Priest of Israel awaited the dawn when he would go to the Romans and, by sacrificing the few, try to save the many.

All his life he had dreaded reconciliation between the Pharisees and the Essenes, for he believed that this would result in strife against Rome that would be destructive to Israel.

He could deal well enough with the Pharisees, there was much in their ways that he respected and they were amenable to reason. The Essenes were more unbending.

Now there was evidence of a much more dangerous alliance. The Essenes and the more extreme Nazarites seemed to be coming together with the Kanaa'im under the persuasive leadership of the man who was now King of Israel. Such fanaticism had to be stamped out. Let Rome deal with the zealots, the Sanhedrin had to know more about the activities at Qumran. They had to have information from the desert community of the Essenes.

The Temple was the repository of the Holy Law, the centre of all authority. The Essenes had long turned their backs upon the Temple. All of the Chassidim regarded the scattered Bets Knesset as the centres of Jewish authority. How could the Sanhedrin hope to supervise such diversity?

Now they had learned from Judah the sicariot that Joshua of Nazareth had directly threatened the very structure of the temple itself. As they had been leaving the sacred complex, crossing the bridge to the Mount of Olives, one of the twelve, still overwhelmed by their success in holding the centre of Judaism, put his hand on Joshua's arm and said, "Look, Rabbi, what wonderful stones and what wonderful buildings."

Joshua had turned and looked over the mighty temple. He looked at the golden stones, some twice the length of a man, all perfectly fitted together, each dressed to catch the light at all times of day, the central part left roughly protruding, the edges cut back to uniform depth and width. This was the work of Herod the Great who had killed tens of thousands of Jews, among them the best of the men and women of Israel.

Joshua had gazed upon this magnificent work and he had said, "Do you see these great buildings? There will not be left here one stone standing upon another that will not be thrown down."

Caiaphas knew that the Essenes had plans to come out of the desert and 'pitch camp in the desert of Judah' – in Jerusalem, which they regarded as a spiritual desert. He knew that there were plans for war upon 'the Sons of Darkness', the Jewish authorities. He had to know how far advanced were those plans. Was the threat to the Temple made by Joshua of Nazareth, the uprising that had once again rocked the Holy City, the beginning of a bid for power by a new union of the Kanaa'im? It certainly appeared to be so.

The High Priest needed a spy in the Essene camp. He thought that he had found one, but it would have to be handled very delicately.

Judah the sicariot sat alone beneath an ancient olive tree on the hill to the east of the city. He sat close to the place where, at long periodic intervals, the carcass of a red heifer was burned. The ashes of these beasts were carefully preserved for the purification of those defiled by contact with the dead. This impurity was one of the gravest and one of the commonest forms of accidental defilement of a priest of Israel and could only be cleansed by sprinkling with water mixed with the ashes of an unblemished red heifer. Judah knew that he had been defiled for he had put the hand of death upon the man in whom he had once had such high hopes, the man who had betrayed him and had betrayed his people.

Judah had been so certain that the small band that gathered around Joshua ben Joseph was the hope of Israel, to rid themselves of the Romans and establish the Jewish commonwealth in *Eretz Israel,* the Land of Israel.

Idly, he played with the tassels on the hem of his shawl. The words from the Book of Numbers drifted, unbidden, through his mind:

'The Lord said to Moses, "Speak to the Israelites and say to

them: 'throughout the generations to come you are to make tassels on the corners of your garments, with a blue cord on each tassel. You will have these tassels to look at and so you will remember the commands of the Lord, that you may obey them and not prostitute yourselves by going after the lusts of your own hearts and eyes. Then you will remember to obey all my commands and will be consecrated to your god. I am the Lord your god, who brought you out of Egypt to be your god. I am the Lord your god."''

Joshua had lusted after the throne of Israel.

They had travelled together as a band of equals. His hopes had, he thought, been confirmed on the road to Jericho when the brothers Jacob and Johannan ben Zebedee had demanded that when they sat at table they should be one on the right hand of Joshua and one on the left. Some of the others had begun quarrelling about precedence and Joshua had rebuked the stormy brothers and the rest, telling them that the first would be last and the last would be first. Judah had sat apart from the argument; he wanted nothing of kudos or preferment. All that he wanted was to serve the Lord by helping to establish the Kingdom of the Lord in Israel.

I will pay to no man the reward of evil;
I will pursue him with goodness,
For judgement of all the living is with the Lord
And it is he who will render to man his reward.

This was from the rule of the Essenes.

Judah had been brought up to be truthful, humble, just, upright, charitable and modest. He had spent his childhood, his youth and his young manhood in study. His teachings in Scripture and in the precepts of the covenant of the Essenes had started when he was very young. At the age of ten he had embarked upon a further ten years of instruction in the statutes. At the age of twenty he was ready to go out into the sinful community of the Jews.

From his youth they shall instruct him in the Book of

113

Meditation and shall teach him, according to his age, the
precepts of the covenant. He shall be educated in their statutes
for ten years. At the age of twenty he shall be enrolled, that he
may enter upon his allotted duties in the midst of his family and
be joined to the holy congregation.

Once free of the stifling constraints of study under the rigid
Chassidic rules in the Essene community at Qumran, Judah
found it difficult to cope with his new, wandering, life. He saw
the misery of his Galilean people under the harsh, uncaring rule
of Herod Antipas. As he walked through the beautiful wooded
countryside he could take no pleasure in the abundant gifts of
nature, for the land was taxed to support a pagan emperor. This
was the Holy Land, this was Eretz Israel, this was the site of the
coming Kingdom of the Lord. Yet there were so many who sold
out to Rome and to the heathen Tetrarch of the Galilee just to
preserve their miserable lives. The Sadducee leadership was in
the pocket of the Romans. The Pharisees, despite their piety,
were too understanding of their enemies. Even the Essenes
seemed to be little more than a debating society.

It was in the town of Sepphoris that Judah had been
recruited to the Kanaa'im. The unhappy young man was in the
town, a zealot stronghold, to seek out those who would oppose
Rome. One evening he was alone with a zealot known as Abner
in a small Bet Knesset. Silently his companion led him to the
Torah scroll that lay partly unrolled upon the *bema,* the raised
platform upon which the sacred scrolls were elevated and read
after they had been taken from the *Aron ha-Kodesh,* the small,
room constructed as an apse, in which they were stored and
protected. Abner pointed to a passage in the Book of Numbers, a
book that Judah knew well. Upon leaving Qumran, Judah was
encouraged to live the life of a Nazarite. The instructions were to
be found in the Book of Numbers:

'The Lord said to Moses, "Speak to the Israelites and say to
them: 'If a man or woman wants to make a special vow, a vow of
separation to the Lord as a Nazarite, he must abstain from wine
and from other fermented drink and must not drink vinegar made
from wine or from other fermented drink. He must not drink

grape juice or eat grapes or raisins. As long as he is a Nazarite, he must not eat anything that comes from the grapevine, not even the seeds or skins.

"During the entire period of his vow of separation no razor may be used on his head. He must be holy until the period of his separation to the Lord is over; he must let the hair of his head grow long. Throughout the period of his separation to the Lord he must not go near a dead body. Even if his own father or mother or brother or sister dies, he must not make himself ceremonially unclean on account of them, because the symbol of his separation to the Lord is on his head. Throughout the period of his separation he is consecrated to the Lord

"If someone dies suddenly in his presence, thus defiling the hair he has dedicated, he must shave his head on the day of his cleansing – the seventh day. Then on the eighth day he must bring two doves or two young pigeons to the priest at the entrance to the Tent of Meeting. The priest is to offer one as a sin offering and the other as a burnt offering to make atonement for him because he sinned by being in the presence of a dead body. That same day he is to consecrate his head. He must dedicate himself to the Lord for the period of his separation and must bring a year-old male lamb as a guilt offering. The previous days do not count, because he became defiled during his separation.

"Now this is the law for the Nazarites when the period of separation is over. He is brought to the entrance of the Tent of Meeting. There he is to present his offerings to the Lord: a year-old male lamb without defect for a burnt offering, a year-old ewe lamb without defect for a sin offering, a ram without defect for a sin offering, together with their grain offerings and drink offerings, and a basket of bread made without yeast – cakes made of fine flour mixed with oil, and the wafers spread with oil.

"The priest is to present them before the Lord and make the sin offering and the burnt offering. He is to present the basket of unleavened bread and is to sacrifice the ram as a fellowship offering to the Lord, together with its grain offering and drink offering.

"Then at the entrance to the Tent of Meeting, the Nazarite must shave off the hair that he dedicated. He is to take the hair and put it in the fire that is under the sacrifice of the fellowship

offering.

"After the Nazarite has shaved off the hair of his dedication, the priest is to place in his hands a boiled shoulder of the ram, and a cake and a wafer from the basket, both made without yeast. The priest shall then wave them before the Lord as a wave offering; they are holy and belong to the priest, together with the breast that was waved and the thigh that was presented. After that, the Nazarite may drink wine.

"This is the vow of the Nazarite who vows his offering to the Lord in accordance with his separation, in addition to whatever else he can afford. He must fulfil the vow he has made, according to the law of the Nazarite."'

Now Abner pointed to another passage in the same book. Judah recognised it immediately. He did not need to read it, but in accordance with his upbringing and his life-long learning he picked up the silver pointer and followed the words, reading aloud:

'Then an Israelite man brought to his family a Midianite woman right before the eye of Moses and the whole assembly of Israel while they were weeping at the entrance to the Tent of Meeting. When Phineas son of Eleazar, the son of Aaron, the priest, saw this, he left the assembly, took a spear in his hand and followed the Israelite into the tent. He drove the spear through both of them – through the Israelite and into the woman's body. Then the plague against the Israelites was stopped, but those who died in the plague numbered 24,000.

'The Lord said to Moses, "Phineas son of Eleazar, the son of Aaron, the priest, has turned my anger away from the Israelites, for he was as zealous as I am for my honour among them, so that in my zeal I did not put an end to them. Therefore tell him I am making my covenant of peace with him. He and his descendants will have a covenant of a lasting priesthood, because he was zealous for the honour of his god and made atonement for the Israelites."'

Using the projecting wooden handles, careful as Judah had been, not to touch the sacred text, Abner closed the scroll and looked deep into Judah's eyes. "We are the Kanaa'im, the zealous ones, as Phineas was zealous in his passion for the Lord, as Judah Maccabeus gathered his zealots around him to fight for the freedom of Eretz Israel. Too many people have gone whoring after the Romans as the Israelites profaned themselves by whoring after the Moabite and Midianite women at Shittim."

Judah felt his heart beating, he was sure that the other man could hear it. Abner went on, "Could you, Judah, show your love for the Lord and your zealousness for him in the way that Phineas did?"

Judah said that he could.

Abner paused for what seemed an eternity. He then drew from beneath his cloak two curved daggers – sicars, and laid them before him beside the Torah scroll. Judah gazed, fascinated, at the dully-gleaming blades. He stretched out his hand. Lovingly he caressed one of the weapons along its length, then, grasping the handle, he raised it high in the air. Abner picked up the other sicar and thrust it back beneath his cloak.

Thus Judah moved inexorably from Essene to Nazarite, to Zealot to Sicariot.

A few weeks later he was in Tiberias, the town built by Herod who, in his sycophancy, had named it for the Emperor. It was a town shunned by pious Jews, but a place that attracted outcasts and those who sought the company of outcasts.

Judah had heard of Joshua ben Joseph, the rabbi who was following the work of Johannen ben Zechariah, now languishing in Herod's fortress at Machaera. It was in Tiberias that he first saw this magnetic man. Judah had heard the stories of miraculous healings of the sick and lame, but this did not interest him. Healing and the containment of contagion had been known since the time of Moses, the rules are written in Holy Scripture. The great Elijah was said to have restored life to a widow's son. Such things did not concern Judah, but they did concern many of the people in the town, some of whom had been attracted there by the nearby mineral springs.

There was a large crowd pressing in upon the rabbi and his handful of followers. One dragged a boat up on the shore and Joshua climbed aboard. The boat was then pushed a little way out onto the lake so that Joshua could be seen, and address the crowd without being overwhelmed.

He was not a tall man, if anything he was slightly below average height, but the breadth of his shoulders and the strength of his arms could be seen beneath the loose, white robe that he wore. His dark hair had a reddish tinge and was worn long in the Chassidic style. His beard was full and dark.

As Judah pushed his way to the edge of the lake he looked for the first time into the eyes of Joshua of Nazareth. They were of the deepest blue, the colour of the Great Sea to the west on a clear summer's day. Those eyes compelled Judah.

Joshua spoke in parables for he was addressing a largely unlearned audience, but they, and Judah, understood that he was preaching the purity of the coming Kingdom of the Lord. When the preaching was over and the crowd dispersed, Judah approached Joshua who was camped by the lakeside eating a meal of fire-blackened fish and unleavened bread. As he came into the circle of light cast by the fire, the rabbi looked up and asked him his name. When the sicariot had told him who he was, Joshua turned to his followers and said, "Now we have our twelfth."

The significance of the twelve was clear to Judah from the outset, and Joshua was the first among equals. One day he had said to them, "The Kingdom of the Lord which we are preparing and which will surely come, is like a great palace with many rooms. Each room has a purpose and men must be skilled in carrying out the functions of the different rooms. The groom is not the treasurer, and the treasurer is not the gardener, neither is he the guard upon the gate. A great house needs many skills for its smooth running. Israel is the greatest of houses and it has many rooms."

They were being prepared for the government of the commonwealth of Israel, the kingdom of the Lord.

Judah had remembered the many rooms and the functions of those rooms as he listened to the argument about precedence on the Jericho road. He had asked Joshua why he did not establish an hierarchy of command.

"Because that would create division, and if a kingdom is divided against itself, that kingdom cannot stand. If a house is divided against itself, that house will never stand. Isaiah asked:

118

'Shall the prey be taken from the mighty?' No one can break into a strong man's house and make off with his goods unless he has first tied the strong man up. Then he can ransack the house. But Nebuchadnezzar bound Shadrach, Meshach and Abednego and threw them into the hottest furnace. The Lord delivered his servants from the fire and King Nebuchadnezzar recognised the power of the Lord and raised Israel up in the Kingdom of Babylon."

Judah could not understand why the rabbi should take upon himself all the danger of leading the group. Was he a prophet?

It was as if Joshua had read his thoughts, for he asked his disciple, "How did Elijah overthrow the eight hundred and fifty pagan priests upon Mount Carmel?"

"He took twelve stones, the number of the sons of Jacob, and with those stones he built an altar. The Lord brought down fire to that altar and the sacrifice was consumed. By that sacrifice the enemies of the Lord were destroyed beside the river of Kishon, and Israel was saved."

The Rabbi smiled, "King David had already known that twelve separate stones, or twelve separate tribes, are nothing until they are brought together in one structure. Then they become an altar to the Lord."

"Teach me, Joshua, for I must know. Are you the builder of the altar?"

"I am, and the altar is Israel."

"Are you also the fire that brings light to our people?"

"Such fire can only come from the Eternal our god. I am the sacrifice."

Joshua had railed against the Sadducees, and particularly against Caiaphas, the High Priest: "You have lost your way, as Aaron, the first High Priest, lost his way when he condoned idolatry even as his brother Moses was receiving the Holy Law from the Eternal on Mount Sinai. You have followed the ways of the heathen Romans as Aaron followed the ways of the heathen Egyptians, the ways of the heathen Assyrians against whom Isaiah struggled. You have ensured your own comfort by encouraging our people to believe that Roman rule is acceptable in the Holy Land. You and your Sadducee kind are the graveyard of Israel. As men paint the walls of a tomb with lime and the

119

whiteness dazzles the eyes of the living, you have whitened the face of Roman rule, but inside there is nothing but corruption. Under Roman rule there is nothing but darkness for the Elect of the Lord. I will return to Isaiah when I say, 'the people that walked in darkness have seen a great light, they that have lived in the shadow of death, upon them has the light shone'."

Joshua had turned his back upon his own Pharisee past because, he said, they had been the salt of the earth, but the salt had lost its taste and was now fit for nothing but to be thrown out and trodden underfoot. "Any light that you may once have had within you is now lost, you have hidden it under a pot where it has died for want of air. The true light of Israel cannot be put out, it cannot be hidden. It must be set high where all can see it and where it casts its glow into the darkest corners. But, as Jeremiah said, 'You are foolish and without understanding. You have eyes and see not. You have ears and hear not'."

He was often challenged by other scholars, even accused of blasphemy. His anger rose against such men: "How dare you speak to me of blasphemy? You, who throw away the wisdom of our people. The precious pearl grows out of the suffering of the lowly creature that gives it birth. A pearl is like a tear, and the wisdom of Israel is the tears of Israel from many generations of suffering. You may be prepared to give that which is holy to dogs, but I will not feed our pearls to swine. You blaspheme every day – by your support for the dogs of Rome, the pigs that subject our land and our people.

"You are without depth of thought or feeling, like the thin soil on a rocky hillside. Your spirit is choked by your fear of Rome as an untended field is choked with weeds. I am the sower who casts the word of the Lord across this land. When you hear the holy word, the shallow soil of your minds gives forth only poor, thin shoots that quickly die in the heat and light of the sun. Your weed-choked spirits strangle the truth. Take care, for much of the good seed that I have sown is already fast-rooted in the fertile soil of Israel."

There were those who dared to suggest that Joshua was the Messiah. One day, with the twelve gathered around him he had been expounding upon the Book of Isaiah when Simon bar Jonah asked him directly if he was the promised one. Joshua smiled,

"The Messiah is not just a man, he is a movement, a cause. There have been many times when we have needed deliverance, and the Lord has always provided that deliverance.

"We have been talking of Isaiah. You must know that the Book of Isaiah was not written by one man, but by two, possibly three men over quite a long period of time. At that time we were again a subject people. The vision of the prophets was such that they knew and, with courage, told their people that only their fidelity to the Lord and the strict following of his ways would bring them deliverance. The times were harsh, Isaiah pointed the way towards salvation, and the times produced the man. As Isaiah said, 'Unto us a child was born, unto us a son was given; and the government was to fall upon his shoulders.' He was known as, 'Wonderful in the council of the Almighty god." His name was Eliakim the son of Hilkiah, and he delivered his people from their oppressors. The government was in the hands of Eliakim. He was the father to the people of Jerusalem and to the House of Judah. The keys to the House of David were in his hands. He and his followers were a messianic movement.

"When Samuel recognised the way out of oppression by the Philistines, he found a way to deliver Israel by unifying the nation under one king. Samuel led the way for the Messiah, and the Messiah of his time was the great King David.

"Moses, our teacher and the founder of our nation was the Messiah of his age, responding to the needs of the time.

"The Messiah is not just a man. The Messiah is Israel and the satisfaction of the need of Israel to be autonomous under the Eternal God, King of the Universe. Our people will, whatever persecution is heaped upon them, live to the end of time and outlive all of their persecutors. I do not know what need we will have of deliverers in the future, but I do know that the people of Israel will always be saved if they maintain the purity of their faith and the uniqueness of their identity, if they hold fast to their Jewishness, and that our salvation will be of the people, not the work of any one man. There have been many times in our history when kings and powers have prevailed over us. Those kings have perished and the powers have passed away. The Romans have the power to destroy the Holy City of Jerusalem, but neither they nor their mortal Emperor have the power that dwells only in the

Eternal God.

"For it is he who has not made me other than an Israelite, who has not made me a slave, who has not made me a woman. He makes the blind see and clothes the naked. He sets the fettered free and raises up his people who are bowed down by oppression. The Eternal God, King of the Universe, and he alone, expands the earth above the waters. He supplies all of our needs and directs the steps of men. The Eternal God, King of the Universe, girds Israel with power and crowns Israel with glory. He grants strength to the weary and removes the sleep from my eyes so that they may be open to see his glory.

"Men have called their gods by many names down the ages, but his people Israel have learned not to diminish their god, the one true god of the Jews, with man-made names. He is as he was in the beginning, is now, and ever shall be. His world is without boundaries and without end. I am only a man, but as a Jew, through my faith in the Lord I will live long after the Emperor, the Empire, and all their powers have crumbled into dust. Today it is Rome that persecutes us. They are not the first, there have been many. Where are they now? In ages yet to come there will be others jealous of the people who are the elect of the Almighty, and they will go the same way as Egypt, of Philistia, of Babylon, of Persia and of Assyria, and Greece – and of Rome!

"Men of Israel, can you not see that the might of Rome is no more than a blot moving across the face of time? Rome is no more than the present evil. The everlasting good is the Lord. Let your faith in the Lord be strong and you will have the strength of the lion and the gentleness of the dove. Arm yourselves in the name of the Lord and you will rise on wings of eagles above the puny works of men. But you will be men who can stand against all evil. We are not contending against mere men, but against empires and powers, against those who rule the world in darkness, against the hosts of wickedness. Put on the whole armour of the Eternal God of our fathers and you will withstand all evil. Whatever dark empires there may be will pass away and they shall be no more. Look at the roads of the Romans. They are broad and straight, but they all lead to Rome. The road I offer you is rocky, it is narrow and hard, but it will take you to the kingdom.

"I look at my people and see that they are poor in spirit, but by the road that I show to them they will enter into the kingdom of the Lord. The people of Israel are in mourning; their comfort can only come from the Lord. We are cast down in our own land, but we will inherit its sacred soil. Rome extracts tribute from us until we go hungry, but we will be filled when we give only to the Eternal God. Yes, we will be persecuted by our enemies, but the kingdom is ours, and it will be ours when all heathen kingdoms and empires have passed away."

As Judah sat on the hard, cold earth of the Mount of Olives, hugging his cloak around him, he realised that he was the only one of the twelve to still have a cloak, the rest had sold theirs.

Memories of the good days with Joshua crowded in on him. There was the priest who had engaged him in debate, then asked him which was the most important of the Holy Laws. Joshua had replied, "As it is written in the Book of Deuteronomy, 'Hear, O Israel! The Lord is our God, the Lord is one. You must love the Lord your God with all your heart and with all your soul and with all your might. Take to heart these words which I charge you this day. Impress them upon your children. Recite them when you stay at home and when you are away, when you lie down and when you get up. Bind them as a sign upon your hand and let them serve as symbols on your forehead; inscribe them upon the doorposts of your house and on your gates'."

"And which is the second of the laws?"

"It is written in the Book of Leviticus, 'Do not hate your brother in your heart. Rebuke your neighbour frankly so that you do not share in his guilt. Do not seek revenge or bear a grudge against one of your people, but love your neighbour as yourself'."

The priest had looked thoughtful. "Unless we follow the second of those laws, and do not do to any man that which would be offensive if done to us, then we have not followed the first law. For our people are the creation and the elect of the Lord and we can only show our love of the Lord by demonstrating our love of his people."

Joshua had smiled upon the priest and told him that he was very close to him in his striving for the kingdom.

There were others who accused him of mocking the prophets and perverting the law. To them he showed his anger and his contempt: "You are the ones who mock the prophets. You are the ones who threaten Holy Law by following the ways of Rome. I have come to fulfil the work of the prophets, to ensure that the law is complete in Israel. Until the end of time not a letter, not a stroke, will disappear from Holy Law. If any man ignores the least of the law's demands, if any man, such as you, teaches others to do the same, then such a man will be the lowest in the Kingdom of Israel. But any man who keeps the law and teaches others to do so, he will stand among the highest in the kingdom."

The Kingdom of Israel!

The only kingdom Judah understood was the heavenly kingdom. There was no place for mortal kings.

Had Joshua always intended to seize the empty throne for himself, or had the success of his campaign turned his head? There was no place for earthly kings in the Holy Land. No man should hold that much power to himself. The last king, imposed by Rome, had been the alien Herod of Idumea – one of the worst tyrants there had ever been. Even the greatest kings of the past, David, Solomon, had been corrupted by their power.

Looking back, Judah now knew that he should have been suspicious long ago. Johannen ben Zechariah had been a true prophet, but the Sadducees would not accept him as such. They feared his strength, his enlightenment, his following.

One day a Sadducee priest had been mocking the memory of Johannen by saying that he had been wandering demented, around the Galilee proclaiming the coming of the king. Joshua corrected the man, telling him that Johannen, who was his cousin, had announced that the promised king had arrived. The Sadducee sneered. "And I suppose you are the one heralded by the Essene?"

Judah now realised that Joshua had not denied this charge. He had said, "Johannen, the son of Zechariah, was a true prophet. He lived for many years in the desert community of the Essenes. But when he returned, as a Nazarite, to the Galilee he saw that the Romans, with your help, had turned it into a desert by the greed of their taxes. He saw that you priests had turned the whole land into a spiritual wilderness. As it is written in the Book of Isaiah: 'Clear a way for the Lord in the wilderness, make a path for the Lord in the desert'."

Judah had thought that this was Essene rhetoric and no more than that. Now he knew that Joshua regarded Johannen as no more than the herald proclaiming the coming of a king to claim the empty throne of Israel. Joshua had not denied the charge that Johannen was his herald. He had his band of followers and, to Judah's shame, he had been a willing member of that band. His entry into Jerusalem had been to wild public acclaim with *lulav,* palm branches, laid beneath the donkey's hooves, the crowd chanting the traditional greeting to a king of Israel. Joshua had bathed in the *mikveh,* the purifying bath, then entered the temple through the Golden Gate, the route to be taken by the Messiah. He had grasped the horns of the altar and proclaimed the *Hallel,* as required of a king of Israel claiming his throne. Even then, Judah believed, because he wanted to believe, that Joshua was still acting as first among equals, that it was he and the twelve, on behalf of the people, acknowledging the acclaim.

As they had crossed the bridge spanning the Kidron Valley to the Mount of Olives, one of the twelve had looked at the stack of stones that had once formed the altar. They had been defiled more than two hundred years ago when the Greek Antiochus had used the altar as a base for a statue of himself in the form of Zeus. Judah Maccabeus had ordered the altar dismantled and replaced, but he had not known what to do with the stones as they had once been consecrated. He had ordered them stacked on the eastern lip of the Temple platform until a prophet should arrive to decide what to do with them. One of the twelve had asked Joshua what should be done. Without hesitation he had ordered that they be broken with hammers until they were no more than dust, then taken out through the Dung Gate and thrown upon the city's rubbish tip. He had then looked over the temple and had prophesied that it would be destroyed. Judah was reassured, although, as an Essene, he had no regard for the temple, he could not imagine a king of Israel threatening its destruction.

But it was the action of a true zealot to threaten the corruption that was Jerusalem. Jews had no place in cities where the sun could only be glimpsed from the man-made canyons of crowding buildings. Judaism was a religion of the land, of the sacred soil of Israel. The people were the people of the land, a land given to them, and only them, by the Eternal God.

When the summer figs had been gathered and the dates were ripe on the palms, the sound of trumpets heralded the New Year. The Feast of Tabernacles, in the month of Tishri, was a time when people dwelt in booths bedecked by the rich produce of the soil. The winter figs came in the month of Marchesvan. Then came the harvesting, and in the month of Chislev the lights of dedication and of the Maccabees were lit, before the sowing of the fields. Through Tebeth and Shebet the sharp-tasting fruits ripened on the trees, to be gathered in Adar. In the middle of this month of Nisan came the Passover, and the harvesting of barley and of flax, followed by the festival of the first fruits. On through Iyyar and into Sivan, when the early figs ripened and Shavuot was celebrated by taking loaves of risen bread made from the flour of the first harvest up to the temple. In Tammuz came the grapes, and in Ab the olives. In Elul the summer figs were ready once again and another New Year approached with its time of reflection on past actions and the chance to atone for past misdemeanours.

Let Greeks and Syrians crowd in the cities, buying and selling in their dark little shops and running their rowdy tavernas. Such were no occupations for Jews. The Jews who did live in cities had lost contact with the ever-ripening seed of Judaism. Cities corrupted and Jerusalem was the capital of corruption.

After leaving the temple they had travelled to Bethany, and it was there in the House of Simon the Priest that Judah had realised the full horror of betrayal. He had always been wary of Simon, who was referred to by the Sadducees as 'the leper'. That dread disease had never touched the priest, but he was an outcast. Although not an official member, he acted as an outside advisor to the brotherhood, the co-ordinating body of the zealots. As Joshua was the leader of the non-belligerent, political wing of the zealot movement, the two men were close friends. But Judah could not trust Simon, the priest had never fully committed himself, and he always stood on the sidelines.

They had taken their evening meal, had recited the *Arvit,* the evening prayer and were relaxing, happy in the success that they had enjoyed in the temple. A young woman, a member of

Simon's household, came into the room carrying a fine alabaster phial. Suddenly she broke open the flask, filling the room with the heavy perfume of precious oil. She handed the alabastron to Simon who poured the contents over the head of Joshua, placed his hands upon the anointed head, and recited the prayer of blessing of a priest.

It all happened so quickly that Judah could at first think only of the waste of such an expensive unguent. He blurted out, "Why are you wasting that ointment? It could have been sold to feed thirty poor families."

Then, as Simon, his hands still upon Joshua's anointed head, gave the sicariot a supercilious look, the full realisation hit him like a hammer blow. The failure to deny the herald, the triumphal entry into Jerusalem, the take-over of the temple, the band of twelve – latter-day tribal elders under an anointed king!

Joshua had not threatened the temple; he had threatened the *Sadducee* temple. He would return there and rebuild the authority with himself enthroned.

The King of Israel turned to the sicariot. "Let them alone. Why do you trouble them? They have done a beautiful thing to me. You will always have the poor with you, and you can always help them. You will not always have me."

Judah stood, uncertain. His hand was beneath his cloak, grasping the handle of the curved dagger. Joshua's mesmeric eyes were upon him. He dashed from the room and out into the night. He did not know how long he wandered in his torment, or where he went. Eventually the walls of the city rose up before him. He knew what he must do. He knew that he would get no support from his own Chassidic people for many of them would welcome strong Jewish leadership, even if it meant exchanging a Roman tyrant for a Jewish one. He must have justice, and there was only one court of justice for the Jews, corrupt though many of its members were. He had to go to the Sanhedrin.

He ran through the streets of the city and hammered and kicked at the door of the house of Caiaphas. A young servant girl opened the door a crack and peered, fearfully, out at him. Judah pushed open the door and burst into the house. The girl flattened herself against the wall. Then an old and dignified man appeared. "It's all right, Miriam," he said kindly to the frightened girl, "I will attend to this."

The man was Annas, father-in-law to the High Priest. Judah spilled out his story. The old man looked grave, then summoned Caiaphas. Again Judah told of his betrayal, and the betrayal of Israel by a man who was, at this moment, the legal King of Israel.

It all seemed to happen in a haze. He was taken through the dark streets to the hall of the Sanhedrin. He wanted to redeem Joshua, to bring him back to the path of righteousness that the rabbi himself had so often preached. The judges questioned him; his answers came automatically, more the product of his education, his many years of debate and dissertation than of any apposite, systematic thought. There was a plan, a plot, for him to lead them to Joshua so that he could be brought before the court. They offered him money for his information and his help. At first he almost spat in their faces, then, irrationally, he thought of what he had said about the waste of the precious oil and how its price could have fed the poor. This was Passover, he thought of the sacrificial lamb. The prophet Zechariah and his husbandry over the flocks of Darius came into his mind. He asked for thirty shekels of silver. He would feed the poor, the lambs of God, with the money with which he had sold the usurper.

I will pay to no man the reward of evil.

The heavy silver coins were tainted. How could he give blood money to the poor?

As the first cold light of dawn crept up behind him, Judah's confusion grew. Had he the right to pass judgement on Joshua? Could he be sure that what he had done was the will of the Lord?

For judgement of all the living is with God.
And it is he who will render to man his reward.

The temple. The temple was already defiled. The temple took tainted money every day. The temple accepted heathen coins in exchange for Jewish coins, but that meant that the temple traded in coins that defied the second law.

In the cold dawn light he rose, stiffly, from beneath the

128

olive tree, a tree old as time, a tree old enough to have been looked upon by King David. At the temple he entered the mikveh to carry out his ritual ablutions. He then walked in through the northern gate. Taking a single shekel from the purse that the judges had given to him, he approached one of the sellers of sacrifice. The man recognised him as one of the Galilean zealots and was about to call the temple guard, but then he looked at the tormented man before him and hesitated. Judah produced the purse and ordered two doves and a year-old male lamb. The tradesman easily recognised his customer as a Nazarite and knew that such an offering meant that he had been in touch with death, but he had not shaved his head as was required. He was surprised to receive a further, stumbling, order for another year-old male lamb, a year-old ewe lamb and a ram, together with their grain offering and drink offering, and a basket of unleavened bread with oil, the offerings of one who has come to the end of his time as a Nazarite. To make the defilement offering, unshaven, and the final offering at the same time was unheard of. As he hesitated, Judah up-ended the purse and poured a stream of heavy coins onto the bench. The trader's eyes popped out, but he reached to count the unexpected bounty before him. "You can't give me this, it's more than ten times the price of your sacrifice..." But Judah had walked away, leaving 29 silver shekels for the man who did not know whether to rejoice, or to call the guard, or to run after the Nazarite to return his money. He decided to rejoice, closed up his stall for the day, hurriedly selected the required sacrifice and handed it over to a Levite with instructions, and then he went home.

Judah walked into the Court of Women, up the curved steps and through the Nicanor Gate into the Court of the Israelites and on into the Court of the Priests. He was following the same route that Joshua had taken only five days ago. The priests and Levites around the altar recognised him immediately and were about to apprehend him, but then they saw his ravaged expression, and let him go. He mounted the ramp to the altar and there he drew his sicar. Savagely, he hacked off his long hair and, as required by the rule of the Nazarites, threw the hair into the altar fire, beneath the sacrifice that sizzled there. This was no calm shaving of the symbolic hair; he slashed until the blood ran from cuts upon his head. When he had finished he dragged himself down the ramp, out into the Court of Israel, through the Court of Women and the Court of the Gentiles. At the northern gate he paused. This was to be the last time that he would set foot in the temple. Judah coughed, and hawked, and spat a great gob of spittle into the outer court of the sacred Temple of Jerusalem.

He found one of the roughest tavernas in the city, run by a one-eyed Greek who would serve anyone but would show no mercy to a customer who offended him, the only offence that he could ever think of was lack of money. Judah placed his single shekel, representing nearly two weeks average wages, upon the counter. He had just released himself from the constraint against any product of the vine, so he ordered a flagon of wine and a bottle of the fierce spirit distilled from the skins, pips and stems of grapes. He gave orders to keep the flagons and the bottles coming until the shekel was used up. The one-eyed Greek was very happy.

Chapter 7

Miriam was becoming desperate.

When Aulus had left her she had waited for a few moments, then put on a cloak and hurried out into the streets. Where to start her search? On leaving the house of Caiaphas she had turned left towards Herod's palace. They were still clearing away the dead, and the girl hurried away. Although Jerusalem had its magnificent buildings, much of the city comprised small dwellings, shops and a few tavernas. There was no order to the city. Curved streets and alleys intersected each other. There was little open space, but a thousand obscure hiding places.

The houses were silent but, she sensed, not sleeping.

Roman patrols were everywhere, some accosted her and, frightened and disgusted, she rushed to escape their coarse jibes.

She peered into dark corners, down alleys, and through gateways into small courtyards. People were camping everywhere. None welcomed her approach for all were withdrawn, silent.

Most in huddled groups were cloaked and hooded, she could not identify the Chassidim by their distinctive long hair. Those who spoke to each other exchanged only brief words in an undertone, she could not pick out the accent of the Galilee.

She moved through the crowded northern quarter as far as the hippodrome and the pool of Bethesda. She walked hurriedly beneath the northern wall of the temple as far as the Antonia where Aulus would now be. The thought of her lover so close should have spurred her on, but she stopped and pressed a hand to her belly. She was suddenly nauseated and bent over, retching, in the shadows of the portico.

Straightening up, she leaned her back against the golden stones and, eyes closed, she took deep breaths. Miriam thrust herself from the wall, knowing that she must continue her search.

The full moon cast its cold light over the city, deepening the shadows into which she peered.

How could she recognise the zealots? She could have already passed them by.

Knowing that dawn could not be far away, she turned her back on the Antonia and passed under the western wall of the temple.

How could Joshua have known? How could the rabbi have guessed?

Miriam had admitted a wild man to the house of Caiaphas, and that man had betrayed Joshua. Knowing that Aulus would want to know, she had listened to all that had transpired before the sicariot had been taken to the hall of the Sanhedrin. When Joshua had been arrested she had made a point of hanging around outside the courthouse that, as a woman, she could not enter. She was there when Joshua was led out, hands bound, surrounded by a detachment of the temple guard, to be taken to face Aulus and Roman authority. The northern rabbi had paused before her, and said: "You shall call him Sirach, and say that he is my son. Now go and sin no more."

How could he have known that she was pregnant?

She had confided only in Branwen, and she knew that the Silurian was one who would never break a confidence.

At first the two women had been thrown together by no more than circumstance. Miriam was the mistress of Aulus, Mordra was the faithful servant of Aulus and Branwen was Mordra's woman. Their paths had to cross. At first Branwen had scorned Miriam as the willing partner of a Roman but, because of her marriage to Mordra, she knew the power of love. It may have been because they were both isolated from the strength of their very different cultures, Branwen by capture, Miriam by her love of a pagan invader, that they struck an empathetic cord. Miriam had never met a woman as strong as Branwen. She could not begin to understand how a woman, and a slave, could be on equal terms with any man.

When the moon changed its face and the flow of blood, the curse of womanhood, failed to occur, Miriam knew. But, as an orphan servant in a city that was not her own, she had no one to turn to. She went to Branwen, and the dark woman from beyond the Empire had first asked her intimate questions about her last flow of blood and what regularity there had been until this month. It was then nine weeks since Miriam had last suffered the curse. They both knew that she was pregnant.

Branwen had bowed her head over the rough kitchen table. For a long time she had held her head in her hands and Miriam detected the salt of tears flowing through her fingers. Then the Silurian looked up, red-eyed, but directly at the Jewish girl. "Do you love him?"

"Yes."

"Does he love you?"

Miriam hesitated, then: "As much as he is capable of love, I believe that he does."

"And was your child conceived in love?"

Miriam's mind went back to the evening when she had known a deep ache in the very presence of her being and had gone to the Antonia in search of Aulus. Mordra had dragged the tribune away from his duties. Their love that night had been the sweetest that either had ever known. Early the following morning she had been less than half awake when she had felt Aulus's hand upon her breast and his hard manhood against her thigh. He had entered her gently, lovingly, and had smiled down at her to bid her "good morning." The most beautiful morning that she had ever known, the day that her child had been conceived.

"Yes," Miriam replied, "He was conceived in love."

Branwen was silent for a long time. Then: "You are a Jewish girl carrying a Roman child, but a child of love. I was once a Silurian girl carrying a Roman child that was a child of hate, the product of Roman rape. I rid my body of that abomination but, perhaps because of what I did, I have not conceived a child in the four years that I have been with Mordra."

"Should I get rid of it?" Miriam whispered, with tears welling in her eyes.

"No!" Branwen had no doubts. "It is a child of love and so must live and be loved."

"How?"

"I don't know." She had gone to the Jewish girl and held her, sobbing, against her breast. Two victims of the careless

133

cruelty that was Rome.

The forum was crowded, and people were stretched out on the stone benches of the amphitheatre, but Miriam wasted little time in these two places. She knew that those she sought would avoid large crowds.

She came to the wall overlooking the Hinmon Valley. All of the rubbish from the whole of Jerusalem was dumped here, and foul smoke from the smouldering waste arose to an uncaring sky.

In the south-west corner of the city she came upon a gateway beyond which there was a circus, a courtyard larger than most. A fire was burning within and people were sitting around in small groups, or in isolation. One man sat alone at the very edge of the dim light cast by the flames. His knees were drawn up and his shoulders were hunched. Without knowing how, Miriam instinctively sensed that this was one of the men she sought.

What to do?

Silently entering the courtyard, she passed behind the man and as she did so she bumped into him. Startled, he turned and looked up at her. His hood fell partly away and she saw the long hair of the Chassidim. She apologised to him, and he turned away without replying, pulling up his hood as he did so.

Aulus was at the opposite corner of the city. To reach him she would again have to risk the dark streets and the Roman patrols.

The sky was streaked with the palest grey. Dawn was not far away. By the time that she could reach Aulus it would be full daylight and the zealot would have disappeared.

The girl reached out and put her hand firmly on the man's shoulder. Again he turned towards her. Now she thought that she recognised him. He had been leading the donkey ridden by the zealot rabbi when he had entered Jerusalem on the first day of this eventful week. She gasped: "You were with the Galilean, Joshua."

There was fear in the man's eyes. "I don't know what you mean," he mumbled, "I don't understand." His accent was of the north.

He got up and walked further away from the fire. He stood in the gateway with his back to the courtyard. Others around the fire were looking up to see the cause of the disturbance. Miriam turned towards them. "This man is one of the zealots," she cried, without considering that she may have ventured into a whole pack of the terrorists. But the man had sought anonymity among those who were strangers to him. A few stood and approached him. He stood his ground. One man took hold of him and dragged him closer to the fire. Roughly he pushed back the hood from his face and head. "Are you one of them?"

"No! I have nothing to do with them. I'm just here for the Passover."

"You're a Galilean. Were you with Joshua of Nazareth?"

"No! Yes, I'm from the Galilee, but so are a lot of people. I don't know this man Joshua. I've never met him."

Miriam had to reach Aulus. Hoping that those in the courtyard would hold the zealot, she ran out of the gate.

As she entered the street, a cock crowed somewhere nearby, heralding the approach of daylight. She paused and looked back. The Galilean was standing stock still, looking up at the still dark sky. There was a look of pure horror upon his face. Again they heard the voice of the cock.

Knowing that the man would do his best to get away and to hide from the light of day, Miriam raced through the streets and up the steps of the Antonia. The guards on the door recognised her, for Aulus had taken her to his headquarters many times. "I must see Aulus Plautius," she gasped, "Let me pass."

The guards stood aside, smirking. When she had entered the building the two soldiers looked at each other and burst out laughing. "She must be desperate for it," one said. His companion agreed, "I'll bet the chief enjoys having that for breakfast."

Mordra was up and busying himself in preparation for the day. His eyebrows raised when he saw Miriam. "Where is he?" she asked. "In there," the Gaul replied, nodding towards the bedroom.

Aulus was lying, dressed, upon his cot. The girl's arrival roused him to full wakefulness.

He rose and put his arms around her. Breathlessly, she told him that she had found one of the leading zealots on the other side of the city.

135

Ignoring his armour, strapping on his sword, Aulus yelled for Mordra to gather two decades of men – now!

Together they dashed across the city, Miriam leading the way. When they arrived in the courtyard it was deserted. Smoke from the dying fire rose straight up to the clear spring sky.

Before returning to the Antonia, Aulus gave orders to his decurion to conduct a house-to-house search. "Every house, shop and taverna in this quarter of the city and as far north as the house of Caiaphas, but don't try to enter that house. Then as far east as the Central Valley. All Galileans with long hair, any Jews armed or concealing arms, anyone suspicious. Bring them in alive. Don't bother with the Bets Knesset, I'll detail other decades to search them."

Miriam stood back, watching Aulus the soldier in action. He turned to her. "Go home. There's nothing more that you can do. You did your best. When will I see you again?"

For the second time within a very few hours her hesitation was just a little too long. "When this is over." The Jewish girl smiled a small, sad smile, turned, and walked away.

Chapter 8

Back at his headquarters, Aulus busied himself detailing more search parties and with preparation for what he considered to be a totally unnecessary trial. He could not accept Pilate's idea of taking advantage of the Passover festival to demonstrate to the Jews that all the arguments were on the Roman side. There was no argument, Rome was in command. Execution was all that was needed, nail them up and be done with it.

Mordra brought him a basket of bread and a jug of goat's milk upon which he made a hurried breakfast.

"Send Galba in," he instructed his slave. When the centurion arrived, his commander looked up. "Have you seen the prisoners this morning?"

"Yes. And last night. The Syrians did a good job; all four can still stand – just. They'll be fully conscious when the nails go in, and should last quite a while on their crosses."

"Provided that they're dead by sunset," Mordra said in an undertone.

"Why?" Aulus turned to the Gaul.

"Because," his slave replied, "today is Friday, so their Sabbath starts after sunset, when you can see three stars in the sky at a single glance. They have to accept naked, mutilated criminals, but on their Sabbath, especially this one in the Passover, I think that it would be wise if they were dead by then, or we could risk a major disturbance."

Aulus nodded. "And these four have caused enough trouble. Thank you, Mordra. Galba, make sure that their legs are broken before the sun goes down."

Death by impalement has been inflicted upon many people in different places, at different times, and in a variety of forms.

The Roman version of this method of execution was one that they had learned from the Carthaginians during the Punic wars. Roman crucifixion was a perverted science. They used their knowledge of the working of the human body, and of mechanics, to refine the cruelty of impalement.

It had been discovered that if the outstretched arms were put at a certain angle before the spikes were driven through the eight small bones of each wrist, the chest was pulled up into the position that it would be in when having taken a deep breath. The body weight then caused the chest to be locked in a position of fixed inspiration, the victim could not breathe out. Suffocation would have happened very quickly, but the knees were bent so that, when straightened the chest wall could fall. Various ways of fixing the feet had been tried; the soles had been placed flat to the upright of the cross, but this often caused the ankles to break and the victim died too quickly. A block had been fixed to the upright so that the buttocks could rest upon it, but this was considered to be too humane. Now the feet were placed each side of the upright of the cross, two more spikes were driven through the heel bones to fix the feet to the upright. The cross was then raised. Whatever pain a man, or woman, may suffer, they would fight suffocation. The only way to breathe out was to straighten their knees by bearing down upon their impaled feet. This could go on for a long time, until they were too weak to push upward, and then they died. If it went on too long and the soldiers supervising the execution wanted to get away, they could despatch the criminal with a spear to the neck, chest or belly, or they could take a club and smash the legs so that they could no longer push upward.

As a final indignity, the victim, be it man or woman, was stripped naked before impalement. To the modest Jews, witnessing the death of their compatriots, this was an added horror.

During the long hours of unbelievable torment, the victims invariably lost control of their bladder and bowels, dying in shame and agony, among swarms of flies, under the hot sun.

It never ceased to amaze Aulus that the natives continued to risk this form of execution. Thousands had died this way and it was the worst form of death that he could imagine, he also knew that it offended against Jewish law by mutilating the victim. It was meant to deter further attempts at insurrection. He knew that

138

a deterrent that was used so often had failed in its purpose, but he could think of no other effective way.

Galba had ordered that the four heavy cross pieces be made ready for the prisoners to carry to their place of execution outside the city wall to the north west, where the four uprights, hammers, spikes, spades, and wedges to fix the crosses were waiting. He had strolled up to the execution site and chatted easily to the soldiers who had been detailed to this unpleasant duty, and who were now passing the time by playing dice as they waited for their victims.

Aulus turned back to his orderly. Have you seen the procurator, or Marcus Lucius?"

"The procurator is up. He's inspecting the defences to make sure that the mob stays out, though he's wearing a toga – I wasn't instructed to polish his armour."

Aulus was well used to the Gallic love of satire. "Don't worry, Mordra, the defences are more than adequate, they were set by a soldier – me. And soldiers man them, not clerks. And Marcus Lucius?"

Mordra kept his face straight. "He's washing in the lavatorium. But I think he's unwell, a vomitorim may have been more appropriate."

Aulus smiled, knowing that when his friend got talking to someone, such as Mordra, who was interested in the same esoteric subjects as himself, he never knew how much wine was lubricating his throat, or when to stop.

Lucius appeared, walking very carefully, his face chalk-white. He groped his way to a chair, and gently seated himself.

"Good morning, Lucius," Aulus said loudly. "Ready for the day's entertainment?"

The scholar looked up blearily. "I'd be more ready if I hadn't been entertained so well last night."

"What you need is to sit through a boring trial, then pop out to watch the executions."

"Must I?"

"Oh, come on, you know you don't like to miss anything. Four men writhing and bleeding away, that'll cheer you up."

Lucius swallowed hard. "Aulus, you're a good friend, but you are also a man of exquisite cruelty."

139

The soldier feigned indignation. "They are criminals."

"I'm not worried about them, I'm concerned about me. My stomach is feeling very delicate this morning. Yes, I'd like to see the executions, I've never witnessed a crucifixion, but I'd rather not think about it at the moment, it's making me feel sick."

"Don't forget the heat, the stink of blood, and of shit, and the flies."

"Aulus! That's enough."

"I'm sorry, Lucius, but you're so keen to see everything and then philosophise about it that I have to laugh."

Lucius attempted a wan smile, with little success. "Alright. I can see the funny side as well – just. If my head and guts were nearer normal I'd laugh with you, but at the moment it hurts."

"Don't worry," Aulus was still cruelly hearty, "it can't last too long. Mordra tells me that they have to be dead by sunset or it will upset the Jews."

"Why should that worry you? We seem to do a lot of things to avoid upsetting the Jews. Why do we indulge them so much?"

Aulus became serious. "Look at a map. This dump is at a crossroads of the eastern world. If we don't keep them as quiet as possible it could hold up some of our trade routes and lines of military communication."

Despite his delicate condition, Lucius still had his enquiring mind. "But they don't even do military service, why not?"

"We tried that once, a few years ago. It was decided that it was time that they served as auxiliaries. Anywhere else in the Empire men clamour to join, then get automatic Roman citizenship, and a nice little piece of land. Not these bigots. Mind you, I'd rather not have them. When they tried it they rounded up some fit ones, put them in uniform and shipped them off to Sardinia. The food didn't suit their palates, and the climate killed them off. Utterly useless as soldiers, proper soldiers that is, not terrorists. Give them an order and they'll spend half a day discussing it."

Lucius nodded, and turned green. Finally Aulus took pity on him. "Mordra, the orange juice and honey, quickly. And have you any of that willow stuff?"

The Gaul had been waiting to dispense the cure that he had administered to his master on a number of occasions. He had a small cup and a large one. He first put the small cup into Lucius's shaking hand. Aulus, amused, watched. "At least this place is well supplied with the remedy. Drink as much orange juice and honey as you can until your bladder is full to bursting, then empty it and drink some more. But first try this Gaulish trick, the Egyptians use it as well, a decoction made from the bark of the *salyx,* the willow tree. It tastes foul but it kills the pain, it also stops fever."

Lucius drank from the smaller cup and pulled a wry face. He then emptied the larger cup, and Mordra refilled it, encouraging him to drink. After four large cups he began to feel a little better. "Very kind. I just wish that you'd given it to me earlier instead of letting me suffer."

Aulus could sympathise. "I'm sorry, but you know how seeing someone else suffering from the revenge of Bacchus is always funny. I don't really believe that suffering ennobles, or is a good thing – except for Jewish terrorists."

As if in response to Aulus's words, Pontius Pilate came into the room, followed by Samuel, their visitor of the previous evening, and Caiaphas, High Priest of Israel. A third man followed behind.

Lucius found that Caiaphas was every inch his idea of a priest. He was tall and stately, bearing himself with all the dignity of his high office. He wore a blue headdress, and over a priest's white tunic a blue robe fringed with golden bells and pomegranates. Upon his shoulders there was an ephod embroidered with bands of gold, purple, scarlet, and blue. On his chest was a gold pectoral inset with twelve different gemstones.

The third man was not a priest but a scribe, his name was Joseph and he was much younger than his companions, perhaps in his early thirties. Caiaphas had brought him as an advisor on points of procedure, and the dissenter Samuel to demonstrate his impartiality and the breadth of advice that he was prepared to accept. Caiaphas introduced Joseph, and told the procurator that, when the trial began, a further twelve Jewish observers would be present, as requested.

Aulus looked up. "Twelve? An interesting number."

Caiaphas was cool. There is no significance in the number, Aulus Plautius, they are simply a representative cross-section of priests, scribes, and rabbis."

Aulus grunted. Pontius Pilate took over, and indicated Lucius. "Marcus Lucius is newly arrived from Rome, he is a philosopher. Like many young men of his background he studied at the academy on the island of Rhodos..."

"Under Georgias," Lucius interrupted, assuming that the High Priest would be interested in scholarly credentials. Caiaphas may have been, Pilate was not. "Quite," he said coldly, "I propose that he keeps the record of the proceedings"

Lucius had not known that he was expected to play the part of scribe, he would have preferred to be an observer only. Pilate had made his decision in order to keep the scholar quiet. Caiaphas nodded his assent towards Lucius, then: "I trust that the procurator would have no objection to one of our people keeping a record on our behalf."

Pilate considered this. "Which language would you employ for your record?"

"Hebrew is usual for legal matters."

The procurator had been expecting this, he turned to Aulus. "Do we have anyone who understands their magic language?"

"My orderly, Mordra."

"The Gaul?"

"Yes."

Gauls and slaves could not be trusted either, but they were better than Jews. He returned to the High Priest. "Very good, Caiaphas, you may keep your independent record, but we will need to see it before you leave. We have someone who is neither Roman nor Jewish who will sit with your scribe as he writes; it seems that we have a Gaulish slave who understands Hebrew."

After their brief conversation of the previous evening, Samuel was secretly delighted that Mordra would be present. Caiaphas gritted his teeth against what he considered to be yet another indignity. But that was all that it was, it could not hurt, and he knew that his scribe would keep a truthful record, perhaps too truthful for the heathen. He inclined his head slightly. "As the procurator wishes."

Pilate felt himself to be in complete control. "It will be as the procurator wishes. We don't need to waste too much time on this, all that we need to do is to establish the facts for the record, then get it over with."

Everyone present knew what the outcome would be. This was no trial in the true sense, it was a means of making an official record of the events and the names of those involved in order to send a report to Rome. No one was under any delusion than that it was anything but a demonstration of Roman might.

They had been standing in the *atrium,* the bare entrance hall to the Antonia. Pilate now led the group into the lower court where the hearing was to be conducted. The lower court was a gloomy place, long and narrow. Their feet echoed on the *lithostrotos,* the pavement of large stone slabs.

Under Mordra's supervision, tables and benches had been set up. There was a chair for Pilate, a judgement seat, and a table for the scribes, and another bearing wine, water, cups, and dishes of fruit. A bowl of water on a tripod stand stood next to the table of refreshments.

Pilate sat, then ushered the others to their seats. Only Mordra and the silent guards remained standing. Pilate took up a paper from the small table at his side. "We have four prisoners: Avram of Beth-yerah who was in the tower of Siloam and who is responsible for the deaths of eighteen soldiers of Rome; Nahum of Achzib, he attacked the citadel and murdered five men; a hill bandit, Joshua who calls himself bar Abbas and comes originally from Cyprus, he led the attack here on the Antonia which killed two Roman soldiers…"

Aulus interrupted. "Three. One of the wounded died in the night."

"Three Roman soldiers." Pilate went on, one soldier more or less was not all that important. "In addition, eight men of the guards upon the gates were stabbed to death. Thirty-four murdered, for they were killed putting down an illegal act. Of course murder and, more seriously, insurrection are capital crimes. The fourth man is Joshua of Nazareth. He does not appear to have killed anyone, but he is the political leader of the terrorists. He also incited the mob not to pay their lawful taxes, and he was preparing to set up an illegal government, he took part in some ridiculous ritual that was supposed to make him king of the Jews. That is sedition, and a capital crime."

Caiaphas felt that he was expected to reply. "Murder and

armed insurrection are crimes under any law. The perpetrators of these acts must pay the price. We cannot let anarchy prevail. If the zealots had their way they would plunge the Land of – the Province of Judaea into blo)dy war, that is what we must prevent at all costs and by any means. Joshua of Nazareth is the leader of the political wing of the zealots. We must cut off the head, but we also need to deal with the body."

Caiaphas had to distance himself, and the Jewish establishment from the zealots. Joshua had been anointed in accordance with the Holy Law of Israel, and Rome had the power to threaten the Law itself as previous occupiers of this land had threatened it. The preservation of Israel depended entirely upon the preservation and strengthening of Holy Law. He went on: "It would appear that Joshua's only belligerent act this week was to take over the temple, a building of Jewish not Roman significance..."

Aulus interrupted him. "It's more than that, and you know it, Caiaphas. Apart from being a religious structure, Herod built it as a fortress. Constructed the way it is it's the strongest point in Jerusalem. Whoever holds the temple has strategic control of the city and the surrounding countryside. And it's much more than that. It's no coincidence that your distant ancestors made Jerusalem your capital city, that it has been fortified and fought over so many times. I'm a soldier, and the first thing that I saw when I came here was that Zion casts a strategic shadow over a vast area, with your temple at its very heart. Don't pretend that you see it only as a place for your religious mumbo-jumbo."

Caiaphas was on his feet. "'He has set his foundation on the holy mountain; the Lord loves the gates of Zion more than all the dwellings of Jacob.' You dare to tell me the significance of the Holy City, of the temple of the Lord our god? The Lord said to us at Horeb, 'See, I have given you this land. Go in and take possession of the land that the Lord swore he would give to your fathers – to Abraham, Isaac and Jacob – and to their descendants after them.' You may have looked upon the temple with your soldier's eye for the past four years. I am a Jew, I have lived in holy contemplation of the sacred temple all my life. I am the High Priest of Israel, and know the dwelling place of the Most High in the inner sanctuary of the temple." With a mighty effort,

Caiaphas controlled his flaring temper, he knew that he was saying much too much. "I do know, Aulus Plautius, the military significance of the temple, and of Zion. I know of every moment in the long history of this city. I also realise that Joshua has demonstrated how easy it would be for the zealots to take over the temple for military purposes. Do you think that we, the lawful civil authority of Israel, would endanger the dwelling place of the Lord by allowing such a thing to happen? Joshua did not take over the temple for military purposes, the fighting was elsewhere in the city. True, some of his followers were armed, but only lightly armed, and there were only thirteen of them. Perhaps his take-over was a demonstration of the ease with which a greater number could use the temple as a fortress; it was a part of his bid for power. Once in the Temple, Joshua was trying to win by winning the hearts and minds of men, to increase his popular support. He is a Pharisaic Rabbi, and he reasons and preaches as a rabbi. Don't forget how widespread is the power base of the Pharisees, the many Bets Knesset, and they include the artisan class, the wealth creators. They are probably the most literate and articulate single section of our society. It is their intellectual strength that we should fear." The High Priest sat, breathing deeply.

Now it was Lucius's turn to interrupt. "But surely the intellectuals are the ones who will move society forward."

Aulus turned to him. "This is not Rhodos, or Rome. We are dealing with Jews, they need to be told what to do, and we are the ones who must do the telling."

Caiaphas knew that he must suppress his anger at these words. "As you know, our people arrested Joshua and he was brought before the Sanhedrin to answer a charge of blasphemy. We questioned him very closely, but he answered all our questions without incriminating himself in our Law. We do not like what he has been saying, but he is very clever and he has made sure that Holy Law and Scriptural writings could support everything that he has done and said. As far as we are concerned, from a purely Jewish point of view, we can find no legal fault in him. You must appreciate that our Laws have developed over more than a thousand years, our Scriptures are highly complex; all of this can be interpreted in many different ways without transgression. Our concern is Joshua's interpretation, and the political action arising from that interpretation that could be destructive to our people. Had he succeeded in his ambitions it would have had serious repercussions upon the people, who are innocent in matters of power politics, and so need guidance from Priests and scholars. We saw his crimes as being purely crimes against Roman authority, but dangerous to Israel. That is why we sent him to you."

Pilate leaned back in his chair. "So what do you suggest that we do with him."

Caiaphas shrugged. "Let your law take its course."

"And am I to take that you do not intend to defend any of these men, no pleas for mercy, no requests for reprieve?"

This was the opportunity that Caiaphas had been waiting for. With an effort he kept his tone non-committal. "We do have an interest in the man who calls himself 'bar Abbas'. We know a great deal about this man, and much that we know convinces us that he has offended in ways that would make him liable to suffer death by strangulation under Holy Law."

Pilate did not care about Jewish Holy Law. "Crucified or strangled, it makes no difference so long as he ends up dead. However I think that I have prior claim because of his insurrection and the murder of Roman soldiers."

Caiaphas felt that he had hooked his fish, now he must play the line carefully before landing his catch. "Yes, he will die, one way or another, but we would like you to give us 'bar Abbas'."

The procurator's mouth fell open. "Why?"

"It could be in our mutual interest."

"In what way?"

The High Priest went off in what seemed a completely different direction. "It is tragic that the great civilisation and culture that was Greece has now degenerated to the point where Greeks themselves no longer believe in the gods – false though they may have been. There was much to admire in them. Now they search for something to believe in, they are in an apocalyptic age, a time of spiritual upheaval in which they hope that they will receive some revelation of a new truth. Some have accepted the Roman gods, and I can understand that for Rome is the power. Many are going down blind roads towards pseudo-philosophies such as astralism and neo-cynicism. Yet others are seeking truth in other religions. Some, like your own legionaries, have embraced the mysteries of the Persian Mithras. Some have looked to the god of Israel..."

Aulus had had enough. "What has this to do with Joshua bar Abbas?"

"He is from Paphos on Cyprus."

"So? You Jews get everywhere."

Caiaphas smiled a little grimly. "He is a Greek."

Pilate was puzzled. "There are lots of Greek Jews."

"He was not always a Jew. He is now circumcised and accepted into the Congregation, but he is a convert."

Mordra could not contain himself. "I knew there was something odd about him. I never thought of a convert."

Pilate roared: "Silence, slave! If I want your opinion I'll ask for it."

Aulus thought of the fair hair and beard, of course, the man even looked like a Greek.

Again, Lucius was perplexed. "I always thought that Jews had to be born Jews."

Elegantly, Caiaphas waved Joseph forward. "I'm sure that one scholar can explain it to another, and it does have some bearing upon today's business."

Although only a little older than Aulus and Lucius, there was a gravity about Joseph that was beyond his years. He spoke with authority on what were, to him, plain matters of law. "We need to differentiate between the nation, which is Israel, the culture which is Jewish or Hebraic, and the religion which is Judaism. Most of us were born into all three, and the three together make us what we are. In the early days our people encouraged conversion. There have even been times in our past when we have forcibly converted those we have conquered, mainly so that we could marry their daughters and so beget Jewish children. We now try to avoid attempts to convert others to our religion, we actively discourage it. The main reason for this is that all other religions are based on faith, a blind faith that accepts all kinds of gods, and usually believes that men are the mere puppets of those gods, without a test in intellectual enquiry. Judaism actively encourages enquiry and the stranger is not

147

equipped to deal with this. Judaism is primarily a religion of practice, of morality, of ethics. My friend here," he indicated Samuel, but did not name him, "no longer has a belief in the Eternal, but, by his practice, by the way in which he lives his life in accordance with Holy Law, he remains a priest and a respected member of the Congregation. If a man is born a Jew, then he lives his life, from the eighth day of his being, in the practice of being a Jew. Those who have been brought up in the shadow of lesser gods may find it difficult, if not impossible to live every moment of their lives within the complex code of being Jewish. But we do not close the door completely, it would be wrong to deny others the opportunity to come to the Lord. It is possible, though very difficult, to convert to Judaism. Those who get through the long process of instruction, learning, and initiation, those who can learn the minutiae of Jewish life, and follow it are, strictly speaking, Jews. However we find it prudent to keep a close watch upon such men after they have been officially accepted because a convert can sometimes be over zealous for his new religion, he may even try to proselytise others, and that would never do. In the case of this man whose name in Israel is Joshua but who originally bore the Greek version of that name – Jesus, there have been certain problems that have worsened as time has gone on."

Pilate did not like long-winded explanations. "What else has he done?"

Joseph went on. "Most recently, over the past two or three years, he has been engaged in outright criminal activity as a hill bandit. You are probably aware that the zealots have been known to use the hill bandits as mercenaries, they certainly did this week. This Jesus/Joshua joined the bandits because he could not live in mainstream Jewish society. He is a man without a proper identity, a Greek who converted in Cyprus then came here in search of something that he patently did not find. He may have been different had he remained among the Greek Jews of Cyprus, he certainly cannot relate to the Hebrew Jews of Israel."

Pilate's impatience was growing. "What's the difference? You're all Jews."

Caiaphas was delighted by this question. Joseph was leading the procurator along the tortuous path that they wanted him to walk. Unhesitatingly the Scribe continued. "There is a very great difference. There are many divisions within Israel, the very name Pharisee means 'separated ones'. However the deepest gulf is between the Hebrew Jews of this land, those of us who are in constant physical contact with our heritage and with the spiritual centre of our religion, the temple, and those Jews who live in other parts of the Empire, whose first language is Greek, whose thought processes are Greek. They have the Jewish religion, and a form of Jewish culture, although a Hellenised version, but they do not have the vital third element which is to be a part of this land."

Pilate had had enough. "This is all very interesting, but this man Joshua or Jesus is guilty of crimes against Rome, in this land, and he will pay for his deeds."

Joseph ignored he interruption. "The zealots are fighting for the independence of the Land of Israel. The mass of the people are uninterested because they just want to get on with their lives, and care little who forms the government. Those of us who hold positions of responsibility can see the danger of the zealots and we are opposed to them, we want them wiped out before they can do untold harm to our people. We are deeply concerned by the presence of a number of Greek Jews among the Kanaa'im." He paused, then: "We wonder what might happen if they took their anti-Roman ideas to other parts of the Empire." He smiled slightly at Aulus. "As you so rightly say, we Jews are everywhere."

Pilate's mind was racing. What would happen to him if he allowed a terrorist movement to get so out of hand in his area of responsibility that it was exported to other provinces, even to Rome itself?

Aulus could not see what all the fuss was about. "You seem to have built a massive case on one Greek who decided that he wanted to be a Jew. Why don't you just kick this bar Abbas out, rescind his conversion?" He knew that they had a time limit upon the executions, and they were wasting time.

Joseph explained that once a conversion had been made it was irrevocable; once a Jew, even by conversion, always a Jew.

Samuel entered into the discussion. "Joshua bar Abbas was influenced by Joshua ben Joseph. They met in Beth Saida. This

Greek who now calls himself Joshua had been trying to behave in an orthodox, Pharisaic manner until he met Joshua of Nazareth. He has since said that he was blind and that Joshua ben Joseph had opened his eyes and made him see."

Aulus wanted to get on with the business of the day. "I do wish that you people would speak in plain language."

Joseph said: "He said that those who follow the more orthodox forms of Judaism are wooden, he actually described them as 'walking trees'. He has only operated on the fringes of the zealot movement, he has supported himself by banditry, but he has also had dealings with the Essenes at Qumran."

Caiaphas was now ready to move a step further with his plot. "You are of course aware, Praefectus, that among the Essenes there are some, not all by any means, but some who could be very dangerous. Unfortunately they are secretive, they live in a closed community in the desert, and access is only granted to their members. We do not know what they are doing. We have a suspicion that they may be influenced by astralism. We know a little of their plots, but only one of their own could tell us what we really need to know. We have reason to believe that they plan to overthrow all established authority, Roman and Jewish. We have heard of plots for an uprising by their so-called 'sons of light' against the 'sons of darkness'."

Again Lucius was interested. "The idea of cosmic forces of light and darkness certainly sounds like astralism, the idea of the heavenly bodies being inhabited by 'spirits of the firmament' that influence men's lives. You know, whichever one is in the ascendant when you are born is supposed to shape the nature of your being, and your fate. Of course the whole thing was discredited years ago, but there are those who have lost the ability to follow established, logical philosophy, or never had it, and because of their limitations of intellect they follow simpler, false philosophies – more like religion than true learning. Such people..."

"Yes, fine." Aulus almost barked. He could see a danger. "Secret societies are not necessarily a bad thing in themselves. The fact that my legionaries get up to all sorts strange rites in their Mithraic temples does not worry me, the army keeps them under control. However I can see that see that if disenchanted

Greeks or religious fanatics form such closed groups they could build a power base without anyone knowing – until it was too late."

Caiaphas was pleased with the way that this was going, but his face still showed grave concern. "You can see why we are concerned, Aulus Plautius. Joshua bar Abbas could be our means of learning a great deal more about these people, if we offer him his life in return for information. I would like to send him to Qumran as a member of their community so that he can tell us everything that the Essenes are doing and plotting. With respect, a Roman could not learn what a Jew could learn, even if that Jew is only a convert. So, give us bar Abbas."

Pilate was not happy. "I can see the value of having a spy at Qumran, but why this man? He has a very serious charge against him. I'm not inclined to let him go."

"It is precisely because he has a capital charge against him, and we could probably bring another one under Jewish Law, that he would make such an effective spy. You know how difficult it is to get into such sects, and virtually impossible to get one of them to turn informer. With Joshua we have the perfect opportunity. We can offer him his life if he co-operates, if he does not, then a choice of two unpleasant deaths."

The procurator was still not convinced. "But I have decided to execute all four ringleaders, including this man. There are four crosses ready. I would prefer you to have Joshua of Nazareth; at least his crimes are incitement, plotting, and sedition, not armed insurrection and murder. And he's a lot cleverer than bar Abbas."

The High Priest now knew that he had won. "I'm sorry, Praefectus, but Joshua of Nazareth is a lot too clever, he would never be persuaded to do it because he would see that it was no reprieve at all. And he's too honourable to play the spy. He's the most dangerous of the four. The best thing to do with the man from Nazareth is to crucify him."

"And risk creating a martyr as a rallying point?"

"No-one can rally to a dead man, especially when they have seen him crucified. His kingly bearing and aspiration will soon disappear when he is on the cross."

"Don't worry, Caiaphas, I'll crucify him for you. I'd hate you to have to be answerable to a king. But you haven't told me how

151

I can let the other Joshua go. I assume that the dozen of your colleagues who are coming know nothing of this plan."

Samuel almost spoiled it. "Perhaps you could release him as an act of mercy."

Pilate looked at him as if the word was unfamiliar to him, which it was. "On what grounds?"

Ignoring Caiaphas's warning look, the priest went on. "You have three to execute. Perhaps you could demonstrate the generosity of Rome – to mark the Passover."

Pilate exploded. "Why on earth would I want to do anything to celebrate your nationalistic festival? No, no! That won't do at all."

Caiaphas had to save the situation. "You could say that we had demanded…"

"Demanded?"

"Requested that you release him to our custody. It would make sense to our people that we should examine him on the capital charge of blasphemy if we let it be known – and we will have our observers here. We could even say that we would hand him back to you when we had completed our examination. By the time that happened they would probably have forgotten all about him, especially if they see the other three executed. When he has served his purpose both Roman and Jewish authorities will have outstanding charges against him. If the Essenes find him out and dispose of him it doesn't matter. Joshua bar Abbas is completely expendable, and his days are strictly numbered whatever happens. You have nothing to lose."

Pilate was deep in thought. Lucius turned to Aulus. "I wish my head had less wool in it. Your treatment has taken away the pain but I still find it hard to concentrate. It's very complicated."

Aulus smiled and lowered his voice to a whisper. "Don't worry, I'll explain all the details later. Both Pilate and Caiaphas are showing, yet again, that their first loyalty is to themselves, not to Rome or the Jews."

Pilate made his decision. "High Priest, you can have your spy, but I want your people to liaise closely with the military tribune and pass on all information from Qumran without delay. When he appears before me I want you to make a plea for him to be handed over to the Jewish authorities for the purpose of further examination. I'll appear to be reluctant, but then I'll let it be known that you people can examine him under your law. I'm still not sure that I like this, but you can have 'bar Abbas'."

Chapter 9

Now that the bargaining for Joshua bar Abbas was over, Aulus was eager to get on with the main business of the day. This was the spring equinox, there were just twelve hours of daylight, and they had already used up almost two hours. He calculated quickly; perhaps another couple of hours for the hearing, say an hour to get the terrorists outside the city wall and fixed to their crosses. That left only seven hours maximum to sunset, not long for the natives to take in the object lesson.

Aulus would have preferred to leave them hanging until they died. Some he had seen had lasted two or even three days, but to achieve that it was necessary to give them something to drink from time to time in order to prolong the agony. Unfortunately he was sure that Mordra was right when he said that it would be better if the zealots were dead before the end of the day. It was part of the contrariness of the Jews to start their day in the evening, as did the Gauls. They didn't even have names for the days of the week, they simply numbered them. When dusk fell this evening it would be their seventh day – the Sabbath. Thought of the Jewish Sabbath gave him some consolation and caused him to smile to himself. He knew that they looked forward to their seventh day all week. When dusk came on Friday evening they welcomed their Sabbath with great song and dance, literally. He did not understand what they were singing about, but Mordra told him that they were psalms attributed to their ancient king David, about singing joyfully, and being jubilant, and thanking their anonymous god. He did not think that they would be doing much singing tonight.

Pilate took him aside and asked for a report. The tribune replied that one of the twelve had been positively identified, but that by the time he had reached the spot where he had been seen he had melted away. "Very interesting," Pilate sneered, "but not

154

very helpful, apart from telling us that some of them are still in the city."

Aulus bridled. "I have doubled the guards on all the gates, and on Hezekiah's tunnel, there are patrols out in strength, and my men are, at this moment carrying out a house-to-house search of the entire city. I have thrown a cordon around the area with the two extra cohorts, and they are searching the surrounding villages."

The procurator turned to Caiaphas. "High Priest, will you wish to call any witnesses from among your own people?"

"I will, Praefectus. The Scribe Joseph here was among the group that challenged Joshua in the Temple. He remained close at hand and paid attention to all that was said, he even joined in some of the arguments."

Pilate gave the scribe an icy smile. "Excellent. Your testimony should be useful."

Caiaphas went on. "We also have one of the twelve."

"The one who betrayed him?"

"Yes, Judah the sicariot."

"I trust that you have him safe."

"There is no need."

Pilate glowered. "Why not?"

The High Priest smiled. "He has nowhere to go, and no-one will take him in. He spent the night sitting on the Mount of Olives, he then went up to the temple, cut his hair, and made sacrifice. He is now lying dead drunk in a taverna not far from here."

Pilate shook his head. "He thought to visit the barber while all this is happening?"

Caiaphas replied patiently. "Cutting his hair means that he has abandoned the Nazarites, and presumably the zealots."

Pilate stood and paced the heavy pavement for a while. Then: "I think that we are now ready to proceed. Let us have the prisoners in."

There was further delay when Caiaphas reminded the procurator of the Jewish observers waiting to be admitted. Joseph went to summon them; they trooped into the court and were shown to the benches.

Lucius seated himself at the scribes' table and assembled his materials. A man was selected from among the twelve Jews and seated at the other end of the table. Mordra sat in the middle, between the two recorders, where he could watch what the Jew was writing, and give to Lucius any information and advice that he may need.

Legionaries with pili lined the long hall, and guarded the door.

Pilate settled himself into his seat of judgement. Aulus, Galba, and the centurion Timocrates sat well away from the Jews. At last all was ready. Pilate looked at the soldiers guarding the door. "Bring in the prisoners."

A decade of guards marched in, surrounding the four men who were a sorry sight. None had been allowed to sleep, and all had passed the long night as objects of the rough and bullying humour of the soldiers. The man who had attacked the citadel had to be supported as his leg wound had worsened during the night, and was starting to stink. The procurator sat back to enjoy this pretence of a trial, and this demonstration of his own authority. "Let us have the first one."

Lucius took up a wax tablet. "Avram of Beth-yerah."

The burned youth was thrust forward. Painfully he drew himself up and looked straight at the procurator, fighting his fear.

Pilate spoke. "You call yourself Avram, and you say that you come from Beth-yerah in the Galilee?"

"My name is Avram." The voice was firm.

Aulus stepped forward. Avram continued to stare at Pilate. Aulus cleared his throat. "This boy was leading the attack on the south east wall and the tower of Siloam. He was guarding the line of retreat through the tunnel to the spring outside the city wall. When I arrived with a century he was on top of the wall armed with spear and sword, issuing orders to his followers. They were well equipped with rocks that this man directed to be hurled down upon my men. Throughout the engagement this Avram was the one giving the orders, and the terrorists were obeying those orders. As well as a good supply of rocks, stacked and obviously prepared in advance, they were armed with spears, swords, arrows, and slingshot."

"Ah," Pilate smiled, "the famous Galilean slingshot. Was it as deadly as we are led to believe?"

"It can be," Aulus replied, "especially in the open. We formed testudo."

The *testudo,* tortoise, was a formation of Roman infantry with shields held all around, and overhead, razor-sharp pili protruding front and rear, and from the sides.

"You had losses?"

"In our attack on both the wall and the tower, it was one operation, I lost eighteen killed, and about as many injured. We brought many of them down with arrows and throwing pili, and then we used scaling ladders and dealt with the rest hand-to-hand. We set a fire at the base of the tower, and it collapsed. I had given orders to take this man alive."

Pontius Pilate turned to the young warrior.

"Do you dispute this account?"

Avram put on an act of bravado.

"Your pet soldier makes it sound easier than it was for him. We gave him what was probably the hottest fight he's ever seen."

Aulus looked at the youth with open contempt.

Pilate went on: "Did you lead the attack on the south east wall?"

"No."

"Then what part, if any, do you say you played?"

Avram's lip curled. "I led the *defence* of the wall and the tower. This city is the capital of Judaea and Israel. You Romans are the invaders. Your people attacked us, we were defending our city."

"This place is no more than a town in a province of the Roman Empire. You have, by your own admission, led an armed uprising against the legally constituted authority. You have murdered imperial soldiers."

"They were casualties of war."

"There is no war. No war exists between Rome and the Jews. It cannot because you are within the Empire and not a sovereign state that could make or receive a declaration of war. Therefore anyone in Judaea who takes up arms against the legal government has not taken part in an act of war, they have disturbed the Roman Peace. Such people put themselves outside the law. They are terrorist bandits and all their acts become illegal. If they kill in pursuit of their aims they have committed

157

common murder." Pilate glanced at Lucius to make sure that his words were being recorded.

Aulus was increasingly conscious of the passing time. He went over to the procurator and spoke quietly to him. "Praefectus, if we don't make progress we won't have time to crucify them today, unless you want to hold them over until Sunday."

Pilate looked queryingly at the soldier. Briefly Aulus explained his reasons for wanting the prisoners dead before sunset. Pilate wanted to be out of Jerusalem and back in Caesarea as quickly as possible. He brought Avram's trial to a rapid close. "Avram of Beth-yerah, according to the evidence of a Roman officer, and on your own admission, you are guilty of armed insurrection against the Emperor, the Senate, and the people of Rome. Furthermore, upon the evidence of said Roman officer, and your own admission, you are guilty of murder. Publish the crime as insurrection and murder. High Priest, do you or any of your people have anything to say?"

Caiaphas half rose. "Nothing, Praefectus."

The procurator fixed Avram with a glassy stare. "You are to die by crucifixion. Sentence to be carried out immediately. Take him away."

Now, the immediate prospect of the four cruel spikes was enough to break Avram's fragile self-control. As he was dragged away he turned to the man from Nazareth. "Joshua, I believed that you were the Messiah, the saviour of Israel. You cannot even save yourself, or us. I would gladly have died for what I believed you were. Now I am going to die for nothing."

Nahum was brought forward, grimacing from the pain that shot up his useless leg. The skin around the wound was puffy, and turning black, oozing dark pus. He was hot and clammy, and his heart was beginning to race. As he took his place before his judge he turned to his king. "Forgive him, Joshua. We are all under the same sentence. I wish with all my heart that I could pay the price on your behalf. The kingdom will come."

Joshua smiled at him. "It will, and when it does you will be there beside me. And you, as a righteous man, must forgive those who torment us. They act out of ignorance."

"Silence!" Aulus bellowed. "Praefectus, this man led the

158

attack on the citadel that was repulsed by the force led by Centurion Timocrates."

The Greek was ushered forward, and gave a brief account in clipped tones. Pilate listened carefully then turned to the crippled zealot. "Did you lead the terrorist attack upon the citadel?"

It seemed that Nahum had used his last reserve of strength in making his cry for the kingdom, he was barely audible. "I did."

"I see no point in asking further questions. I'd rather get him to his cross while he's still alive. High Priest?"

"Nothing to add, Praefectus."

Again Pontius Pilate gave his predetermined judgement. "Nahum of Achzib, you are guilty of armed insurrection against the Emperor, the Senate, and the people of Rome. You are further guilty of murder. The sentence is death by crucifixion. Sentence to be carried out immediately. Take him away and publish his crime."

As Nahum was half dragged, half carried from the court, Lucius leaned to Mordra. "How do we publish the crime?"

The Gaul was grim. "The nature of the crime is inscribed upon a tablet which is then hung upon the cross so that everyone can see it."

Now things were moving well. Aulus was beginning to enjoy himself. He just hoped that they would not waste too much time pretending to bargain for the Greek. "Praefectus, Joshua who calls himself bar Abbas carried out a direct frontal attack upon the Antonia, leading four or five hundred men."

"How were they armed?"

"Spears, clubs, a few swords, arrows, and slingshot."

"Did they do much damage?"

"Not to this fortress. We had a few injuries and three deaths. However, when we had broken their initial assault, and blocked their retreat I had to go to Siloam. The senior centurion commanded here, and he captured this man."

"Very good. Primus Pilus, step forward."

Galba, his equipment highly polished, the very picture of a veteran Roman fighting man, stepped smartly up.

"Right, Primus, give us an account of the battle. A brief account will do."

"Sir. It wasn't much of a battle. They were beneath us and

all in front, no attempt at encirclement. They had no armour to speak of. We were able to pick them off more-or-less at leisure. This man Joshua was wearing some sort of armour and carrying a sword. He was giving direct orders, he was obviously in command. After we'd broken their initial assault and sent a force to the portico behind them to cut off their retreat, all we had to do was mop up their wounded and stragglers."

"Thank you, Primus." Pilate returned his gaze to the fair-haired bandit. "Did you lead this abortive attack upon the Antonia?"

"I attacked the Antonia." Joshua growled.

Aulus said: "It was a badly conceived, and badly led attack, Praefectus, but under proper leadership it would, I think, have been the main thrust against Roman authority."

"Perhaps." Murmured Pilate. "You are plainly guilty of insurrection and murder," then, in an attempt at humour, "but I think that your greatest crime was military incompetence." No one smiled. "However, it is the intention that matters. Obviously we can trust the military judgement of the tribune and the Primus Pilus regarding the conduct of the attack, but that is not the point. The point is what you intended as the outcome." Pilate was playing for time, giving Caiaphas the opportunity to make his plea.

The High Priest rose. "Praefectus, this man's military prowess, or lack of it, is no concern of ours. Regarding his attempt to attack this fortress, we recognise that Rome must judge a crime against Rome. From our point of view, under Jewish Law, this man who is known as Joshua has much to answer. He has been heard to make some wild claims that are deeply offensive to our people, and almost certainly serious offences under our Holy Law. We would appreciate it if we could be given the opportunity to examine him on a possible charge of blasphemy before you proceed further with your charges against him."

Pilate blustered. "He has a capital charge, under Roman law, hanging over him. I don't see why I should delay and let him go, even into your custody."

"Purely for further examination, Praefectus, then we would return him to you for your verdict and sentence, although blasphemy is a capital offence under Holy Law."

The pantomime continued. "I would have thought that you would prefer me to give you the other one, the man from Nazareth, he's the one who took over your temple."

"As far as that one is concerned, we have complete faith in Roman justice. We request that you give us the one who calls himself bar Abbas."

Pilate appeared to think it over. "On condition that you return him to us as soon as you have completed your examination, you may have bar Abbas."

Caiaphas inclined his head. "We are very grateful."

Pilate turned to one of the decurions. "See that he is taken, properly secured, and handed over to the Jewish guard. Make sure that they guard him well, and satisfy yourself with the custody arrangements before you leave. Oh, don't forget to have them sign a receipt for him."

Relief, confusion, puzzlement fought each other on the Greek's features as he was led, bound, away from what he was certain would be an immediate sentence of death.

As he emerged from the Antonia, ten legionaries around him, and a decurion leading the way, the few Jewish spectators could not believe their eyes. Unlike the other two who had emerged previously, he was not carrying the crosspiece for his execution. Had he been reprieved? An uncertain, wavering cheer arose, and quickly died.

Chapter 10

As Joshua of Nazareth was brought forward Caiaphas recalled the words from the First Book of Samuel:

'Then Samuel took a flask of oil and poured it on Saul's head and kissed him, saying, "Has not the Lord anointed you leader over his inheritance?"'

Only a priest could anoint a king to 'save them from the hand of their enemies'. Only a priest could anoint the Priest King who was to be the Messiah, that longed-for, only vaguely understood man who would save Israel until the end of time. Simon of Bethany was of the *Cohanim,* the hereditary priesthood. He was not a member of the Sanhedrin, but Caiaphas knew that Pilate associated all priests with the high court of Israel. They were on dangerous ground.

The procurator called upon the scribe Joseph. "You saw this man in the temple; what did he say and do there?"

Although the Scribe spoke quietly, he betrayed a latent outrage. "Most of what he said was his interpretation of our Holy Law, and the words of the prophets. I cannot fault his reasoning, only his premises, and I would certainly doubt his conclusions. There were two things that he said that were obviously subversive. You know about his incitement not to pay imperial taxes? That was bad enough, but the other thing that he said could be even more disturbing."

"And what was that?"

"This was not broadcast to the mob, but I managed to overhear him in some of his discussions with his inner circle. Judah the sicariot has since confirmed much of what I heard. Joshua warned his followers that they would see wars and hear of wars, he said that such conflict was inevitable. Nation would rise against nation, kingdom against kingdom. He said that they were to bide their time until the time was right, allow their enemies to destroy each other. He said that such widespread conflict would be the birth-pangs of a reborn nation – Israel."

This was something that Aulus could understand. "This can only mean that he was anticipating the break up of the Empire. The Jews would take advantage of the chaos and try to recreate their kingdom."

Lucius was in a world of his own. "Out of chaos there came order and the world was formed. The titans ruled the earth until the birth of the gods…" He suddenly realised that everyone was silent, staring at him. He blushed, dragged himself away from the Greek creation myth, and mumbled: "Sorry. Just thinking."

Joseph had not finished. "He also talked about the destruction of Jerusalem."

This was what Pilate could not understand. "Your so-called capital city?"

"Yes. According to Judah, as he was approaching Jerusalem he saw a fig tree and wanted to eat the fruit. As this is the month of Nissan even the early figs will not be ripe for another two months. He cursed the tree, and when they saw it again it had withered and died."

Pilate was scornful. "I'm not impressed by the tricks of magicians."

Joseph was patient with the closed mind of a Roman. "I think that it was meant to be a parable, an allegory. He looked out over the city and said that as the tree had been destroyed so Jerusalem would be destroyed and not one stone would be left standing on another. This is part of Essene ranting. And he threatened to destroy the temple built by Herod."

Samuel the priest butted in. "Forgive me, Joseph, Praefectus, but I think he also said that he would rebuild it."

"What he said, and I was there," Joseph did not hide his exasperation, "was that he would tear down the temple and rebuild it in three days."

Aulus was tired of all this. "Now that really would be a miracle," he said with heavy sarcasm.

The attempt at irony was lost on Samuel. "I think he was talking about building the temple in the hearts and minds of men.

163

It was a metaphor."

"I had realised that, priest."

Pilate always felt that he could cut through intellectual meandering to what really mattered. "I don't care if he was proposing to rebuild the temple metaphorically. The important thing is that he threatened to destroy it."

Lucius had thought of a legal point. "If I may, Praefectus. As the temple is a religious building it is surely the responsibility of the Jewish authorities, and may be outside Roman jurisdiction."

Now his friend exasperated Aulus. "As I keep telling everyone, it's more than a religious building, it's a perfect fortress. They may use it to pray in, but they could just as easily use it to fight from, and that is something well within our jurisdiction – which, anyway, is absolute."

The procurator wanted to move on. "Did the Sanhedrin get anything useful out of him?"

Caiaphas replied: "You must understand, Praefectus, that we were examining him for blasphemy, which we were unable to prove. However there were some things that could be apposite. We asked him about his relationship with Johannen ben Zechariah, did he consider the Essene to be his herald, because the coming of the Messiah is expected to be heralded? He replied by quoting from our prophet Isaiah: *'Hear! A voice calling: "Clear a way for the Lord in the wilderness, make plain in the desert a highway for our God."'* We had to admit that that he was proclaiming the coming of a heavenly kingdom, not an earthly one. Yes, Joshua has the perverted Essene notion that the Holy City is a spiritual desert; that the only righteous ones are to be found in the Judaean desert. He has spoken in derisive terms of the Roman roads leading to Roman ways, and his narrow road being the only way forward for the Jews. We do not like the emphasis that the Chassidim put upon such things, the ways in which they interpret Holy Scripture for their own purposes, but Joshua's arguments can be supported by Holy Writ, and there was no blasphemy.

"One of the Sanhedrin Priests who had not been in the temple when Joshua was there, pointed out that he had said: 'The very stone that the builders rejected has become the head of the corner.' And that he had been claiming to be the keystone, the head of Israel. But he reminded us that this was a quotation from the Psalms. The passage goes on: *'...O give thanks to the Lord for he is good; His steadfast love endures for ever!'* He had been uttering a song of praise and thanksgiving.

"He has sought out some unsavoury company, not only zealots and bandits, but people I can only describe as sinners. We asked him why he did this. He told us that those without sin had no need of him, for he had come to return those who had strayed from the narrow path of the Lord back to observance of Holy Law."

"Then why," Pilate wanted to know, "if he has done no wrong in your law, did you send him, bound, to us?"

Now Caiaphas was careful. "Because he was the leader of the zealot Nazarites. If the Kanaa'im had succeeded in overcoming the Jerusalem garrison it would have been only a short time before reinforcements were sent from the coast, and perhaps from Syria and Egypt. Our people would have been crushed. Jerusalem could have been laid to waste. The actions of these people endanger everyone, they are a cancer that must be cut from the otherwise healthy body of Israel."

Pilate raised an eyebrow. This was probably the first time that he had received a completely honest answer from the High Priest.

"Are you Joshua ben Joseph of Nazareth?" Pilate read from the wax tablet before him, then looked up at the prisoner.

"I am."

The procurator went on: "We have ample evidence of your incitement to the people not to pay their lawful taxes. Do you deny this charge?"

"Your emperor has no entitlement to the produce of this land. This is the Holy Land of Israel. All, all that is within this land must be saved from the heathen because it is the property of the Eternal God, king of the Universe, and is exclusively earmarked for the sustenance of his chosen people."

Pilate gave a short laugh. "Wrong! This land, all that it produces, and everyone in it, including you, all is the property of the divine Tiberius, Emperor of the world."

Joshua looked pityingly at the man who sat in judgement

upon him. "Pilate, how small your mind must be, how little you know. Your emperor is not the first to claim divinity. The Egyptian pharaohs made 'hat claim long ago. Where are they now? Two hundred years ago, here in this land, we were ruled by the Seleucid Antiochus. In his madness he claimed to be the living embodiment of the pagan god Zeus, that he was the Greek god in human form. He found that he was mortal. After a series of crushing defeats at the hands of my people he took to his bed and died. You may follow what gods you choose when you are not in our land, even Tiberius if you must. Yes, there are many gods – and even goddesses. All people who dwell on earth sing to their own gods, but they are the gods of other peoples and of other lands. Here, in this the land of the Jews, there is only one god. It is written in Holy Scripture that not only his people Israel will worship him, and no other, but that the same applies to 'the stranger within our gates'. You, Pilate, are the strangers in the Holy Land. Whilst you are here you will, like us, recognise no other god."

The Roman ruler of Judaea was amazed that this insignificant rabbi dared to speak in this way. He had spent the night being flogged, and subject to the rough jokes of the legionaries. Whatever they had done to him, his forehead was cut and torn, and dried blood stained his hair and beard. He was bound, and heading for horrific death, yet he compounded his crime by mocking Rome and the Emperor. What he had just said was another capital offence to add to those that he had already committed. "Well," said the procurator of Judaea, "we are now in no doubt that you did commit this act of incitement. We will crucify you for that. We will also crucify you for what you have just said, and for your actions this past week, and for your deep involvement with the zealots. It's only a pity that we can't bring you back to life so that we can keep on crucifying you again and again. You deserve no less.

"Tell me, do you claim to be the Messiah-king?"

"I am part of the messianic movement."

"What is that supposed to mean?"

"Who do you say that I am?"

Caiaphas interrupted. "If you are claiming to be the Messiah you have shown little regard for your people. By your actions in the Temple you have deprived them of their right to make sacrifice to the Lord."

Joshua turned to him. "They will have their sacrifice," he said wearily, "but it is not by sacrifice that Israel lives, it is by Holy Law. Israel has no need of a temple to worship the Lord. We need only the hearts of good men. Where ten Jews are gathered together in the name of the Lord, wherever they may be, he is in their midst."

Pilate turned to another subject. Tell me, Caiaphas, which comes first? I accept that you have your religious laws, but you are also part of the Empire. If there is a direct clash between your so-called holy law and imperial law, which would you obey?"

"Where there is a direct clash between Holy Law and he law of the land, then secular law takes precedence."

Pilate looked at Joshua. "What do you say to that?"

"The High Priest knows as well as I do that the rule that he has just quoted only applies to Jews in other lands, the guests of other people, and, as I have said before, all people, including heathens such as you, who are in our land are subject to our Holy Law. There is no other law in Eretz Israel, the Holy Land."

Pilate smirked. "It is not your land, it is Roman land, and here Roman law prevails above all others." He again addressed the High Priest. "We have heard that this man has been trying to set himself up as king of the Jews, presumably within the rules laid down in Jewish law. Had he been successful it would, of course, have meant secession from the Empire, by force if necessary as we have already seen. Is what he says correct, High Priest, do you only recognise your own laws in this province?"

"You must understand, Praefectus, that Joshua of Nazareth speaks for himself, not for Israel. In our culture all men are encouraged to question, even to dissent. What he has said is the view held by one section of our society, a very small section I may add. He has put the extremist view. I am the one who speaks on behalf of the vast majority, on behalf of Israel."

Pilate was not prepared to let go of this matter. "And if he had succeeded in becoming king of the Jews, in he eyes of your people, would he have broken any of your laws?"

Caiaphas had to regain control of this argument. "If I may say so, Praefectus, I think that you hypothesis is a little overextended. *If* he had succeeded, *if* the people had recognised his claim..."

"What were they doing last Sunday when he came riding into the city on a donkey but greeting him as a king?"

Caiaphas was beginning to sweat. "There is more than that to being recognised as King of Israel."

"What, Caiaphas, what are the conditions that you people would demand before you made a man a king?"

Aulus stepped forward. "If I might suggest, Praefectus, my orderly has taken a great interest in these people and their ways. Perhaps a non-Jewish view would be of value, and," he glanced poisonously at Caiaphas, "a lot shorter by avoiding all the different interpretations that Jews love to put upon everything they talk about."

Pilate looked sourly at the Gallic scholar. "What can you tell us about Jewish kings?"

"Well, they haven't had a proper one for a long time, but there are criteria." Mordra knew that he was going to enjoy this. "As I understand it there are seven criteria; and they can come in a variety of orders, depending upon the circumstances. First, a man has to be a Jew. This may sound to be self-evident but it rules out any foreign kings such as they, and others, have had. Also, they sometimes have difficulty in defining who is or is not a Jew. They seem to have more rules defining rejection than they have for acceptance as a Jew. Although they are a patriarchal people, the first requirement for Jewishness is to be the child of a Jewish mother. I suppose that this makes sense – we all know our mothers, but can perhaps be less certain of the identity of our fathers. If they are all satisfied that the candidate is Jewish, then they can proceed. If there is no king at the time, or if a successor is in the offing, for whatever reason, then there is expected to be a herald announcing his coming. The candidates for kingship must have support, a following, even if no more than a bodyguard at first. Fourth, the man has to receive public acclaim to show that he has the support of the people. He must go to the temple, grasp the horns of the altar, and make a public declaration in a prescribed form of words. A priest must anoint him with sweet oil in the name of their god, and before witnesses. Finally, he must be successful in holding his kingdom or he will be deposed, perhaps killed, and replaced. And that is how a Jew becomes a king."

Pilate looked satisfied. "High Priest, is what this slave says correct?"

"It is, Praefectus, in its essentials. However..."

"I don't need any complicated details. I find this most interesting. I'm quite prepared to accept his Jewishness." He sniggered. "When we strip him for his execution we will all be able to see that he's a Jew. It seems that this wild Essene, Johannen wasn't it, was his herald. He's dead isn't he?"

"Yes," Aulus replied, "Antipas had his head off."

"Good. We know that he had his little band of beggars following him around, and having some pretensions of being a shadow government. He had his public acclaim when he did his donkey trot last Sunday, and he has been anointed. We cannot say that he held his kingdom, but," he stared hard at Caiaphas, "what did he do when he went into the inner temple on his first day there?"

The High Priest was silent. Pilate went on: "He got off his donkey, took a ritual bath, entered the temple by the Golden Gate – the route of the messiah. He went into the inner part where only Jews may venture. Did he grasp an altar and utter some form of words that were supposed to make him into your king?"

Caiaphas knew that the Roman governor would find out, he might as well tell him. "Yes, he grasped the horns of the altar and proclaimed the Hallel."

"The what?"

"The 'form of words'. The Hallel is an exaltation and praise of the Lord."

"So, I think that six out of seven is good enough to say that he is the king of the Jews – according to your 'holy law'."

Lucius looked up from his records. "I think that we could say that he also satisfied the final criterion. He did hold his kingdom. He controlled the temple for three days; a short reign, but an apparent success while it lasted."

Pilate thought that he may have misjudged the scholar. He could talk sense at times.

Now he was all bustle as he brought the trial to its inevitable conclusion. "Joshua ben Joseph of Nazareth, by your own admission you have incited the people of Judaea not to pay their due taxes to Rome. In my presence here today you have mocked the Roman Empire, and the divine majesty of the Emperor Tiberius. You are a known leader of the zealots, and the head of their so-called brotherhood. You have set yourself up as an illegal pretender king. I wonder if the mob will be so ready to acclaim you when they see the life ebbing from your naked body. You were to save your people from these terrible Romans. You can't even save yourself. Your own High Priest can't wait to see you on the cross. These Sanhedrin people, the very cream of your society, all want your blood. Your god has not come down on a cloud of fire to rescue you. No great horde of bandits has stormed the Antonia to save you. Even one of your closest friends put the kiss of death upon you, sold you out for thirty silver coins. Are you going to tell me that it was your intention to bring about unity of the Jews, the most argumentative people on earth?"

Joshua appeared to be unruffled. "As the Lord our God is one, so the kingdom is one."

"Yes! One province, one little province of a great Empire. And that's what it will always be. Are you still trying to say that you are a king. Are you the Messiah?"

Joshua ben Joseph of Nazareth looked steadily at Pontius Pilate, his deep blue eyes did not flicker. "It is as you say."

There was an intaking of breath throughout the court. Pilate turned to the High Priest of Israel. "Caiaphas, what do you say we should do with this man?"

The High Priest felt suddenly light, he was a little dizzy. He had not seen that the procurator had just, for the record, guaranteed his complicity in a regicide. All that he could see was that he had saved his people from the excesses of the zealots, and the dreadful retribution that the Romans could visit upon Israel. In his euphoria all that he could say was: "Let Roman law take its course."

Pilate turned back to the king. "A charge of sedition has been proved against you. You are to die by crucifixion. Sentence to be carried out immediately."

Lucius stood up. "Do we publish the crime as sedition?" There had seemed to be so many charges against Joshua.

Pilate paused. "No. Let them write upon the tablet: 'The King of the Jews'."

Samuel was indignant. "Surely, Praefectus, you mean a pretender who tried to claim the empty throne of Israel."

Pilate looked at Joshua, and gave one of his wintry smiles. "He believes himself to be a king, and so do his followers. According to your own law he is your king. Write: "The King of the Jews'. I want all of Jerusalem to see how Rome treats their king. Take him away."

Unprotesting, still with the quiet dignity that had disconcerted Aulus and Galba, Joshua of Nazareth, King of Israel, was led out to his death.

Caiaphas could feel nothing but relief. He had helped to remove a grave danger from his people. "A satisfactory outcome, Praefectus."

Pilate nodded and remained silent as the stately, blue robed figure led the Jewish observers from the lower court. Aulus loosened his cuirass. The trial over, he was now off duty until he went to see how his men were conducting the executions, and that could wait a while. He sat and poured himself a cup of wine. "Perhaps now we'll see some peace."

Pilate stood and walked to the refreshment table. He reached for the flagon, then paused. "A satisfactory outcome, yes, but it's a dirty business. Whenever I have to deal with *lestai,* with bandits I feel that I have been handling vermin." Pontius Pilate went to the bowl of water on its tripod stand, and, very carefully, very thoroughly, he washed his hands. "I sometimes think that my hands will never be clean again. But it was worth it. We now know that we have heard the last of the 'King of the Jews'."

Chapter 11

Nahum was the first to die, but he was dying before the first nail was driven in. He was half carried, half dragged from the Antoina, and a bystander, a Passover visitor from Cyrene in North Africa, was pulled from the side of the road and made to carry the crosspiece. The soldiers, repulsed by the stink from Nahum's suppurating leg wound, refused to carry him, and dragged him by the arms along the road surface.

On arrival at the place of execution the crosspiece was assembled to the waiting upright. As his executioners stripped his clothing away they recoiled from the smell and the sight of the blackening skin, and the foul pus that oozed from the untreated wound. Nahum had lost consciousness and had to be revived with water before the execution could proceed. The zealot's arms were angled properly, and he moaned as long nails were driven through his wrists and into the rough wood. His knees were bent, his feet placed each side of the upright, and two more nails were hammered through his heel bones.

The base of the cross was positioned at the lip of the hole that had been dug. Ropes were attached to the ends of the crosspiece, and two soldiers strained on these as two others heaved behind the head of the upright.

When almost at the vertical, the base of the cross thudded into the hole, wrenching flesh and bone against the nails. The cross was positioned upright, and wedges hammered in to secure it, every hammer blow sending a shock up the wood, and along the tortured nerves of the hanging man.

He felt his chest tighten, he tried to force the air from his lungs, he could not breathe. Automatically he tried to straighten his knees, but one would not work, and he forced down on the impaled heel of his one sound leg. A flame of agony shot up his leg, but he was able to release the trapped breath from his body.

Through a haze of agony and delirium, Nahum gazed for the last time over the Golden City. His mind was in turmoil; would he be resurrected crippled and in pain? Would the kingdom come before he died? A scream came into his fogged brain. Was he screaming? Again his chest was locked, again the reflex straightening of his knee, and the flaming pain. The screaming was coming from somewhere to his side. He turned his head and saw Avram writhing on his cross.

Every time that the youth straightened his knees the breath came out in an animal scream of torment. Every time that he slid up the cross, and then slumped down again the wood chafed his burned flesh.

Time after time after time, Nahum was forced to push down on his one good leg. Every time the pain exploded in his heel, scorched up his leg and spine, and into his head. Every time that he slumped back down, his impaled wrists became the focus of his agony. The poison that was spreading rapidly through his body was making his heart race, and forcing him to breathe more rapidly. There was only pain. His body, his mind, his soul were nothing but pain. The world was a whirling holocaust of pain.

Merciful blackness came over him.

Something wet and sour was forced into his mouth. A legionary had dipped a sponge into wine vinegar, and raised it to him on the end of a pilus. He was revived to return to his world of pain.

There were some words that he should say. He could not speak. There were some words that should now be in his mind. What were the words? Israel – the Lord – there was one – who was that one? Joshua – eternal. He could not find the words. Time was measured in the agonies in different parts of his body; the pain in his chest, the pain in his foot and leg, and the pain in his hands and arms. He could not know how many minutes, or days, or years of pain he had known before he was dimly aware that another cross was being assembled beneath him, another man was being stripped naked, thrown down upon the cross. He heard fresh cries as more nails were hammered home.

Twice more he sank into merciful unconsciousness. Twice more he was revived by a bitter sponge forced between his parched lips.

He could not breathe. His skin was turning dusky red as foul air was trapped in his tortured body. With a mighty effort he forced down, the heel bone shattered, the nail tore through the skin, held for a moment on the powerful tendon, then broke away in a spray of dark blood. He was hanging, helpless, his chest bursting. For a few moments he thrashed from side to side, then, with a long, deep, guttural croak, death released Nahum from his torment.

Avram had carried the heavy timber on his scarred shoulders along the endless, too-short road to his death. He had appealed to the silent people who lined the route. He had called upon his mother's name. He had fallen to the ground and lay with the wooden beam across his back. He had been kicked, the weight of the crosspiece was lifted from him, he had been hauled to his feet, and the crosspiece had been laid upon him again. He did not know how many times he had fallen and sobbed into the dry dust. Every time he was brutally brought back to his last walk.

Rough hands were upon him, ripping his clothing away. His hands tried to hide and shelter his virgin manhood, the indelible mark of a Jew. Grasping his upper arms, two legionaries flung him, face up, onto his cross. Someone held his arms while another man pulled down on his ankles to position him for impalement. He felt strong hands around his lower arms, the harsh prick of nail points over his wrists, then unspeakable pain with every stroke of the hammers. More hands, now upon his legs. His knees were bent, his feet were placed each side of the upright. The pain travelled a precise path from his feet, along the outer parts of his lower legs, up the backs of his thighs, across his buttocks, into his lower back, up his spine, and came shrieking out of his mouth.

The world turned as the cross was raised to the upright position. Four points of absolute agony were all that he knew as the base of the cross found its hole in the ground.

He must tell them. They had to know that he had been betrayed, that Joshua was not what he had thought him to be, he had to speak. He could not speak, he could not breathe. He felt his knees straightening. He screamed aloud at the pain that shot up from his impaled feet, the pain of the rough wood against his burned back. His body fell, taking his weight upon his impaled wrists to add to the agony of the scouring wood against his back.

He saw Joshua being brought to his torment. May he suffer as I am suffering. The adventure was over. There was never any glory. Why? Why? Why? Turn back time, let me be a child again, with my mother.

He could smell his own excrement. Mother, mother, I'm dirty, clean me – please! People were looking up at him. What was in their faces? Was it disgust? Pity? Horror? He was naked, he was filthy, and he was not fit to live. He would die. He would refuse to breathe and he would die. He hung from his impaled wrists, the pain in his arms building and building, his hands like claws. His chest was burning, blowing up, there were splashes of red darkness before his eyes. His legs straightened, and the breath came screaming from his lungs.

Beneath him Joshua cried out as the nails were driven in. Joshua deserved to die. The promises that Joshua had made had led to this bare hill, to this cross.

In the Antonia, Aulus was beginning to receive reports from his patrols. About thirty men had been rounded up and were in the praetorium. He knew that he would have to go to the citadel to question them. The tribune looked at Lucius, and ordered Mordra to take his friend to see the executions. Now that the time had come, neither man wanted to witness what was happening outside the city wall, but Lucius did not want to appear cowardly, and Mordra had no choice.

Leaving the Antonia they crossed the Central Valley and followed the narrow, uphill road to the gate that lay to the north of the citadel. Through the gate, and they turned right towards their destination. Lucius did not want to take this path, he walked slowly and counted every step. From the Antonia it took him 1,894 steps to reach the killing place. He tried to imagine what each of those steps would have meant to the three condemned men who had gone before him.

The sight that greeted them was worse than any of his imaginings. Two men were already hanging. He thought, he hoped, that one was already dead, but a legionary soaked a sponge in a jar, attached it to a pilus, and forced it into the dying

175

man's mouth. He revived, and Lucius gazed in horror as his one sound leg straightened against the vicious spike, and the breath came shuddering from his tortured body.

The smells were as bad as the sights. Lucius covered his nose and mouth but could not escape the stink – blood, faeces, sweat, urine, burned flesh, pus. He tried to brush away the flies that had fed on all of this, and now buzzed around his head.

Joshua had now been stripped, and the Roman scholar watched those who were sworn to protect the Roman way of life as they drove the nails into the rabbi's wrists and heels. Lucius recoiled as the cross dropped into the prepared hole, and he saw the sudden stress of flesh on nails, the beginning of the dreadful cycle, every fourth heartbeat, of pushing down on the impaled feet in order to force breath from the body.

Mordra looked away from the three crosses, and his eyes roamed over the sullen crowd. Why did these people come? Were they trying to offer support, or was it just sick curiosity? He was surprised at the number of women who were there. He did not know it, but most of them were Galileans who had believed in Joshua, and could not now believe what they were seeing. He saw a familiar figure at the edge of the crowd. Miriam's eyes were wide in her pale face. She could not look away from the rabbi on the cross. Mordra approached, gently he said: "Miriam, do you think that you should be here? It's not a place for you."

Slowly she turned her face up to him. "I won't be here long. Tell Branwen that I am leaving Jerusalem today. Thank her from me, and tell her that I will do what Joshua wants me to do."

Mordra did not know what had transpired between the two women. Branwen and he shared most things, but this was women's business. Later, when he told his wife, she did not know what Joshua had wanted Miriam to do, and she worried for that lonely girl and her unborn child.

He did not know what else to say, and stood silent at Miriam's side. He saw Lucius stagger, and rushed to his aid.

"I'm all right," the Roman told him, "but I don't think I can stand much more of this."

"Neither can I." Mordra replied. He looked back to where Miriam had been standing, and she was gone.

They were preparing to leave when Samuel stopped them. Ignoring Lucius, he said: "Well, Mordra the Gaul, now whose side are you on?"

"Not the Sanhedrin's, nor that of any man who could do this, whatever the justification."

The priest's presence gave Lucius the chance that he needed to relieve some of his impotent anger. "You know that I sat through that sham of a trial; I kept the record. I could not stoop to be a man like you, or your colleagues, who could send their fellow-countryman to us knowing that this would be the end. And when I look up there and see what Rome can do, in my name, then I am deeply ashamed that I am a Roman."

The two men turned their backs on Samuel, and he walked away from them. Mordra was looking around, trying to see Miriam before they left this cursed spot, when Aulus arrived with Galba and Timocrates. All five looked up at the hanging men. Joshua's lips were moving but he could not breathe, he could not speak. "Is that one dead?" asked Aulus, pointing to the limp body of Nahum. "Decurion, give him the sponge to revive him."

The decurion obeyed, but Nahum did not stir. "Shall I give him a prod, sir?"

"Yes." The soldier drove his pilus up under Nahum's ribs and into his chest. Straw coloured fluid gushed out, followed by a trickle of black blood. "Dead, sir." The decurion reported unemotionally. "Leave him there," said Aulus. "Let the Jews look at him for a few hours yet. Take him down when the sun is a hand's breadth above the horizon. I want them all dead and down by then."

Timocrates looked at the wooden tablet hanging on Joshua's cross. "So, this is the King of the Jews. I can see that he is surely their messiah – much good may it do them." He and Galba laughed together, and Aulus joined in.

The soldiers of the execution squad were getting bored. Any surviving zealots would keep well away from here and the natives who were silently watching the slow deaths would cause no trouble. They resumed their game of dice.

Lucius looked appealingly at Mordra who could only shrug helplessly. With Aulus there, neither felt that they could leave.

177

Again Joshua's lips moved soundlessly. Avram was opening and closing his mouth, dumbly gibbering, and as his knees straightened yet again, urine spurted from him.

The soldiers gathered up the poor clothing of their victims, and used it as stakes in their game of dice.

On and on, through the long, hot afternoon, the two men went slowly, agonisingly to their cruel deaths. Too slowly the sun descended. Lucius tried to will it towards setting. Tribune and centurions, eyes fixed upon the dying men, spoke in low tones of the prisoners who had been rounded up. They expressed their disappointment that they had not been able to identify any zealots among them. Mordra was sure that, innocent or guilty, those men would not leave the praetorium unscathed.

"Another one dead, sir." The decurion reported to Aulus. In death, Avram looked even younger, about twelve years old. All his agony, his shame, had been wiped away; his hatred of Rome, and his fear were no more. The boy seemed to sleep upon the cross. The sun was approaching the Great Sea. "Get those two down," Aulus ordered. Ladders were put up behind the crosses. The nails were knocked loose with hammers, and pulled from the wood with heavy pincers. Ropes had been passed around the arms of the two dead men and, without ceremony, they were lowered to lie crumpled on the bloody ground. Noisily weeping women approached with rolls of white linen cloth. The cloths were spread, the bodies gently laid upon them, and carried away to their burial.

Joshua still lived. "Another few minutes and we'll break that one's legs," said Aulus.

Again, the rabbi pushed down to free the breath from his body. Again the unspeakable agony. He looked over the Holy City of Jerusalem, every stone burnished gold by the dying sun. He looked over the Mount of Olives, and he looked up at the deep blue of the sky. He could not utter the words, but they were in his brain and in his heart: "Shema Yisroel, Adonai Elohenu, Adonai – Ehaaaaad!" With the final word drawn out, he had heaved down upon his feet, and had cried aloud his last proclamation of the oneness of the god of Israel.

Joshua of Nazareth, King of Israel, was dead.

"Decurion," Aulus called, "I think that one's finished. Give him a prod."

The decurion drove his pilus into the inert body of Joshua. As with Nahum, there was a gushing of straw-coloured fluid that had built up in the lining of his tormented lungs, followed by a trickle of dark blood. "Dead, sir." The decurion reported. Aulus glanced casually at the limp body, then to his left, to the dying sun. "Get him down, decurion."

The tribune stood between Galba and Timocrates. He placed a hand on the shoulder of each Centurion. *"Probus,"* he said, *"consummatum est."* – Good, it is finished.

Chapter 12

When Branwen saw her husband's face she gasped and clutched her hand to her breast. He sat heavily; she stood close beside him.

"You've come from *y moel yr angau ofnadwy.*" It was a statement, not a question. He put his arms around her, and his tears stained her dress. Their language said it – 'the bare hill of terrible death' – that so well described the skull-like promontory where he had been made to witness the most profound act of deliberate cruelty that he had ever seen. Gently she stroked his hair as he hugged her close. Mordra was a strong man, a son of warrior people. As a youth he had gone on cattle raids, and had killed other men. With Aulus, he had penetrated the Germanic forests, and seen the efficient butchery of the army of Rome. Here in Judaea, Jewish life was cheap to the occupying army. But the deaths that he had witnessed today, a boy, a dying man, and a scholarly politician, who wanted nothing but to rid their land of the vileness that was Rome, these were not honourable killings, there was no *chwarae teg,* no fair play by which the Gauls, and the British set such store. The manner of those deaths! He had heard all about crucifixion, but this was the first time that he had seen it. He had seen the lowest depths to which men could sink out of their hatred and fear of their fellow men. For the Romans did fear the Jews, as they feared all who had ideas that they could not understand. This was why they had persecuted and all-but destroyed the Druids in Gaul.

What he had seen today was not done by iron nails. It was done by arrogance. It was done by dogma. It was done by ignorance. The Romans believed that they were always right, they believed that they had absolute knowledge, with no test in reality. This was what men could do when they aspired to the status of gods.

He looked up at her. "We must get out of the empire, this evil empire. You are right, we must get to Prydain. I don't know how long it will remain free of Rome, but we must go there, perhaps do something to keep your people free. I want a spear in my hand again, and I want my spear to taste Roman blood."

Her heart leapt. She had faith in Mordra's determination and his strength. He was already planning.

"I'll do as you suggest, I'll cultivate Marcus Lucius. You must help me. If he can get a lawyer as well as an historian he will be even keener. He told me that he wants to study our laws as well as our religion."

"Yes!" Her eyes were shining, as he had never seen before. "And we'll both complete our studies, and enter the *Gorsedd*."

Mordra stood, and they embraced. Branwen went on: "The sacred grove of the *Cantref o Nudd,* the territory of the hundred Nudd Valley settlements, lies at an angle between the water meadows of the River Nudd, and one of its tributaries the *Afon Clydach,* the stony river. There's a path through *Dyffryn Clydach,* the Vale of Clydach, we call it *coed bach,* the little wood, and it leads to the *Gelli Derwen,* the oak grove where only Druids, and those who are about to join the *Gorsedd,* the Assembly of Druids, may go. We will go there. This man Marcus Lucius is our key…"

Mordra felt her stiffen against him. He turned and saw Lucius standing behind him. They had been speaking in their own tongue that was unintelligible to the Roman.

He had vomited until he was empty, and then retched until his stomach felt like a hard fist within him. "I'm sorry," he muttered, "I don't mean to intrude."

Branwen swallowed her hatred of all things Roman, and started to greet him in Latin. Mordra interrupted her in Greek. "I think that Marcus Lucius would prefer Greek." She looked gratefully at her husband. He had told her that she did not need to speak the language of Rome. And to Lucius: *"Kalispera-sas. Ti kanete?"* Good evening. How are you?

Lucius tried to smile. *"Eho to stomachi-moo."* I've got a stomach upset. He gestured to a chair. *"Boro na katsso etho?"* Can I sit here?

Mordra stepped forward to assist him to the chair. *"Leepa*

me." I'm sorry.

Branwen left the room, and returned with a jug and two earthenware cups. She poured two generous measures of a clear liquid, and handed one to each man. Mordra sipped the raw spirit. Lucius took a gulp, and coughed. *"Efkharisto poli."* Thank you very much.

Branwen smiled. *"Parakalo."* You're welcome.

Mordra completed the formalities. *"I Branwen, ke I Marcus Lucius."* This is Branwen, and this is Marcus Lucius.

The Roman saw before him a woman who was not a classical beauty, but was more. She had strong, attractive features that were pleasing to the eye. Her dark hair was carefully braided, and the braids were coiled artfully upon her fine head. There was kindness in her eyes, but also, he thought, wariness. She was slender, and carried herself with grace. He did not know why, but he took an instant liking to Branwen. She disguised her feelings. He turned to Mordra. "I hope that you don't mind my visiting you like this, I want to keep out of the way of Aulus Plautius for a while."

Mordra nodded, he understood. Lucius went on: "Pilate's gone. He left for Caesarea when we were – out there." He emptied his cup, Branwen indicated the jug, he nodded, and she poured.

Lucius sat hunched, taking occasional sips. Mordra and Branwen watched him, waiting. Eventually, he looked up. "Why can't they just behead them or something?"

It was Branwen who answered him. "That's what my people would have done."

"Your people?"

"The Silures, I'm from Ynys Prydain."

Something began to dawn upon Lucius's face. "Prydain? What's it like?"

Branwen gave a low laugh. "I have to admit to a prejudice." She paused, and a distant look came into her eyes. "You know what it's like in an apple orchard, especially in the spring when the trees are alive with blossom, and the lazy bees move from flower to flower, or in the late summer with the smell of the fruit that are heavy on every branch?"

Lucius nodded, she had conjured an idyllic picture.

182

Branwen went on: "In our language an apple orchard is *afallon,* which is also the name that we give to the most perfect part of the Otherworld, paradise. My home is near the end of a beautiful valley with many waterfalls. The trees grow thickly; the pastures are rich where cattle, sheep and goats grow fat. The river flows through the port and into a sparkling sea that provides a variety of fish. There's barley for beer, and blackberries for wine; the corn grows high, and fruits are heavy on the trees."

"So you live on more than apples?"

"We live on iron. On the left bank, above the port, are the foundries and workshops. Iron, and copper, and tin lie beneath our feet. In places the iron seeps out of the ground as deep orange water. We take iron from the earth and work it until it is fine finished goods."

"And you live among all that?"

"No. On the right bank of the river is our settlement, and there are many more up the valley. We have our religious and academic centres by the river, and our hospital on the hillside."

Lucius's thoughts could not turn away from the horrors of the day. "And you give your criminals a quick and merciful death?"

"There's more to it than that. Yes, we decapitate those who have committed serious offences..." Her mind went back to a legionary killed by a powerful back swing from his own sword, his head hurled into the broad waters of a river mouth. Mordra looked steadily at her. She threw off the thought. "We also take the heads of our enemies killed in battle. The difference is what we do with them."

"What is that?"

"The heads of our enemies, lost in fair play, we take back to our settlement as trophies, and we keep them in an honoured place that we call *Caerpennau,* the Fort of the Heads. This ensures that the enemy warrior can be reborn in the Otherworld. It's a similar thing with executed criminals. We reunite them with their heads so that they can pass to the Otherworld, and when they cross the threshold back to this life we trust that they will offend no more. The heads of those seen to be unfit for rebirth are thrown into the river or the sea."

Lucius was fascinated. "Tell me about the Otherworld."

183

Branwen wanted this man to be pliable. Without asking, she refilled his cup. "You know that some of the Jews believe in resurrection of the dead?"

Lucius nodded, she continued: "We have a similar belief, but ours is more specific. There are two parallel worlds, this one and the Otherworld, which is a superior place, a place of happiness, although those who have done evil in this world, and have been buried with their heads, can be punished there so that, when they return, they will live in closer harmony with their neighbours. There is but a curtain between the two worlds, and beings from the Otherworld can cross to visit us as guides and mentors. When a loved one dies we mourn for our loss, but it is also a time of rejoicing for that person's rebirth in the Otherworld. And when a child is born we rejoice at the gift of that child to us, but we also mourn that person's death in a better place."

"So you believe that your people spend eternity passing between the two worlds?"

"We do, but we can break the cycle by giving the head of an evil-doer to the gods and goddesses of the waters for the fish to eat them."

"And who decides who is an evil-doer whose offences are so grave that he must be destroyed for ever?"

"The judges. It can be one judge."

Mordra could see where Branwen was leading this conversation. He decided it was time to guarantee Lucius's interest. "I think that you should know something of our education, you may recall that I mentioned it last night. We all attend the Druid school from the age of three. Some of us remain in full time education for more than eighteen and a half years. To be precise, the law demands eighteen years and 223 days. In the last year and a half, the student has to produce some original work in his own discipline. I was working upon the earliest origin of our people, and I was coming to the conclusion that we are not descended from the Greeks, as many believe, but that they and we may be the two branches of the same tree. If the student is successful he is awarded a golden wand. He is a professor and can enter the Assembly of Druids. A Druid is a member of our intellectual class. they may be any type of scholar, or a priest. I was within one year of completing my studies when I had to enter the service of Aulus Plautius. Branwen still had two and a half years to go when she was abducted by legionaries and ended up here."

Lucius was dumbfounded. "But Branwen's a woman."

Branwen's laughter was genuine. "I'm a Silurian woman. In our society, and that of Gaul, women have the same rights and duties as men."

"But, how?"

"How? Do you think that women have no brains? You and the Greeks sit on your women, you make them into no more than decorative objects for the pleasure of men. You confine them to simple work within the household, and you do not allow them to be real people. Don't you realise that you are wasting half of your most precious resource – the working of the human brain? In my land, and that of my – of Mordra, women can do anything that a man can do, except that most of us avoid much of the work in iron because that is better suited to the male physique, just as such tasks as spinning and weaving are better done by the dextrous hands of women. We can be heads of families, we can lead tribes and nations, even into battle. A woman can be a Druid just as easily as a man."

Lucius could still not come to terms with this. "And what would you have done if you had been able to complete your studies?"

Mordra spoke quietly. "Branwen is a lawyer, she would have been a judge."

Lucius sat back, his eyes wide. He knew that he had drunk three cups of strong spirit on an empty stomach. He recalled something that he had learned as a student on Rhodos regarding such a spirit: 'one cup gives an appetite for dinner; two cups give a stronger appetite; three cups are a disaster, and you will not eat dinner'. He had taken too much, but he knew that it had not affected him in the slightest. He looked from one to the other, his mind racing. He sighed. "I think that it was Ippokrates who complained that life was so short, and the craft so long to learn. I know what he meant. I came here to study the Jews because I am interested in the link between religion and law. I want to visit your land for the same reason. As I am here I will start with the

Jews, but you make me more eager to go to Ynys Prydain."

Mordra felt that he was closing a trap. "You can study both while you are here."

"How?"

"Both Branwen and I have compiled quite a library of notes. You are welcome to use them, but there is one problem."

Lucius could guess. "Language?"

"Yes. Since coming to Judaea I have kept most of my notes in Greek, Branwen sometimes does the same. We have our own alphabet, but that is mainly used for the secrets of religion and magic. Most of us write in our own language but in the Greek alphabet, that is the Druidic way."

Branwen could see another bond to tie Lucius to them. "We will teach you our language. In that way you can read all that we have written about Prydain and Gaul as well as about Judaea, and when you visit my people you will be able to understand each other."

The thought that had been going through Lucius's mind had to be uttered. "What is the price of a slave in your society?"

Branwen felt her heart quicken. "There are no slaves in our society, not slaves as you know them, like me and Mordra. But we do have indentured servants who are bound to one master. They are mostly captured warriors, minor criminals, or those who have fallen upon misfortune. Even so they may marry freely, have their own possessions, even land, and pass their possessions on to their children."

"Do you buy and sell them?"

"We usually hire them out. The price of the hiring is a cup of wine. Very rarely are they sold."

"And how much are they?"

"They are only sold if there is some major change in a family's circumstances or fortunes. The price is a jug of wine."

Lucius could hardly believe his ears. "A jug of wine?"

Branwen's confidence was growing. "It's only a token price." She was deliberately talking like a lawyer. "A contract of agreement has to have a value put upon it in order to make it binding upon both parties, so we have set a price that everyone can afford to pay." She laughed. "Of course, Silurian wine is made from blackberries and is very strong." She glanced at

Mordra. "Much better than thin Gallic wine."

Branwen asked him if he would care to dine with them. Lucius suddenly realised that his stomach was now feeling perfectly normal. He had started the day suffering the effects of too much wine and had witnessed an act that he was trying, without success, to forget. Was it the spirit he had drunk, or the company that he was in? He was starting to relax, and said: "I would love to dine with you. There is so much that I want to learn about the Keltoi." The look that his hosts gave him made him realise that he had used an unfortunate word. "I'm sorry. You don't use that name to identify yourselves?"

Branwen was solicitous. "It's not your fault, Lucius. I suppose that must be the name that they use on Rhodos, or the Latin 'Celtae'. No, we don't use those words, we find them dismissive of our highly developed culture, and they are words coined by people who have done us little service by their descriptions of our people. Oh yes, all the people of temperate Europe share in one culture, but we identify ourselves by the nation and region to which we belong. Mordra and I are from different peoples." She smiled at Lucius's embarrassment. "Even though we are both 'Keltoi'."

Mordra stood up. "Then you'd better start learning our customs." He led the puzzled Roman to a small lavatorium where water poured into a stone bowl. On a ledge there was a cake of some strange, sweet-smelling, fatty substance.

"It isn't only Jews who go in for ritual washing, we do too," said Mordra, dipping his hands into the bowl and picking up the fatty cake. The Gaul demonstrated.

"This is soap." He rubbed the cake between his hands, and foam appeared. When Lucius tried it he was most pleasantly surprised. He had always thought that the *strigil,* the skin scraper, the most efficient means of cleansing the skin. This soap made his hands feel different, cleaner, and left them smelling like a field of flowers.

Branwen had earlier received a message that Aulus would dine that night in the praetorium. The three ate well; Lucius drank little, and they talked of a world that Lucius did not yet know.

Lucius managed to avoid Aulus for more than a week. This

was not difficult as the tribune was fully engaged in trying to round up the remaining zealots. Aulus knew that his friend would be happy discussing obscure prospects with Mordra, and he only once gave him a passing thought. This was when they crucified five more zealots, or, to be precise, suspected zealots. Aulus had thought of inviting Lucius to the executions, but he had seen what effect crucifixion had upon him, and decided that this would be beyond a joke. The five had been found in the upper room of a house close to that of Caiaphas, in the southwestern quadrant of the city. One of the patrols found three men and two women apparently holding a meeting of some sort. This was enough for the soldiers. They had been questioned minutely, and brutally, in the praetorium, and had denied all knowledge of the zealots, and of those who had died a few days earlier. They were Galileans, two of them from Nazareth, yet they claimed that they had never heard of Joshua until his public execution. Then one of them slipped up by referring to the dead rabbi as King Joshua – that was enough.

One of the women was an old crone who was the object of much coarse humour when she was on the cross. The other was a beautiful girl of fifteen, and the soldiers were happy to have her as a prisoner. As she struggled on the cross, the scars, the bruises, the blood of her multiple rapes were plain to see. This time the execution squad had bets on who would last the longest. The winner was a skinny man in his mid thirties who, with careful reviving, took over thirty hours to die; much better than the mere six hours that Joshua had hung there.

The Priest Simon of Bethany was crucified, together with his wife, his sons, his grandsons, and his entire household, including a servant girl whose only crime had been to fetch a phial of consecrated oil.

Aulus did not set foot in the Antonia. He ate and slept in the citadel. There were two auxiliaries to discipline for sleeping on duty. Aulus knew about the Chassidic belief in resurrection, and was concerned that someone would remove the body of Joshua, then claim that he had come back to life. For this reason he took careful note of where the rabbi was buried. A Pharisee called Joseph who was a member of the Sanhedrin provided the tomb, and he and another Pharisee called Nicodemus supervised the burial according to Jewish ritual. Aulus was satisfied with this, and even more pleased when he saw the great stone wheel that formed the door of the tomb rolled into place. He was now confident that the 'King of the Jews' would remain secure until he rotted, and his bones were transferred to an ossuary. To avoid tomb robbery he put a guard in place, and thought that all would be well. He was not prepared for the fact that, when Joshua had been no more than three days dead, both men would sleep on duty. They may have been given drugged wine, but that was no excuse. When their relief arrived in the morning, accompanied by the centurion of the guard, they were snoring like pigs. The door of the tomb had been rolled away, and the body of the rabbi had disappeared. The centurion had never been angrier. Viciously he kicked the two men into wakefulness, then whipped them all the way to the praetorium with his vine staff, which broke just as they arrived at the citadel. He reported to Galba, who reported to Aulus, whose first reaction was two hundred lashes each. This would have been a fatal flogging. After about fifty lashes, Aulus called a halt.

"Crucify them."

Galba could not disguise his shock.

"They're soldiers, sir."

"Are they?" said Aulus grimly. "They were auxiliaries, not Roman citizens. Only the gods can know what a problem they may have unleashed. They are the enemies of Rome. Crucify them as they deserve."

Four decades guarded the execution site as they went to their deaths. Galba did not want the Jews to witness these executions, he knew that they would enjoy them. Both men had been filled with wine laced with mulberries and poppy juice before they were stripped for their deaths. After an hour, Galba ordered that the two men be despatched with pili.

The Romans could not find any of Joshua's inner circle of followers. They took out their frustration on those they did round up. Aulus was not surprised that the Sanhedrin had let him down again. The sicariot who had betrayed Joshua could not be found. He very much wanted this man. He had turned informer once, he would do it again, and his knowledge of zealot names and of zealot activity must be profound.

A century was sent to the Galilee with a request to Herod Antipas to search in his territory. The Tetrarch gave his permission, but little practical help. A few Jews were killed, many more were beaten, some women were raped, but the zealots had melted away. In Nazareth, the carpenter's shop was closed up, the family was nowhere to be found. The building was torched, and the legionaries took some satisfaction from its destruction.

Aulus gave a great deal of thought to an assault upon the Essene community at Qumran; the place must be stuffed with zealots. He discussed it with Galba and Timocrates, and the Primus Pilus suggested that he speak with Caiaphas first. There was now a spy in place there. It was Caiaphas's opinion that Joshua bar Abbas should gather as much information about the strength and the distribution of the zealot Essenes before an attack was launched. In that way they could not only wipe out the desert community, but also be able to target Essene pockets throughout the land, thus ensuring their complete destruction.

Half way through the week, Aulus returned to the Antonia in a foul temper. He told Mordra to send Branwen to the house of Caiaphas with a message for Miriam. He desperately needed her. Branwen made a pretence of going on the errand, and returned with the news that the girl had left Jerusalem. No one knew where she had gone. Aulus was incensed. For a day and a night his only companion was a constant supply of harsh spirits. Mordra carried his master to his bed where he tossed and vomited, then spent another day in deep sleep. When eventually he opened his eyes, a bolt of white-hot pain shot through his head. He dare not try to rise from the pillow. His mouth felt that it was full of sand. He did not know, or care, that his room had been cleaned and his bed linen changed as he had slept. He groaned and slowly rolled his head from side to side, but the pain would not go away. Where was Mordra? Why wouldn't he come? Let the terrorists have this fleapit of a land, it wasn't worth the trouble. They would never be stopped until the last Jew had been wiped from the face of the earth, and it was too much effort to crucify all of them. Even then their bones would, like dragon's teeth, become new bandits growing from the cursed soil of this 'holy land'. His stomach lurched. A shadow fell across him. Shielding his eyes from the light of the oil lamp, wishing that he could not smell the burning oil, he looked up at Mordra, flagon in hand, standing by his bed. The Gaul put a strong arm under his shoulders, cradling his head in the crook of his elbow and a cup was raised to his dry lips. After five large cups of sweet fruit juice, he tasted the bitter essence of the willow tree, then more fruit juice. "I need to pee," he mumbled. Mordra hauled him out of bed and indicated a bucket on the floor. Relieved, he flopped back on the bed, and reached for more orange juice and honey. Mordra left a full flagon at his side.

Lucius was at his language lessons with Branwen when Mordra returned. "He's awake," was his brief report. Lucius looked up. "I don't suppose he's in a fit state for a discussion?"

"Definitely not what you want to discuss. You're going to have to wait until he's in a better mood, and I can't think when that is going to be."

Lucius had spent all his waking hours with these two fascinating scholars. As Mordra had brought news of what was happening outside, he liked Jerusalem less and less, and became ever more determined to get out of this land, back home to Samnium, and then to the island of Britain – Ynys Prydain. Branwen, without care, had asked him: "Is this the honourable code of your soldiers? Killing unarmed men, old women, raping girls. Do they not know how to play fair?" Lucius had no answer. He had already accumulated a small lexicon of British words, adding to them and using them all the time. One of the first phrases that he had learned was *chwarae teg,* fair play, and his new friends tried to explain the concept to him.

Haltingly, he had suggested to them that it might be possible to take them from Aulus. If he could, then he would want nothing more than for them to accompany him to Prydain. The two had looked dumbfounded, as if such a thought would never have occurred to them. Branwen remained silent, praying. Mordra expressed grave doubts as he fought to keep a straight face. This made Lucius more determined.

Despite herself, Branwen could not help liking Lucius. There were times when she almost forgot that he was Roman. He had been genuinely distressed by the brutality that he had

191

witnessed. Mordra had told her that, at the foot of the crosses, he had expressed his shame in being of a people who could be capable of such cruelty. On first meeting he had approved of the Silurian way of quick and humane execution, and the honouring of noble enemies who had died fairly. She was increasingly aware that he was moving away from the sordid life of Rome.

They had told him no lies. They had not pretended that British society was perfect, even detailing its imperfections. But they had shared their Druidic knowledge of their culture with him. She smiled to herself as she conjured a picture of Lucius with flowing hair, and a moustache, dressed in breeches, and a multicoloured cloak, perhaps a golden torc about his neck – a Roman Silurian! She threw off the thought. She reminded herself that Lucius was a Roman. Instead she made herself picture Mordra dressed as he should be. She had only ever known her husband clean shaven, with short hair, and wearing a Roman tunic. She wanted to see him as a Gaul.

That evening Mordra and Branwen were to visit two Jewish friends; the couple who had invited Mordra to their Seder, the Passover feast that, after recent events, now seemed a lifetime ago. He told Lucius that it would be unwise for him to accompany them, and they left him to his silent study of the Jews from Mordra's Greek language scrolls. He was eager to perfect his knowledge of the British tongue so that he could read about that island.

The evening was not a success for Mordra and Branwen. It was the evening of the day that the Romans had dedicated to their god Saturn. To Mordra and Branwen, and to their Jewish hosts, it was the evening of the start of a new day, the first day of the Jewish week. Sabbath was over. Joel and his wife Judith were Pharisees, and the first friends that Mordra had made among the natives. They had witnessed the marriage of this pair who came from beyond the world that they knew. The invitation had been given a little over a week ago, at the end of the Seder. None of them could have imagined how their worlds would turn in so few days. There was a careful trust between the two couples, but Joel and Judith could not, this night, forget that their guests were the employees, albeit unwilling, of he who they considered to be the most evil man in Jerusalem, Aulus, the representative and personification of Rome.

Mordra and Branwen wanted to reach out to their gracious host and hostess, but they were constrained by all that had recently occurred. All were aware that there was an unbridgeable cultural gulf between those from around the Great Sea, especially the Jews, and those from temperate Europe. How could they communicate their shared hopes, their dreams, and their fears?

They had expressed their thanks, and departed as early as they considered it decent to do so.

Returning to the Antonia through the darkened streets, a hand reached from a black alcove and grabbed Branwen by her braided hair. Mordra's spring was checked when he saw the waning moon reflected on the curved blade held to his wife's throat. A hoarse voice came from the darkness. "You are Mordra, servant of the butcher Aulus Plautius?"

"Yes. What do you want?"

"To talk."

"Release her, and I'll talk."

The sicar was still at Branwen's throat. Again the hoarse voice: "They say you are a friend of the Jews."

"I am a friend of all reasonable men."

"The Romans?"

"No. I said of reasonable men."

The killing skills of a Gallic warrior were useless. The exchange was in Aramaic, but Mordra was thinking in the quick, persuasive tongue of Gaul.

He heard a scream, and his heart stood still. Then Branwen was by his side, her assailant writhing on the ground. Branwen had sensed a slight relaxation in the man who held her. He was distracted by his conversation with her husband, and had lost vital concentration. In one fast, smooth movement she had grasped and turned the man's right wrist to thrust the dagger away from her, and, with her left hand, she had reached between his legs to squeeze and twist the soft, vulnerable flesh. Mordra kicked the dagger away, and Branwen picked it up. Mordra reached down and hauled the man up by his cloak. The hood fell away to reveal coarsely hacked hair, and a terrified, bearded, pain-filled face. Mordra thrust him against the wall, and held him with his forearm under the chin and hard against the throat. "Who are you?"

The Gaul had to withdraw his forearm slightly to allow the man to reply: "Judah."

Mordra glanced at the dagger held low and ready in his wife's hand. "The sicariot, one of Joshua's twelve?"

"Yes."

"What do you want?"

"To talk."

"Then talk, now."

There was a tremor through the man's body. "Are you a friend of the Jews?"

"I told you."

There was a sob, then: "I cannot tell my people. I cannot try to make them understand."

"I'm not surprised, you betrayed their king."

Again the sicariot sobbed. "Someone must know why. No Jew, no Roman, someone."

Mordra glanced at Branwen, she nodded. He looked into the deep pits of the Jew's eyes. "We will listen, and I can promise you that Aulus Plautius will never know." He released the man and stood back. Branwen was a little to his side, half crouched, the dagger ready. Judah took a deep breath, and rubbed his bruised neck. "Not here."

"Where then?"

"There is a cave in the Hinmon Valley."

Mordra gave a harsh laugh. "With the city's rubbish? What an appropriate place. Where in the valley?"

"On the western side. You will see half the head of the statue of Antiochus, the Maccabeans threw it there. Directly above it you will see a myrtle tree growing out of the rock. There's a cave hidden by that tree. I'm there all the time."

"Living on the city's garbage?"

"I am living, as Johannen did, on carob pods, and whatever I can find."

Branwen did not take her eyes off the sicariot. "See him. We may learn something. Or I could take his head now, everyone will thank me for it." She had spoken in Aramaic.

For a few moments Mordra considered the two options,

then: "I'll see you. I don't know when, just be there."

The stricken man backed away. "I'll be there. I have nowhere else to go."

Lucius looked up from the scroll that he was studying as they entered. He could see that they were both troubled. Mordra sat at the table opposite him, and Branwen brought a flagon of wine and three cups. "How much of a loyal Roman are you," Mordra asked, "and how much of an objective academic?"

"I like to think that I'm an academic before all else." There was no response. "And what little I've learned in the past week has more than whetted my appetite for more. I think that I'm beginning to learn that my only loyalty is to learning – my only loyalty! Loyalty has to be earned, it cannot be demanded. I am Roman by accident of birth, no more than that. What is happening here at the moment is releasing me from any automatic loyalty that I once thought that my birth demanded of me."

Mordra took a deep draught of wine, and he looked into Lucius's eyes, attempting to plumb the depths of his soul. "We have just met with Judah."

"Judah?"

"The sicariot who betrayed Joshua."

"Where? Here in Jerusalem?"

"Yes. In a dark alley. He wants to meet with me, he has something to tell me."

"What? Are you going to meet him? When?"

Branwen laid the sicar on the table between them and said: "We cannot tell you when, or where. But Mordra has agreed to meet him. I want to go with him, but he thinks it better if he goes alone. Aulus Plautius must not know. Mordra will decide whether to tell him anything after he has met with this man."

Lucius's eyes were fixed on the wicked dagger. Mordra smiled. "In his society, as in yours, only men are warriors. Another waste of half your resources."

Lucius gazed at the dagger, then up at Branwen. He had much to learn. He drank his wine, and nodded his agreement. He knew that he had taken his first steps away from Rome, and towards that world beyond the north wind that he longed to see and understand.

195

Chapter 13

Aulus suspended the operation in search of the zealots. They were beaten for the time being, and the little gang that had surrounded Joshua must now be long gone. A few dozen had been crucified, which should be enough to keep the population quiet. He was satisfied by their sullen silence, but he did not want to antagonise them further. The hill bandits must have suffered more heavily than the true zealots; travellers and caravans entered Jerusalem unscathed with no reports of any sightings.

After a few visits to the army's brothel he began to be reconciled to losing Miriam, although he could not think why she had deserted him. Sitting with Lucius one evening, mellowed by wine, he had said: "It was nice to have a regular woman. I'll find myself another one I think. Nothing as regular as you and Paulina, I'd never consider marriage outside Italy. One day I'll have to do something to continue my family's ancient and noble name, but not yet. Miriam can be replaced while I'm here, anyone can."

This gave Lucius the chance that he had been waiting for. "That's true, no one's indispensable. Although I've been finding Mordra to be a rare scholar, just what I need as a collaborator. I wonder if you'd consider selling him to me."

"Mordra? No way, he's much too useful to me."

"But we agreed that no one's indispensable."

"We did, but I have to think of my comfort. Oh, I don't doubt that I could find an orderly as good as Mordra, but his main value to me is what he knows about the Jews. He was a good source of information in Gaul and Germania, but since coming here – he is indispensable. As long as I stay in Judaea I must have Mordra with me."

"And when you leave Judaea?"

"I depends where I'm sent."

Lucius fell silent, he could see no way out of this impasse.

When he reported this conversation, Branwen was still optimistic.

"One refusal is not necessarily final."

"You sound like a lawyer," Lucius said ruefully.

"I am a lawyer," she replied, "that's why I must think of some other way to proceed, and I'm a Silurian lawyer. We're famous for our cunning. It's also why you need me."

Lucius had to laugh. "The three of us should make the most formidable academic team in the world." It was the first time that he had said anything to indicate that he regarded Branwen as an equal. The British girl smiled to think how far he had progressed in so little time.

Mordra was not with them. He had gone to the Hinmon Valley to meet with Judah the sicariot.

The Gaul, not wanting to be observed, skirted the forum and the amphitheatre, and left the city by a gate into the Central Valley. He walked around the outside of the southern wall, and into the noisome Hinmon Valley. All the rubbish from the whole of Jerusalem was dumped and burned here, and the stink offended his nostrils. The wall turned sharply to the north, protecting the western side of Jerusalem, and the citadel. Soon he saw the shattered visage of Antiochus IV poking out from the garbage. Mordra knew that when Judah Maccabeus and his army had overthrown the Greek garrison of Jerusalem they had found he Temple desecrated. The houses of the priests had been pulled down to give the defenders a clear field for their arrows and spears. The gates had been burned, and there were shrubs growing up through the cracked paving stones. The stone altar had been profaned by being used as the base for an obscene statue of Antiochus in the form of Zeus. Those early zealots had brought down the statue and smashed it into pieces. The remains were thrown upon the rubbish here in the Hinmon Valley. They dismantled the altar, but did not know what to do with the stones. True, they had been defiled, but before that they had been dedicated to their god, and their god was eternal. Judah ordered that they be stacked on the eastern lip of the temple platform

197

where they would remain until a prophet should come and tell them what to do with them. The Maccabeans had quarried virgin stone, and used it, not dressed, to build a new, pure altar.

Looking up from this reminder of a hated Greek ruler, Mordra saw the dark green leaves of a myrtle tree, the white flowers had not yet budded. He scrambled up the slope and pushed the branches aside to look into the maw of a shallow cave. The dark shape of a man huddled against the far wall. "It's Mordra the Gaul," he announced. The man hesitated, then came forward towards the light. It was the sicariot. He would not leave the shelter of the cave, and Mordra had to crawl in and find a seat on a rough, low ledge jutting from the side. "What do you want to tell me?" The Gaul allowed his contempt to come out in his tone.

The Jew moaned, "I am a man who has seen affliction by the rod of his wrath.

He has driven me away and made me walk in darkness rather than light."

Mordra began to regret that he had come on this errand. "I too have read the Book of Lamentations. I am familiar with your people's writings."

Judah looked up at him.

> "Rejoice greatly, O Daughters of Zion!
> Shout, Daughters of Jerusalem!
> See, your king comes to you,
> righteous and having salvation,
> gentle and riding on a donkey,
> on a colt, the foal of a donkey.
> I will bend Judah as I bend my bow
> and fill it with Ephraim.
> I will rouse your sons, O Zion,
> against your sons, O Greece,
> and make you like a warrior's sword."

"And that's from one of your prophets," Mordra said, "Zechariah I think. If I want to know your canon of writings, I can read for myself. You cannot know if you are of the tribe of Ephraim. If you have nothing better to tell me you will make me regret that we left your head on your shoulders."

Judah gave a low sob. "Ephraim was the name of my father. I have betrayed him, as I have betrayed Israel.

"Joshua ordered the twelve to go up to Jerusalem for Passover. He warned us of extreme danger, but he did not say what that danger would be. He said that he doubted that he would survive. We went through Jericho and Bethphage to Bethany where Joshua told two of the twelve to find a mount for him. They found a tethered colt and started to untie it. When the owner challenged them they told him that it was for Joshua of Nazareth, and he gave them the loan of the animal.

"'See your king comes riding on a donkey'.

"We went slowly up to Jerusalem so that we could gather a following from those who were camped on the approaches to the city. There were many Galilean Chassids who elbowed aside any dissenters so that he could enter the Holy City to loud acclaim. People laid palm branches and their clothing beneath the hooves of his colt, and greeted him with the traditional word of acclaim for a king of Israel. They called him 'Son of David!' We went up to the temple, and entered the mikveh. Then we followed him around to the eastern wall and through the Golden Gate, the route of the Messiah."

"I saw all of this," Mordra interrupted him, "I was there and saw you go into the ritual bath, then enter the temple. I watched Joshua on the three days that he was there."

If Judah was surprised he did not show it. He seemed incapable of expressing any normal feelings. "You cannot have seen him in the Court of the Priests."

Mordra gave a humourless laugh. "I respect my own life and I believe what the warning sign says."

A low stone wall, beyond which no Gentile may venture, surrounded the inner courts of the temple, and bore prominent warnings in Greek and Latin that 'No foreigner may enter within the balustrade and the enclosure around the temple area. Anyone caught doing so will bear the responsibility for his own ensuing death'.

"But I have been told that he proclaimed the Hallel from the horns of the altar. Is this true?"

"Yes," Judah replied. "He strode through the Court of Women, we tagged behind. Not glancing to right or left, he went

199

up the curved steps leading to the Nicanor Gate that opens into the Court of the Israelites. Joshua and we went beyond into the Court of Priests." Judah's eyes were unfocussed; he was back in the temple on that recent, distant day. "To his left lay the stone altar. The air was heavy with the mixed odours of blood, incense, and charred animal fat, but because of the constant breezes there are no flies and golden spikes atop the walls prevent scavenging birds from nesting. The attending priests and Levites stood back as he walked round the altar, ascended the ramp, and reached out his hands to grasp the bloody, horn-like stone projections on the northern side of the sacred edifice. Raising his head, he proclaimed the Hallel in a loud voice."

Mordra was not satisfied. "You, and the priests must surely have known what that signified."

"I did."

"So you stood there, with a sicar beneath your cloak, and allowed this man to make himself your king?"

Judah gazed down at the earth floor of the cave. "I still believed, because I wanted to believe, that Joshua was proclaiming the Kingdom of the Lord."

"Are you completely stupid?"

"I think that I am." He looked up and Mordra saw the agonising torment in his eyes. "I was stupid to follow Joshua. I was stupid to believe that he would establish the Holy Republic of Israel." He paused. "And I betrayed him."

"And you regret that?"

"I don't know! I cannot know. 'Do not judge, or you too will be judged. For in the same way as you judge others, you will be judged, and with the measure you use, it will be measured to you'."

"Now that sounds like another quotation, but I can't identify it."

"Joshua said those words to me – at the Seder."

Mordra wanted to get back to the events in the temple. "What were the priests doing when Joshua was making himself your king?"

"There was total silence when Joshua uttered the words of the Hallel. You are right, the priests knew what was happening, but they said and did nothing. Joshua released his grip on the horns of the altar, turned and descended the ramp. He walked around the altar, and up the steps of the Sanctuary. Standing with his back to the great doors, he looked around the Court. Most of the people in the Court of the Priests were Sadducees but he could see beyond to the Court of the Israelites, which was packed with his own followers. Around the altar there was a knot of Sadducee priests and scribes, his gaze rested upon them. Then he descended from the Sanctuary, and strode from the temple."

Judah leaned back against the wall of the cave, eyes closed. Rhythmically he began to beat upon his breast with a clenched right fist. The mournful words came from his livid lips: *"Yisgadal ve'yiskadash sh'mey rabbo deevro chiroosey, ve'yamlich malchoosey be'chayeychown, u'vyowmeychown u'vchayey de'chol baiss Yisroel, ba'agolo uviman koreev ve'imroo Omaine."* 'Magnified and sanctified be his great name in the world which he has created according to his will. May he establish his kingdom during your life and during your days, and during the life of all the house of Israel, even speedily and at a near time, and say you, Amen.'

With the first phrase Mordra had recognised the *Kaddish,* the Jewish prayer for the dead. He had heard it often – too often. Standing, he allowed Judah to come to the final words: *"Owsseh sholowm bi'mrowmow, hoo yasseh sholowm oleynee ve'al kol Yisroel, ve'imroo Omaine."* He who makes peace in his high places, may he make peace for us and for all Israel, and say you, Amen'.

Mordra then placed his hand, gently, upon the hunched shoulder of the sicariot. "I will come again tomorrow. Do you want me to bring you some food?"

Judah made no reply. Mordra forced his way around the myrtle branches, and slithered down the slope into the foul valley. Placing his hand upon the head of Antiochus, he looked up to where he knew the cave to be. He could not avoid a sense of utter hopelessness. *"Pwy fydd yma 'mhen can mlynedd?"* He asked himself in his own language – 'Who'll be here in a hundred years?' It was an old saying among his people.

Mordra had once looked up from a copy of Homer's Odyssey and pointed out to Branwen that Ithaca, the name of

Odysseus's home island was also the Greek word meaning 'homesickness', and that it was similar to their word *'hiraeth'*, meaning a deep, grieving longing of the heart that their people experienced when they were away from their own land with little or no prospect of return. Even as he had said it he had known that he was making a mistake. His wife's longing for the freedom of Nudd was greater than was his' for Romanized Lutetia.

Now the previously optimistic Branwen was suffering the depths of hiraeth. Lucius had again gone to Aulus with an offer to buy Mordra. He had not reported the full conversation to the Silurian, but he had told her that the tribune was prepared to sell her, but never the man that neither Roman yet knew was her husband. Branwen was faced with a direct choice between her two great loves, Mordra and Siluria. She knew that she could never give up the man who was everything that a man could be, and more to her than anyone who could live in this world. If Aulus would not sell Mordra, then she would remain tied to a Roman whose trade was mindless, unfair butchery. She would never again look upon the clouds kissing the hills across her valley. Never again step into the sacred oak grove by the water meadows. Never again hear the happy laughter of the myriad streams and waterfalls of *Cwm Nudd,* the beautiful valley of the river dedicated to the father god of her people.

Lucius had, wisely, only told Branwen the outcome of his conversation with Aulus, not the details. He had again gone to his friend with an offer to purchase Mordra, and he had again been rebuffed. "I'll tell you what," Aulus had said, "I'll let you have his woman. She's a surly bitch, and I've certainly had better cooks."

Lucius had bitten his tongue. He would never have described Branwen as surly, and he had enjoyed several delicious meals in their company, although he had noted that Mordra did as much of the cooking as Branwen. Outside the army he did not know of male cooks, but he was prepared to believe, rightly, that this was another aspect of the culture that he was desperate to explore.

Aulus had offended him further when he had said: "You take her off my hands and you'll have something to warm your bed, and remove a distraction from Mordra."

Lucius began to see how far apart he and Aulus had grown. He loved his wife Paulina and would not think of being unfaithful to her. Based upon his own love for his wife, he could see what Mordra and Branwen had. How could the insensitive Aulus regard people, even slaves, even women, as no more than commodities? Without realising it, he had taken yet another step away from Rome.

Aulus took a step towards him, and sniffed. "You smell like a whore's breechcloth. Have you been washing with soap?" Lucius said that he had. Aulus shook his head. "You're spending too much time with the Celtae. A Roman shouldn't pick up their habits. You'll be going native next and getting yourself circumcised."

Mordra returned from the Hinmon Valley, and made straight for the lavatorium to wash away the muck that he had walked through and sat among. Returning, he sat heavily upon a bench. Lucius looked at him expectantly. Branwen, still using Greek, although she knew that this irritated Lucius who was eager to improve his British, asked: *"Krasi?"* rather than the British *'gwin'*, both words meant 'wine'.

Mordra replied in the same language: *Ochi, poto."* 'No, spirit.'

Branwen poured three cups of clear spirit and asked: "You met with the sicariot?"

"I did," Mordra replied, "but I can't say that I enjoyed it." He gave them a resume of his meeting with Judah, but was careful, in Lucius's presence, not to give any clues to the location of the sicariot's hideout.

"What's your impression?" Branwen wanted to know.

"That he's a bit more than half mad with guilt and grief," her husband replied.

"I'm not surprised," was Lucius's opinion, "after what we saw on that bare hill."

Mordra knew that he did not need to explain that Judah would not have been anywhere near the crucifixion site. He stood and excused himself. The many years that he had spent in training his memory in endless verses of Druidic wisdom were often of infinite value to him. He could recall every single word of his exchange with Judah the sicariot. He must now get it down on paper while it was still fresh in his mind.

203

Chapter 14

Two of Joshua's zealot followers had succeeded in escaping from Jerusalem and headed out towards the coast, hoping to make it to the Jewish port of Joppa, away from Roman Caesarea. As they descended towards the town of Amwas, noted for its two warm healing wells, a place that the Greeks had renamed 'Emmaus', they discussed their hope for the resurrection of Joshua. "You know," Cleopas said, "when my father died, I thought that I was seeing him everywhere. Whenever I saw a man of similar build and aspect I thought that it was him."

"What did you do?" his companion, Simeon, asked.

"I left the city," Cleopas replied.

"Did that help?"

"Yes. I knew that, logically, my father could never be anywhere else because he had not left Gortyn in his entire life."

They were walking slowly, and a stranger came up behind them, travelling in the same direction. With the curiosity that is normal to Jews, he asked them: "What are you discussing as you walk along?"

They stopped in the middle of the road. Cleopas, his face downcast, asked him: "Are you only a visitor to Jerusalem and do not know the things that have happened there in recent days?"

"What things?" he asked.

"About Joshua of Nazareth," they replied. "He was a prophet, powerful in word and deed before the Lord and all his people. The High Priest and all our rulers handed him over to the Romans to be sentenced to death, and they crucified him, but we had hoped that he was the one who was going to redeem Israel."

"When did this happen?" the stranger wanted to know.

"Three days ago, on the third day of Passover."

Ahead of them the sun was dipping towards the Great Sea as they entered the town of Amwas. The stranger acted as if he was going further, but they urged him: "Stay with us, for it is nearly evening. The day is almost over."

Together they found a taverna. As they sat for their evening meal, the stranger looked at the two zealots and said: "I think that I am the oldest." They were still within the eight days of Passover. The stranger picked up a cake of unleavened bread and said: "Blessed are you, O Lord our God! King of the universe, who created the fruit of the earth." He broke the bread and handed a portion to each of the zealots. Looking from one to the other, the stranger asked them if they believed that Joshua was the Messiah.

"We once believed that he was," Simeon replied, "but then we saw him die."

The stranger shook his head. "Have you not read the words of the prophet Jeremiah?" he said: "'Woe to the shepherds who are destroying and scattering the sheep of my pasture!' declares the Lord. Therefore this is what the Lord, the god of Israel, says to the shepherds who tend my people: 'Because you have scattered my flock and driven them away and have not bestowed care upon them, I will bestow punishment on you for the evil you have done,' declares the Lord. 'I myself will gather the remnant of my flock out of all countries where I have driven them and will bring them back to their pasture, where they will be fruitful and will increase in number. I will place shepherds over them who will tend them, and they will no longer be afraid or terrified, nor will any be missing,' declared the Lord.

'The days are coming,' declares the Lord,
'when I will raise up to David a righteous Branch,
a King who will reign wisely
and do what is just and right in the land,
In his days Judah will be saved
And Israel will live in safety.
This is the name by which he will be called:
The Lord Our Righteousness.

'So then the days are coming,' declares the Lord, 'when people will no longer say, 'As surely as the Lord lives, who brought the Israelites up out of Egypt,' but they will say, 'As surely as the Lord lives, who brought the descendants of Israel up out of the land of the north and out of all countries where he had banished them.' Then they will live in their own land.'"

"Do you understand these words?"

The two zealots looked at each other, then Simeon spoke: "You are a rabbi?"

"I am."

"Then tell me how Jeremiah can speak to us, down six centuries, about the dreadful events of the past few days."

"Think of the words of Isaiah:

'but those who hope in the Lord
will renew their strength.
They will soar on wings like eagles;
they will run and not grow weary,
they will walk and not be faint.'

"The exiles will be gathered in, because a Jew cannot truly live as a Jew outside the Holy Land. You," he looked into Cleopas's eyes, "are a Greek. But a Jew cannot be a Greek any more than he can be a Roman. The Hellenic Jews can do nothing in the Diaspora. It is only in the Holy Land that we can thrive – after we have driven out the heathen. The Lord will return the scattered flock to its own pasture, and the shepherd, the king, will return Israel to its glory"

Simeon, a Galilean, could take no comfort from ancient prophecies. "But Joshua, the man we thought was our king, our shepherd, is dead."

"But Israel lives. And the Messiah is not just a man, he is a movement. The Messiah is Israel." The stranger rose and left them.

The following morning the two zealots rose early, but their companion of the previous evening had gone. As they had invited the rabbi to stay the night with them, they regarded him as their guest. It was the Greek custom not to ask a guest his name, but to wait for him to reveal it, which this man had not done.

They held no discussion, but retraced their steps and returned towards Jerusalem.

Mordra returned to the Hinmon Valley carrying a package

206

of unleavened bread that he had bought from a Jewish baker, a flask of oil, a net of oranges, and a skin of rough village wine. If the sicariot was grateful, he did not express it. The Gaul sat on the low, rocky ledge and got straight down to business. "What happened when you left the temple on that first day?"

Judah was not calm, but he seemed to be numb. In a flat monotone he continued his story. "We returned to Bethany where we lodged at the house of a priest known as Simon the leper."

Mordra raised an inquisitive eyebrow at this epithet, but Judah went on: "Joshua talked long into the night, reviewing zealot policy for the benefit of Simon's household and the neighbours who had come to hear him. It was the familiar, fundamental message: 'Our forefathers carried the tablets of the Law in the Ark of the Covenant. But we must carry the Law in our hearts and minds.'

'When the Children of Israel possessed the land of Canaan, the simple tabernacle at Shiloah was sufficient to house the Ark, and for the great Samuel.'

'We would be right to question whether Solomon built the first temple out of his love of the Lord, or out of his own pride. We know that, as soon as the temple had been dedicated, Solomon built altars and shrines to Canaanite gods for the wives of some of his followers. Solomon, the temple builder, defiled himself, and the Lord showed his anger to that proud king.'

'Each Temple has been defiled – by Nebuchadnezzar, by Antiochus, by Pompeii. And now the priests, the scribes, and the Levites defile it.'

'There are 17,000 men employed by the temple and the Sanhedrin, one-third of the population of Jerusalem is either a priest, a scribe, a Levite, or a judge. What do they do? How can they justify the money that they take from the poor to maintain their comfortable lives? At this moment they are building a new court for the Sanhedrin. How much space do 71 men require? They already have a court. Or are they thinking of employing more people because their own skills in judgement are not enough?'

'The love of the Lord, and obedience to the Law depend upon the pure hearts of individuals. Even the most complex

207

communal rites need no more than ten men coming together in the name of the Lord.'

'Israel does not need a temple, for a temple will always corrupt itself by becoming a place of idolatry. Israel does not need priests who only hold their priesthood because their fathers did before them. Israel does not need Scribes because their scholarship is empty, and only serves to excuse the activities of the priests, not to enlighten the people. Israel does not need Levites because without a temple we do not need temple servants. Israel needs true scholars and teachers, men who preserve and pass on the love of the Lord, and the love of his people through obedience to Holy Law. The priests and the scribes accuse me of breaking the law of the Sabbath, and other laws. I have not come to destroy the Law but to fulfil it. To the end of time not a word, not a point must disappear from the Holy Law of Israel.'

'Why should we use man-made coins that we have to purchase at a loss in order to sacrifice animals? Nature abounds in this land, and the Lord will provide sacrifice as he provided the ram for Abraham to sacrifice in place of his beloved son Isaac. Why should men profit from our sacrifice to the Lord?"'

Mordra could see the holes in this argument. The Jews could not use Roman coinage in the temple, and had to exchange it for coins that did not have a portrait on them. This was in accordance with their second law. The men who exchanged coins had to charge a commission. It was their livelihood. Similarly the sellers of sacrifice had to purchase animals that had to be pure in accordance with Jewish law. Priests examined them for any blemish, and the traders had to make a costing for those that were rejected. Unlike the distant, nomadic Abraham, the inhabitants of Jerusalem could not hope to find a convenient ram caught in a thicket. All the traders had to pay a rent on their stalls. Mordra believed that these men were fully aware of the holiness of their trade. If they were to work for nothing they would soon be joining the ranks of the poor for whom the Nazarites claimed to have such concern.

But Judah went on, quoting Joshua: "'We have had too much contact with the Greeks and with the Romans, and with many others whose ways are not our ways. Some of our people have adopted the ways of the strangers, and have adulterated Judaism with them, especially within the Diaspora. Let others follow their own gods. The Lord commands us to have no other god before him. You cannot graft aspects of an alien culture upon what already belongs to the people. No one sews a patch of unshrunk cloth on an old garment. If he does the new piece will pull away from the old making the tear worse. And no one pours new wine into old wineskins. If he does the wine will burst the skins, and both the wine and the wineskins will be ruined.'

'This ancient land is the land of the Jews. The stranger who dwells here, or who visits, must follow Holy Law as we do, and no other law.'

'Brothers, we must cleanse this Holy Land of the foreign invader. We must re-establish the kingdom of our god in the land of Israel. For this we must devote all that we have, our very beings, to our cause. We must keep to the Law. We need no treasure on earth. Consider the flowers that grow in the fields, they do not work, yet even Solomon was not dressed in finery to rival theirs. We must give all that we have to the poor, and to the fight for the future, not to the priests or to the Emperor. How hard it is for the rich to enter the kingdom of the Lord.'

"At this, Simon our host, who is not a poor man, was dismayed and asked: 'Who then can enter the kingdom of the Lord?' Joshua replied: 'With man this is impossible, but not with the Lord; all things are possible with the Lord.'

"One of the twelve reminded him that we had given up everything to follow him on the Nazarite path. 'I tell you the truth,' Joshua replied, 'no one who has left home or brothers or sisters or mother or father or children or fields for me and the truth will fail to receive a hundred times as much in this present age (homes, brothers, sisters, mothers, children and fields – and with them, persecutions) and in the age to come, eternal life. But many who are first will be last, and the last first. We will throw down those who are in high places over us – Jew and Gentile. We will elevate the people to the government of Israel.'

"The following morning, as we were leaving Bethany, Joshua stopped before a fig tree. It is not yet the season for figs, and he gazed long upon the large leaves and the tiny, young fruits. He then turned to us and said: 'If the fruits of this land do

209

not feed only the people of this land, then may no one else ever eat of those fruits again.'"

Judah leaned back against the wall of the cave. Mordra felt that he had heard enough for one day. He wanted to get back and record what Judah had said. Leaving the sicariot, he again picked his way through the Hinmon Valley, and back to the Antonia.

Branwen pulled herself out of her despair the only way she knew, by using her fertile mind. With a lawyer's training she surveyed the pros and cons of their position. Aulus Plautius was prepared to let her go. She was thankful that she had never shown him the respect to which he believed himself entitled and that she had made no effort to provide him with appetising food and that he did not know of her scholarship – not that he would have believed it of a woman. The only reason why he wanted to keep Mordra was his need for information about the Jews. This was an obvious disadvantage, and it had to be turned into an advantage. Lucius was Roman, and no Roman could be trusted, but he was eager to visit Prydain. She had already begun to spin a web to entrap him, starting to teach him her language and introduce him to her culture. She was prepared to go much further, to reveal Druidic secrets in order to whet his appetite to the point where he would do anything to get Mordra away from Aulus, and back to civilisation.

As Mordra emerged from the lavatorium he was happy to see his wife recovered.

"How was our pet assassin today?" she asked.

"Starting to stink," her husband replied. "He never sets foot outside that cave, for anything, so you can imagine what it's like."

She wrinkled her nose in distaste. "And did he have anything interesting to say?"

"Yes. Much of it we already knew, but he did put some flesh on the bare bones and, of course, he tells it from the zealot point of view. I'll visit him again, I think that he still has a lot to tell us. I just hope that he doesn't go completely mad and kill himself before he outlives his usefulness."

"Do you think that a possibility?"

"Highly likely, the state he's in. Now, what's cheered you up?"

210

"What's the one thing that cheers up a scholar?"

Mordra pretended to ponder the question. "Thinking."

Branwen laughed. "Thinking. And that's what I've been doing. We have all the advantages on our side, except that Aulus Plautius is dependent upon your knowledge of the Jews, and your contacts among them."

"A pretty big disadvantage," he put in.

"But the only one, and we must find a way to turn it into an advantage. We'll find a way; our brains against their Roman brains, they have no chance."

"You say their brains. Which side do you put Marcus Lucius on?"

"His own. That's why I'm working on him so that his interests and ours completely agree."

Mordra was caught up in her enthusiasm. "You make me ever thankful that I married a *Cymreigydd,* a British scholar."

She looked at him coyly. "I hope that wasn't the only reason you married me."

He took her in his arms. "Oh, no. I can think of a few other good reasons."

Describing her as a Cymreigydd caused Branwen to start playing a word game beloved of their people. "When I get him among my *cymrodyr,* comrades, we'll soon turn him into a *Rhufeiniwr Cymroaidd,* a British Roman."

Mordra stepped back and smiled at his wife. "Are you thinking of a *cymrodedd,* a negotiation and compromise?"

"I am," Branwen replied, "but I intend to make sure that we gain much more than we lose. Now, it's late. We should go to bed, and you can consider some of the other reasons why you married me, apart from my mind."

Chapter 15

"We must never let the Greeks take over." Judah's eyes burned in the gloom of the filthy cave. Mordra was convinced that the sicariot had now gone completely mad. Gently, he said: "It is the Romans who are your enemies, not the Greeks."

Judah was contemptuous. "I'm not talking about the Seleucids, they were two hundred years ago. It's the Greek Jews who are the greatest danger; greater even than the Kittim."

Mordra was relieved that he had been mistaken. Judah was still rational. "Who are the Kittim? And why should the Greek Jews present a danger?"

"The Kittim? That is the Essene name for the Romans, and the Romans can be destroyed by the sword and by the strength of the Lord. But the Lord built for us a sure house in *Eretz Israel,* the Land of Israel, whose like has never existed from former times until now. Those who hold fast to it are destined to live for ever and all the glory of Adam shall be ours. This is the land of the Jews, and the Jews are the people of this land – and of no other! The power of the Lord that produces the flowers of the field is the power that drove my youth. The power of the Lord that drives the rivers and the springs is the power that drives my blood. The power of the Lord that brings the drought will turn my blood to wax. For I am of this land, and this land is mine, the gift of the Lord."

Mordra could understand this easily enough; it was the belief of his people that they were at one with their land, and that what affected the land affected men in the same way. This was the basis of many of their religious rituals and he knew that the Jews, like the Gauls, had rituals tied to the seasonal growing cycle and the produce of the land. "So are you saying that a Jew can only be a Jew if he lives here in Judaea or in the Galilee?"

"No," Judah replied. "That is the danger. The Greek Jews

are still Jews just as I am, but they have cut the ties that once bound them to this land, and they have drifted with other currents." He studied Mordra carefully. "Look at me and you do not see a Roman or a Greek, you see my beard, you see the way I dress and the tasselled shawl that I wear. You see a Jew. I look at you and I see a Roman, but I know that you are a Gaul. Did you always look as you do now, when you lived in your own land?"

Mordra was uneasy. "Why is it important to you to know how I dressed in my own land?"

"Just tell me." Judah had taken control of their conversation.

"I wore breeches, a tunic, and a cloak – fine one in summer and a heavy one in winter. Like you, I had a cowl that I could pull over my head." He began to feel the tug of hiraeth. His clothing and appearance since joining Aulus's service had been functional. But he was now being forced to remind himself that there were other reasons why he had changed his appearance. "I wore a golden torc around my neck, and smaller ones on each wrist."

"Your hair and beard?" Judah's voice was soft with sympathy.

"My hair was long, dressed and whitened with lime. At work or in battle we tie it in pigtails. I wore a moustache."

"You were a warrior? Captured in battle?"

"I was not captured in battle. My land had been completely pacified before I was born and was becoming more and more Roman. Unlike you, my people have accepted the Roman presence. But all my people are warriors. At the end of the winter when our food stocks are low we go on cattle raids, and we can be raided. We all learn the skills of the warrior."

"Even your women?" Judah recalled how easily that fierce woman had disarmed him, and the pain that she had inflicted upon him.

"Men and women have the same responsibilities, the same rights, and the same opportunities in our society."

Judah could not understand this. He returned to his theme. "If you were to return to your land, would you dress as a Roman or as a Gaul?"

The question stung Mordra. "I'm a slave and I dress as a Roman slave. I would only dress as a Gaul if I were a free man among free people."

213

"But Rome rules the entire world."

"No." Mordra was ever conscious of his wife's efforts to return to her homeland. "Have you heard of a land called Ynys Prydain, the Island of Britain?" Judah tilted his head back, a negative response. Mordra pressed the question. "Or of the people from beyond the north wind?"

Judah almost smiled. "Oh yes, I've heard the legends of a race of giants and mighty warriors from beyond the north wind."

"It's no legend. Across the narrow sea from Gaul there is an island that we call Ynys Prydain. Its people are not giants, just a little taller than you or the Romans, as I am. But they are mighty warriors. My wife, Branwen, is from that land, and she's taller than you."

Judah was amazed. "She's an Amazon."

Mordra gave a short laugh. "Not an Amazon. She's a woman of a people called the Silures."

The Jew fell silent. There was much that Mordra wanted to know. "Why do you make such an issue of the way we dress? What is the threat from the Greek Jews?"

Judah remained silent. Mordra stood, he was becoming impatient. "Why do you use   Essene name, Kittim, for the Romans? I know that you are, ᴄ were, a Nazarite, have you also been an Essene?"

The sicariot looked up at the tall man looming over him.

"Rise up, O Hero!
Lead off your captives, O Glorious one!
Gather up your spoils, O Author of mighty deeds!
Lay you hand on the neck of your enemies
and your feet on the pile of the slain!
Smite the nations, your adversaries,
and devour the flesh of the sinner with your sword!
Fill your land with glory
and your inheritance with blessing!
Let there be a multitude of cattle in your fields,
and in your palaces silver and gold and precious stones!

O Zion, rejoice greatly!
O Jerusalem, show yourself amidst jubilation!

Rejoice, all you cities of Judah;
keep your gates ever open
that the host of the nations
may be brought in!
Their kings shall serve you
and all your oppressors shall bow down before you;
they shall lick the dust of your feet.
Shout for joy, O daughters of my people!
Deck yourselves with glorious jewels
and rule over the kingdoms of the nations!
Sovereignty shall be to the Lord
and everlasting dominion to Israel!"

Mordra was fascinated. "Do you learn your lore by verses?"
Judah ignored him, and went on:

"The heavens and the earth will listen to his Messiah,
and none therein shall stray from the commandments of the holy
ones.
Seekers of the Lord, strengthen yourselves in his service!
All you hopeful in your heart, will you not find the Lord in this?
For the Lord will consider the Pious Chassidim and will call the
righteous by name.
Over the poor his spirit will hover and will renew the faithful
with his power.
And he will glorify the pious on the throne of the eternal
kingdom.
He who liberates the captives, restores sight to the blind,
straightens the bent.
And for ever I will cleave to the hopeful in his mercy.
And the fruit of the land will not be delayed for anyone.
And the Lord will accomplish glorious things which have never
been before.
For he will heal the wounded, and revive the dead and bring
good news to the poor."

Mordra was silent. He was sure that he was hearing some of
the secret lore of the Essenes, that mysterious sect that had its
dwelling in the desert at Qumran. Judah went on: "Yes, the

215

Hellenic Jews are Jews. But they are far removed from the eternal source that is the land of Israel. They have been tainted by their contact with the stranger's ways. They have compromised Holy Law by following the laws of the lands in which they live. Our struggle is not their struggle. Jew and Greek must be forever apart. If the Greek Jews are allowed to enter our movement they will destroy it, and in so doing they will destroy Israel. I dress as a Hebrew, as a Jew of this land. Look at the Hellenic Jews, they dress as Greeks. A Jew should look like a Jew as a constant reminder to himself, and to all who see him, of his Jewish identity. I know that I am a Jew. Do you know that you are still a Gaul? Do my Hellenic brethren still know their Jewishness? Yes, they pray in the Hebrew tongue, but they now read Holy Scripture in Greek!" He closed his eyes and leaned back against the rough stone. He spoke as if from far away. "Now my sons, be careful with the heritage that is handed over to you, which your fathers have given you. Do not give your heritage to strangers, and your inheritance to knaves so that you become humiliated and foolish in their eyes and they despise you, for, although sojourners among you, they will be your chiefs. So hold to the words of Jacob, your father, and seize the laws of Abraham and the righteousness of Levi and mine. And be holy and pure of all fornication in the community. And hold the truth and walk straight, and not with a double heart, but with a pure heart and a true and good spirit. And you will give me a good name among you, and a rejoicing to Levi, and a joy to Jacob, delight to Isaac, and glory to Abraham, because you will keep and walk in the heritage which your fathers will have left you: truth and righteousness and uprightness and perfection and purity and holiness and priesthood according to all that you have been commanded..." Judah gave a deep sigh, and began to snore. Mordra, knowing that he had heard another snatch of Essene lore, left him, scrambled down the valley side, and picked his way through the foul fumes of the rubbish that lay outside King David's Golden, Holy City.

Bethlehem, a hillside Judaean village to the south of Jerusalem, had been sacred to the Jews for a millennium. The tomb of Rachel, Jacob's wife and the mother of Joseph and

216

Benjamin, was located there. It was there that Ruth had lived with her second husband Boaz, there that their descendant David was born, and there that he had been anointed King of Israel. Two hundred years after the time of David the prophet Micah proclaimed that a new leader would come out of Bethlehem, a descendant of David who would return the Hebrews to their former glory after they had suffered exile and humiliation.

It was to Bethlehem that Cleopas and Simeon, the two men who had returned from Amwas after meeting the nameless rabbi, had gone to avoid the dangers of Jerusalem. Both men knew of Micah's prophecy, Cleopas, from Crete, was an exile and Simeon, a Galilean, knew humiliation. In Bethlehem they had met with others who had hoped that Joshua of Nazareth was the promised Messiah.

Aulus's men were scouring the Galilee, centre of the zealot movement. Bethany, the scene of Joshua's anointing, was being terrorised by the Romans. Jerusalem had become the capital city of death. A mixed bag of survivors had, by instinct, found their way to David's birthplace. They were suspicious of everyone and of each other, but gradually the torn remnants of the zealot network began to re-form as past allies were recognised. Small groups came together and Cleopas and Simeon, knowing some of the men there, had joined such a group. No one asked another man's name, if they identified themselves at all it was by their place of origin.

Ten men huddled round a table in a small, dimly lit room. Three, including Simeon, were Galileans. Cleopas was the only Cretan. The rest were from Cyprus, Egypt, Ephesus, and Cyrene. They had been silent for a very long time, then Cleopas spoke: "I'm obviously not a Judaean, I'm an Idaean, that's one of the names by which Cretan Jews are known, because of Mount Ida. My home island is like a great ship with three masts and the masts are the three great mountains of Pachnes, Ida, and Dikti. It is said that the father of the Greek gods, Zeus, was born in the Dikteon cave. I was born in Gortyn, one of the mighty city-states of ancient Crete. According to the Greek religion, it was in Gortyn that Zeus transformed himself into a bull to bring back the fair princess, Europa, from Phoenicia. There is a plane tree beside a stream in Gortyn where, it is said, Zeus married Europa

217

and she later gave birth to the great king Minos thus becoming the mother of Europe.

"The Carthaginian Hannibal sought refuge in Gortyn after his defeat. A hundred years ago the people of Gortyn helped the Romans to conquer Crete, and it is now the capital of Crete and Cyrene with a population of some 300,000.

"As a Cretan Jew I am doubly favoured. The Cretans are as old as the Jews; King Minos lived at the same time as Abraham. I can talk of Zeus, of Poseidon, of Hera, and Athena, and my neighbours worship them. But I am a Jew and I have only ever followed the eternal god of Israel, something that my neighbours respect as much as I respect their right to follow the Olympian gods.

"I am deeply ashamed that the Gortians of a hundred years ago betrayed Crete. After my father's death I left home and took the difficult journey over the mountains, heading north and west, until I came to a deep bay where the Romans had built a mighty port and a town called Soudin because the bay is shaped like a channel or a pipe, with huge water cisterns in the hills above to feed the town. Across the bay there is an *akrotiri,* a peninsula of fertile land guarded to the east by a long range of hills. I went there, to the far north of the akrotiri, to a village called Stavros because the hill above it is like an upright stake. There were no Romans in Stavros, but neither were there any Jews. I learned of a town to the west of the akrotiri, a place called Xania, where many of the fishermen were Jews whose fathers had settled there countless years ago. I have lived happily enough in Xania but, as a Jew, I had to visit the Temple of Jerusalem." Cleopas gave a humourless laugh. "And I had to pick this year to come here."

One of the Galileans growled a parody of the Passover question: "Why is this year different to any other year of your life?"

"Because this was the Year of King Joshua."

"It was," the Galilean replied, "but he was King of Israel, not of Crete."

The man from Ephesus joined in. "He was king of all the Jews, whether Greeks like me and this man here," he nodded towards Cleopas, "or of Hebrews such as you."

The Galilean was not to be placated. "A Jew can only be a

true Jew in the Holy Land, in Eretz Israel."

Simeon did not know which side to choose in this argument. "My friend here may be a Cretan, and I do not know whether or not a Jew can live as a Jew in the Diaspora. But he is here now, and he was by my side in the attack on Herod's citadel." He looked at his fellow Galilean. "Did you take up arms, did you shed your blood, did you offer your life for the kingdom of the Lord in Israel? This Cretan did."

"Yes," the man replied, "I followed Joshua bar Abbas in the attack on the Antonia."

An Egyptian, a man from Alexandria, was scathing. "I will not tell you what I may have done, or not done. I may have been at the citadel, or the Antonia, or at Siloam, perhaps all three. But I will tell you this: perhaps a thousand men fought in the uprising, and we know that we lost more than half. Less than five hundred survivors, but when the tale is told and retold you will find ten thousand men who will claim to have fought for Jerusalem on that day."

The angry Galilean rose to attack the Egyptian. His friend, the third northerner present, dragged him back to his seat. "We are all Jews, whether Greeks or Hebrews. Do you want to save Israel, or to destroy her?"

There was a brooding silence, and then Simeon spoke again. "A few days ago my friend and I decided to leave this land, to escape to Crete. We were on our way to Joppa when we met a rabbi on the road to Amwas. He reminded us that, at this time of year, we celebrate the fact that the Lord brought us out of Egypt" He turned to the Egyptian and smiled slightly. "Then he said that the day was coming when we would celebrate the return of all Jews from their places of exile, back to Eretz Israel."

A middle-aged man spoke up. "I am Ananias from Cyprus." The company was dismayed that he had revealed his name in these dangerous times. But the Cypriot went on. "Yes, the Temple is in Jerusalem and, like our Cretan friend here, I believe that all Jews need to visit the holy site. That is why my wife and I are here. But I do not believe that a man can live as a Jew only in the land of Israel. Our god is the god of the world, king of the universe. I have a home in Paphos. I have land producing rich crops. My children and grandchildren are in Cyprus. I have many friends, both Jew and Gentile, and I'm an active member of the Greek community as well as of the Jewish community. Yes, the only Temple is here, but in Paphos we have a fine synagogue." He looked around the table as if counting the other nine men present. "And we have no problems in forming a *minyan*, we can easily have ten times ten Cypriot Jews at prayer in Paphos."

The belligerent Galilean would not be satisfied. "And tell me, Cypriot, do you read the Holy Scriptures in Hebrew or in Greek?"

Ananias remained calm. "Of course the *Sefer Torah*, the five books of Moses, is in Hebrew. When the scrolls are taken from the ark and I am called up to read a portion, then it is read in Hebrew. I pray in Hebrew; I read Holy Scripture in Hebrew, and I also read the Alexandrian translation in Greek."

"Ha!" the Galilean replied. "You take the Sefer Torah from the 'ark'. No! It is kept in the *ehal* or the *Aron-ha-Kodesh.* Speak Hebrew, the language of the Lord."

The Ephesian was getting angry. "And is Aramaic the language of the Lord?"

The Galilean ignored him, and went on. "You talk about your fine 'synagogue', another Greek word. Why can't you call it the Bet Knesset as we real Jews do?"

The Ephesian was growing ever more impatient. "The Holy Land of Israel is our source, and we Greeks are ever conscious of that. But we are no less Jews because we live in other lands. We could say that we have to work harder at our Jewishness because we are not daily treading the sacred soil. I will defend our orthodoxy. We also have a very deep concern for the freedom of this land, and a strong desire to rid it of the heathen. Do you not see that we of the Diaspora have a need for a free Eretz Israel? It ensures our identity, our dignity, and our survival. There could easily come a time when we will need this land as a refuge. That is why there are Greeks like this Cretan, and perhaps others here, who will fight for this land."

The Egyptian spoke up again. "In Alexandria we have the largest Jewish community outside this land. Two hundred years ago the Maccabeans wrote to us several times with an appeal for support against the Seleucid Greeks. They did not ask us to rise up in our part of the Greek Empire; they asked for fighters to come here, they asked for diplomatic support, they asked for money because the temple treasury had been robbed and because wars cost money. We gave all that was asked. Now you are taxed very heavily, and the Romans will probably increase your tax burden, and it still costs money to wage war. In Alexandria we have a prosperous Jewish community that is willing to help you."

"Right," said the Galilean, "you give the money, we'll give the blood."

Ananias glanced out of the window and saw that the sun was approaching the horizon. Looking around the table he said: "I think that I am the oldest here." He stood, drew his shawl over his head, and faced north towards Jerusalem. "Blessed be the Eternal for ever!"

The other nine chanted: "Amen! Amen!"

The Cypriot went on, the other nine joining him in the prayer, not in unison, but each man praying alone although conscious that he was part of a minyan of ten Jews. "Blessed from Zion be the Eternal, who dwells in Jerusalem. Hallelujah! Blessed be the eternal God, the God of Israel, who alone performs miracles: And blessed be the name of his glory for ever, and may the whole earth be replete with his glory. Amen! Amen! The glory of the Eternal shall endure for ever; The Eternal rejoices in his works. The name of the Eternal shall be blessed from now and until evermore. For the Eternal will not forsake his people for the sake of his great name, for the eternal promised to make you his people. And when all the people saw it they fell upon their faces and exclaimed: The Eternal, he is God! The Eternal, he is God! And the Eternal shall be king over all the earth; on that day the eternal shall be known as one, and his name One. Be your mercy, O Eternal! Extended towards us, and deliver us from among the heathen, that we may render thanks unto your holy name, and glory in your praise. All the nations whom you have made shall come and prostrate themselves before you, O Lord! And ascribe glory to your name. For great are you, and the performer of miracles, are you, O God! alone: Whilst we are your people and the flock of your pasturage, we will give thanks unto you for ever, from generation to generation recounting your praise. Blessed is the Eternal by day, blessed is the Eternal by night, blessed is the Eternal when we lie down,

221

blessed is the Eternal when we rise. For in your hand are the souls of the living and the dead, you in whose hand is the soul of every living creature, and the spirit of all human flesh. To your hand do I commend my spirit, you redeem me, O Eternal, God of truth! Our God who is in heaven, do you unify your name, and establish your sovereignty in perpetuity, and reign over us for evermore.

"May our eyes behold and our hearts rejoice, and our souls exalt in your salvation in truth, when it is said unto Zion, your God does reign! The Eternal reigns, the Eternal has reigned, the Eternal will reign for evermore. For the sovereignty is yours, and you shall reign for evermore in glory, for we have no sovereign but you. Blessed are you, O Eternal! The King who in his glory shall perpetually reign over us and all his works."

Chapter 16

Marius, the legate commanding the Tenth Fretensis Legion, sat on the roof of the praetorium of Caesarea. Two scrolls lay before him on a low table. The breeze from the Mare Internum stirred his grey hair as he gazed out over the busy forum with its fine column and statues. To the left of the forum lay the beautiful Temple of Neptune with its Corinthian columns and red tiled roof. Beyond lay the great harbour sheltered by a massive breakwater some 420 fathoms in circumference, designed not only to protect vessels from the rough winter seas, but also to prevent the harbour silting up with sand carried by the prevailing southern current. Swarms of workers carried bales of wool, and amphorae of wine, oil, and dried fruit, the produce of the land of the Jews. Along the quay a group of travellers waited while a vessel's master, manifest in hand, checked the cargo being loaded on board his merchantman. Two giant towers flanked the harbour entrance, and then the great sea stretched purple blue, a school of dolphins breaking its surface.

The legate picked up the two scrolls, one in each hand as if weighing them. They were reports, both in Latin, of the recent uprising in Jerusalem, one written by the commander of the Jerusalem cohort, the other by the procurator of Judaea. Marius smiled when he thought how two very different men could write two such very different reports on the same subject. Pontius Pilate, who had not been there until the fighting was over, was ready to take credit for the defeat of the terrorists. He was carping in his repeated criticism of the army for having allowed a thousand armed Jews into the city. The report from the Tribune, Aulus Plautius, was coldly factual. The legate placed Pilate's report back on the table, and re-read the other one. Aulus's sparse wording brought back memories of so many battles. Marius could understand how easily so many zealots secretly entered

Jerusalem, packed to bursting for Passover. The three operations had been conducted in the highest traditions of the Roman army. Yes, there had been perhaps avoidable deaths caused by the collapsing tower, but this was understandable in the conditions under which Aulus had fought and the tribune had accepted full responsibility. The capture of the ringleaders had been efficiently achieved. The pretence of a trial was a complete waste of time. They should have been nailed up immediately, and repeatedly revived so that they could have spent longer on their crosses as an example to the natives. Marius was of the opinion that Aulus had been right to ensure that the criminals were dead before the Sabbath came in. He did not approve of Pilate's agreement to release one of the men so that he could spy on the Essenes. Roman artillery and a couple of cohorts would soon sort out Qumran. Aulus's report pleased Marius because it confirmed his judgement in having the right men in Jerusalem.

He had one legion, ten cohorts, to garrison the whole of this troublesome land. Ideally Jerusalem should be garrisoned with twice the force that he had available, three times that at Passover, but Judaea, with its difficult terrain and impossible population, made him spread his inadequate forces thinly. This report told him, yet again, that he had been right to deprive himself of his first cohort and to trust those 480 legionaries, with auxiliary support, to control that city and the surrounding countryside. Had the potential threat come from outside Jerusalem then the single cohort would have been more than enough, for the city was a mighty fortress. But the threat from the zealots came from within; anyone could be a terrorist, any wandering holy man a sicariot. Not only had his senior tribune proved his worth once more; with satisfaction Marius read of Primus Pilus Galba and Centurion Timocrates. He approved of Aulus's commendation of these men and had added his endorsement in his report to Rome.

For the past four years he had made his second cohort the first for the rest of Judaea, and its senior centurion an unofficial Primus Pilus, and he allowed Aulus complete freedom to manage the so-called Holy City. Aulus Plautius was a man after his own heart, even though they were of very different backgrounds. Marius had joined the army as a simple legionary, and had progressed by natural aptitude to his present position. He knew the science and the art of soldiering from the bottom up. Aulus was not one of the effete upper class tribunes who were obliged to spend a few years behind the standard. He was an instinctive soldier who loved the army. Marius would have liked to keep Aulus under his command, but he knew that the young man had more to offer, and so he must be recommended for a higher post in the service of the Empire. When he sent his full report to Rome, Marius had made such a recommendation.

The legate's pleasant reverie was broken when a decurion came to tell him that the procurator had arrived and was demanding to see him.

"Ave, Legatus." Pilate was his usual bustle.

"Ave, Praefectus." Marius was cool. Once, in a letter to his wife, Marius had confided that on first meeting it had been mutual hate at first sight – and since then the relationship had deteriorated! His wife, sharing the ironic humour of her soldier husband, had replied with a riddle: *"Si cervicibus tenus procuratori sepulti in harenis erunt, quidnam?"* – 'What do you have when you have procurators buried up to their necks in sand?' To which Marius had replied: *"Parum harenarum."* – 'Not enough sand'. The two had exchanged riddles for many years; Marius had started the habit when, short of news, he had written: *"Qui centurio galeam amplissiman gerebat?"* – 'Which centurion wore the biggest helmet?' And his wife had replied: *"Is qui capitis amplissimi."* – 'The one with the biggest head'.

Now the legate looked at the humourless man before him and could not help but pity him for his dour, narrow views, and his unsatisfied, complaining wife.

Pontius Pilate was predictable: "What is the army doing? They managed to defeat the terrorists, belatedly, because they should never have allowed them into Jerusalem in the first place. I want them all dead, even if it means killing every dirty Jew in Judaea. Your fancy tribune has crucified a few, now he seems to have given up. I must have more action."

Marius stayed calm. "Others have tried to destroy the Jews; it can't be done. Aulus Plautius has done enough to keep them quiet. As you say, he's crucified a few, enough to set an example. He sent a force up to the Galilee where they knocked a few heads, and burned the carpenter's shop of the family of Joshua in

Nazareth. Among those crucified was the priest who anointed Joshua. Not even terrorists can regroup without leaders, and their leaders are dead. If Aulus were to go further is could stir up the natives yet again. He has calmed the situation, and I trust him to keep it calm."

"The 'situation' should never have arisen in the first place."

"Perhaps it would not have done if you had allowed me to send reinforcements when Aulus first requested them, as he requested them last year, and the year before that."

"That was his fault for not making the problem as clear as he should have done. According to his first report he was only concerned about a handful of Nazarite tramps behind Joshua of Nazareth – a man who I ordered crucified."

"After the army had killed a majority of the zealots, and captured the ringleaders."

Pilate would not back down. "The army did not capture Joshua, the Jews did and handed him over to me."

"To you? I understand that Aulus had questioned him, and had had him locked up in the praetorium before you arrived in Jerusalem. And had it not been for your arrival, Aulus would have nailed him up there and then so that he could have spent a whole day on the cross rather than the few paltry hours that were left after an unnecessary trial."

The procurator gave a sour smile. "When I sent my report to Rome I demanded that Aulus Plautius be relieved of his command."

Marius was stunned. "Why?"

"Because of his incompetence in allowing the terrorists into the city."

Marius was about to explode, but he took a deep breath and forced himself to remain calm. "Praefectus, may I remind you that your place is there." He gestured to his right, to the magnificent administrative buildings, Pontius Pilate's palace, overlooking the north east corner of the harbour. "My place is here in the praetorium, and Aulus Plautius is under my command."

"And may I remind you, Legatus, that as procurator of Judaea I control everything in the province, including the army."

"Only a soldier can command soldiers. If you knew the first thing about military matters, you would know that there was no way that Aulus could have stopped the zealots forming in Jerusalem at this time of year. Had he had three cohorts, as he requested, instead of one then I doubt that they would have dared to attack." Marius knew that this argument was going nowhere. He decided to end it. "However you will no doubt be pleased to learn that when I sent my report to Rome, and a copy of that of Aulus Plautius, I too recommended that he be relieved of the Jerusalem command."

Pilate could not believe his ears. Marius was beginning to enjoy himself. He went on: "Based upon his record over the past four years, and because of the efficiency with which he put down the uprising, I recommended him for promotion. As there is no higher post in Judaea, except mine, he should soon be leaving the province." Marius sat back and took delight in the procurator's reaction to this news. Pilate was getting his wish, but in a way that could give him no pleasure.

Left alone, Marius began to chuckle. Soon he laughed aloud until the tears ran down his cheeks. He had thought of something that he could say when he next wrote to his wife. The wild boar standard of the Tenth was enough to control the Jews. He did not need a second pig – Pontius Pilate.

Lucius would later wonder if his negotiation with Aulus would have gone differently if they had known of this confrontation going on 65 miles away on the coast.

Branwen had worked out a scheme that she had revealed to Lucius and Mordra. They had discussed it, refined it, and now Lucius presented it to his old friend. "There's no point in arguing about who should own Mordra."

"I'm glad you've come to realise that," the tribune replied, "because I own him."

"Of course you do. But it doesn't really matter who owns him."

"Why not?"

"Because what he does in Jerusalem is of value to both of us. Apart from his orderly duties, which you've already said anyone can do, his value is his knowledge of the Jews, their languages and customs, and his contacts among them. That has military value to you, and it has scholarly value to me."

"So?"

"So there's a way in which he could be more useful to both of us."

"How?"

"First, relieve him of his orderly duties so that he can devote all his time to the Jews. He has a lot of talent and you're just wasting it by having him as a servant."

Aulus took a deep draught of wine. "I see your point. I'll get Galba to find me an auxiliary as an orderly. But you said that was the first way in which he could be more useful. What's the second?"

"The second way is even more important. But first, I think that we agree that as long as you are in Judaea, Mordra should be here to give you the benefit of his special knowledge."

"Absolutely. He's done a lot of work on the Jews over the past four years. I'm not going to lose that. As long as I'm here he's here."

"I intend to return to Samnium before much longer, just to visit Paulina and Marcus, then I ll be back here to continue my study of the Jews, with Mordra's he'., of course."

Aulus nodded. Lucius went on: "In the present situation there's a big disadvantage, and ﹖ barrier to Mordra achieving his full potential."

"What's that?"

"All Jerusalem knows that he's your slave. He recently told me that a Jew addressed him as 'the property of that butcher Aulus Plautius'."

"Ah," said Aulus, "now I see where this is heading."

"Of course you do. As long as he's your slave there's only so far that he can go with the Jews. If he were known to be the property of a harmless scholar he could go farther. You know how the Jews regard scholars. They'll always hate you because of your job, but I may be able to get a little closer to them even though I'm also a Roman. They can't resist scholarship. Mordra and me as a team, independent of the army, could be of infinite value to you."

"So you want me to give the Gaul to you?"

"No. I want you to sell him to me."

"What's the difference? I don't need your money."

Lucius smiled, knowing that he was quoting Branwen. "A

contract of agreement has to have a value put upon it."

"Oh, Lucius, you know that you could always tie me up with your philosophical clap-trap. I just give orders and expect them to be obeyed. Everything that you've said seems to be so sensible, so obvious. There's got to be something wrong with it, but I can't see what at the moment. Give me a few days to think about it."

The philosopher knew when to stop. Too much argument could be worse than too little, and he was eager to report back to Mordra and Branwen.

Aulus decided to let him stew for more than a week, although he had already made up his mind. Lucius, as much as his two new friends, was on tenterhooks. When Branwen had devised the scheme she knew that she was postponing her return to Siluria, but Aulus would never allow Mordra to leave Jerusalem as long as he was tribune of the garrison. Pontius Pilate could be procurator for another six or eight years; Aulus Plautius could remain in Judaea for a very long time, unless the zealots killed him.

After nine days Aulus said, casually, to Lucius: "I think that you should have Mordra, provided that he stays here."

Lucius's mouth opened, and closed again. A slow smile appeared on his face. "Right," he said. "I've drawn up a bill of sale."

"Do we need all that formality?"

"Oh yes, we do, old friend. You might change your mind."

Lucius went off, and returned with legal documents transferring the ownership of Mordra from one to the other. There was a proviso that Mordra should remain in Judaea for as long as Aulus needed him there. When he saw the price, Aulus raised his eyebrows, threw back his head and laughed. "Is that all you value him at?"

"He's worth a lot more than that," Lucius replied, "but there is a poetic nicety in the price that I'm prepared to offer."

"What's that?"

"Apparently the price of a slave in Gaul is a jug of wine." The tribune nodded. "I'm offering you more than that, a whole amphora – Italian."

"I'll take it." Aulus laughed, and, taking up a stylus he signed the two copies with a flourish.

Lucius had not finished. "What about his woman?"

"What about her?"

"I think that you may want to get rid of her as well."

"You can have her, I'll throw her into the bargain."

Lucius presented other scrolls. "I've drawn up a similar agreement for her."

Aulus scanned the second bill of sale. "I must make an amendment to this."

Lucius's face fell. "What amendment?"

Aulus grinned. "She isn't worth Italian wine. You can have her for a skin of that piss the Jews make."

The documents were signed and they shook hands on the deal. Aulus put his arm around his friend's shoulder. "You can't continue to live in the Antonia and those two certainly can't if Mordra's supposed to be distanced from the army."

Lucius had already thought of this. "I've taken a lease on a house."

"You were confident. Where is it – if I'm allowed to know?"

"Here in the city, in the south west corner. You know where your men rounded up those five zealots, three men and two women? Well, that house is now available and I'm – we're – moving in there."

Lucius did not then know, although Mordra was to discover that their new home was the house in which Joshua of Nazareth had sat his last Seder, celebrated his last Passover.

The philosopher returned to the lower rooms of the Antonia. With a huge effort he adopted a solemn face. Mordra and Branwen looked up expectantly, and saw no hope in Lucius's expression. "No luck?" Mordra was resigned.

"Not much." Lucius replied. "I went to him with four bits of paper, and came away with only two."

Mordra's shoulders hunched, but Branwen did not dare hope that she understood what the Roman had said. Lucius unrolled two documents upon the table. They knew them, Branwen had dictated them for Lucius to write. It still took some time before they could take it in. Then there was jubilation as the three scholars hugged each other, whooped and wept for joy. *"Gwin!"*

'Wine', Branwen shouted.

"Oes, gwin!" 'Yes, wine', Lucius replied in the British tongue.

But the Roman had not finished. He allowed his friends, and himself, to enjoy several cups before he stood and called for silence. He drew two more documents from beneath his tunic, saying, solemnly and in British: *"Tegwch I bawb."*, 'Fairness for all'; he was beginning to understand the concept of fair play. He handed the first document to Branwen, the second to Mordra. Husband and wife read, re-read, and read again, not sure that they had read aright. They looked up at Lucius, whose grin threatened to split his face. "Yes," he said. "You are both free. Your slavery is over."

Branwen burst into tears, and threw her arms around Lucius's neck. Mordra hugged them both.

It was some time before Lucius could give his final piece of news. "Tomorrow we all move out of the Antonia. I've leased a house in the city where we will establish our little *Athrofa Prydeinig,* our British Academy.

Chapter 17

Mordra spent a long day with Judah the sicariot. The Gaul sat as close to the cave entrance as he could. He was gagging from the stench of the man and of his increasingly disgusting habitat. Despite the bread, oil, fruit, and wine that he was providing, Judah's physical condition had deteriorated rapidly. His tufts of hair were greasy and matted with old blood from the wounds that he had inflicted on himself when, at the base of the altar, he hacked away at his Chassidic hair. There were sores around his mouth, his teeth were filthy, and his breath stank.

There was still much that Mordra wanted to know – before it was too late. "Where you an Essene before you joined Joshua's Nazarites?"

"Yes. From early childhood until I was past twenty I spent my life in an Essene community."

"Where?"

"Somewhere between Jericho and En Gedi."

"At Khirbet Qumran?"

Judah did not answer.

"Can you tell me about the Essenes?"

"No. According to the Essene rule: 'He shall conceal the teaching of the Law from men of injustice, but shall impart true knowledge and righteous judgement to those who have chosen the Way'.

"The Essenes are a closed community; those who would enter must bring all their knowledge, power, and possessions into the Community. We do not want others to know our secrets. There then follows a long period of learning before a man is fully accepted. After that he may go on further to study the precepts, the knowledge, the wisdom of the Community, and in Holy Law, and scriptural interpretation, as I did."

Mordra nodded. "I can understand that. It may surprise you

to learn that I received a similar education, and we too have our secret lore. Tell me, do you learn by memorising verses?"

"Some is in verse, most is not, but yes, we do read and re-read until we have committed our lore to memory."

Mordra was satisfied with this, and knew that he would get little further information about the secretive sect from this tormented man. "Why did you join Joshua's inner circle, and why did he accept you?"

"He accepted me because he needed twelve men of different talents and experience to form the executive group of the zealot brotherhood, and to form the core of the *Knesset*, the ruling assembly of Israel when the Kittim have been expelled and the Sadducees stripped of their power."

Mordra smiled at the way in which Judah expressed these impossible dreams as if they were about to come true. The sicariot went on: "I was born a Pharisee and my father Ephraim dedicated me to the Essene way when I was a very young child. As a member of the Community I had no personal possessions, I never needed any. The only thing that I have ever owned was my sicar, and your wife took that from me." He said this without rancour; it was a statement of fact. "Some go out from the Community to teach the Word in Israel. I returned to the Galilee and lived the Nazarite way of life. But I saw the misery of my people at the hands of Herod Antipas and his Roman masters. The zealots are not a single group but are drawn from all the Chassidic peoples, be they Pharisees, Essenes, or Nazarites. I joined the Sicarii."

"So, did Joshua accept you into his little band because of your skills as an assassin?" Judah was silent. Mordra pressed him. "I can accept that your scholarship is extensive, but Joshua had a towering intellect. Did he want an Essene or a sicariot?"

"The zealots have many sicarii. Joshua did not take me because of my knife."

"Then why?"

"Perhaps to fulfil a prophecy. He may have needed someone to betray him."

Mordra lost patience. "You call yourself a scholar? You are only trying to justify your treachery. If Joshua had *wanted* to be crucified he could have surrendered to Aulus Plautius at any

233

time. He didn't need to go through all that palaver of betrayal and appearance before the Sanhedrin. And even I know that your prophets are not soothsayers, they are much more than empty fortune-tellers gazing at the stars or rummaging among the entrails of a pigeon, then pretending to have visions of future events; no man can know the future. Joshua was far too clever to knowingly take a viper into his group. Don't try to excuse your actions by blaming your prophets. You did what you did for I know not what reasons; but I will not accept that you were the instrument of some divine purpose. Why did you go to the Sanhedrin?"

Judah gazed at the dirt floor. A lizard gazed back at him. The stillness of the little creature made it look as if it was carved from stone. Judah raised his head, the lizard scuttled off towards the warm, clean sunlight. "I should not have gone to the Sanhedrin; I should not have trusted the Sadducees."

Mordra waited. Eventually Judah continued. "The Essene Community is a long, hard day's walk from Bethany, it usually takes longer than a day. Jerusalem was less than an hour away from where I was. The Sanhedrin was closer. Joshua had allowed himself to be anointed by Simon. You called me stupid, and I am, but I finally realised that he had made himself King of Israel. Joshua had spent time in the Community. He is an accepted Essene, and the rules have provision for returning those who have transgressed, back to the Way. Had I gone to the Community we could have returned Joshua to the path of righteousness and he would still be alive. But I went to the Sadducees, and he's dead."

"The Sanhedrin paid you."

"Yes, I asked for thirty shekels. I thought that I would feed the poor."

"And did you?"

"No. I drank one shekel; the rest went up in smoke."

Mordra did not fully understand this reply, but he went on: "Do you want to tell me about it?"

The sicariot tilted his head back, then: "When I realised that Joshua had made himself king my first instinct was to kill him. He had betrayed me, he had betrayed Israel. My hand was on the sicar beneath my cloak. Oh, the others would have killed me, but it did not matter, there was nothing left to live for. But judgement is not mine it is the Lord's. I went to the Sanhedrin to redeem Joshua. I returned to Bethany and met two of my companions who were on their way to Jerusalem to prepare for the Seder."

"And the Seder?"

"You seem to know much about our way of life. Do you know about Passover?"

"I too sat Seder this year, not for the first time, as a guest."

If Judah was surprised that this Gentile knew so much about Jewish ways, he did not show it. "It is in the rule of the Essenes: 'And when they shall gather for the common table, to drink new wine, when the common table shall be set for eating and the new wine poured for drinking, let no man extend his hand over the firstfruits of bread and wine before the priest; for it is he who shall bless the firstfruits of bread and wine, and shall be the first to extend his hand over the bread. Thereafter, the Messiah of Israel shall extend his hand over the bread, and the congregation of the Community shall utter a blessing, each man in order of his dignity'. This applies to all communal meals, but can you imagine the extra significance at this year's Seder, with Joshua?"

Mordra said that he thought he could.

Judah's narrative speeded up as he recalled the events of that evening.

"You must understand that none of us knew that the uprising was to be the following morning until then, although we knew that it would be soon. He did not want us to take part in the fight, but he knew that we must be ready to defend ourselves. He asked if we had swords, and two were found. He told us that this was not enough. I didn't need a sword; I had a deadlier weapon. He told the rest to arm themselves. As we had no money, he said that those who were unarmed should sell their cloaks to buy a sword. Nothing was said, but we were all aware that Joshua had been involved in secret talks with the various zealot groups. I later learned that I was the only sicariot in Jerusalem not to be involved. He had spoken of the uprising as we left the temple for the last time. He had intimated that the day was upon us, but we did not then know that this year's Passover was to be the time. He was elated, yet despairing. As he drank the first ritual cup he said: 'I will not drink of this fruit of the vine from now on until the day when I drink it anew with you in the Lord's kingdom.' The whole table experienced great excitement when he said that. Nazarites do not drink wine, except at Passover. Now Joshua was telling us that the day of the kingdom of the Lord, the expulsion of the Kittim, the realisation of the Chassidic dream, was upon us. But then he said: 'This very night you will all fall away on account of me, for it is written in the Book of Zechariah:

"'I will strike the shepherd,
and the sheep of the flock will be scattered.'

'But after I have risen, I will go ahead of you into Galilee' We thought that he meant when he had risen from the table.

"Simeon bar Jonas, who never thinks before he speaks, said: 'Even if all fall away on account of you, I never will.'

"'I tell you the truth,' Joshua answered, 'this very night before the cock crows, you will disown me three times.' But Simeon still declared: 'Even if I have to die with you, I will never disown you.' And the rest around the table, except me, said the same."

"Was that when you left the Seder and returned to the Sanhedrin?"

"Yes."

"Why? You had learned that your long-dreamed-of uprising was about to happen."

"Joshua said to me, and to me directly: 'Do not judge, or you too will be judged. For in the same way as you judge others, you will be judged, and with the measure you use, it will be measured to you.' This is Essene argument; but Joshua had not been redeemed. He was still the king of Israel; and Israel can have no earthly king."

Mordra shook his head. As a Gaul from a pacified Roman province he knew all about awful compromises and the loss of national identity. Why couldn't the Jews accept what was happening? Judah went on: "If the Temple guard took Joshua, rather than the Romans, I believed that he had a chance. We used to meet in a place at the base of the Mount of Olives called Gethsemene because there is an ancient oil press there. I was sure that Joshua and the other eleven would not be in Jerusalem

236

or in Bethany, but would be at Gethsemene. I led the temple guard there and pointed Joshua out to them. He saw me, and saw what I had done. He was so pure, so innocent, he took me in his arms and kissed me on both cheeks, and then they arrested him."

"And what did the other eleven do?"

"Simeon, characteristically, drew his sword and attacked the man who was holding Joshua. He took a swipe at his head. The man turned but he lost an ear. Then Joshua told them to put up their swords. Jews, not Romans, were taking him, and Jews should not kill Jews in battles or skirmishes.

"One of the twelve, I don't know who, had sold his cloak and was dressed in no more than his shift. As he ran off a guard grabbed for him and stripped him naked; as such he ran away from the olive grove."

"And what were you doing during all this excitement?"

"Hiding among the trees."

"Olives don't give much cover."

"No. Joshua saw me as he was being taken away." Tears sprang into Judah's eyes as he recalled the look that Joshua had given him, the forgiveness that he had seen in the doomed man's expression. "For the rest of the night I sat on the hill, alone. In the morning I went to the temple and completed the ritual for cleansing my soul, and the ritual for ending my days as a Nazarite. I then got drunk for I don't know how long; it was the first time that I had tasted strong drink. When the owner of the taverna threw me out I came here."

There was one more thing that Mordra wanted to know. "You have told me what Joshua did on his first day in the temple, how he made himself your king. I saw him attack the temple tradesmen on the second day. On the third day he was beyond the Court of the Gentiles and so I could not follow him. What happened on that last day?"

Judah laid his head back against the rocky wall of the cave. Water seeped down and moistened the dried blood on his scarred head. "The Essenes do not recognise the temple as the centre of Judaism. Our love of the Lord and our obedience to Holy Law reside in the hearts of true men, not in vain buildings. Most Nazarites see no purpose in the blood sacrifice of animals. Our gifts to the Lord lie in how we live our lives and how we deal with our fellow men. The temple is a defiled place. Such men as Antiochus, and Pompeii, and others, have defiled it so many times in the past and now it is defiled daily by the corruptly comfortable priests who should be supporting the poor instead of their own easy lives. The temple can never be redeemed. We are ever conscious that the hated Herod, built the present temple.

"We returned to the temple on the third day, again entering by the Golden Gate. At the foot of the curved steps leading from the Court of Women to the Court of the Israelites, a group of priests awaited us. 'Rabbi,' their leader said, 'we would speak with you.' Joshua nodded, then demonstrated his contempt for them by saying, in a low voice and in Latin: *'Vade mecum.'* – come with me. Thus he acquiesced to their request, and at the same time told them who he regarded as the true masters of the Sadducees.

"At each corner of the Court of Women there is a chamber, each with a specific purpose. One holds wood for the altar fires. priests, who reject any wormy timbers, must inspect even the firewood. Another stores oil for the altar fires and for the lamps, especially for the great seven-branched menorah, and for the eternal light. The third booth in the Court of Women is the Chamber of Lepers. It is here that priests examine those suspected of having leprosy. In the second of our holiest books, the Book of the Exodus, there are clear instructions on the manifestations of infectious diseases, the differences between leprosy and less serious conditions, and instructions on the management of such diseases.

"The fourth booth is the Chamber of the Nazarites, and it was there that Joshua led the priests. It must be remembered that although the political wing of the zealots is drawn from the Nazarites, not all Nazarites are zealots. They are an established and respected sect, if for no other reason than that few men could give up everything for their god, and lead such ascetic lives. Because the Nazarites have no homes they are granted a meeting place within the temple. The priests asked him the obvious question. 'By what authority are you here, and who gave you authority to say and do the things you have?' Joshua replied: 'I will ask you one question. Johannen ben Zechariah's works – were they from the Lord or from men? Tell me!' The priests withdrew from him to discuss the question among themselves. When they returned they answered: 'We don't know.' Joshua said: 'Neither will I tell you by what authority I am doing these things.' He then left them to address the crowd. He told a parable: 'A man planted a vineyard. He put a wall around it, dug a pit for the winepress and built a watchtower. He then rented the vineyard to some farmers and went away on a journey. At harvest time he sent a servant to collect from them some of the first fruits of the vineyard. But they seized him, beat him and sent him away empty-handed. Then he sent another servant to them. They struck the man on the head and treated him shamefully. He sent another, and that one they killed. He sent many others. Some they beat, others they killed. He had but one left to send, a son, whom he loved. He sent him last of all, saying: "They will respect my son." But the tenants said to one another: "This is the heir. Come let us kill him, and the inheritance will be ours." So they took him and killed him, and threw him out of the vineyard. What then will the owner of the vineyard do? He will come and kill those tenants and give the vineyard to others'

"He then quoted from the Psalms:

'The stone that the builders rejected
has become the capstone;
the Lord has done this,
and it is marvellous in our eyes.'

"I suppose you think that this parable was an attack upon the Roman interlopers in this land?"

"Is it?"

"No. It is an attack upon the Sadducees. The stone that the builders rejected represents the righteous Chassidim, rejected by the Sadducees. The tenants had not taken the vineyard by force as the Greeks and then the Romans had taken the Land of Israel. The owner had willingly leased it to them. The vineyard is the Land of Israel, planted by the Lord our god. The tenants are the ruling Sadducees, those who control the temple and the Sanhedrin. The servants are the prophets who have come with their periodic warnings and with their reminders that the produce of this land is the property of the Lord and of his chosen people. The son could only be Joshua himself as a prophet and the political leader of the zealots. He was reminding the priests that if they killed him then others would come after him; the zealots would probably destroy the Sadducees and the 'vineyard', would be handed over to the Chassidim. The sons of light would come up from the desert of Judaea and pitch camp in the spiritual wilderness that is the desert of Jerusalem, and wage war upon the sons of darkness

"But Joshua's reference to the produce of this land going only to owner and to the rightful tenants must have given the priests another idea. One of the Scribes came to him and said: 'Rabbi, we know that you are a man of integrity. Men don't sway you, because you pay no attention to who they are; but you teach the ways of the Lord. Is it right to pay taxes to the Emperor or not? Should we pay or shouldn't we?' Joshua knew that they were trying to trap him and he told them so. Nevertheless he told them to bring him a denarius and let him look at it. He had specified a Roman coin, which is not allowed beyond the Gentile barrier, but there were people who had collected coins when he had attacked the money-changers the previous day, and some one produced a denarius. He held the coin in his hand, looked at it, then held it up. 'Whose portrait is this? And whose inscription?'

'Tiberius.' They replied. He then flung the coin from him and said: 'Then give to Tiberius that which is his. But give only to the Lord that which is the Lord's.'"

Mordra had heard this tale before. "And so he sealed his fate by telling your people not to pay Roman taxes."

"Rome has no right to the produce of the Holy Land."

"I tend to agree with you, apart from that which is bought from farmers and vintners at a fair market price. Remember that I too am from an occupied country. But Pontius Pilate certainly doesn't see it that way."

"Pilate is a heathen animal."

"There I certainly agree with you, and I've met him. What did Joshua do next?"

"He spent the rest of the day discussing points of Holy Law with all who came to him. For the last time he was doing the work of a rabbi. Some scribes, who, being Sadducees do not believe in resurrection, asked obscure and outdated questions about remarried widows and who their husbands would be in the life after death. Joshua gave a good Pharisaic answer by telling them that our god is not the god of the dead but of the living.

"Another asked him a question to which everyone knows the answer – which is the most important Law? He quoted the first Law, then referred back to Rabbi Hillel who had taught 'the whole of Torah' to a man sanding on one leg – 'Do not do to any man that which would be offensive if done to you.' His questioner understood. 'To have regard for my fellow Jew is more important than all burnt offerings and sacrifice.' Joshua commended the man and told him that he was close to the Kingdom of the Lord.

"He asked: 'How is it that there are those who say that the Messiah is the son of King David? David himself declares in his Psalms:

'The Lord said to my Lord:
Sit at my right hand
Until I put your enemies
Under your feet.'

'David calls him 'Lord'. How then can he be his son?'"

Mordra sat up at this. "Are you saying that Joshua was not trying to claim descent from David? I thought that was supposed to be one of the requirements for your Messiah."

Judah chose not to answer this question. Instead he went on: "Joshua was sitting at the door of the chamber of Nazarites, watching people put money into the thirteen rams' horns used for collecting for the temple treasury. Many rich people threw in large amounts, some looking round as they did so to make sure that they were being observed. A poor widow came and put in what could only have been a very small amount. Turning to us, Joshua said: 'I tell you the truth, this poor widow has put more into the treasury than all the others. They gave out of their wealth, but she, out of her poverty, put in everything – all that she had to live on.'"

Mordra laughed aloud. "I would say that that is self-evident, if slightly exaggerated. She probably kept something back for herself. I'm sorry, but I have to remind you that, unlike your poor widow, Joshua chose a life of self-inflicted poverty. He was born into a prosperous family and could have returned to his trade and made a good living at any time. I find that there is an arrogance in such men when they identify with those who cannot avoid or escape their poverty."

Judah did not respond to this criticism. He seemed barely aware of Mordra's presence, but continued his narrative. "As he was leaving the temple for the last time, through the Golden Gate and across the causeway, one of the twelve pointed out the pile of stones left by Judah Maccabeus when he dismantled the altar that had been desecrated by Antiochus. For two centuries they have lain there, awaiting a prophet who would decide what to do with them. 'Look, Rabbi,' said the man; I don't remember whom, 'the massive stones of the altar.' He was obviously expecting Joshua to make the prophetic decision, and he was not disappointed. Joshua did not hesitate. 'They must be smashed with hammers until they are little more than dust, then taken out through the Dung Gate and thrown into the Hinmon Valley.'

'Does the Lord demand the stink of the blood of animals? He who keeps the Law brings offering enough. He that takes heed of the commandments offers a peace offering. He who does good to his fellows offers fine flour, and he who helps the poor sacrifices praise to the Lord. To depart from wickedness pleases the Lord; and to forsake unrighteousness is the sin offering. We are poor men, but you will not appear empty-handed before the Lord, for all that you do is done because of Holy Law.'

"He then turned and looked upon the temple. 'Do you see all these great buildings? Not one stone here will be left on another; every one will be thrown down.' He then reminded us of the coming war of the sons of light upon the sons of darkness, and he went on: 'The Lord will deliver us from evil; he will guide us from temptation. The wise man does not hate the Law; but the Sadducee hypocrites are like a ship in a storm. A man of understanding trusts in the Law; and the Law will calm the storm and allow him to rise above the waters. Therefore do not be content just to bind the words of the Lord upon your hand and before your eyes, for the hypocrites do that so men can see them. Bind the Law also to your hearts where only the Lord can see.'

"As we sat beneath the gnarled old trees on the Mount of Olives, his first four followers sat closest to Joshua and, returning to the topic of the rising of the sons of light, asked him: 'Tell us when these things will happen. And what will be the signal that they are about to begin?' Joshua said to them: 'The signal is when he who is called upon to do so proclaims the Hallel from the bloody horns of the altar.'

'So the time is now?'

'The beginning is now. No one knows the day or the hour of the ending, only the Lord. We have a long and stony path to follow, and I may not be with you all the way.'

"We were all afraid at this. Didymos Judah said: 'How can we achieve the Kingdom of the Lord without you to lead us?'

"It was then that I knew real fear." He gave Mordra a penetrating stare. "You've probably realised that I'm a coward. The sicar is a cowardly way of killing. I lacked the courage to kill Joshua when he made himself king. I went to the Sanhedrin, my enemies, rather than to the Essenes because I was afraid that the Essenes would reject me for breaking the trust that Joshua had placed in me. Yes, I was a member of Joshua's inner circle, the last to join, and I joined the political wing. I was the only sicariot not to be a fighting zealot. What Joshua now told us loosened my bowels with terror. He said: 'Have I not prepared you? You, or your sons, or any that come after us will inherit the kingdom; no matter how long it takes. What will you do? I will tell you. Watch out that no one deceives you. Others will come, claiming to act in the Lord's name and deceiving many. But I have taught you the way of truth and the only way to the kingdom. When you hear of wars and rumours of wars, do not be alarmed. Such things will happen, but the end of the Roman Empire is still to come. Nation will rise against nation, kingdom against kingdom. There will be earthquakes in various places, and famines. These are the beginnings of the birth-pains of freedom from Rome and from any that would oppress us at any time in the future to the end of time. You, as long as you live, must be on your guard. You will be handed over to the local councils and flogged by the petty authorities. On account of me you will stand before governors and kings for their judgement.'

'Whenever you are arrested and brought to trial, do not worry beforehand about what to say. Just say whatever comes to mind at the time, for it is not you speaking, but the lessons that I have given to you from the Lord. There will be civil war. Brother will betray brother to death, and a father his child. Children will rebel against their parents and have them put to death. All men will hate you because of me, but he who stands firm to the end will be saved.'

'The next time that the temple is attacked, or desecrated in any way, then let those who are in Judaea flee to the mountains. Let no one on the roof of his house go down or enter the house to take anything out. Let no one in the field go back to get his cloak. How dreadful it will be in those days for pregnant and nursing mothers! If we can decide the time, let it not be in winter, for that will cause greater distress to the people, and the winter is no time to start a campaign. So be on your guard. I have told you everything ahead of time. But in those days, following that distress, remember the words of Isaiah:

> 'The sun will be darkened,
> and the moon will not give its light;
> the stars will fall from the sky'
> and the heavenly bodies will be shaken.'

'Now learn the lesson from the fig tree: as soon as its twigs get tender and its leaves come out, you know that summer is near. Even so, when you see these things happening, you will know that it is near, right at the door. I tell you the truth, this generation will certainly not pass away until all these things have happened. Be on guard! Be alert! You do not know when the time will come. It is like a man going away: he leaves his house and puts his servants in charge, each with his assigned tasks, and tells the one at the door to keep watch. Therefore keep watch because you do not know when the owner of the house will come back – whether in the evening, or at midnight, or when the cock crows, or at dawn. If he comes suddenly, do not let him find you sleeping. What I say to you, I say to everyone: watch!'"

Judah gave a deep and shuddering sigh. "Was it then that I decided to betray Joshua, knowing that the Sadducees would either strangle him or hand him over to the Kittim? I had

244

operated only on the fringes of the zealot movement; I had never risked my life for Eretz Israel. Now Joshua was telling us that we would never know peace, that we would be attacked, persecuted, flogged. He was telling us of endless war and I do not know how to fight.

"From there we went to Bethany, to the house of Simon. Joshua was anointed and I betrayed him. Did I want to redeem him? Or did I only want to return to the joys of the Nazarite life, spending all our time in argument, debate, and discussion; not working because, as Nazarites, we would always be housed and fed? Did I do what I did only out of fear for my own skin?"

Judah fell silent. Mordra had no answers to these questions and his mind was reviewing everything that he had learned from this sad man. Could he tell any more? Probably not. The Gallic historian looked long and hard at the young Jewish zealot. Then he took his leave and scrambled, for the last time, back into the valley of garbage.

His route back was now shorter. He entered the city through the Zion Gate and made his way to his new home. When he entered the house he had to suppress his laughter. Branwen was directing Lucius to put this here and that there, and the patrician Roman was obeying her every command. Now Lucius also knew where Mordra had been to meet with Judah. They looked at him expectantly. "Well," said Mordra, "I think that was my last useful talk with him. If he doesn't decide to kill himself he'll soon die of his own filth. I'll write up what he said today and, when I've done that I'd like both of you to read my notes on him. I think that, as far as we're concerned, he's now served his purpose. There are things that he will never tell us, mainly about the Essenes, and I'm not sure that what he has told me is of much use. You two can decide.

Branwen was solemn. "So you think that he has no more to give us?"

"I think not," her husband replied. "Why?"

"Then I think that we should give him to Aulus. If you have wrung everything useful from him then we can give him to the tribune as an earnest of our good faith. From what you say he's close to death, one way or another. He'll either kill himself if he sees soldiers approach, or be killed as the arrest him. Knowing how the Romans question their prisoners, I can't see him living long enough to be crucified. Give him to the tribune. From what you've said I think that he would welcome martyrdom."

Lucius had to laugh. "May the gods help me when we go to Prydain. If the Cymreig are half as ruthlessly cunning as you, I don't stand a chance."

Branwen knew some turmoil, and a little guilt at this remark. She was using Lucius, and still told herself that she did not really care what might happen to him if she were to get him to Siluria. Yet she was beginning to like the Roman. He had not only purchased them; much more importantly, he had freed them. Perhaps there were some Romans who were not animals.

Mordra intervened. "Yes. We've had all that we can get from this man. I'll go to Aulus Plautius tomorrow to tell him where to find him. I am sure that he would welcome death, whether by his own hand, or that of others, or, most of all, by crucifixion so that he could share that horror with his beloved Joshua."

What Mordra did not know was that Judah had spent his time in writing a long account of the zealots from the time of Mattathias and his five sons to the present day. He had put down a detailed account of the current zealots, with all their names and activities. He had unburdened himself of all his hopes, and disappointments, in Joshua ben Joseph of Nazareth. At the back of the cave there was a pile of writings that Judah knew would be of immense value to future historians.

The following day Mordra returned to the Antonia to speak with Aulus. "I've found the man who betrayed Joshua."

The tribune was all attention. "Where is he?"

"In the Hinmon Valley."

Aulus screwed up his nose. The Gaul went on. "Above the remains of the head of Antiochus there's a myrtle tree. Behind that tree there's a hidden cave. Judah the sicariot is living in that cave."

The soldiers were quickly assembled. They crossed the city from the Antonia, passing the forum and the amphitheatre, and out through the Dung Gate into the Hinmon Valley. They thrust the tree aside, and found nothing but an empty, stinking cave.

246

The decurion glanced inside, and recoiled. He did not blame Mordra, because it was obvious that this shallow cavern had, until very recently, been inhabited. Disgusted by the stench, and frustrated in his search, he ordered his soldiers: "Clean it!" They collected dry foliage, brought oil and burned out the cave and the tree that had guarded its entrance. The futile writings of Judah the sicariot were reduced to ashes.

When Branwen learned of the wasted military expedition to the rubbish dump, she could not help but feel some satisfaction, and relief that the information that they had given to Aulus had not taken Judah to a cross. She put her arms around her husband's neck and kissed him, then stepped back. Ugh! You're bristly."

Mordra smiled at her. "Only my upper lip. It's time that I had a moustache again and I feel that my hair should be a little longer."

Tears stood in Branwen's beautiful brown eyes. "Mordra the Gaul *is* a Gaul!" And then they went, happily, to bed.

Chapter 18

Bethlehem had now become the centre of the zealots' attempts to regroup. There was no taverna in Bethlehem, but a caravanserai on the outskirts of the village had been taken over by the native Hebrews. In addition to lodgings, the caravanserai provided protection. Built of local stone and sun-dried brick, and walled to keep out brigands, it had long been a welcome sight at the end of a day of dusty travel. Such havens were always built around a source of water, and a sweet well was to be found in the courtyard where travellers could feed and water their animals, and fill their water skins. Some of the poorer zealots slept in the courtyard, but in bad weather they took shelter in the arcades that constituted the ground floor and served as stables. A stone staircase led up to an open corridor fronting a series of tiny, bare rooms available to those who could afford them. Shaded during the day by blankets and mats hung up to air, the more affluent could be somewhat removed from the clatter and smells of the busy courtyard below. Those Hebrews who had shelter in the courtyard and stables were better accommodated than the Greeks.

Those of the Greek Jews who remained in Judaea had moved a little to the east of Bethlehem, and were living in sweltering caves. Most from the Diaspora had returned to their various homelands after the terrors of the Passover uprising. The majority of the remaining Greeks were wanderers, with the exception of the Cypriot Ananias who had decided to prolong his stay in the Holy Land. He had found lodgings in a house in nearby Etam and, daily he left his wife there to take the half-hour walk to meet and to pray with the zealots.

Bethlehem was now the one zealot stronghold in the whole of Sadducee dominated Judaea, but Aulus had concentrated his efforts upon those places that were more obviously associated with Joshua and his followers – the Galilee, Bethany, and Jerusalem itself. Mordra, for his own reasons, chose not to inform his one-time master of the historical importance of Bethlehem, a short walk of some six or seven miles from the Holy City. As far as the tribune was concerned it was only a place where a couple of dozen Jewish children had been killed twenty-four years ago.

One of the tragedies of the Jews was that the Hebrews and the Greeks could never agree. They were all of the line of Abraham and of Isaac and of Jacob. Whatever their lingua francas, Aramaic or Greek, they were united by their mastery of the Hebrew tongue. They prayed the same prayers, they all bound the words of their god in leather phylacteries upon their arms and their heads, and they had those same words in mezuzim upon the doorposts of their houses and upon their gates. They all strove to follow the 613 complex rules of Holy Law. They were all Jews, but they were very different Jews. The Hebrews believed themselves to be the only true Jews, living in the Holy Land, and with easier access to the temple. The Greeks saw themselves as the custodians of the Holy Word in alien lands, as representatives of the eternal God, King of the Universe, and as a light to lighten the Gentiles.

Eight men, not enough to form a minyan, cooked a sparse meal over a low fire in a deep cave. Seven were Greeks from various parts of the Empire; the eighth was the Galilean Simeon who had turned back from Amwas with his Cretan friend Cleopas.

Simon, the Cyrenean who had been dragged from the crowd to carry the beam of Nahum's cross, had come up to Jerusalem for Passover. He had taken little previous interest in the activities of the zealots. What he had witnessed on that terrible day had brought him to the zealot cause. At his home in North Africa he too was under Roman rule, but he had never given it much thought. He was a Jew living in a Gentile land, and it was of little concern to him which Gentiles formed the government. He had always paid imperial taxes, perhaps grudgingly because no one likes paying taxes, but without demur.

As he had borne the heavy timber towards the bare hill, Nahum being dragged along by his side, he had wondered what

249

crime could be so heinous that it deserved this cruelty. When he had witnessed the deaths of three men who had struggled for the independence of the Holy Land, and the nature of those deaths, he experienced a deep loathing of the masters of the world. He still had much to learn. Turning to Simeon the Galilean he asked:

"Why do the Hebrews have so little regard for the Jews of the Diaspora?"

"I don't know," Simeon replied, "You are different to us, and there are those who are suspicious of anything that is different. Don't forget that the Diaspora is very old. It is now eight hundred years since Jews first started to establish communities in other lands and any society undergoes many changes in such a length of time, your changes have been different to ours. But there are many differences between the people of this land." He gave a short laugh. "I have heard it said that wherever you have two Jews you will find three points of view. I think that we are jealous of the security that you have found in your own lands. You have no reason to fight for Cyrene, or for Crete, Cyprus, Cilicia, or anywhere that Greek Jews have settled; but this is the Holy Land and we of this land must fight to rid it of the heathen."

"This is my first visit to Judaea." Said the Cyrenean. "I had no idea of your suffering under Rome until less than two months ago, at Passover."

"Is that why you're still here?" The Galilean wanted to know.

"I don't know why I stayed. I just felt that I had to do something."

"I'll tell you why you stayed," Cleopas said, "because as Jews we all need a free and independent Eretz Israel. I was born in a mighty city, six times the size of Jerusalem, where we had three synagogues, and where the Jews were fully accepted in Cretan society. I later moved to a small fishing town where we have enough Jewish families to maintain a small synagogue. I have also lived for a short time in a Cretan town where I was the only Jew. None of my neighbours expected me to follow Zeus, even though the king of their gods was born on Crete. No one remarked the religious differences because in the Greek world all men can follow their own gods. But we now live in a Roman world. The Romans pretend to give religious freedom but they only allow Roman ways, and those ways do not include the Eternal.

"Has it not occurred to any of you that the holocaust could start outside Judaea?" The other seven remained silent. Cleopas went on: "Look at the Alexandrian Jews; they are a prosperous and highly visible group in that great city. We know that Rome wants the wealth of its empire, and that Egypt is a land of untold riches. They could turn the Egyptians against the Jews, destroy them and confiscate their property, and the Egyptians would prefer the Jews to suffer rather than themselves. A madness could start that would spread throughout the Empire, and what could the scattered Jewish communities do to prevent it?"

Simeon thought that he could see the answer. "Your only refuge would be the Holy Land, if it were free and under nothing but Jewish control. Perhaps that's what the rabbi meant when we were in Amwas."

"Perhaps;" Cleopas agreed, "and that is why we scattered Jews need to fight for the zealot cause. But not only as a refuge. A free Eretz Israel would be a force in the world. The Knesset could apply diplomatic pressure. A Jewish army could enforce the Knesset's demands. Eretz Israel would be the shield to all Jews throughout the world."

A Parthian could not accept this proposition. "But the threat of the holocaust is a warning that if we do not follow the way of the Lord then he will destroy us by fire as he destroyed the cities of the plain."

"That is one interpretation," Cleopas agreed, "but there could be others. Yes, the Hebrews are right to envy us our security – for now. But we are all in a vulnerable position; we are minorities, and visible minorities, in our homelands. I cannot imagine my neighbours turning against me because I am a Jew. But the sons of Jacob, who fared so well when their brother Joseph took them into Egypt where he was one of the most powerful men in the land, could not have imagined that their descendants would be reduced to slavery, and ordered to put out their children to die.

"We could easily become scapegoats if some tyrant, especially a Roman Emperor with all the means that such men have at their disposal, chose to blame us for real or imagined ills.

251

The fate of the goat sent into the desert to die for the sins of men would be nothing compared with what could happen to our people. Remember that Amos warned that we could be burned in our thousands and in our tens of thousands. How easy it would be to pick us off in our scattered communities, one by one, a few hundred or a few thousand at a time. By the time the Jews of Crete had learned that the Jews of Cyprus were under attack it would be over, they would be dead. That would be far easier than attempting the destruction of the entire population of this land; others have tried to do that and they have always failed, the Lord has destroyed them."

The brooding silence brought about by these words was broken by the arrival of another Galilean. "You must come to the caravanserai. The twelve are there."

"What twelve?" Some one asked.

"Joshua's twelve."

"There are only eleven, if they're still alive."

The man was jubilant. "No. There are twelve again, Judah's place has been taken by Matthias – a good man." He went off to round up the inhabitants of the other caves.

The courtyard of the caravanserai was packed to bursting. This was the festival of Shavuot, marking the end of the grain harvest, and a time of rest before the grape harvest. People were on their way to Jerusalem, each with two loaves of risen bread made with flour from the new crop.

The walls of the caravanserai offered a little protection from the hot wind that was blowing up from the desert, but the men standing on the balcony had torn away the sheltering mats and blankets, and they stood exposed to the hot blasts. These men were the eleven of Joshua's inner circle, and the man Matthias who had been elected to replace the traitor Judah. Their faces were alive with a burning ecstasy, and a man standing behind Cleopas laughed and said in a loud voice. "They look like they have had too much wine."

The Cretan turned, angrily, and said: "I very much doubt it, it can be no more than the third hour of the morning."

The man in the centre of the twelve raised his arms, his long hair blowing across his face. He looked the very picture of an

252

ancient prophet. "I am Simeon bar Jonas," he announced. He spoke in halting Hebrew for he knew that not all there would understand his Aramaic. As well as Judaean and Galilean Hebrews they were Parthians, Medes and Elamites, residents of Mesopotamia and Cappadocia, Pontus and Asia, Phrygia and Pamphylia, Egypt and the parts of Libya near Cyrene; visitors from Rome (both born Jews and converts to Judaism), Cretans and Arabs. Simeon introduced his companions. "These are ten of the men chosen by Joshua to form the zealot executive council, and soon to be the government of Eretz Israel; and also Matthias who we have elected to replace Judah ben Ephraim." His arm was around the shoulders of this newcomer to their band. One by one he indicated the others. "Here is Johannen, Jacob, and Andreas. That is Philippos, and the scholar at his side is Didymos Judah. Then we have Ben Talmai, and Mattathias who once collected the temple tax. The last three are Jacob ben Alpheus, Simon the Zealot, and Judah ben Jacob. We twelve are set to continue the work of King Joshua and to establish the Kingdom of the Lord in Israel.

"Fellow Jews, let me explain to you; listen carefully to what I say. This is what the prophet Joel spoke:

'In the last days, the Lord says,
I will pour out my spirit on all people.
Your sons and daughters will prophecy,
young men will see visions,
your old men will dream dreams.
Even on my servants, both men and women,
I will pour out my spirit in those days,
and they will prophecy.
I will show wonders in the heavens above
and signs on the earth below,
blood and fire and billows of smoke.
The sun will be turned to darkness
and the moon to blood
before the coming of the great and glorious day of the Lord.
And everyone who calls
on the name of the Lord will be saved.'

"Men of Israel, listen to this: Joshua of Nazareth was a man accredited by the Lord to you by miracles, wonders and signs, which the Lord did among you through him, as you yourselves know. This man was handed over to you by the Lord's purpose and foreknowledge; and you, with the help of wicked men, did put him to death by nailing him to a cross."

At this, a great cry went up from the courtyard; the stronger voices rose above the roar: "We are not Sadducees."

"Rome killed our king."

"We followed Joshua."

And more.

Simeon held up a hand. "You are Israel. I do not accuse you but those who we allow to rule us, who act in your name."

The crowd fell silent. Simeon went on. "But the Lord raised him from the dead, freeing him from the agony of death, because it was impossible for death to keep its hold on him."

There was a low murmur among those who heard these words. Had they heard aright? Men turned to their neighbours and did not dare ask the question. If Joshua had been resurrected, then the Chassidic belief was vindicated and, more significantly, now could be the apocalyptic age, the end of the world they knew – and a new beginning!

Although he spoke in the language common to them all, there were many who had difficulty with Simeon's outlandish Galilean accent. He was aware of this, and spoke slowly, deliberately. "David said about him:

'I saw the Lord always before me.
Because he is at my right hand,
I will not be shaken.
Therefore my heart is glad and my tongue rejoices;
my body also will live in hope,
because you will not abandon me to the grave,
nor will you let your Holy One see decay.
You have made known to me the path of life;
you will fill me with joy in your presence.'

"Brothers, I can tell you confidently that the patriarch David died and was buried, and his tomb is here to this day. But he was a prophet and knew that the Lord had promised him an oath that he would place one of his descendants on his throne. Seeing what was ahead, he spoke of the resurrection of the anointed one, that he was not abandoned to the grave, nor did his body see decay. The Lord has raised this Joshua to life, and we are all witnesses to the fact. Exalted to the right hand of the Lord, he has received from the father the promised Holy Spirit and has poured out what you now see and hear. For David did not ascend to heaven, yet he said:

> 'The Lord said to my Lord:
> "Sit at my right hand
> until I make your enemies
> a footstool for your feet."'

"Therefore let all Israel be assured of this: the Lord has made this Joshua, whom you crucified, both King and Messiah."

There was turmoil, a swelling babble of voices, at these words. There was hope that a risen Joshua would lead them to the final victory over Rome. There was anger that Simeon was again implicating those who had followed the zealot cause, in the death of Joshua. A man cried out to the twelve: "Brothers, what shall we do?"

Jacob answered. "The promise is for you and for your children and for all who are far off – for all whom the Lord our god will call. This is Shavuot, I need not remind you that it is not only a celebration of the grain harvest, it is the day that Moses our teacher returned from Sinai bearing the tablets of Holy Law from the Lord. Today is the first day of a new age!"

Simeon paused, then called out: "Save yourselves from this corrupt generation."

Jacob raised his arms and beckoned to the crowd. "Who is on the Lord's side? Let him come to me!"

Most surged forward. Some held back, uncertain. What would the zealots do to any who would not join? Didymos Judah sensed their fear. "Let any who doubt depart from here; you will go unharmed. I too have doubted Joshua; I have doubted the Lord. Go away and think on what you have heard here today, and the spirit of the Lord will enter your hearts as it entered mine."

Jacob lowered his inviting arms, and looked approvingly at Didymos Judah. "For those who will not join us today, there is always tomorrow. Go in peace."

Those who chose not to stay hurriedly gathered their belongings. Those with camels or donkeys untethered their beasts. There was a minor exodus towards Jerusalem, with offerings of bread for the Temple.

About three hundred remained in the caravanserai. In typical Jewish fashion they split into groups to discuss the points that Simeon had made; men going from one group to another to add their opinions.

Simeon settled himself at the entrance of one of the arcades. Behind him, unconcerned, a donkey ate from a stone manger. Simeon was satisfied. "You know," he said to no one in particular, "Joshua took me from my trade as a fisher; he said that he would make me a fisher of men. I did not understand him at the time, but today I have cast the Lord's net and have brought so many to the Way." He looked around him. "Who would have thought that we would have our new beginning in such a place? I know that Micah promised that a new leadership would arise in Bethlehem and bring Israel to new glory, but how could we have known that it would happen in a place like this? From this day, this simple inn will be a sacred place."

There were those who were as unimpressed by this remark as they were with a very ordinary caravanserai. One of them expressed their feelings. "Do you intend to make this place the new zealot headquarters? Aulus Plautius won't leave it standing for long if you do."

"No." Simeon replied. "There is only one place where we should be – Jerusalem."

"Oh yes," another man was scornful, "if the Roman butcher won't come to us, then we must go to him, perhaps spread our arms before him so that he can drive in the nails."

Jacob entered the discussion. "There is one place that the Romans will not go. We will establish ourselves in the temple, in the Booth of the Nazarites."

The man was not satisfied. "And do you think that the Romans will respect the sanctity of the temple if they see this crowd march in there?"

"We will not march in." Jacob replied. "Joshua the Messiah made his entry through the Golden Gate in accordance with requirements. We will enter singly, in twos and threes, small groups."

"And what about the priests and the temple guard?"

"What about them? The Sadducees would be the last people to bring the legionaries into the temple. Neither will they inform the Romans, because a siege of the temple would halt its holy function."

Men nodded at this, one added: "And prevent people giving their money."

Another asked: "Do we become Nazarites, must we give up all our possessions?"

"You need no treasure on earth." Simeon told him. But Andreas, knowing that Greek Jews could not take easily to the Nazarite way, said: "Those who wish may join us as Nazarites, but this is the dawn of a new age. Men must live as they see fit, provided that they live in accordance with Holy Law, and as followers of the Messiah."

Ananias had been carried away with what he had heard. "I have land in Cyprus; I will sell it and bring the money that I raise to Jerusalem to further this holy cause."

Simeon rose, tears in his eyes, and embraced the Cypriot. "You are a true brother."

Jacob ben Alpheus as planning ahead. "We will meet in the Court of Women, at the Nazarite Booth, but we will also establish ourselves, secretly, within the city; there are obscure little houses, some where we have supporters, there are cellars and dry cisterns, Bets Knesset. We will go to the Galilee, but not to Nazareth, we have little or no support there; and do the same there, mingling with the people. For this we need men who are plainly not Nazarites, who can pass unnoticed."

There were those who were inspired by Ananias's generous gesture, they did not want to be outdone. "As we are to share in the Kingdom of the Lord, so we must share all that we have." Simeon warmly approved of this.

Some one wanted to know how David could have foreseen the coming of Joshua as the Messiah. "King David was a

257

thousand years ago."

"But the Lord is eternal," Ben Talmai told him, "and Joshua was anointed as David was anointed. The Lord works through his anointed ones."

"From today," Jacob added, "the Lord works through all men who accept his Way. From today all of you are the Lord's anointed."

In the early afternoon, as the sun passed its zenith, they broke off their discussions to recite together the hundred and forty fifth Psalm of King David. Then, facing north to Jerusalem: "O Lord! Open my lips and my mouth shall declare your praise." And they recited the eighteen blessings, followed by the required prayers for the afternoon.

They then resumed their endless talk until it was time for their evening prayers; then again as the first stars of the new day were joined by the pale moon and the endless points of light in the eternal night sky.

Chapter 19

As these momentous events were unfolding just a few miles to the south, three scholars were in deep discussion in the upper room of a house close to the palace of Caiaphas in Jerusalem.

The three had quickly settled into their new home. Lucius had insisted they hire servants, and a Jewish man and wife came daily to cook, clean and attend to the comforts of what Lucius continued, light heartedly, to insist was the *'Athrofa Prydeinig gan Caersalem'*, the British Academy of Jerusalem. He was working on his British language lessons and only making a few mistakes. Lucius was of the opinion, justifiably, that they only needed a woman coming in daily, but Branwen had insisted that they needed a couple, sharing the tasks, and she would supervise to ensure that the man did as much work as the woman. The Silurian girl had organised the accommodation into comfortable living quarters and the large upper room as their library and *efrydiaeth*, their study – she was reluctant to use the Latin *studium*, study, or perhaps more properly, and closer to the British, *meditatio*, room for thought, for this room of academic endeavour. Latin had been the language spoken by the men who had raped her, the brute who had claimed her and taken her to Massilia and whose head had, long ago, fed the fishes. Occasionally she threw in the odd Latin word or phrase when speaking to Lucius. She did this out of the irony that came so naturally to her people, but recently she was doing it less and less. They spoke mostly Greek, but increasingly in *Prydeinig*, in British.

They sat at a large table, big enough to accommodate a dozen or more people for a meal. Piles of scrolls lay before them. It had taken ages for Lucius's baggage to arrive from Caesarea, but now he had all the documents that he had brought from Samnium in preparation for his study of the Jews. Unrolled before them was the second of the five books attributed to Moses. It was a copy of the Greek translation that had been made in Alexandria. Lucius consulted his notes on this book. "I've broken it down into sections, there's a lot of sections. There seems to be a jump of about four hundred years from the previous book, which, I must say, is often a bit fantastic, to this book which is far more rational."

Mordra had read these words in both Greek and the original Hebrew. Branwen had dipped into them, and she had been particularly interested in this second book. Lucius went on. "The first section tells how the Jews were oppressed in Egypt."

Mordra interrupted. "They weren't Jews then, they were Israelites, then Hebrews; they did not become the Jews until about six hundred years ago."

Lucius smiled, he was enjoying himself. "May the gods preserve me from pedants. All right, the ancestors of the Jews if you like. Next we have the birth of Moses, then his chequered career, first in the court of the Pharaoh, then in Midian, and his contact with their god. Then we have his return to Egypt and his leadership of the – Israelites; the ten plagues up on the Egyptians; the first Passover and the departure from Egypt. We then have an account of various tribulations that they suffered until they came to Sinai three months after their escape from Egypt, a very eventful three months if this is to be believed. This is where it starts to get really interesting. From this point on, for most of the book we have their laws. I must admit to some problems here because about half of these laws refer to the temple, but that had not yet been built, they hadn't even arrived here."

Branwen had an immediate answer. "I see your point, but I can't accept that all the laws that the Jews now have date from the time of Moses. Some of the temple laws may have existed in embryonic form because they had a portable sanctuary that they called the Tent of Meeting. But I am sure that these laws were amended and augmented after Solomon built the first temple here in Jerusalem."

"Of course," Lucius agreed, "Perhaps they had a little more than the first ten rules when they were wandering in the desert. Most of the rest are about ritual and the conduct of a settled

260

people rather than a rabble taking what must have been a very circuitous route from Egypt to the Jordan. Look at how I've categorised them – idols and altars, Hebrew servants, personal injuries, protection of property, social responsibility, laws of justice and mercy, laws about their Sabbath. Then they go on to something rather esoteric about angels preparing the way, and about the confirmation of the covenant between their god and that shadowy figure Abraham.

"Next comes something very specific: sacrifice; the box in which they carried the law; a fine table with golden dishes; a lampstand with seven branches."

Mordra butted in again. "I've never seen it because it's in the forbidden part of the temple, but I'm told that the lampstand, the menorah is huge, and that it's patterned on the seven branched *salvia judaica*, the sage, another example of their affinity with the land and it's produce. When Judah Maccabeus cleansed the temple he could only find enough consecrated oil to rekindle the lamp for a day, but he lit it and, miraculously, it burned for eight days – so they say. Now, in all Jewish homes you will find an eight branched lamp patterned on the *salvia palaestina* sage; they light this at the Feast of Dedication, which also commemorates the Maccabees."

"It must be of immense importance to them," Lucius went on, "because this book makes much of the oil for the lamp, and the tabernacle, the altar, priestly garments in great detail, and other matters of ritual. Then the whole lot is repeated.

"Now, what I find interesting about the Jews is that they call their law Holy Law and believe that the will of their god is the authority. It is incumbent on them to obey the divine commandments. However, they also seem to believe that they have free will to obey or disobey their law. From time to time prophets come along to put them back on the right path. But if their god is all powerful, as they believe, how does he allow those who regard themselves as his chosen people to disobey him?"

Branwen took a sip of wine. Lucius looked at her. "Do you actually enjoy that stuff?"

"I've tasted worse." Branwen said. "Gallic wine is too thin, Italian wine is little better. This is made from fatter grapes than you can grow further north. But no grape wine is good, wine should be made from blackberries."

"You've mentioned these black berries before, what are they?"

"When we get to Siluria I'll show you. Does it matter where a law comes from? Why do people obey laws? The purpose of law is survival. Civilised societies devise laws by common consent so that people can live together in harmony. Anyone who transgresses those laws will, by the consent of society, suffer appropriate sanctions. This holds the civilised society together, and people's behaviour, like the laws governing that behaviour, results from rational thought. If a people, such as the Jews, believe their laws to come from a god, it makes little difference because the judges are men, and men carry out any sanctions against transgressors. I think the only important difference comes in amendments to the law. If you believe your laws come from your gods then it is difficult to change them. Times change, circumstances change, social needs change, and if your laws are known to be man-made then such laws can be amended more easily.

"There are three perceived sources of law: a god-given law such as that of the Jews, a law imposed by a tyrant, in the steps of Draco, and a law that comes from common consent. A divine law is difficult to amend, although Mordra tells me that the Jews are examining, updating, and amending their 'holy law' right now. A Draconian law cannot be changed during the life of the tyrant, or the tyrannical regime. Laws made by men are made by councils, by assemblies, which may be powerful, but they are also accountable and can be replaced. I think that there is more chance of fair play under laws known to be made by men."

"Or women?"

Branwen laughed. "Don't try too hard, Lucius. I know that it's difficult for you, you're only an ignorant Roman. At home we had dogs, some were male – dogs, others were female – bitches, but we refer to them all as dogs because they are of the specie dog. I am a human being of the specie man, I'm of the female gender but I'm the same specie as you."

"I still have a lot to learn, haven't I?"

"You have, but you're working very well."

"Thank you very much, teacher, or should I say *diolch yn*

fawr, athro?"

Branwen clapped her hands. "Very good! You're my star pupil."

Lucius beamed, then it occurred to him. "I'm your only pupil."

Branwen just smiled. Lucius was serious again. "In Prydain, are your laws man-made, or are they attributed to your gods?"

"If our gods had made our laws there would be complete confusion, we have so many gods. They are more harmonious than the lesser number of Greek or Roman gods that are always falling out, but our gods serve us in different ways to any of the deities I have met around the Mare Internum."

"I think I'll wait until I get there before you explain your gods to me, I'll understand them better when I see their own land. I still can't understand the Jewish god, but I think that I've got a little closer here than I did in Samnium."

Branwen was impressed with this. "I shouldn't have called you an ignorant Roman, I hope you know I was only joking. That was a profound observation. All gods belong to the land that gave them birth. They are the gods of that land and of the fertile cycle of growth in that land among the people of the land. You cannot export gods."

Lucius was surprised at his delight in receiving Branwen's approval. He had come to respect her intellect, to regard her as an academic equal. He regarded himself to be fortunate in his unswerving fidelity to Paulina, in his friendship with Mordra, and his respect for the love between his new friends. Branwen was a lovely woman, she was also a stimulating scholarly companion. He felt no sexual desire for her, but he wanted her friendship – which he did not think he had yet fully attained. It was only two months since he had arrived in what was then the tumult of Jerusalem. How far had he travelled in this square mile of a city, in that time? Here he was, in discussion that would have pleased his Rhodian tutors – and, for the first time in his life, with a woman, or was it with a man of the female gender? "From what you've told me, it seems that your sanctions against lawbreakers are not extreme, yet Julius made much of the cruelty of the Gauls, about human sacrifice and burning masses of people in wicker baskets."

"We've discussed this before," Mordra said, "but I seem to remember that you were a little drunk at the time. Don't forget that we are an ancient people and our ancestors may have been much more savage in the distant past. We're about as old as the Jews and our culture had its origins long before Romulus and Remus were suckled by a wolf on the Capitoline Hill. The wicker man that Julius described is something that I'd never heard of until I read his biased account of the conquest of my people. His description of the Druids is something that you can judge for yourself when you meet the Druids in Siluria, but don't forget that if Branwen and I had been allowed to remain in our own lands then we would both be Druids by now. Can you see either of us doing the things that Julius spoke of?"

Branwen came back. "Why do people break the law, whatever they think is the origin of that law?"

Lucius frowned. "Out of self interest, I suppose."

"That's a good a way to put it as any, but I don't think it's quite that simple. Self interest, yes, but perhaps also an inability to live properly in human society, greed, and the belief that the transgressor can get away with it. An imposed law, be it from a god or an autocratic ruler, is often seen to be against the interest of many individuals. A law arrived at by consent, because it is seen to be for the good of society, is more likely to be obeyed because it is seen to be in the interest of the majority. Transgressors are, by definition, antisocial people who need to have sanctions applied."

Lucius shook his head. "You speak of sanctions, not punishment."

"Because punishment is useless. The offence has already been committed and punishment will not turn back time and prevent that offence. Punishment is only revenge. Sanctions are designed to prevent re-offending."

"But you told me that you behead criminals."

"A judge, or in the absence of a judge, a lawyer, can order execution." Her eyes were troubled. She would never be able to forget the powerful swing of a legionary's sword, the sickening jar that went up her arm as the neck was severed. Bone, sinew, muscle, veins sliced through, the blood jetting from the stump of the neck and drenching her. The ugly head, with eyes staring, rolling away from the still quivering body. "There are those whose offences are so deep that they cannot be allowed to live in this world or the Otherworld. Their heads are given to the gods of the waters, to be food for the fishes; in this way they cannot pass into the Otherworld and are forever destroyed. There are others who are decapitated but are united with their heads in death, separated from their bodies by a slab of stone. They will pass into the Otherworld and when they are reborn in this world we trust that they will not re-offend. For lesser offences people can be exiled, or indentured as servants, or denied access to religious ritual and so be separated from the gods."

"And do these sanctions work?"

"Yes. But our society is very different to yours."

"In what way?"

Mordra came into the discussion. " The aim of our people is survival in harmony with the land in which we live. Yes we are a warlike people, but there are reasons for this. The first need of all people is survival. At the end of winter we raid other tribes to take their cattle, and they raid us. Another thing about us may be more difficult for you to understand. Julius described the Gauls as a people who fought like madmen with no fear of death. This is true; we do not fear death because we do not fear the finality of death, it is simply a journey from this world to the Otherworld, which is a better place. The army of Rome is a formidable force. I have seen them fight. But they do not fight with any joy, as we do; they are efficient because of their training, their discipline and their comradeship. And they do not wage war in order to survive but to impose the Roman way on other people."

"You're right!" Enlightenment suddenly came to Lucius. "I can begin to see why our laws, and the application of those laws, differ from yours. The Roman way is about power. The power of a privileged social class, to which I belong, over the mass of the plebeians, the power of Rome over conquered peoples. The patricians are a tiny minority, but we hold an immense power over vast numbers of people. If you look at the entire Roman army, legionaries, auxiliaries, marines, praetorians, there are probably about a quarter of a million men. But they impose Roman peace over almost the entire world."

"And how do they do it, Lucius?" Branwens voice was low, gentle.

The Roman took a deep draught of wine. "By fear, by cruelty. It is not long since we saw three men die by crucifixion. Yet people are still being crucified. If that punishment was designed to prevent men offending against Roman law then it has plainly failed. You are right Branwen, it is nothing but revenge."

Mordra refilled the three cups. "Perhaps you judge your people a little too harshly. The rulers of Rome control people, both in Italy and throughout the Empire, by other means. They give people pleasures, such as the circuses. Roman citizens are not directly taxed, and citizenship is a source of pride. But it is an illusion that makes them believe that they are part of the glory that is Rome. That illusion makes them continue to function, to work, quietly and obediently. The only glory is enjoyed by the few and is the product of the sweat and toil of many. There is not one Rome but two, the rich and the poor. The Roman way, and Roman certainty, can also lead your people into an error of judgement. Your view of yourselves colours your view of other peoples; you judge all by Roman standards, Roman ideas."

Across the city, in the Antonia, Aulus was entertaining his commanding officer Marius. The legate had arrived unannounced from Caeserea and demanded an immediate tour of inspection. They went first to the praetorium in Herod's citadel where Marius first awarded circes to Galba and Timocrates in recognition of the part that they had played in the Passover uprising. He then carried out a detailed inspection of the barracks. As a one-time legionary he knew exactly where to look and what to look for; he was satisfied with the condition of the praetorium, the weapons, and the battle-readiness of the men. He spoke easily to many of the soldiers. His Latin was as rough as theirs, his language as coarse, and his humour as basic and ironic. At the end of the tour there was not a man who would not have followed him beyond the gates of Hades.

He then went around the city, looking, with a practised eye, at the standing preparations for any trouble that may arise, approving of the permanent guard on the vulnerable pool of Siloam. He complimented Aulus on all that he had done and was continuing to do. Back in the Antonia he relaxed and shared the first flagon of wine with the tribune. "You've done a good job, Aulus, I'll be sorry to lose you." The tribune sat up. Marius laughed. "Don't get too exited, you're not going anywhere yet, I need you here for a while to make sure that any further problems are properly dealt with. But you'll be out of Judaea before the end of the year, quite a bit before if our masters in Rome have their way."

"Can you tell me where I'm going?"

"I can, and I'm not sure you'll like it, it's another trouble spot."

"I like trouble spots, it's what I'm paid to do."

"I know, Aulus, I know. When you were first sent here I was warned about you, that in Gaul you'd gone out of your way to find trouble, going into Germania to kill off as many savages as you could find. You're going to Pannonia, the place has never been properly pacified."

Aulus was delighted. Marius frowned. "My problem is your replacement. In all the other nine cohorts I only have a couple of half-decent tribunes, the rest are upper class idiots, all breeding and no brains, who are just filling in their time until they can take their father's seats in the senate. I can't trust Rome to send me a proper soldier as a replacement, and anyway I'd rather promote from within, someone who knows the place and knows what he's doing."

Aulus did not hesitate. "Galba only has a couple of years to serve, but he would be the ideal man. He's a superb soldier, the men respect him and would follow him anywhere."

"Leaving the first cohort without a Primus Pilus?"

"Timocrates. He's a few years younger than Galba, the perfect man. Those two already work together like a well oiled machine."

Marius smiled. "You have just confirmed my decision. I'd already decided that Galba is to be promoted to command the cohort and that Timocrates is to take his place. Now, a bit more about your orders." He took a drink. "Good stuff this. Do you give Pilate Italian wine on his infrequent visits here?"

"No." Aulus replied. "The local brew is good enough for him."

Marius nodded. "You're to take command of the Ninth Hispana Legion in Pannonia."

Aulus's jaw dropped. His commander was enjoying this. He stood and raised his arm in salutation. "It's a bit premature but, Ave Legatus." Aulus still could not speak. Marius had not finished. "There's just one thing. The Empire's had nothing out of Pannonia yet in all the years we've been there, not a single denarius. At the moment, and for the foreseeable future, it's a job for the army. It's certainly no place for civilian clerks. They'd have even less to do there than whatever it is they do in the rest of the Empire. There's no procurator and no sign of appointing one. The commander of the Ninth will, in effect, be the governor of the province."

Chapter 20

A forty-year-old man had made a career as a professional beggar at one of the gates of the temple. Daily he had been brought there and had spent the day from early morning to late afternoon with his legs bent painfully beneath him. He made a reasonable living, but for years he had watched the Nazarites with envy and resentment. They, too, were beggars, but holy beggars, and their lives were so much better than his. Although they had nothing they needed nothing. They were well fed, people housed them, they even had their own meeting place within the temple.

Now two Nazarite were approaching the seven steps leading to the outer gate, the gate where the poor beggar had his daily pitch. He knew that these men carried no money, but he called upon everyone who passed him. The two stopped and looked down at him; the taller of the two, a powerful man, said. "Look at us!"

The beggar gave them his attention, thinking they were going to give something to him. The big man said. "Silver or gold I do not have, but what I have I give to you. In the name of Joshua the Messiah, walk." He reached down with his right hand; the beggar was mesmerised, he took the man's hand and allowed himself to be pulled, slowly, agonisingly, to his feet. He massaged the circulation back into his legs, he bent his knees, his hips, his ankles, loosening the stiffened joints. He began to walk. He followed the two men into the outer court, walking, trying to jump, and praising the Lord. He was convinced he was being invited into the Nazarite fold.

While the beggar held for support to Simeon and Jacob, who were fulfilling their pledge to return to Jerusalem, he was making so much noise that people turned to stare. The two Nazarites leaned him against the pillar of the colonnade, and Simeon addressed those whose curiosity had brought them close.

"Men of Israel, why does this surprise you? Why do you stare at us as if by our own power and godliness we had made this man walk? The god of Abraham, Isaac and Jacob, the god of our fathers, has glorified his servant Joshua. You handed him over to be killed, and you disowned him before Pilate. You disowned the holy and righteous one, before the cock had crowed you denied him three times." Simeon paused, then went on. "You killed the author of life, but the Lord raised him from the dead. We are witnesses of this. By faith in the name of Joshua, this man whom you see and know was made strong. It is in Joshua's name and the faith that comes through him that has given this complete healing to him, as you can all see.

"Now, brothers, I know that you acted in ignorance, as did your leaders. But this is how the Lord fulfilled what he had foretold through all the prophets, saying that his anointed one would suffer. Repent, then, and turn to the Lord, so that your sins may be wiped out, that times of refreshing may come from the Lord, and that he may send the Messiah, who has been appointed to you – Joshua. He must remain in heaven until the time comes for the Lord to restore everything, as he promised long ago through the prophets. For Moses said, 'The Lord your God will raise up for you prophets like me from among our people; you must listen to everything they tell you. Anyone who does not listen will be completely cut off from the people.'

"Indeed, all the prophets from Samuel on, as many as have spoken, have foretold these days. And you are heirs of the prophets and of the covenant the Lord made to your fathers. He said to Abraham, 'Through your offspring all peoples on earth will be blessed.'"

A detachment of the Temple guard pushed through the crowd and grasped the two men, who did not resist. As it was evening they decided to imprison them overnight and deal with them in the morning. Simeon and Jacob were marched to the far end of the Court of the Gentiles, to where the new meeting hall of the Sanhedrin was almost completed. To the west of the new building lay the pinnacle of the Temple with a flat roof, designed by Herod as a watchtower and a defensive position. The two Galileans were thrown into a small room in this structure.

The following day the Sanhedrin began to assemble on the

horseshoe of benches. First to arrive were Annas, father-in-law of the High Priest, with Jacob and Alexandros, two members of his family. Other members drifted in until about two dozen of the 71 members were settled in their places, more than enough for a quorum. Another two dozen or so occupied the public benches at the back of the hall, a few because they regularly watched the proceeding, most because they had witnessed the arrest of Simeon and Jacob and wanted to see some fun; one because he had given up his miserable life as a beggar at the gate of the temple and now wanted nothing more than to be accepted among these men. Caiaphas made his entrance and sat upon the raised chair at the crown of the horseshoe. The prisoners were brought in.

The commander of the guard told of what had happened in the outer court on the previous evening. Caiaphas wanted to know if anyone else had witnessed the occurrence. Three men stood and were asked to give their accounts, which were fairly similar. Caiaphas then asked the two Galileans by what power and in whose name they had done this. Jacob stepped forward. "Rulers and elders of the people! If we are being called to account today for an act of kindness shown to a cripple and asked how he was healed, then know this, you and all the people of Israel: It is by the name of Joshua, the Anointed One, of Nazareth, whom you crucified but whom the Lord raised from the dead, that this man stands before you healed. He is 'the stone you builders rejected, which has become the capstone.'

"Salvation is found in no-one else, for in this age there is no other name under heaven given to men by which we must be saved."

Caiaphas stood and strode from the hall; the rest of the judges followed him. Alexandros was dismissive, "They are only unschooled, ordinary men. What real harm can they do?"

"They may be unschooled," Jacob told him, "but they have been identified as two of the twelve who followed Joshua."

"Then give them to Aulus Plautius," was Alexandros's response.

"No!" Annas was emphatic. "We have had enough crucifixions. The Sanhedrin must deal with these men, and do it quickly and quietly."

271

"I agree," Caiaphas nodded, "and don't forget the beggar they claim to have healed, he's here for all to see and there are many who will believe that to be an outstanding miracle."

"He was no more crippled than I am. He's a professional beggar who must have uncoiled his legs every night when he got home."

"You can't know that, Alexandros," said Annas, "and even if it's true, it is not what people want to believe. And, who knows, it could be a genuine healing miracle."

"Then what are we going to do about these Nazarites?" Another judge wanted to know.

Caiaphas thought for a moment. "We must warn these men to speak no longer in the name of the dead rabbi. We can easily discount their wild claims of resurrection, but there are many, too many, who would like to believe it. We must stop this thing from spreading." The judges marched back into the hall and took their seats. Caiaphas fixed the prisoners with a stern look. "The Sanhedrin commands you not to teach or speak at all in the name of Joshua of Nazareth."

Simeon replied. "Judge for yourselves whether it is right in the sight of the Lord to obey you rather than the Eternal God of Israel. For we cannot help speaking about what we have seen and heard."

Caiaphas was cool. "I am the High Priest of Israel, I tell you what is right, and wrong, in the sight of the Lord and in accordance with his Holy Law. If you disobey the Sanhedrin's command you will be flogged. If you continue on your present path you will sooner or later, commit blasphemy for you have neither the education nor the native intelligence that Joshua had. And you know the punishment for blasphemy. I suggest that you leave Jerusalem today, return to the Galilee and peacefully resume whatever occupations you had before Joshua led you in his dangerous ways."

Jacob was inclined to argue that all Jews, not only the Priests, had access to their god, but he did not want to waste his time with the empty, authoritarian mind of a Sadducee.

On their release, Simeon and Jacob went back to their own people who had taken up the occupation of a small house in the north of the city. They reported all that the priests and the elders had said to them. When they heard this they raised their voices together in prayer to their god. "Sovereign Lord," they said, "you made heaven and the earth and the sea, and everything in them. You spoke by your spirit through the mouth of your servant, our father David:

> 'Why do the nations rage
> and the people plot in vain?
> The kings of the earth take their stand
> and the rulers gather together
> against the Lord
> and against the Anointed One.'

"The judges of our nation met together with the Gentiles to conspire against your holy servant Joshua, whom you anointed. They did what your power and will had decided beforehand should happen. Now, Lord, consider their threats and enable your servant to speak your word with great boldness. Stretch out your hand and perform miraculous signs and wonders through the name of your holy servant Joshua."

After they prayed, the little house was shaken by their exhilaration. Again and again they expressed their determination to preach boldly the word of the Lord in the name of Joshua ben Joseph of Nazareth, the King and Messiah of Israel.

Chapter 21

"He's there again." Branwen was at the window of the upper room, looking down into the small open space in front of the house. The southern wall of Caiaphas's palace loomed above her to the left. Before her was the outer wall of an open circus with a double tower at it's centre. Mordra joined his wife at the window. A now familiar figure stood with his back to the circus, gazing up at them this was the fourth day that he had taken up this position. "He's dressed like a Greek," Mordra murmured, "I've no idea who he could be. Perhaps it's time I found out."

The Gaul descended, then looked down at the young man, perhaps in his early twenties. He was bearded, his head was covered, and he wore a Greek tunic. Mordra addressed him in Greek. "What do you want?"

"Is this the Academia Britannicus?"

Mordra laughed. How had this Jew picked up Lucius's joking name for their house, and why had translated it into Latin? "I suppose it is. What do you want there?"

"I'm looking for a man called Mordra the Gaul."

"You're looking at him."

"You are Mordra?"

"Yes."

"I'm told that you are a friend of the Jews."

"People keep telling me that. My usual reply is that I'm the friend of all reasonable men. But is it reasonable to stand every day looking up at our window?"

The young man looked down and shuffled his feet in the dust. "Who else is in there, is the Roman?"

Mordra was becoming impatient. "If it's any of your business, no, Marcus Lucius is on a brief visit to his home in Italy. My wife is the only person in residence."

"Is she a Gaul?"

"You want to know a lot. No she isn't a Gaul, she's British – hence the 'Academia Britannicus'."

A look of puzzlement crossed the Jew's face. Mordra was not inclined to explain the role of women in his and Branwen's society. The young man drew himself up."My name is Nikolaos; my home is in Cilicia in the city of Tarsus. I am a student of Gamaliel."

Mordra nodded. "I know Gamaliel."

"It was he who suggested that I speak to you."

"Why?"

"I have joined the followers of Joshua of Nazareth."

Mordra reached out a hand and took the man's upper arm. "You'd better come in."

Together they crossed to the small portico and passed between the four Doric pillars that gave the house an air of pretension. Mordra guided his guest up the inner stairs to the book-littered room where Branwen was waiting.

Mordra made the introductions. Branwen's eyebrows raised.

"So you're a zealot; taking a risk, aren't you?"

He looked from one to the other. "I want to talk about scholarly matters." Mordra nodded; the Jew looked at Branwen, expecting her to leave. Mordra sighed. "I'm tired of explaining this. Our culture is very different to yours. This lady is a scholar, she's a lawyer in her own land, she will understand everything you say – and will probably be well ahead of you."

Nikolaos shook his head. He could not begin to understand what the Gaul was saying. "Gamaliel has told me that Britain is a place beyond the Empire."

"It is," said Branwen, "for now."

"I need to talk to people unsullied by Rome."

Branwen gave a humourless laugh. "I don't know where you'll find them. Sit down though, you can talk to us." Nikolaos sat. Branwen was offhand. "I don't suppose I can offer you any refreshment."

Nikolaos brightened. "Do you make your own wine?"

"No, we buy it."

"Judean wine?"

"Of course."

"Then I'll take a cup of wine with you."

Silently, Mordra left the room and returned with a flagon and three cups. He poured and handed cups to the other two. Nikolaos raised his cup. *"L'chai'im!"*

Mordra repeated the toast. "Hardly appropriate to be drinking 'to life' in these times."

"But it is." The young man replied. "Have you heard how Jacob and Simeon healed the crippled beggar at the temple gate?"

"I have, and I've seen that beggar many times; I often wondered whether he was restored every evening after he had been taken home."

"No! He was a cripple. Joshua had the gift of healing, and now it has been passed on to the twelve."

Mordra smiled. "I do not underestimate the importance of healing. I have a sister who is a physician in Lutetia – yes another woman." Whilst in Gaul, Mordra had been able to maintain contact with his family, and since coming to Judea he had kept in correspondence with them. "But I understood that Joshua was supposed to be your king, your Messiah even. I would have though that he would have left the medical arts to others."

"He did more than that." Nikolaos's eyes were shinning. "Like Elijah, he raised people from the dead."

Mordra had had enough. "Joshua was a Nazarite, and as such he could not approach a dead body."

"Joshua was above such rules. He saved people from the tomb."

"Joshua bound himself, and his immediate followers, by those rules."

Branwen sipped her wine and steadily regarded the Cilician. "We too believe that there is life after death in this world and that people return from the Otherworld to be reborn. But I think that you are talking about something entirely different. Do you claim that Joshua raised people from the dead before their funeral rites were completed, before they had been buried?"

"Yes."

"Then I think that we have nothing more to say."

Nikolaos could not accept dismissal from a woman. He turned to Mordra. "Your ways are different to ours, but I came here to tell how they can be the same."

"Then you are wasting your time. We are of different peoples."

"Yes, people are different, but there is only one true god."

Branwen stood and turned her back. "We have our gods, and they are true to us. You have your god who is true to you. Different people have different truths."

There was a note of desperation in the Jew's voice. "All men have the same needs; peace, freedom, life, a settled existence."

Branwen turned back to face him. "Yes. But your god cannot give those things to my people. From what I've seen he cannot give them to his own people."

Nikolaos could not believe that he was having this discussion with a woman. "What of the Roman gods?"

"What of them?" Mordra asked. "There are no Roman gods, they are Greek gods with different names."

"Yes!" Nikolaos cried. "Different names. The god of Israel has no name, but the god of Israel does for his chosen people what the Greek gods do for the Greeks, I would think what your gods do for you. Our god is the one true god of Israel. Can you say that your gods are not the same as our god, but divided into many parts and with different names."

Mordra nodded. "You have a point. As it happens I don't even follow the gods of my own people, but I can see that all gods serve the same, or a similar, purpose." Nikolaos was about to speak again, Mordra held up a hand. "And I think that I can anticipate where your argument is leading. What is the point of having dozens of gods and goddesses, all doing different things, when it would make more sense to have one, all-powerful, god doing everything?"

A look of joy came over Nikolaos's face. Mordra went on. "But I don't even follow my own gods, so I certainly could not follow another, however powerful he may be, who was the product of a culture that is not my own. To follow the Jewish god a man must be a Jew and I have no intention of being circumcised."

"I'm not sure that it would be necessary." Nikolaos replied. "Our god is the King of the universe, more than just the world. All men, Jew or Gentile can, through Joshua, follow no other god but ours,"

"What has Joshua got to do with it? His only concern was to rid your land of the heathen and to establish a pure, Jewish state here."

"I am a Greek."

"But a Jewish Greek."

"And when I return to Cilicia I will return to the Greeks, as well as to the Jews of Tarsus."

This young man did not impress Branwen. "And will you tell the Greeks to abandon their ancient gods and goddesses and start following the Jewish god?"

"I will."

"Then may all the gods help you."

"Tell me," Mordra wanted to know, "have you discussed this with Gamaliel, or with any of your fellow students?"

"I have tried to."

"And what did they say?"

"I have only spoken to one student, another Cilician called Saul. He became very angry, he would not listen. He believes that Joshua was a blasphemer."

"And Gamaliel?"

"He suggested that I speak to you."

Branwen and Mordra exchanged exasperated glances. Mordra decided that it was time to get rid of their guest. "What gave you the idea that this house was the 'Academia Britannicus'?"

"I heard this lady talk about it, in the market place, to the Roman."

Branwen laughed. "I remember; I was joking with Lucius and taunting him with Latin as I sometimes do."

Mordra had an idea. As an historian he was prepared to use any source of information. Standing, he ushered Nikolaos towards the door. "You will never convert us to belief in your god, or to your Jewish way of life. But you may visit us again if you wish. Anything you tell us about the followers of Joshua, be they Greeks or Hebrews, will remain a secret, the Romans will not hear of it."

"What about the Roman who lives here?"

"He is a scholar before he is a Roman. And he isn't here."

Lucius was in Samnium, in his family's villa beneath the mountains. The infant Marcus was on his knee. When Lucius had first returned, the child had turned away from him. It had only been a few months, but he did not know this man who was his father. After a few days all was well and Marcus would chuckle on Lucius's knee. Now he was silent, sullen, perhaps in reaction to the argument that went on and on between his parents. Paulina was angry. "Are you honestly asking me to take this child to a filthy province where the natives are at war with Rome?" They were going over the same ground. Lucius gave the same answers. "In the first place Judea isn't filthy, the Jews are very hygienic people, they have laws about it. And the house that I have there is cleaner than this villa. I have Jewish servants, very clean. And the Gauls and British wash more than we do."

"And the zealots, killing every Roman they set eyes upon?"

"The zealots are finished. You know Aulus, he's seen to it."

"And you want me us to share a house with barbarians, with slaves?"

"They are not slaves, they were but now they are free. And they're more civilised and more learned than anyone I know in Rome."

"Learned! That's all that matters to you isn't it? If a man can read a few books and talk endlessly about them you think he's something special. And the idea of a woman taking an interest in such things, it's against the laws of nature."

Now Lucius was becoming as angry as his wife was. "What do you know about the laws of nature? Have you read any of the natural philosophers?"

"You know I haven't."

It had seemed to be such a good idea when they had talked about it in Jerusalem. Lucius was eager to return home and visit his wife and young son. Branwen had said, casually, "Do they have to stay in Italy? There's plenty of room here for Paulina and Marcus, and for a nursemaid."

It had seemed so obvious. He would have his wife and child with him all the time. Paulina would have a ready-made friend in Branwen, and he and Mordra could really get down to work – and Branwen as well of course.

Perhaps he had had too much contact with the remarkable

Silurian woman, he had forgotten that he was married to a patrician Roman whose outlook was much narrower. Paulina had never had the opportunities that British women took for granted.

He could not say that the argument had ruined his visit. He loved the time that he spent with Marcus. He was already planning for the boy's education, looking forward to visiting him in his alma mater, the Academy of Rhodos. Young as he was, he believed that time spent in another land would be a useful experience for the child. Paulina was as loving and as dutiful as ever. Their nights together were still as sweet. During the days he enjoyed her company, until he brought the conversation back round to the subject of living for a while in Judaea.

They both knew what the outcome would be. It was Paulina who acknowledged it first. "You're my husband; if you say that we must go to Judaea, then we must go."

"I'd rather you were happier about going."

"How can I be?"

Lucius was as optimistic. "I'm sure that when you get there you'll find it very interesting and that you'll be happy there."

Paulina had decided that it would be otherwise.

Chapter 22

Whenever an adult joined the Essenes he was expected to bring all of his possessions with him to give them over to the community. When a child, such as Judah who had later become a sicariot, was dedicated to the Essenes, his father was expected to make a substantial contribution. They lived a communal life with a rigid hierarchy determined by length of time in the community, and the amount of learning accumulated there. All of their bodily needs were met from communal funds, their spiritual and intellectual needs were satisfied by the lore of Essenes, and detailed study of Holy Writ.

When a man became a Nazarite he simply walked away from all earthly things, leaving his family, his home, his job and his possessions. He subsisted by begging food and lodging from Jewish households. If he were refused, he placed a mark on the doorpost of that house so that all other Nazarites may avoid it; this also pleased the occupants of that house because these holy men never again solicited them.

The sect of the Essenes and the cult of the Nazarites were peculiar to the land of Israel. There were Chassidim in the Diaspora, in fact the Pharisees were the majority in other parts of the Empire, but the Essenes had no focus outside Judaea, and Nazarites had little hope of subsistence where Jewish homes were a small minority.

The Hebrews who were busily reconstituting Joshua's following took naturally to the mendicant and the communal life. The caravanserai at Bethlehem had become their commune and was almost exclusively theirs. The owner was happy enough with this arrangement. He even saw it in his interest to join them. Apart from those festivals that drew people to Jerusalem, his trade was often sparse; now he had a guaranteed full occupancy, and a young man, Didymos Judah, as the treasurer who paid up fully and regularly. Those travellers who came to the inn were harangued by the zealots. Most looked upon it as an evening's free entertainment, a few took a genuine interest, even fewer were annoyed by it – it was the Jewish way.

Similarly, the Hebrew zealots in their scattered secret places in Jerusalem and in the Galilee shared all that they had, no one claimed that any of his possessions was his own. There were no needy persons among them. Those who owned lands or houses sold them, and brought the money from the sales to whomsoever of the twelve was the leader of the local group. This money was carefully accounted and used to support the community.

The Greeks were less than happy with this. Some, being wandering men, had little or nothing to offer. Those who did own property in their own lands were reluctant to deprive their families and to pour money into a land that was not their own. They had no experience of the Essene or the Nazarite ways of life. This was a constant source of friction between Hebrews and Greeks. The turning point came with a Cypriot called Joseph. He had been almost a year in Judaea and had fought with the zealots at Passover. In Cyprus he had a field that lay on a stony hillside and was of little value to him, but was coveted by his Gentile neighbour, for no other reason than that he wanted a bulwark between himself and the Jew. Joseph, who among the zealots had adopted the name of Barnabas, wrote to his brother with instructions to sell the useless field. This done he brought the money to Simeon in Jerusalem.

One man who witnessed the public handing over of this money was dismayed. Ananias knew that he had been carried away with emotion when he had promised to sell his land and bring the proceeds to the cause. Had he not known it, his wife, Sapphira, soon told him what a fool he had been. "We have worked and sweated on that land," she shrieked when he told her what he had done. "Your father, your father's father, and his father toiled on that land. What of our sons and grandsons, do you want them to be paupers?"

Ananias knew that he had made a mistake, but he did not know how to get out of the pledge that he had made. When Sapphira had calmed down she thought of an answer. "Let us sit down and think about the value of each part of our land. There's that field under the escarpment. Every time it rains the rocks roll down and it takes weeks to shift them. It costs us more time to maintain it than it is worth. If we go through the whole property, a field at a time, we will see which we will be better off without. We will then write to Reuben with clear instructions. That way we can gain something out of this thoughtless promise of yours."

"But I'll still have to give the money to Simeon."

"Will Simeon know how much land you have sold, and the price? Give him something, but keep a reasonable amount for us."

Ananias wrote to his eldest son, and money was despatched to Jerusalem in the care of a trusted servant. The Cypriot was delighted with the price that his hard-headed son had got for the land. He divided the proceeds into two equal parts and took half to Simeon. He could not know how Simeon saw through his deception, but he suspected Joseph. Simeon said, "Ananias, how is it that evil has so filled your heart that you have lied to the Lord and have kept for yourself some of the money you received for the land? Didn't it belong to you before it was sold? And after it was sold, wasn't the money at your disposal? What made you think of doing such a thing? You have not lied to men but to the Lord."

A sicar flashed. The Cypriot looked, unbelieving, at the wooden handle of the knife that protruded from beneath his left ribs. He looked into Simeon's unforgiving eyes, staggered, fell, and was dead before he struck the floor.

There were half a dozen men in the room, they were stricken with fear, they knew that there was nothing they could do, they were outlaws. Simeon nodded to two of the hardier men; they wrapped the body of Ananias in his shawl and carried him out to his burial.

About three hours later, Sapphira, worried that her husband had not returned, went to Simeon. He showed her the bag of money that Ananias had handed over and asked her. "Tell me, is this the price that you and Ananias got for the land?"

"Yes," she said, "that is the price."

Simeon said to her. "How could you agree to test the Spirit of the Lord? Look! The feet of the men who buried your husband are at the door, and they will carry you out also."

Again the sicar flashed. Then the young men came in, and

finding her dead, carried her out and buried her beside her husband.

Simeon rose and made his way to the temple. The booth of the Nazarites remained the meeting place of the inner circle, but they often overflowed to the Court of the Gentiles where they met beneath the colonnades and addressed the crowd. The temple guard did not dare to come near them because tough men always surrounded them, and they wanted to avoid a riot. A whisper went round the court that two people had died because they had not obeyed Simeon. There were those who wanted the big Galilean brought before the Sanhedrin. Others, and they were the ones that prevailed, said that Simeon was a man of peace, but the Lord struck down the wicked and whoever it was that had died must have been brought to account before the throne of the Eternal.

When Caiaphas heard rumours of deaths among the zealots, and that the Hebrews had killed Greeks, he did not know whether to believe it. If they were fighting amongst themselves it could only be a good thing, but his concern was the zealot presence in the temple. If there were trouble between the various factions it would be the right time to clear the sacred site of these troublemakers. A detachment of the guard was ordered to arrest Jacob and Simeon and to put them into gaol. But during the night one of their supporters among the gaolers opened the door and let them out. Once free the two men looked at each other and Jacob said. "We will go back to the temple and tell the people the full message of the new life."

At daybreak they entered the temple, stood beneath the colonnades and began to speak in the name of Joshua. When Caiaphas assembled the Sanhedrin, he sent to the gaol for the two prisoners. But when the guard arrived at the gaol they did not find them there. So they went back and reported: "We found the gaol securely locked, with the guards standing at the doors, but when we opened them, we found no one inside." The judges looked at each other, nonplussed. Then a Levite came from the temple and said. "Look! The men you put in gaol are standing in the Court of the Gentiles preaching to the people." The guard was despatched and re-arrested the two. They did not use force because they wanted to avoid spilling human blood in the temple precincts.

Simeon and Jacob were ordered to make their hair dishevelled as was required of anyone who appeared before this august court. Caiaphas spoke. "We gave you strict orders not to preach in the name of Joshua ben Joseph of Nazareth. Yet you have filled the temple with your preaching and are determined to make us guilty of his blood."

Jacob replied. "We must obey the Lord rather than men! The God of our fathers raised Joshua from the dead – whom you killed by handing him over to the heathen to be nailed to a cross. The Lord has exalted him to his own right hand as King and Messiah. We are witnesses of these things, and so is the Holy Spirit, whom the Lord has given to those who obey him."

When the judges heard this they were furious. It was close to blasphemy; and these men were surely close to death. But the he wise Gamaliel, the most prominent rabbi in the land and a man who was respected by all, stood up and ordered that the two men be put outside for a little while. Then he addressed the court. "Men of Israel, consider carefully what you intend to do to these men. Some time ago Theudas appeared, claiming to be somebody, and about four hundred men rallied to him. He was killed, and all his followers were dispersed, and it all came to nothing. After him, Judah the Galilean appeared in the days of the census and led a band of people in revolt. He too was killed, and all his followers scattered. Therefore, in this present case I advise you: leave these men alone! Let them go! For if their purpose or activity is of human origin, it will fail. But if it is from the Lord, you will not be able to stop these men. You will only find yourself fighting against the Lord."

His speech persuaded them. They called Jacob and Simeon in, and had them flogged. They then ordered them not to speak in the name of Joshua, and let them go.

The two men rejoiced that they had got off so lightly. They saw their wounds as trophies that they had suffered for their cause. Despite his pain, Simeon walked on air. Let the cock crow now, he had not denied his king. Day after day they preached in the temple. Now the Nazarites among them no longer only asked for food and a bed for the night, they went from house to house preaching the coming of the Kingdom of the Lord in Israel.

285

Chapter 23

The troubles between the Hebrews and the Greeks escalated. A fiery man called Stefanos was emerging as one of the leaders of the Greek Jews in Jerusalem and, with a small group, he went to Jacob who was the designated leader of the Hebrew faction. "We all appreciate that your ways are different to our ways." Stefanos said. "It is not our custom to raise money in the way that you do, but we have made a considerable contribution both in money and in our efforts. Many of us shed our blood for Judaea at Passover. Some of our number have been crucified since then."

"Huh," said Simeon, "and some of you tried to defraud us of what is due to the Lord."

Stefanos knew that he was on dangerous ground with this man, but he pressed on. "We are not all like Ananias and his wife. We are fighting the same cause. I have given everything that I had and I challenge you to find that I held anything back. Yet our people are not receiving their just subsistence from the common fund. We have widows here, and orphans, of men who sacrificed their lives at Passover and they are being overlooked in the daily distribution of food."

"What do you want?" Simeon wanted to know. "That we should neglect the work that we are doing in order to wait on your tables?"

Jacob stepped in. "Brothers, choose seven men from among you who are known to be full of the spirit and of wisdom. We will turn this responsibility over to them, and make them a cadre among the brotherhood."

Stefanos withdrew to discuss this proposal with his companions. They liked it. The more they talked about it the more they liked it. They would have a distinct Greek presence in the zealot brotherhood. Stefanos emerged as the natural leader of the seven; and they selected Philippos, Procorus, Nicanor, Timon of Antioch, a convert to Judaism, Parmena, and Nikolaos of Tarsus. They presented these men to the brotherhood, who prayed and laid their hands upon them.

Despite, or perhaps because of, his elevation among the zealots, Nikolaos fell into the habit of visiting Mordra and Branwen, and telling them of what he saw as the successes of the followers of Joshua. He continued in the hope that he could persuade them to his own way of thinking. He was fascinated by the thought of taking the word of the Lord to the legendary land beyond the north wind. He was welcomed into their house for the information that he could give, given wine, and listened to. Carefully selected bits of useless information were passed on to Aulus. The zealots continued to thrive, and continued to divide themselves into two ever more separate camps.

One day Nikolaos arrived and proudly presented a scroll to the two scholars. "What's this?" Mordra asked.

The young Greek beamed. "One of the Hebrews, one of the twelve, Didymos Judah, has written down all the sayings of Joshua that he can remember. He wrote it in Aramaic, but we have translated it into Greek. We are sending copies to every Jewish community in the world. The Hebrews are distributing it here. When you have read this, you will know the truth, the one true god."

When he had departed, Branwen and Mordra sat down together at the big table, the table where Joshua had sat his last Seder, unrolled the document, and read:

'These are the secret words which the living Joshua spoke and Didymos Judah wrote.

And he said: Whoever finds the explanation of these words will not taste death.

Joshua said: Let him who seeks, not cease seeking until he finds, and when he finds, he will be troubled, and when he has been troubled, he will marvel and he will reign over the all.

Joshua said: If those who lead you say to you: "See, the kingdom is in heaven", then the birds of the heavens will precede you. If they say to you: "It is in the sea", then the fish will precede you. But the kingdom is within you and it is without you. If you will know yourselves, then you will be known and you will know that you are the sons of the Living God. But if you do not know yourselves, then you are in poverty and are poverty.

Joshua said: The man old in days will not hesitate to ask a little child of seven days about the place of life, and he will live. For many who are first shall become last and they shall become a single one.

Joshua said: Know what is in your sight, and what is hidden from you will be revealed for you. For there is nothing hidden which will not be manifest.

His disciples asked him, they said to him: Would you that we fast and how should we pray and should we give alms and what diet should we observe?

Joshua said: Do not lie; and do not do what you hate, for all things are manifest before heaven. For there is nothing hidden that shall not be revealed and there is nothing covered that shall remain without being uncovered.

Joshua said: Blessed is the lion which the man eats and the lion will become man and cursed is the man whom the lion eats and the lion will become man.

And he said: The man is like a wise fisherman who casts his net into the sea, and drew it up from the sea full of small fish; among them he found a large and good fish, that wise fisherman, he threw all the small fish down into the sea, he chose the large fish without regret. Whoever has ears to hear let him hear.

Joshua said: See, the sower went out, he filled his hand, he threw. Some seeds fell on the road. The birds came, they gathered them. Others fell on rock and did not strike root in the earth and did not produce ears. And others fell on the thorns. They choked the seed and the worm ate them. And others fell on the good earth; and it brought forth good fruit. It bore sixty per measure and one hundred and twenty per measure.

Joshua said: I have cast fire upon the world, and see, guard it until the world is afire.

Joshua said: This heaven shall pass away and the one above it shall pass away, and the dead are not alive and the living shall not die. In the days when you devoured the dead, you made it alive; when you come into light, what will you do? On the day when you were one, you became two. But when you have become two, what will you do?

His disciples said to Joshua: "We know that you will go away from us. Who is it who will be great over us?"

Joshua said to them: Wherever you have come, you will go with Jacob the righteous for whose sake heaven and earth came into being.

Joshua said to his disciples: Make a comparison to me and tell me who I am like.

Simeon bar Jonas said to him: You are like a righteous angel.

Mattathias said to him: You are like a wise man of understanding.

Didymos Judah said to him: Master, my mouth will not at all be capable of saying whom you are like.

Joshua said: I am not your master, because you have drunk, you have become drunk from the bubbling spring, which I have measured out. And he took him, he withdrew, he spoke three words to him. Now when Didymos Judah came to his companions, they asked him: "What did Joshua say to you?"

Didymos Judah said to them: "If I tell you one of the words which he said to me, you will take up stones and throw at me and fire will come from the stones and burn you up."

Joshua said to them: If you fast, you will bring sin upon yourselves, and if you pray, you will be condemned, and if you give alms, you will do evil to your spirits. And if you go into any land and wander in the regions, if they receive you, eat what they set before you, heal the sick among them. For what goes into your mouth will not defile you, but what comes out of your mouth, that is what will defile you.

Joshua said: When you see him who was not born of woman, prostrate yourselves upon your face and adore him; he is your Lord.

Joshua said: Men possibly think that I have come to throw peace upon the world and they do not know that I have come to throw divisions upon the earth, fire, sword, war. For there shall be five in a house: three shall be against two and two against three, the father against the son and the son against the father, and they will stand as solitaries.

Joshua said: I will give you what the eye has not seen and what the ear has not heard and what hand has not touched and what has not arisen in the heart of man.

The disciples said to Joshua: Tell us how our end will be.

Joshua said: Have you then discovered the beginning that you inquire about the end? For where the beginning is, there shall be the end. Blessed is he who shall stand at the beginning, and he shall know the end and he shall not taste death.

Joshua said: Blessed is he who was before came into the beginning. If you become disciples to me and hear my words, these stones will minister to you. For you have five trees in paradise, which are unmoved in summer or in winter and their leaves do not fall. Whoever knows them will not taste death.

The disciples said to Joshua: Tell us what the Kingdom of Heaven is like.

He said to them: it is like a mustard-seed, smaller than all the seeds, but when it falls on the tilled earth, it produces a large branch and becomes shelter for the birds of heaven.

Miriam said to Joshua: Who are your disciples like? He said: They are like little children who have installed themselves in a field which is not theirs. When the owners of the field comes, they will say: Release our field. They take off their clothes before them to release the field to them and to give back their field to them. Therefore I say: If the Lord of the house knows that the thief is coming, he will stay awake before he comes and will not let him dig through into his house of his kingdom to carry away his goods. You then must watch for the world, gird up you loins with great strength lest the brigands find a way to come to you, because they will find the advantage which you expect. Let there be among you a man of understanding; when the first fruit ripened, he came quickly with his sickle in his hand, he reaped it. Whoever has ears let him hear.

Joshua saw children who were being suckled. He said to his disciples: These children who are being suckled are like those who enter the Kingdom.

They said to him: Shall we then, being children, enter the Kingdom?

Joshua said to them: When you make the two one, and when

290

you make the inner as the outer and the outer as the inner and the above as the below, and when you make the male and female into a single one, so that the male will not be male and the female not be female, when you make the eyes in the place of an eye, and a hand in the place of a hand, and a foot in the place of a foot, and an image in the place of an image, then you shall enter the Kingdom.

Joshua said: I shall choose you, one out of a thousand, and two out of ten thousand, and they shall stand as a single one.

His disciples said: "Show us the place where you are, for it is necessary for us to seek it."

He said to them: Whoever has ears let him hear. Within a man of light there is light and he lights the whole world. When he does not shine, there is darkness.

Joshua said: Love your brother as your soul, guard him as the apple of your eye.

Joshua said: The speck of dust that is in your brother's eye you see, but the beam that is in your eye, you do not see. When you take the beam out of your eye, then you will see clearly to take the speck of dust out of your brother's eye.

Joshua said: If you do not fast from the world, you will not find the Kingdom. If you do not keep the Sabbath as Sabbath, you will not see the Lord.

Joshua said: I took my stand in the midst of the world and in flesh I appeared to them. I found them all drunk, I found none among them thirsty. And my soul was afflicted for the sons of men, because they are blind in their hearts and do not see that empty they have come into the world and that empty they seek to go out of the world again. But now they are drunk. When they have shaken off their wine, then they will repent.

Joshua said: If the flesh has come into existence because of the spirit, it is a marvel, but if the spirit has come into existence because of the body, it is a marvel of marvels. But I marvel at how this great wealth has made its home in this poverty.

Joshua said: Where there are three gods, they are gods; where there are two or one, I am with him.

Joshua said: No prophet is acceptable in his village, no physician heals those who know him.

Joshua said: A city being built on a high mountain and

fortified cannot fall nor can it ever be hidden.

Joshua said: What you will hear in your ear and in the other ear, that preach from your housetops, for no one lights a lamp and puts it under a pot, nor does he put it in a hidden place, but he sets it on the lampstand, so that all who come in and go out may see its light.

Joshua said: If a blind man leads a blind man, both of them fall into a pit.

Joshua said: it is not possible for one to enter the house of a strong man and take it by force unless he binds his hands, then he will ransack the house.

Joshua said: Take no thought from morning until evening and from evening until morning for what you shall put on.

His disciples said: When will you be revealed to us and when will we see you?

Joshua said: When you take off your clothing without being ashamed, and take your clothes and put them under the feet of the little children and tread on them, then you shall behold the son of the Living One and you shall not fear.

Joshua said: Many times have you desired to hear these words which I say to you, and you have no other from whom to hear them. There will be days when you will seek me and you will not find me.

Joshua said: The Sadducees and the Scribes have received the keys of knowledge, they have hidden them. They did not and they did not let those enter who wished. But you, become wise as serpents and innocent as doves.

Joshua said: A vine has been planted without the Lord and, as it is not established, it will be pulled up by its roots and destroyed.

Joshua said: Whoever has in his hand, to him shall be given and whoever does not have, from him shall be taken even the little which he has.

Joshua said: Become passers-by.

His disciples said to him: Who are you that you should say these things to us?

Joshua said to them: From what I say to you, you do not know who I am, but you have become as the Sadducees, for they love the tree, they hate its fruit and they love the fruit, they hate the tree.

Joshua said: Whoever blasphemes against the Lord, it shall be forgiven him, and whoever blasphemes against the son, it shall be forgiven him; but whoever blasphemes against the Holy Spirit, it shall not be forgiven him, either on earth or in heaven.

Joshua said: They do not harvest grapes from thorns, nor do they gather figs from thistles; for they give no fruit. A good man brings forth good out of his treasure, an evil man brings forth evil things out of his evil treasure, which is in his heart, and speaks evil things. For out of the abundance of the heart he brings forth evil things.

Joshua said: From Adam until Johannen the Essene there is among those born of women none higher than Johannen, so that his eyes will not be broken. But I have said that whoever among you becomes as a child shall know the Kingdom, and he shall become higher than Johannen.

Joshua said: It is impossible for a man to mount two horses and to stretch two bows, and it is impossible for a servant to serve two masters, otherwise he will honour the one and offend the other. No man drinks old wine and immediately desires to drink new wine and they do not put new wine into old wineskins, lest they burst, and they do not put old wine into new wine, lest they spoil it. They do not sew an old patch on a new garment, because there would come a rent.

Joshua said: If two make peace with each other in this one house, they shall say to the mountain: "Be moved", and it shall be moved.

Joshua said: Blessed are the solitary and elect, for they shall find the Kingdom; because you come from it, and you shall go there again.

Joshua said: If they say to you: "From where have you originated?" say to them: "We have come from the light, where the light has originated through itself. It stood and it revealed itself in their image." If they say to you: "We are his sons and we are the elect of the Living God." If they ask you: "What is the sign of the Lord to you?" say to them: "It is a movement and a rest."

His disciples said to him: When will the repose of the dead come about and when will the new world come?

293

He said to them: What you expect has come, but you do not know it.

His disciples said to him: Twenty-four prophets spoke in Israel and they spoke about you.

He said to them: You have dismissed the living one who is before you and you have spoken about the dead.

His disciples said to him: Is circumcision profitable or not?

He said to them: If it were profitable, their father would beget them circumcised from their mother. But the true circumcision in spirit has become profitable in every way.

Joshua said: Blessed are the poor, for yours is the Kingdom of Heaven.

Joshua said: whoever does not hate his father and his mother will not be a disciple to me, and whoever does not hate his brethren and his sisters and does not take up his cross in my way will not be worthy of me.

Joshua said: Whoever has known has found a corpse, of him the world is not worthy.

Joshua said: The Kingdom of the Lord is like a man who has good seed. His enemy came by night, he sowed a weed among the good seed. The man did not permit his workers to pull up the weed. He said to them: Lest perhaps you go to pull up the weed and pull up the wheat with it. For in the day of the harvest the weeds will appear, they will pull them and burn them.

Joshua said: Blessed is the man who has suffered, he has found life.

Joshua said: Look upon the Living One as long as you live, lest you die and seek to see him and be unable to see.

They saw a Samaritan carrying a lamb on his way to Judaea. He said to his disciples: Why does this man carry a lamb with him?

They said to him: In order that he may kill it and eat it.

He said to them: As long as it is alive, he will not eat it, but only if he has killed it and it has become a corpse.

They said: Otherwise he will not be able to do it.

He said to them: You yourselves, seek a place for yourselves in repose, lest you become a corpse and be eaten.

Joshua said: Two will rest on a bed: the one will die, the one will live.

Salome said: "Who are you, man, whose son? You did take

your place on my bench and eat from my table."

Joshua said to her: I am he who is from the same, to me was given the things of the Lord.

Salome said: "I am your disciple."

Joshua said to her: Therefore I say, if he is the same, he will be filled with light, but if he is divided, he will be filled with darkness.

Joshua said: I tell my mysteries to those who are worthy of my mysteries. What your right hand will do, let not your left hand know what it does.

Joshua said: There was a rich man who had much money. He said: "I will use my money that I may sow and reap and plant and fill my storehouse with fruit, so that I lack nothing." This was what he thought in his heart. And that night he died. Whoever has ears let him hear.

Joshua said: A man had guest-friends, and when he had prepared the dinner, he sent his servant to invite the guest-friends. He went to the first, he said to him: "My master invites you." He said: "I have some claims against some merchants; they will come to me in the evening; I will go and give them my orders. I pray to be excused from the dinner." He went to another, he said to him: "My master has invited you." He said to him: "I have bought a house and they request me for the day. I will have no time." He came to another, he said to him: "My master invites you." He said to him: "My friend is to be married and I am to arrange the dinner; I shall not be able to come. I pray to be excused from the dinner." He went to another, he said to him: "My master invites you." He said to him: "I have bought a farm, I go to collect the rent. I shall not be able to come. I pray to be excused." The servant came, he said to his master: "Those whom you have invited to the dinner have excused themselves." The master said to his servant: "Go out to the roads, bring those whom you shall find, so that they may dine. Tradesmen and merchants shall not enter my house."

He said: A good man had a vineyard. He gave it to husbandmen so that they could work it and he would receive its fruit from them. He sent his servant so that the husbandmen would give him the fruit of the vineyard. They seized his servant, they beat him. A little longer and they would have killed him.

The servant came, he told his master. His master said: "Perhaps they did not recognise him." He sent another servant; the husbandmen beat him as well. Then the owner sent his son. He said: "Perhaps they will respect my son." Since those husbandmen knew that he was the heir of the vineyard, they seized him, they killed him. Whoever has ears let him hear.

Joshua said: Show me the stone which the builders have rejected. It is the corner-stone.

Joshua said: Whoever knows the all but fails to know himself lacks everything.

Joshua said: Blessed are you when you are hated and persecuted. You will find a place, where you will not be persecuted.

Joshua said: Blessed are those who have been persecuted in their hearts. These are they who have known the Lord in truth. Blessed are the hungry, for the belly of him who desires will be filled.

Joshua said: If you bring forth that within yourselves, that which you have will save you. If you do not have that within yourselves, that which you do not have within you will kill you.

Joshua said: I will destroy this house and no one will be able to build it again.

A man said to him: Tell my brothers to divide my father's possessions with me.

He said to him: O man, who made me a divider? He turned to his disciples, he said to them: I am not a divider, am I?

Joshua said: The harvest is indeed great, but the labourers are few, but beg the Lord to send labourers into the harvest.

He said: Lord, there are many around the cistern, but nobody in the cistern.

Joshua said: Many are standing at the door, but the solitary are the ones who will enter the bridal chamber.

Joshua said: The Kingdom of the Lord is like a man, a merchant, who possessed merchandise and found a pearl. That merchant was prudent. He sold the merchandise, he bought the one pearl for himself. You also seek for the treasure which fails not, which endures, there where no moth comes near to devour and where no worm destroys.

Joshua said: I am the light that is above them all, I am the

296

All, the All came forth from Me and the All attained to Me. Cut a piece of wood, I am there; lift up the stone and you will find me.

Joshua said: Why did you come out of the desert? To see a reed shaken by the wind? And to see a man clothed in soft garments? See, your kings and your great ones are those who are clothed in soft garments and they shall not be able to know the truth.

A woman from the crowd said to him: Blessed is the womb which bore you and the breasts which nourished you.

He said to her: Blessed are those who have heard the word of the Lord and have kept it in truth. For there will be days when you will say: "Blessed is the womb which has not conceived and the breasts which have not suckled."

Joshua said: Whoever has known the world has found the body, and whoever has found the body, of him the world is not worthy.

Joshua said: Let him who has become rich become king, and let him who has power renounce it.

Joshua said: Whoever is near to me is near to the fire, and whoever is far from me is far from the Kingdom.

Joshua said: The images are manifest to man and the light which is within them is hidden in the image of the light of the Lord. He will manifest himself and his image is concealed by his light.

Joshua said: When you see your likeness, you rejoice. But when you see your images which came into existence before you, which neither die nor are manifested, how much will you bear?

Joshua said: Adam came into existence from a great power and a great wealth, and yet he did not become worthy of you. For if he had been worthy, he would not have tasted death.

Joshua said: The foxes have their holes and the birds have their nests, but the son of man has no place to lay his head and rest.

Joshua said: Wretched is the body which depends upon a body, and wretched is the soul which depends upon these two.

Joshua said: The angels and the prophets will come to you and they will give you what is yours. And you, too, give to them what is in your hands, and say to yourselves: "On which day will they come and receive what is theirs?"

Joshua said: Why do you wash the outside of the cup? Do you not understand that he who made the inside is also he who made the outside?

Joshua said: Come to me, for easy is my yoke and my lordship is gentle, and you shall find repose for yourselves.

They said to him: "Tell us who you are so that we may believe in you."

He said to them: You test the face of the sky and of the earth, and him who is before your face you have not known, and you do not know to test this moment.

Joshua said: Seek and you will find, but those things which you asked me in those days, I did not tell you then. Now I desire to tell them, but you do not inquire after them.

Joshua said: Give not what is holy to the dogs, lest they throw it on the dung-heap. Do not throw the pearls to the swine, lest they make them into manure.

Joshua said: Whoever seeks will find and whoever knocks, it will be opened to him.

Joshua said: If you have money, do not lend at interest, but give to him from whom you will not receive back.

Joshua said: The Kingdom of the Lord is like a woman, who has taken a little yeast and has hidden it in dough and has made large loaves of it. Whoever has ears let him hear.

Joshua said: The Kingdom of the Lord is like a woman who was carrying a jar full of meal. While she was walking on a distant road, the handle of the jar broke. The meal streamed out behind her on the road. She did not know it, she had noticed no accident. After she came to her house, she put the jar down, she found it empty.

Joshua said: The Kingdom of the Lord is like a man who wishes to kill a powerful man. He drew the sword in his house, he stuck it into the wall, in order to know whether his hand would carry through. Then he killed the powerful man.

The disciples said to him: "Your brothers and your mother are standing outside."

He said to them: Those here who do the will of the Lord, they are my brothers and my mother. These are they who shall enter the Kingdom of the Lord.

They showed him a gold coin and said to him: "Caesar's

men ask taxes from us."

He said to them: Give the things of Caesar to Caesar, give the things of the Lord to the Lord and give me what is mine.

Joshua said: Whoever does not hate his father and his mother in my way will not be able to be a disciple to me, for my mother is only a woman but my true mother gave me the life.

Joshua said: Woe to them, the Sadducees, for they are like a dog sleeping in the manger of oxen, for neither does he eat nor does he allow the oxen to eat.

Joshua said: Blessed is the man who knows in which part of the night the robbers will come in, so that he will rise and collect his sword and gird up his loins before they come in.

They said to him: Come and let us pray today and let us fast.

Joshua said: Which then is the sin that I have committed, or in what have I been vanquished? But when the bridegroom comes out of the bridal chamber, then let them fast and let them pray.

Joshua said: Whoever knows father and mother shall be called the son of a harlot.

Joshua said: When you make the two one, you shall become the sons of man, and when you say: "Mountain be moved." It will be moved.

Joshua said: The Kingdom is like a shepherd who had a hundred sheep. One of them went astray, which was the largest. He left behind ninety-nine, he sought for the one until he found it. Having tired himself out, he said to the sheep: "I love you more than ninety-nine."

Joshua said: Whoever drinks from my mouth shall become as I am and I myself will become he, and the hidden things shall be revealed to him.

Joshua said: The Kingdom is like a man who had treasure hidden in his field, without knowing it. After he died, he left it to his son. The son did not know about it, he accepted the field, he sold it. And he who bought it, he went, while he was ploughing he found the treasure. He began to lend money to whomever he wished.

Joshua said: Whoever has found the world has become rich, let him deny the world.

Joshua said: The heavens will be rolled up and the earth in your presence, and he who lives on the Living One shall see neither death nor fear, because I say: Whoever finds himself, of him the world is not worthy.

Joshua said: Woe to the flesh which depends upon the soul; woe to the soul which depends upon the flesh.

His disciples said to him: "When will the Kingdom come?"

Joshua said: It will not come by expectation. They will not say: "See, here," or "See, there." But the Kingdom of the Lord is spread upon the earth and men do not see it.

Simeon bar Jonas said to them: Let Miriam go out from among us, because women are not worthy of the life.

Joshua said: See, I shall lead her, so that I will make her male, that she too may become a living spirit, resembling you males. For every woman who makes herself male will enter the Kingdom.

The secret words of Joshua ben Joseph of Nazareth, King and Messiah

According to Didymos Judah, one of the twelve.'

They sat back. Branwen exhaled a long breath. "I don't think I've ever read such a bad piece of writing in my entire life."

Mordra shook his head and gave a low laugh. Branwen was irritated. "The spelling isn't too bad, and I've seen worse grammar, but the syntax is all over the place. I thought that Jews were supposed to be educated."

Her husband put an arm around her. "Not all of them. Joshua seems to have surrounded himself with some of the lesser educated ones, men with only basic education, apart from Judah the sicariot, and although he has spent most of his life in study it seems to have been by rote. I don't think that he has much native intelligence. If I could find him again I'd like him to see this, compare it with his memory of what Joshua may or may not have said. It is strange that a rabbi should tell his followers to be 'as little children'. That's anti-intellectual and not how rabbis think. He is even supposed to have said; 'a child of seven days', one day before a boy is circumcised to become a Jew. To be fair, I think that it is largely a problem of translation, and not only from one language to another. You can translate words, but, as you know,

300

you can't translate the idiom of one people to that of another. I think I'll ask Nikolaos for a copy of the Aramaic original."

"Is it worth it?"

Mordra thought for a moment. Perhaps not. Forget the language, what do you make of the content?"

"Not much."

"Neither do I."

Branwen scanned the scroll again. "It's a dreadful litany; all this 'Joshua said, Joshua said, Joshua said'; lightly relieved by 'he said, they said'. Perhaps the key is in the opening and closing words – 'These are the *secret* words of Joshua. Do you think that there could be a code here, such as that of our secret verses; only one born to their culture can understand it, as only we can fully understand Druidic wisdom?"

"I think that you have put your finger on a possibility. The litany can be no more than an attempt at authenticity – 'These are the words of Joshua'. The trouble is that it is only quotations of his words, they are taken out of context. Some of these sayings are familiar, you've read them in what Judah told me. But he quoted Joshua in context, and that gave the sayings some meaning. I can also detect some Greek revisionism in this."

"How do you mean?"

Mordra gathered his thoughts. "There was that bit about eating lions. Jews don't eat the flesh of lions because it's against their dietary laws. Yet we have a further passage about eating all that strangers, that means Gentiles, set before them. As you know, Jews do not normally eat or drink anything in a Gentile house. Remember Nikolaos asking us if our wine was Gentile or Jewish? But I wonder if the Jews of the Diaspora have learned a degree of compromise."

Branwen nodded. "I found that interesting about not giving pearls to swine. I've never seen a pig in this land."

Mordra laughed again. "When Joshua said that, he was talking about the Romans. The wild boar badge of the legion is a very useful image to them. But there were some pigs brought into the Galilee for the benefit of the Gentiles in Tiberias; Joshua sorted that problem out."

"What did he do?"

"He crossed the lake to the region of the Gerasenes on the

east bank, which was the source of the illegal meat supply. It seems that he drove a large herd of pigs down a steep bank and into the lake where they drowned."

"He was taking a risk, the Gerasenes lost a valuable herd."

"Yes, they might have been able to fish out a few and sell them, but they must have lost a fortune. Of course he had his twelve around him, but I believe that he had to leave very quickly." Mordra's smile faded. "Going back to this account, he was advocating nudity at one point; not very Jewish, but it could be Greek. Even in the privacy of their own homes they are always fully dressed, not like us. Then there was that about circumcision. This has to be revisionism because I can't imagine a rabbi giving the answer that this Didymos Judah says he gave, that rite is absolutely central to their culture. Do you remember Nikolaos's reaction when I told him that I had no intention of being circumcised?"

"Yes," Branwen replied, "and I hope you never do, I prefer you as you are. But he also said that it may not be necessary in order to join their sect."

Mordra was solemn. "Don't forget that from what Nikolaos was saying, the Greek Jews may be thinking of trying to introduce their god into the Gentile world, trying to convert the uncircumcised to a form of Judaism without being Jewish."

"I can't see how that's possible. But, as I said to Nikolaos," his wife was as solemn as he, "if they try to do that – may all the gods help them because, if they do, they are facing nothing but death."

Chapter 24

Lucius stood on the upper deck of the gently tossing ship. He looked with eager anticipation at the approaching towers guarding the entrance to the harbour of Caesarea.

Paulina lay, miserably, below. The infant Marcus was under the care of Scylla, the Greek slave from Sicilia who was his *pedagogus,* his governess.

Paulina had travelled in an uncomfortably jolting carriage, down through increasingly unfamiliar countryside to the bustling port of Puteoli with all its stink of the sea and of those who sail upon the sea. She had first been sick while they were still tied up to the harbour wall. When they had put to sea her misery had worsened. Despite Lucius's ministrations, she refused to try to eat anything, taking only sips of ever more disgusting water. She knew that Judaea would be even more horrible than the trials of getting there.

On his previous visit, Lucius's baggage comprised mainly books and the minimum of clothing. Now they had a pile of crates containing all the necessary (and, he thought, largely unnecessary) items for the comfort of his wife and child. He instructed the ship's captain to see that this heap of baggage was safely delivered and, carrying Marcus in his arms, led Paulina along the quay to Pontius Pilate's palace. Scylla had been left to supervise the unloading and the transport of the baggage. Lucius would have preferred to go straight to Jerusalem, but he knew that Paulina would need to recover from the voyage and so he led the way to the only possible accommodation for a patrician family.

The young woman had to admit that the palace was much more magnificent than anything that she had expected to find in this land. Entering through a gateway protected by two square towers, she found herself in a broad courtyard. A wide flight of marble steps led to a colonnaded frontage with a red-roofed gatehouse at its centre. Through this gate, and the main body of the palace rose before her. She admired the symmetry of the white building with its pillars, square towers, and a gatehouse identical to the outer one.

The Major Domo, ever on duty when a ship arrived from Puteoli or Ostia, was at the gate. He easily recognised Lucius from his visit earlier in the year, and he led the family to one of the ever-prepared guest suites. Having seen the couple and their child settled, he went to round up servants who would attend to their needs and comfort.

The suite was at the seaward end of the palace. Paulina went to the broad window and looked out over the harbour, a reasonable distance away, and out over the dark sea, gazing towards the west. Lucius busied himself with instructions to the servants, telling the one in charge not to trouble the procurator, who he knew to be a busy man, and did not need to know that they had arrived. Paulina overheard this. "Will we not dine with the procurator?"

"Not if I can help it," her husband replied, "he's the worst kind of upstart plebeian, and he doesn't like me either." He looked fondly at the beautiful woman as the sun dipped towards the horizon, bringing a rose-red blush to her marble-white skin.

They stayed for four days in the provincial capital, Paulina enjoying the sophistication of the city. She had complete confidence in the Sicilian girl, and so she had the leisure to explore Caesarea with Lucius as her only guide. She loved the broad thoroughfares, the shops, and the magnificent buildings. They visited the great theatre just outside the city's' southern wall. Walking in the forum, a delicate parasol shielding her from the glare, they discussed their friend Aulus; and the man she invariably referred to as 'the odious Pilate'.

They had been unable to avoid the procurator, or his miserable wife, even in so large a building. Pilate felt obliged to greet his patrician guests; in the rigid social structure of Rome they were on a higher plane than he, as an equus, was. In Paulina's presence he had been coolly polite to Lucius, and as gracious as he was able to Lucius's wife. He also had some good news. "I see that your friend Aulus Plautius is to leave us."

Lucius's heart leapt. Could he now get Mordra and Branwen out of Judaea and to Prydain? "Leave you?"

"You didn't know?" The procurator was supercilious. "He's been appointed to the command of the Ninth Legion."

Lucius was delighted for his friend. "The Ninth. Where are they?"

Pilate was taking some pleasure in the exchange. He knew something that this clever aristocrat did not know. "Pannonia. I'm sure that he'll enjoy it, a completely disorganised province. The army has done nothing with the place in the forty-odd years they've been there. It has no civil administration, so Rome has never got anything out of it."

Lucius took satisfaction from this. As legate of the Legion, and with no procurator, he would be governor of the province – exactly what Aulus wanted.

Livia, the wife of Pilate, gave a sour smile. "The sooner he leaves Judaea the better, but I can't think why they've promoted him. He should never have crucified that rabbi. When my husband returned from Jerusalem and told me what had happened, I had a dream that told me to beware of the followers of that Jew."

Lucius bit his tongue. There was no point in telling this stupid woman of her husband's glee in sending the three men to their crosses, nor of how he had demonstrated his contempt of the 'vermin' as he had washed his hands.

As they strolled in the forum, they again expressed their pleasure in Aulus's good fortune and both agreed that it was well deserved. Paulina was less happy with her husband's plans to travel to the edge of the world. "And I suppose that your Celtic slave friends will be very pleased."

Lucius could not avoid irritation. "'The Celtae' is a dismissive term that they do not like. Mordra is a Parisian, a Gaul, and Branwen is Silurian and British. They are no longer slaves, and they only fell into slavery because of conditions imposed by Rome. Their social structure is very different to ours, but in their own lands they are the equivalent to patricians." Paulina was not convinced.

The following morning they departed for Jerusalem. They formed an impressive train: a carriage for Lucius and Paulina,

305

another for Marcus and Scylla, and six camels bearing their luggage. They slept that night in the ancient city of Shechem, where Abraham, Jacob, and the twelve sons of Jacob, the Patriarchs of Israel, are buried. They were accommodated in a caravanserai that Lucius found to be perfectly adequate, despite his wife's complaints.

It was late in the following afternoon when they passed through the Damascus Gate and entered King David's city. As they had approached, Paulina had gasped at her first sight of Jerusalem. She could never have imagined that it could be so lovely. Nowhere had she seen a building to match the massive Temple. Lucius smiled to himself. He knew that they were approaching the city at the best time of day; the lowering sun turned the ancient stones to burnished gold.

As they halted outside the house, Paulina received another pleasant surprise. It was not the hovel that she had been expecting. Four pillars guarded the entrance. A row of five windows, shaded with blinds, marked the upper floor. On the left there was a square tower, topped by a dome, this was where her husband had his *studium,* his study. To the right of the house there was a huge villa, more than a villa, a palace.

Stiffly, they emerged from the carriage to be met by two elegant people, both taller than either she or Lucius. The man's fair hair fell around his ears, and a carefully tended moustache adorned his upper lip. The woman wore a long, slender, rich red gown; her hair was braided, the braids dyed in different colours and coiled artfully about her fine head. Their expressions were open, welcoming. Surely these could not be the barbarians!

Introductions were made. They were ushered into the spacious entrance hall where fruits, tempting tidbits, sherbet, and wine were ready. Lucius could not wait to share the good news. "Have you heard about Aulus?"

"I've seen him several times," the Gaul replied, "but I've heard nothing out of the ordinary."

Lucius was happy that he was the one to bring the news. "He's been promoted to legate."

Mordra was puzzled. "What about Marius?"

"As far as I know, Marius is fine. Aulus is leaving the Tenth, he's been given command of the Ninth."

Branwen sat up. "Where?"

"Pannonia. He isn't leaving immediately. Pilate would like to get rid of him tomorrow, but Marius insists that he stays a little longer – to ensure that Jerusalem stays quiet. But he will be going before the end of the year, two or three months at the most."

Branwen released a long breath. "I thank Ogma for giving me the ability to draw up those bills of sale. And I'll always be grateful to you, Lucius, for giving us back our freedom. Now Aulus Plautius can't take us with him," she laughed. "By the way, where's Pannonia?"

Her husband answered her. "It's part of what used to be known as Illyricum, to the north of the Adriatic Sea, it was divided into Pannonia and Moesia."

"Is it?" Branwen mused. "Then it must be close to the long valley of the river named for the goddess Danu. People of our culture."

"Yes," said Mordra, "the area between the great river and the sea."

Lucius had a question. "Was Ogma your tutor who taught you law?"

"No. Ogma is the patron god of the Druids, the god of eloquence and learning." She was distracted from the conversation by the arrival of Scylla, carrying the infant Marcus. "And this is Marcus? What a beautiful child." Early in her marriage, Branwen, still scarred by her dreadful experiences, had taken steps to avoid conception, using the sponge soaked in vinegar. Later, as her trust in Mordra had deepened, and as her maternal longing overcame her despair at their slavery, she had abandoned this precaution. She was now sure that what she had done to herself to abort the foetus that the brutal legionary had forced upon her had condemned her to a lifetime of sterility. Now she hoped to share in the joy of this child of Paulina and Lucius. The Roman mother experienced a surge of warmth at Branwen's reception of her precious Marcus. The two men saw the opportunity to leave their wives to their mutual pleasure, and to take themselves off to the studium.

Settled comfortably, with a flagon of Judaean wine, Lucius wanted to know everything that had happened since he had departed for Samnium. Mordra was eager to tell him. "We now have a contact inside the zealot brotherhood." Lucius was amazed, then rapt as his friend related how Nikolaos had come to them, and had become a frequent visitor, and how he had been elected to the new, Greek, party among the leaders of those who had followed Joshua. Mordra handed over a scroll that he had ready and waiting. "You must read this. A man called Didymos Judah, one of Joshua's original twelve, has written down all the sayings of the rabbi that he can remember. The only problem is that this is a Greek translation of the Aramaic original, and we don't think a very good one. But you must read it. I want to know what you make of it."

In a Bet Knesset across the city, the Rabbi Gamaliel was seated behind a desk brightly illuminated by two oil lamps in tall stands at either side. A group of young men, their heads covered with their shawls, sat and stood around the room. Two were seated on a rough wooden bench to the left of the desk, leaning slightly forward to catch every word from this great teacher. Another leaned across the front of the desk, yet another leaned towards Gamaliel from the side, an expression of enquiry upon his handsome face. Behind him a student held his left hand to his beard, the forefinger crooked across his mouth. Two more stood at the back of the room; one turned sideways and looked over his right shoulder. The other, the Cilician, Saul, had his arms folded, a confident look upon his face, his eyes steady under their thick brows that met over the bridge of his hooked nose. The other Cilician, Nikolaos, sat alone on a second bench to the right of he desk. A Torah scroll, one of the five books of Moses, the book of Holy Law, was unrolled upon the desk. The rabbi's eyes twinkled; he would give them something to think about. "The Lord may say: 'If only my people would forsake me and keep my Torah.'" The students stiffened, the rabbi went on, "'because the light of my Torah will bring them close to me.'"

A student was quick to respond. "That puts practice above faith."

Another replied: "Faith is not enough. We cannot understand the Lord, he is above all human understanding, and faith cannot be proved or disproved. We can only show our love of the Lord by the practice of keeping to his Holy Law."

Yet another said: "The Torah is central to Judaism, it emphasises that the will of the Lord is to be found in his revealed teachings, that the words of the Torah are the stairway to heaven."

Saul spoke up. "But I think that it implies something else, of wider significance: that the pursuit of spiritual experience is less important than being part of a collective tradition. We are the chosen of the Lord, and the only way in which we can attempt to repay him for his great gifts to us is through our Jewishness and we can only hold to our Jewishness by our obedience to his Holy Law."

Gamaliel smiled. "But we don't all do it in the same way. We Pharisees live our lives in a different way to other Jews. The Sadducees have their way, the Essenes theirs, and what about the Samaritans?"

"Yes," a man was quick to reply, "but all who live in the light of Torah are Jews. The paths we tread may be different, but they all lead us to the Lord."

The rabbi was content with the way the discussion was going. "We are nine in this room, one short of a minyan, but we do not need the tenth man in order to explore our hearts and our minds. Seven of us are Hebrews. We have spent our entire lives in touch with the sacred soil of Eretz Israel. Two are Greeks, who do not, in their homelands, have the privilege of being a part of the Holy Land that the Lord gave to us, and only to us. Yet all nine of us are, equally, Jews. We all live our lives in the light of Torah."

Saul and Nikolaos puffed up with pleasure at these words. Then Gamaliel posed the question that he had been leading up to. "Can a Gentile follow Holy Law?"

There was a stunned silence in the room. Saul was the first to break it. "No!" The Lord gave Holy Law to Moses, not to Pharaoh! It is the Law of the Jews."

The Rabbi slowly nodded. "But are we not a light to lighten the Gentiles? How, practically, are we to shed that light?"

Nikolaos said: "Any man, Jew or Gentile, can follow Holy Law. It is the perfect law because it comes from the Eternal God, King of the Universe. Why should we deny access to Holy Law to those who are not Jews?"

Saul was becoming angry. "Even the blasphemer Joshua did not make such a proposition. You are associating with those who were with him, ask them. If a Gentile wants to live his life in the light of Holy Law, then he must cease being a Gentile, he must become a convert, be circumcised, and live his life as a Jew."

Gamaliel gave the stormy Cilician a stern look. Saul was a good man, a clever student, but he must learn to control his temper.

The discussion went on and, as ever, did not reach a conclusion upon which all could agree.

Lucius put down the scroll. "I agree that this is probably a bad translation and we've both seen plenty of those. But, even allowing for that, I can't make much sense of it and I don't think that the original could be much more rational."

"Branwen wonders if it could be in code. Our secret lore is often couched in terms that can only be understood by the initiated. And if it's an Aramaic code, then translation into Greek would scramble it still further."

"That's a possibility. But some of these saying we already have from your interviews with Judah, and he put them into context. Whatever the rest might mean, do you think that it's worth spending more time on it?"

Mordra did not hesitate. "No."

"Neither do I. We now know that we won't be here much longer. I suggest that we pick up what we can from your friend in the brotherhood, then leave them and do something much more interesting in Siluria." He picked up the scroll. "Didymos Judah. That means that this Judah is a twin. I wonder what the other one's like." They both laughed. Lucius rolled up the scroll and dropped I onto the big table. "As far as these ramblings are concerned, I think that we file it, and forget it."

Chapter 25

When Nikolaos next visited the house, he was again made welcome. Then he saw Lucius and stopped dead. "The Roman!"

Lucius had been warned. He stepped forward. "Before anything else I'm a scholar. And I am told that you are a student of the great Gamaliel. Scholarship knows no ethnic boundaries. Next, I regard myself as a friend of Mordra. If you trust him, then you can trust me. Yes, I am a Roman, but I am in your land to learn more of your religion, your laws, and your way of life. I would not be able to do that if I were to go running to Aulus Plautius or Pontius Pilate with information that I have gained, in confidence, from you or any other Jewish source. Pilate is not my friend. I despise the man and what he does. Aulus Plautius is my cousin and a friend from early childhood, but the tribune of the Jerusalem cohort is often a stranger to me. I witnessed the death of Joshua. The men who did that deed did it from the lowest depths of human degradation."

Nikolaos was thoughtful. His mind turned over the Roman's words. He moved towards Lucius, looked deep into his eyes, and grasped his hand. He then followed them to the upper room.

Branwen would dearly have loved to join them, but she was trying hard to build a bridge between herself and Paulina. The only plank in that bridge was Marcus. His mother doted upon him, and the girl from Nudd would have been happy to take over from Scylla. Apart from the child, Branwen had been unable to find any common ground with his haughty mother.

A skin of wine hung on a peg in the studium. Mordra went towards it. Nikolaos produced a cup. "I hope that you don't mind, but I knew that you would offer me wine, you always do. It isn't just the food and drink, but also the vessels that have to be in accordance with Holy Law."

Mordra smiled. "I did know that. I've seen you give the

311

Gentile cup a surreptitious wipe on your previous visits. Now, are you people and the Hebrews still talking to each other?"

"Yes. In the brotherhood we all talk together."

"Talk *with*, or talk *at*?"

"Have you ever witnessed a Jewish scholarly discussion?"

"I have. And, would you believe, even taken part."

The young Jew learned more about this man from the north every time they met. He had difficulty in seeing how a stranger could have learned so much about their ways, how he had gained such understanding. Only Jews knew Jews. Everyone else was a stranger – or an enemy. "In the Bet Knesset of Gamaliel there are just two Greeks, myself and Saul and he and I do not agree. But in that place we do all talk together." He laughed. "Sometimes we all talk at the same time."

Lucius could understand this; it had been his experience as a student on the island of Rhodos. "We all do that. Have you ever thought that there is no such thing as an exchange of ideas in academic discussion? Lectures impart information and ideas, tutorials give us structured, supervised, discussion. But when we are among others of like mind, we are stimulated to delve into our brains, and we organise our thoughts by talking to ourselves, in the presence of stimulating company."

Nikolaos was surprised to discover that it was not only Jewish scholars who proceeded in this way.

Mordra was satisfied that their guest seemed to have accepted Lucius. "How do two Greeks, who disagree, fare in the school of the foremost rabbi?"

"Gamaliel stresses that we are all Jews, and equally so." Nikolaos thought that it would like to put his latest ideas to two Gentiles, it would be a start. "We had a very interesting discussion a few days ago. You know that our god is King of the Universe. Therefore he must be king of the whole world, of Jew and Gentile?" Mordra nodded. The young man went on. "You may also know that the Lord has also told us that we are a light to lighten the Gentiles." Again Mordra nodded. Lucius came in. "I am interested in your emphasis upon light and darkness. I think that they are co-terminal with good and evil. The Persian Zoroastrians have also developed this idea and I know that the Essenes refer to the 'sons of light' and the 'sons of darkness'."

312

For the first time in his short life, Nikolaos was in discussion with men who were not Jews, but who could reason and argue like Jews. He was enjoying it. "The Torah is the light of the world, it is the perfect law because it comes from the one true god. Why can't the Gentiles follow Holy Law? If you did then you would bathe in the light of the Lord."

Mordra shook his head. "It's the perfect law to you because it is your law, you believe that it comes from your god. We have our laws, the laws of our people. To follow your law a man must be a Jew."

"Why?"

"I recall that one of your laws is: 'On the eighth day the boy is to be circumcised.' That means that to follow your law a man must be a Jew. And what about your dietary laws? In my country we enjoy nothing more than a boar hunt, and the boar is a staple in our diet. Throughout Europe farmers, butchers, shopkeepers have built up their livelihood upon our dietary habits, which are largely based upon what's available and what can be grown. To follow your law all of that would have to be overturned, it's hardly practical."

Nikolaos could think of no answer to Mordra's point about diet. "The rules regarding circumcision are to be found in the twelfth chapter of the Book of Leviticus, and they are uncompromisingly specific. But, in the Book of Deuteronomy we are told, twice: 'Circumcise your hearts'."

Lucius was not sure where the young man was heading. "I have to agree that, if there is an hierarchy of the body's parts, then the heart is more important than the penis; you can't live without a heart. And I appreciate that what is in the heart of man is more important than any external signs that are put upon him, especially if those external signs are put upon him when he is too young to make his own choice."

Nikolaos smiled and said: "Then, if the Lord is in the heart of a man, then surely that man will want to follow Holy Law because it is the Law of the Lord. And if a man follows Holy Law, then the Lord will enter his heart."

Both of his hosts liked this argument. They did not agree with it, but it was a neat piece of reasoning.

Much as he was enjoying the exchange, Mordra wanted to

313

get down to something of more practical value. "I have to tell you, Nikolaos, that we will be leaving Judaea soon, and I doubt that we will ever return. We have important work to do on the Island of Britain. How do you see the brotherhood going in the immediate future?"

Without thinking twice, Nikolaos said: "The brotherhood in Judaea will disappear very soon. Its members will be reabsorbed into mainstream Chassidic life, be they Pharisee, Essene, or Nazarite. In the Galilee it may last a little longer. The best of their men and, most important, the best of their leaders, died at Passover. Before he died, Joshua nominated Jacob as his successor, and this was ratified at the meeting when they appointed Mattathias as the replacement for Judah. By the way, there were two men proposed for the replacement, the other one was Joseph, called Barsabbas," (The two other men raised their eyebrows at this his epithet, Nikolaos did not notice their reaction.) "who was bitterly disappointed not to be chosen. But Simeon bar Jonas is a strong, a driven man. He regards himself as Joshua's beloved disciple, the man who should lead them. It is not only the Greeks and Hebrews who disagree. There are further divisions within each camp. They will either tear themselves apart, or realise the futility of their struggle. You will never again see anything like the Passover uprising. The future is with the Greek Jews."

"And what will they do?" Lucius wanted to know.

"Whatever you may say, they will take the word of the Lord, the spirit of the Lord, Holy Law, to the Gentiles."

Lucius struggled not to appear contemptuous. "But I thought that the whole point was the fight against Rome; the determination to rid your Holy Land of the heathen invader."

"Rome will depart." Nikolaos had all the blind confidence of youth. "Israel will live long after your seven hills have crumbled into dust and your empire has been forgotten. That is the inevitable will of the Lord. We are living in the day of a new age. The light of Israel will blaze through the Gentile world, and all people who live on the earth will learn to sing to the Lord with a joyful voice."

When the young man had left, the two friends poured more wine. "What do you think?" Lucius wanted to know.

314

Mordra frowned. "I think that the last thing that he said was probably true. The zealots here are finished, at least for the present. The Greek Jews are everywhere. They may want to take some spiritual message out to the rest of the world, but the rest of the world will probably interpret it as a political message."

Lucius was troubled. "From what I've seen in the few months that I've been here, I have learned that the Pax Romana is far from benign. From what I have learned from you and Branwen, I know that the Greeks are not the only ones with a civilisation and a culture older, and perhaps more sophisticated, than ours."

Mordra interrupted. "But Rome is the present power in the world."

"But is it a power for good?"

"It makes no difference. Branwen and I know this as well as anyone can know it. Rome rules."

"But not in Prydain."

"No," Mordra said sadly, "not in Prydain, yet."

"If the Greek Jews take their ideas to the rest of the world, what do you think will be the result?"

Mordra knew the answer only too well. "Chaos. At the moment most parts of the Empire are living in peace. If these people stir up the populations, then Rome will do what they did to the Druids in my land, and what they are doing to the Jews here. I have to agree with Nikolaos that the power of Rome will pass away, all empires have their day then die. Where are the Persians, the Greeks, so many others? In their day they were invincible, but the sun set upon them and their day died. But we must think of the present, and of the immediate future."

"Should we go to Aulus?"

"Yes."

The tribune was surprised to receive a message saying that Lucius and Mordra wanted to see him. Lucius was his oldest friend, and Mordra had come to him a number of times, unannounced, with scraps of information since he had taken up his new life. This looked official. Branwen decided that her presence at the meeting would not help – she was only a woman!

Aulus received them in the lower court, the place where

official business was conducted. It was the first time that Lucius had set foot there since the trial of the zealots and it was the first time that the two cousins had met since Lucius's return. "Pilate tells me that congratulations are in order."

"He told you then?"

"I think that he was glad of the opportunity to gloat that you are leaving Judaea."

"Aulus laughed. "I can see that. But I don't suppose that he wanted me to go on promotion."

Wine was poured. Cups were raised and drained. Mordra lounged in his chair as easily as his companions did. Oddly, Aulus had no difficulty in accepting this. Now that the Gaul was no longer his slave, he could almost accept him as an equal. He had always been uncomfortably aware of Mordra's social standing among his own people.

Lucius came to the point of the meeting. "Mordra has told you of his new contact on the zealot brotherhood, a Greek. We spoke to him at some length yesterday, and we think that you will be interested in what he had to say."

"What was that?"

The two scholars started to give a detailed account of what they had learned. Aulus stopped them. "Galba should be here to hear this. He's to take over command of the cohort, with Timocrates as his Primus Pilus." His new orderly was waved forward and sent to summon Aulus's successor. When Galba arrived, Lucius rose and saluted him. "Ave, Tribune. Congratulations!" The old soldier was both embarrassed and delighted. Mordra noted a marked change in the man; he was more relaxed, he had acquired a new confidence.

They resumed their tale. Mordra was at pains to point out that the Jewish authorities were apparently as disturbed as they were by the activities of the followers of Joshua. Aulus already knew this. When Rabbi Gamaliel's name was mentioned, Mordra stressed that he was not a supporter of the zealots. They outlined the growing divisions and manifold splits between the current zealots, and they all saw this as a development that was useful to those who would maintain order, Romans and Jews. Mordra used the example of Nikolaos himself and his fellow-student Saul two Greek Jews from the same city in Cilicia, both students of

316

Gamaliel, yet they held opposing opinions about the followers of Joshua. They related Nikolaos's opinion of the limited future of the zealot brotherhood. The four discussed this at length, and ended by agreeing that Nikolaos's assessment was probably right.

They then went into deep discussion of the role of the Greek Jews, what Nikolaos had said about taking Jewish ideas, and the Jewish god, out into the Greek world – into the Empire. Lucius reminded Aulus, and told the other two, of why the Jews had recently been expelled from Italy, and of the dangers of oriental cults. All four could see that this posed a new threat. Aulus said: "At least there are few Greeks in Pannonia, and I don't think there are any Jews. They're all Celts there; that should be a real challenge." Lucius and Mordra exchanged glances at Aulus's use of this name.

Aulus turned to Galba. "What you do after I've gone is your own affair, but, if it's any use, I'll tell you what I would do."

"I'll be glad of any advice that I can get."

"I think that you can leave Caiaphas and his gang to deal with the Hebrews. We've heard how he drags a few of them out of the temple from time to time, gives them a flogging, then kicks them out. Sooner or later they're going to get tired of that, and give up. There are certainly no signs of them reorganising properly to become any sort of threat to good order. And the more they fall out among themselves, the better. I think we all agree that the Greeks are the problem, or the potential problem, I'd concentrate on them."

Galba slowly nodded his agreement. "We might get the Sanhedrin to help us with them as well."

"How?"

"Well, from what Lucius and Mordra have said," Lucius raised an eyebrow at this new informality. "and I'm certainly prepared to bow to their superior knowledge in these matters, these Greek Jews seem to be saying things that the Sanhedrin are not going to like. How would it be if the Sanhedrin strangled a few of them for so-called blasphemy?"

Aulus threw back his head and laughed aloud. "You're going to be better at this job than I ever was. And I suppose that, given the chance, you'll hand them over to the Sanhedrin, just as the Sanhedrin handed Joshua to us."

"Given the chance, yes," Galba replied. "It's surely better to have Jews kill Jews than to have Romans kill them. That way there's less danger of repercussions."

"With your full co-operation of course."

"Of course." Galba reached for the flagon, poured himself a generous measure, and sat back with a satisfied look on his face.

Aulus's new orderly, a Syrian auxiliary, was hovering uneasily in the background. "Dodi," his master called, "Down to the cellar and get some more wine. Italian wine, none of this Jewish piss." Turning to his companions, he said: "Tomorrow the retiring tribune and the tribune-elect will go to Caiaphas and have a very interesting chat with him. I'm not inviting you two bookworms. Don't think that I don't appreciate what you've done, because I do, but our conversation with the High Priest is going to be at a lower level than your elevated minds would like. Now, let's all get drunk."

The two soldiers walked through the city in undress uniform, dark red tunics and no armour, no swords, just a short dagger worn on the right. Aulus wore his colourful British cloak against the winter chill. Galba was muffled in the old cloak that had served him so many times as a blanket. They were going to visit the High Priest of Israel.

Caiaphas was almost affable in his welcome. "Welcome, Legate."

Aulus's was not really surprised. These Jews had spies everywhere. But there was more to come. "I am sure that the Celtae will benefit from your firm sense of order, I hear that Pannonia is in need of control."

Annas joined in the congratulations. "And we are happy that the new tribune is to be a man who knows Israel. A new broom can often sweep away he grain with the chaff." He very nearly smiled at Galba.

The two Romans glanced at each other, Aulus nodded slightly. So, these men were privy to the internal affairs of the proper authority. they would now demonstrate their knowledge of what the Jews were doing. Galba had already seated himself, Aulus joined him. "I suppose that you know that there is now a Greek party in the zealot brotherhood."

"We do," the High Priest replied, "and we have their names – and provenance."

Galba needed to stamp his new authority. "We will return to these men later, but first, let me say that I think that we can work together more closely. It is now seven, nearly eight months since the Passover disturbance. We need to maintain the Roman Peace. You need to maintain order, and your own authority. I would prefer to avoid any more crucifixions because they could stir up the people – but I will not hesitate to use that sanction if there are any more crimes against Rome. I know that you all believe that the Empire will end some day and that you will have your land back for yourselves. I don't' know about that. All that I know is that I have less than two years to serve before I retire, and I intend to spend that time in a peaceful province – by whatever means."

Annas's eyes narrowed. "Where do the Greeks come into this?"

Aulus answered, indirectly. "I think that the time has come for us to stop playing games. The Empire is here, for ever, but because of your unusual religion, and the fact that you have a law that you attribute to your god, we are of the opinion that there are many aspects of administration that are better left to you – perhaps even more than before."

It was now the turn of the priests to exchange meaningful glances. Aulus saw this, and went on. "I never know which of you is the real High Priest." Caiaphas was about to speak, but Aulus did not allow him to do so. "I've been here for the better part of five years, and I have learned something of your ways in that time. I know that you can have only one High Priest; ever since what-was his name, Aaron? Yet you both bear the title. Now, I know that you, Annas, held the office from the time of Augustus's census, for some ten years; and that the High Priest used to hold office for life, under Jewish convention. I also know that since we took over, it was a Roman procurator who appointed you, Caiaphas, to your office. Just who is the leader of the Jews?"

It was Annas who answered. "Both my son-in-law and I represent Israel, equally. As you have said, it is better to leave the finer points of Jewish Law and practice to us."

319

Caiaphas still wanted to know what the Romans knew about his Greek co-religionists, and their activities in Judaea. "You said that you would return to the topic of our Hellenic brethren."

Galba was now satisfied that it was time to pursue his predetermined agenda. "It is the opinion of Aulus Plautius and me that that the Hebrew followers of Joshua are best left to you. They fall directly under your jurisdiction, and we are confident that you will be able to deal with them. The Greeks are a different matter."

"In what way?" Caiaphas wanted to know.

"Because," said Aulus, "what was the Greek world is now a part, and a major part, of the Empire. We do not want these people to export revolution."

The priests appreciated his directness, Annas said; "So you want us to deal with the Greeks as well?"

Galba had been waiting for this question. "This is where we could best work together, to our mutual advantage."

Annas and Caiaphas remained silent, waiting for him to continue. It was Aulus who took up the theme. "We have been informed that the Hebrew zealots are tearing themselves apart. A man called Jacob is their designated leader, but there seems to be an ignorant Galilean fisherman, Simeon bar Jonas, who covets the leadership. We wiped them out in the spring; and you were kind enough, or sensible enough, to give us the most dangerous man of all of them. Our information is that the Judaean zealots are finished, and we are more than happy to let you get on with dealing what's left of them under your law. Any executions that you sanction, Rome will endorse. It is only with regard to the Greeks that you will need to work together with Tribune Galba, to destroy them before they can spread their poison outside Judaea."

"And how," Annas asked, "are we to do that?"

Galba knew the answer to that question. "As you know, I was not born into the officer class. I started my military career as a simple legionary. Aulus Plautius has said that one of my strengths is that I know the army from the bottom up. I think that we can apply this principle to our current problem with the Greek Jews. We need to have someone who is as committed as you are to mainstream, sensible, Jewish life, but who is at a much lower level than your elevated position, more in daily contact with ordinary Jews."

The priests could see the sense in this. Aulus developed the prearranged argument. "In the school of Rabbi Gamaliel there are two Jews from Cilicia. Nikolaos is one of the seven Greeks on the council of the brotherhood. He is drawn to the followers of Joshua. The other, Saul, abhors the followers of Joshua. Although he is a Pharisee, he seems to be much closer to your sensible Sadducee point of view than are most of those in the Diaspora. I would suggest that you cultivate this Saul, and use him as a tool to deal with the Greeks – who are already starting to spread dissent towards the Decapolis, among the Greek Jews of those ten cities in Syria which are now, of course, Roman."

Caiaphas knew all of the students of Gamaliel. The venerable Rabbi was, all Jews agreed, deserving of the unqualified respect in which he was held. The Sanhedrin, of which he was a member, often feared his ability to go straight to the heart of a question, and his unerring citations of Holy Writ. But Saul of Tarsus? A young man, impressionable, clever, perhaps this young Cilician could be recruited to help to put an end to all the dangerous nonsense that was bedevilling the prospect of a strife-free Israel until the Romans departed. If they had a reliable agent rounding up the troublemakers, then the Sanhedrin would be able to keep their hands clean. "Legate Aulus, Tribune Galba, I look forward to closer co-operation between our two administrations,"

The two soldiers walked back to the Antonia, satisfied with what they felt that they had achieved. "Do you trust him?" Aulus asked.

"No." Galba replied. "He is prepared to talk about what appears to be in our mutual interest, but he's still a Jew, whatever his testimonies may be."

"So, what do you doubt, the number of times that he protests, or the veracity of his testimony?"

"Remember the old proverb, sir: *'Ponderanda sunt testimonia, non numeranda.'*

All testimonies aggregate not by their number, but their weight."

Chapter 26

Nikolaos and Saul followed their academic course in the Bet Knesset of Gamaliel, but they prayed in one of the Greek synagogues of Jerusalem. Both usually attended the Synagogue of the Freedmen, founded by men from Cilicia and Asia who had been enslaved by the Roman General Pompeii, and later freed. Of late, Saul had taken to visiting the Libyan Synagogue, which was frequented by Jews from Alexandria and Cyrene; because it was here that Stefanos had taken to preaching.

It had been with some trepidation that the young student had answered the summons to attend the palace of Caiaphas. Once there, he had been overjoyed to be complimented on his fidelity that he had demonstrated by his opposition to the followers of Joshua. He had said that he would do anything to bring errant souls back to the Lord. Annas and Caiaphas told him exactly what he would do. He was given the authority to spy upon the zealots, and to round them up, and he was told to report regularly to the High Priests. It was then that he had told them that Stefanos had been preaching against the sanctity of the temple, and that he had accused the Hebrews of being intractably evil.

This was what his new employers wanted to hear. If Stefanos were to repeat these sermons before the Sanhedrin, then he would almost certainly be found guilty of the most serious offences. Saul was instructed to listen to all that Stefanos had to say, and to summon the temple guard the next time that he heard blasphemy from his lips.

Now Saul listened with mounting anger, and with mounting satisfaction, to Stefanos's latest diatribe. How could this man, who was known to be a member of the zealot brotherhood, say such things about the Holy Land of Israel? He was saying that this land was not the spiritual centre of Judaism, that the Lord revealed himself in other ways, in other places. Saul slipped out of the synagogue and made his way to the temple. With the approval of most of the congregation, Stefanos was hauled off to answer to the Sanhedrin.

Saul sensed a new importance as he stood before that august body. He looked around the horseshoe of benches. He was conscious that the public benches behind him were full, and men stood in all available spaces. He directly addressed Caiaphas seated on the elevated presidential chair. "I have heard Stefanos speak words of blasphemy against Moses and against the Lord."

"And what were these words?" Caiaphas was grave.

"This fellow never stops speaking against the Holy Temple, and against the Law. For I have heard him say that the risen Joshua of Nazareth will destroy the temple, and change the customs that Moses handed down to us."

The High Priest asked Stefanos: "Are these charges true?"

Stefanos stood, dishevelled but proud before his accuser and his judges. "Brothers and fathers, listen to me! The God of glory appeared to our father Abraham while he was still in Mesopotamia, before he lived in Haran. 'Leave your country and your people,' the Lord said, 'and go to the land I will show you.'

"So he left the Chaldeans and settled in Haran. After the death of his father, the Lord sent him to this land where you are now living. He gave him no inheritance here, not even a foot of ground. But the Lord promised him that he and his descendants after him would possess the land, even though at that time Abraham had no child. The Lord spoke to him in this way: 'Your descendants will be strangers in a country not their own, and they will be enslaved and ill-treated for four hundred years. But I will punish the nation they serve as slaves,' the Lord said, 'and afterwards they will come out of that country and worship me in this place.' Then he gave Abraham the covenant of circumcision. And Abraham became the father of Isaac and circumcised him eight days after his birth. Later Isaac became the father of Jacob and Jacob became the father of the twelve patriarchs"

Annas interrupted him. "We are all of the seed of Abraham. We do not need a history lesson from you."

Stefanos ignored the interruption, and went on. "Because the patriarchs were jealous of Joseph, they sold him as a slave into Egypt. But the Lord was with him and rescued him from all

323

his troubles. He gave Joseph wisdom and enabled him to gain the goodwill of Pharaoh, king of Egypt, so he made him ruler over Egypt and all his palace.

"Then famine struck all Egypt and Canaan, bringing great suffering, and our fathers could not find food. When Jacob heard that there was grain in Egypt, he sent our fathers on their first visit. On their second visit Joseph told his brothers who he was, and Pharaoh learned about Joseph's family. After this, Joseph sent for his father Jacob and his whole family, seventy-five in all. Then Jacob went down to Egypt, and he and our fathers died. Their bodies were brought back to Shechem and placed in the tomb that Abraham had bought from the sons of Hamor at Shechem for a certain sum of money.

"As the time grew near for the Lord to fulfil his promise to Abraham, the number of our people in Egypt greatly increased. Then another king, who knew nothing of Joseph, became ruler of Egypt. He dealt treacherously with our people and oppressed our forefathers by forcing them to throw out their newborn babies so that they would die.

"At the time Moses was born, and he was no ordinary child. For three months he was cared for in his father's house. Then he was placed outside, Pharaoh's daughter took him and brought him up as her own son. Moses was educated in all the wisdom of the Egyptians and was powerful in speech and action.

"When Moses was forty years old, he decided to visit his fellow Israelites. He saw one of them being ill-treated by an Egyptian, so he went to his defence and avenged him by killing the Egyptian. Moses thought that his own people would realise that the Lord was using him to rescue them, but they did not. The next day Moses came upon two Israelites who were fighting. He tried to reconcile them by saying, 'Men, you are brothers; why do you want to hurt each other?'

"But the man who was ill-treating the other pushed Moses aside and said, 'Who made you ruler and judge over us? Do you want to kill me as you killed the Egyptian yesterday?' When Moses heard this, he fled to Midian, where he settled as a foreigner and had two sons."

Caiaphas leaned forward, about to halt of this long, familiar tale. Annas put a hand upon his arm and whispered: "Let him go on. The more he says, the more chance there is that he will condemn himself." Caiaphas sat back.

Stefanos had barely noticed this exchange. "After forty years had passed, an angel appeared to Moses in the flames of a burning bush in the desert near Mount Sinai. When he saw this, he was amazed at the sight. As he went over to look more closely, he heard the Lord's voice, 'I am the God of your fathers, the God of Abraham, Isaac, and Jacob.' Moses trembled with fear and dare not look.

"Then the Lord said to him, 'Take off your sandals; the place where you are standing is holy ground. I have indeed seen the oppression of my people in Egypt. I have heard their groaning and have come down to set them free. Now come, I will send you back to Egypt.'

"This is the same Moses whom they had rejected with the words, 'Who made you ruler and judge?' He was sent to be their ruler and deliverer by the Lord himself, through the angel who appeared to him in the bush. He led them out of Egypt and did wonders and miraculous signs in Egypt, at the Red Sea, and forty years in the desert."

Stefanos paused. Caiaphas shook his head. "Thank you for telling us what we have all known since earliest childhood, that we re-tell every year at Passover."

The Greek glared at the High Priest. "The Lord performed his wonders through Moses in Egypt, at the Red Sea, in the desert, not in the land of Canaan. Moses came face to face with the Lord on holy ground at Mount Sinai, not in the land of Canaan. Abraham came to this land, but he did not even own a foot of ground in the land of Canaan. The covenant is with the people, not with the land. Moses saw this land, but he did not set his foot upon it. The Lord performed his wonders in other lands."

Saul interjected. "The Lord is King of the Universe. He may perform his wonders and his miracles in any land. But this is the land that he gave to us, his chosen people. The Lord gave to Joshua the strength to overcome the armies of the five Canaanite kings. He threw down the walls of Jericho, he gave the land of Canaan to our forefathers. It was towards this land that Moses led the Israelites for forty years in the desert."

Stefanos looked with hatred at the young student. "This is

that Moses who told the Israelites, 'The Lord will send you a prophet like me from your own people.' He was in the assembly in the desert, with the angel who spoke to him on Mount Sinai, and with our fathers; and he received living words to pass on to us.

"But our fathers refused to obey him. Instead, they rejected him and in their hearts turned back to Egypt. They told Aaron, 'Make us gods who will go before us. As for this fellow Moses who led us out of Egypt – we do not know what has happened to him!' That was the time they made an idol in the form of a calf. They brought sacrifices to it and held a celebration in honour of what their hands had made. But the Lord turned away and gave them over to the worship of the heavenly bodies. This agrees with what is written in the book of the prophets:

'Did you bring me sacrifices and offerings
for forty years in the desert, O house of Israel?
You have lifted up the shrine of Molech
and the star of your god Rephan,
and the idols you made to worship.
Therefore I will send you into exile beyond Babylon.'"

"Yes, yes," Caiaphas was growing weary of this. "We are all familiar with the words of the prophet Amos. And you've skipped ahead. Amos was four or five hundred years after Moses. You will find that the members of this court know more than you do about the works of the twenty or so prophets who have come since Moses."

"And what have they achieved?" demanded Stefanos. "The Lord has sent his prophets, he had given us his Holy Law, but still Israel is in sin. You, the priests and the judges of Israel, delivered his greatest prophet, Joshua of Nazareth, into the hands of our enemies to be crucified."

One of the judges rose to his feet. "He defiled the temple with his claim of kingship."

"The temple is a sink of iniquity. The Temple is defiled – by you!" Stefanos roared. Our forefathers had the tabernacle of the testimony with them in the desert. It had been made as the Lord directed Moses, according to the pattern he had seen. Having received the tabernacle, our fathers under Joshua brought it with them when they took this land from the nations the Lord drove out before them. It remained in the land until the time of David, who enjoyed the Lord's favour and asked that he might provide a dwelling place for the God of Jacob. But it was Solomon who built the house for him.

"However, the Most High does not live in houses made by men. As Isaiah says:

> "'Heaven is my throne,
> and the earth is my footstool,
> what kind of house will you build for me?
> Or where will my resting place be?
> Has not my hand made all these things?" says the Lord.'"

There was uproar in the court at these words. Stefanos shrieked above the tumult: "You stiff-necked people, with uncircumcised hearts and ears! You are just like your fathers: you always resist the Holy Spirit! Was there ever a prophet your fathers did not persecute? They even killed those who predicted the coming of the Righteous One. And now you have betrayed and murdered him – you who have received the Law that was put into effect through angels but have not obeyed it."

The crowd at the rear of the hall began to surge forward. The guard quickly formed a cordon to hold them back and to keep them from this blasphemous Greek. Caiaphas stood and raised his voice above the din of the screaming mob. "Get him to the prison!"

As Stefanos was hustled from the court, the men in the crowd gnashed their teeth in the traditional sign of the hostility of the righteous for the wicked.

Closely guarded, and with a howling mob close behind, Stefanos was hurried down the thoroughfare that led to the western aspect of the temple. He was to be imprisoned in the secure rooms of the pinnacle that had accommodated so many of his comrades.

Back in the Court of the Sanhedrin, the judges had no doubt. The man was clearly guilty of blasphemy, having insulted the Lord by all that he had done through Moses, and through

Joshua, his General and conqueror of Canaan. He had denigrated the Lord's gift of Eretz Israel to his chosen people, his sacred house here in David's Holy City. He had exalted the prophets, who were only men, over Torah that came directly from the Lord. He must die by strangulation. All that the court required was the approval of the Roman authorities to carry out the sentence of death. It was a formality. Aulus and Galba had already given verbal sanction, but the correct procedure must be followed.

As Stefanos and his guard walked under the towering western wall of Herod's Temple, some one lifted a stone from the stack that the builders had left there for the work that was being carried out to construct a new court for the Sanhedrin. Stefanos seemed to sense what was happening, he tried to dodge but was too firmly held. He managed to turn his head and the heavy stone smashed his left shoulder and drove him to the ground. The guard stood back. The mob grabbed the injured man and dragged him round the corner of the Temple, and along outside the southern wall to a small gate that led out of the Holy City, tugging off his outer garments as they did so. He was hurled into a pit, with a cracking of bones. As the stones pelted down upon him, he tried, several times to rise and to escape the pit. Then he raised his voice for the last time: "Shema Yisroel, Adonai Elohenu, Adonai Ehad!" Then he was silent. His body twitched and then was still as more stones rained down to cover him.

The young man Saul of Tarsus stood at the lip of the pit and looked down with satisfaction.

The noise of the mob had been heard in the Antonia. At a leisurely pace, Galba arrived at the scene of death with a decade of legionaries. "What's going on?" he wanted to know.

"We have stoned a blasphemer." The mob was elated.

Galba glanced down into the pit. "I didn't give my permission. But never mind, it's done now. I hope you're not going to leave him there, he'll be stinking by tomorrow. Get him out and get him buried."

Chapter 27

When Galba returned to the Antonia he told the three soldiers who were waiting for him about the stoning. Timocrates said: "Is that the man they were trying before the Sanhedrin? They didn't waste much time."

Galba chuckled. "The mob beat them to it. Before the judges could get my official approval to strangle him, the mob took over and pelted him with stones."

There was a satisfied look on Aulus's face. "It looks like your plan is working; they're killing each other."

The fourth member of the quartet was Cornelius, a centurion who had been sent from Caesarea with Aulus's orders to report to Rome before going on to his new appointment in Pannonia and to escort him back to the seaport for his departure. Aulus was beginning to relish his new status, a centurion to escort a legate!

They had been discussing the zealots at some length, and Cornelius had expressed his envy. "There aren't any in Caesarea, of course. I think you're lucky to be here in Jerusalem among the lot of them." Galba had made a mental note, a man who wanted to come to grips with the terrorists could be very useful. Unfortunately he had already promoted a decurion to the vacant post, and did not yet have a place for another centurion. Cornelius went on. "I regard myself as a religious man. I give my allegiance to Mithras and I can't see that I will ever swerve from that path. But, you were telling me that those friends of yours have learned that some of the natives are talking about taking their religion to people who aren't Jews."

"Not the natives," Aulus said, "but some of the Greek Jews."

Cornelius smiled. "It would be a bit of a joke if one of us volunteered to join them. Do you think he'd be accepted?"

"It's a thought," Galba replied, "but you should talk to

Lucius and Mordra about it. If a Roman joined them it could be very useful indeed, if it could be done."

Cornelius began to back off. "I wasn't thinking about actually joining, not for real. But if one of us approached them, if nothing else, it might throw them off balance."

"How would you do it?" Timocrates wanted to know.

"Well, I'd have to know a bit more about them first, talk to your friends. I think that I'd be thinking Mithras but talking Jewish god, that would make it more convincing. I'd go to them, tell them that I'd 'seen the light', and ask to be told more about their 'one true god'."

"It could be useful," Galba said, "You being based in Caesarea would make it easier, they know my men too well. But I'm not sure that it could be done. I don't think that even these people are that stupid."

Thoughtfully, Cornelius sipped his wine.

I was the darkest time of the year, the winter solstice. This had once been the tenth month of the Roman calendar, but since the calendar had been revised in the time of Julius Caesar, it was now near the end of the twelfth month.

The Jews had already celebrated the dedication of the temple, and the zealots among them had lit the eight lamps in remembrance of Judah Maccabeus

From the 17th to the 24th of the month the Romans had been celebrating the Saturnalia, a time of revelry when, even in the army, all manner of licence was permitted. Everyone had enjoyed the Brumilia on the 25th of the month, when there were parties and the exchange of gifts.

On that same day, the soldier followers of Mithras celebrated the birth of their god by lighting their temples, where white-robed priests officiated at the altars where boys burned sweet incense.

And on that day, those Egyptians who still followed their ancient gods celebrated the birth of Horus, who was, they said, born of a virgin as the saviour of mankind. In their temples they built a model crib in which a figure of the infant Horus lay, with a statue of his virgin mother Isis at his side. A palm tree was cut and decorated, a young tree to symbolise the new born sun. It was the one time of the year when Egyptians ate the flesh of the goose, symbol of the earth god Seb, because if the god Osiris, husband of Isis, were offended, he could only be placated by the gifts of a large goose and a thin cake.

Paulina had eagerly anticipated the *Natalis Solis Invicta,* the Birthday of the Unconquered Sun, on the 25th, when she showered her beloved Marcus with gifts. She too had caused a young tree, a pine, to be set up and decorated with candles to encourage the sun in its weakest hours with their heat and light.

Branwen had been happy to add evergreen plants, Silurian symbols of immortality. At home she would have used the mistletoe, ivy, and holly. The mistletoe never touched the ground when growing, and its name meant 'all-heal' because of its medicinal powers.

Mordra, the atheist, was tolerantly amused by all this religious nonsense. He had always enjoyed the joyous celebrations that marked the mid-point of the winter season of Samhain. He recalled the time that he had spent among the savages of Germania where the natives believed that their god Wotan would drive his chariot through the sky from the frozen north, with gifts for all who honour him at what they called Yuletide.

Aulus had been invited, and was looking forward to, the *cena,* the dinner on the day after Brumilia. He wanted to spend some time with Lucius before he departed; but he was uneasy about visiting him in his new house. Four years of Branwen's indifferent cooking had been more than enough. It proved to be an evening full of surprises. He liked the look of Paulina; she was undoubtedly beautiful, she seemed to be docile enough, and she had already produced a son. The perfect Roman wife. Having seen Mordra many times over the past few months, he had become accustomed to seeing his ex-slave turning back into the Gaul he once had been – and more, a mature, confident man, so far removed from the twenty-year-old he had met in Lutetia more than ten eventful years ago. The first surprise was the elegant lady at Mordra's side. A long dress of brightest blue adorned and accentuated her slender figure. Her long neck supported a proud head with perfectly proportioned features and crowned by a sophisticated coiffure. But most of all, it was her bearing, she comported herself like a princess. Where had Mordra found this woman? Then, with a shock, he recognised Branwen as she extended a long-fingered hand to him in greeting. For more than four years he had never really looked at her.

"You are welcome, Aulus Plautius," she said, the gracious hostess. "I know that it is a little belated, but I would like to congratulate you upon your promotion."

The next surprise was the sumptuous meal laid out before him. He recognised many of the dishes from his time in Gaul; where had they found the ingredients? He turned to his hostess. "I must compliment your cook. This is really excellent; I haven't tasted anything as good since I left Lutetia."

Mordra smiled. "Rachel, one of our servants, is competent enough, although with Jewish food. She's a good assistant, but Branwen is mistress of the kitchen."

"Aulus frowned. "Then why did I never eat like this when she was mistress of my kitchen?"

"Because," Branwen smiled openly at him, "you were not my guest, and I was only your slave."

Aulus, his mouth full, almost choked upon his laughter. "So, for more than four years you deliberately fed me slops because you were my slave? How did you two eat?"

"Very well," said Mordra.

Paulina was the only one at the table who could not see the humour in this.

When the cena was over, Paulina, the good Roman wife, rose and departed to her room and to Marcus. Aulus expected Branwen to go. Women did not sit at table after dinner, when the men usually drank too much and sank into ribald stories. Instead, Branwen brought fresh cups and rough spirit, and then she resumed her seat.

At a loss for what to say in the presence of a woman, Aulus could only think to tell of the stoning to death of the Greek that had occurred that morning. "So," Branwen said, "the Jews can be as heavy handed as the Romans in dispensing their brand of justice."

Aulus looked at her in amazement. Mordra stepped in. "You will remember, Aulus, that even in Romanized Gaul the role of women is very different to what you are used to. Branwen is a lawyer, had she been able to complete her education she would have been a judge."

The Roman sat back, still trying to come to terms with this. "Then tell me, lawyer, how would you deal with these things in your country?"

Branwen took a sip of spirit, rolling it around her mouth before she answered. She set the cup upon the table and looked directly at the Roman soldier. "You need to understand that our attitude towards offenders is very different to yours. You believe in punishment, we believe in prevention. Once a crime has been committed, punishment cannot undo that crime; it is no more than revenge upon the offender."

"But if the 'revenge' is death, that person cannot offend again."

"That person, no, but others can. Especially if you are dealing with political offenders, then you may well be creating martyrs as rallying points. You kill people so often, yet others continue to commit the very same crimes and so you kill them, and on it goes without end and without improving the situation. And a person risking a sentence of death is more likely to be protected by his comrades and friends, so you never catch them. Of all those you crucified earlier this year, you only executed one of the top leadership of the zealots, only one member of the brotherhood, Joshua; after eight months the rest are still at large, presumably well protected."

"Don't tell me that you never execute people under your laws, because I know that you do."

"Yes we do," Branwen replied, "but our whole ethos is different to yours. We usually reunite them with their heads after death so that they can enter the Otherworld. It is only the most desperate criminals whose heads are thrown into the waters so that their cycle of life is forever ended. We have a principle that we call *chwarae teg,* fair play. Let me illustrate it for you. A flock of sheep strayed into another man's garden and ate his crop of woad. The man who had lost the crop demanded that the sheep be slaughtered and that he should have the carcasses as recompense for his loss. The judge ruled that the sheep be shorn, and that the injured man should have the wool. The following year the sheep would regrow their wool, and the woad would grow again in the man's garden. That is chwarae teg."

Aulus remained silent. Branwen smiled at him. "We should think carefully before we slaughter a sheep because, living, it can provide us with wool and with milk for many seasons. A living cow or a goat will produce milk time after time. But if slaughtered, you can only eat it once. When you nail a man to a cross, do you really know what you have killed, what you may have destroyed – out of your revenge? And do you ever think that such a man may been seen as a martyr. Do you ever wonder what you may have created out of his destruction?"

Although Lucius was enjoying his friend's discomfiture, he thought it only fair (chwarae teg) to rescue him from what he knew must be a most disconcerting discussion. "When do you leave us, Aulus?"

"Tomorrow. Marius has a nice sense of what is proper. He's sent a centurion to escort me to Caesarea. Then I take ship for Ostia, on to Rome, then to Pannonia."

"It's a wonderful opportunity for you. A whole province to sort out."

"Yes, I'm looking forward to it. The only problem is that I could do with a Gaul to help me with the natives, but I haven't got one any more."

Mordra put a hand on the shoulder of his one-time master. "I don't know of any, Aulus, at least no nearer than Gaul itself. I'm sure that you'll find someone in Pannonia to help you out. It's only a pity that you never learned our language properly. But you still have time to pick it up."

Aulus gritted his teeth. He had been addressed informally, and clapped on the shoulder by a man who had been his slave and effectively dismissed by that man. He turned to Lucius. "I wonder if you'd consider two, or perhaps three amphorae of wine – Italian of course?"

"Nothing to do with me," Lucius told him, "but I don't think that you could persuade a free man to sell himself so cheap."

Aulus wrapped his coloured cloak close around him as he walked across the city, back to the Antonia. Damn the British! Their woollen clothing was the best in the world – 'a living sheep will produce wool season after season.' But the zealots weren't producing wool, they were producing revolt against the laws of Rome, and slaughter was the only answer. His face felt raw as a

334

few flakes of snow fell from the cold night sky. The year had less than a week to run. In six days it would be the month dedicated to the god Janus, the month and the year in which he would become commander of the Ninth Legion and governor of Pannonia. When he had finished with the Celtae there, he wanted nothing more than to take his legion, and other legions, to the Isle of Britain where he would show that disturbing woman, and all her people, how Roman law worked.

Back in the Antonia, among his own kind, his black mood soon began to lighten as he passed the rest of the night in wine, and soldiers' tales, and happy reminiscences with Tribune Galba, Primus Pilus Timocrates, and Centurion Cornelius.

The following morning, having partaken of the juice of the willow bark, and orange juice and honey, the two soldiers rode out of the Jaffa Gate. That night, Aulus refused to find a caravanserai. He preferred to sleep on the frost-hard ground, beneath the stars, wrapped in his British cloak. Gazing up at the eastern sky, he looked at the constellation of Orion, the hunter, and at the three stars in his belt, known to some as the 'three kings'. Directly below Orion, and a little to the left, the brilliant dog star Sirius dominated the winter skies.

Galba had the greatest respect for Aulus, but he was of the opinion that his late commander's patrician background was something of a handicap, it limited his outlook and did not allow him to talk easily with all classes of people. One of Tribune Galba's first actions was to have a long talk with Lucius and Mordra, and, oddly, with Mordra's woman who he found to be a person full of surprises. What had happened to the sullen slave girl who he could easily ignore? He needed, first hand, their knowledge of the Jews. He needed to establish a new relationship with these people, one that would be useful to him. He then went to Caiaphas and Annas. His first meeting with the High Priests was somewhat marred by the presence of the young man Saul. He did not know why, but Galba took an instant dislike to this Cilician. The priests were full of the young student's praises, and Galba already knew that he could be useful, but he would prefer not to liaise with him directly. He was setting up his own web for the control of the population of

335

Jerusalem and surrounding area, for the destruction of what was left of the terrorists, and the prevention of the export of revolution outside Judaea.

Together, Galba and his contacts were successful. As far as they were aware, the followers of Joshua were melting away from the city, and there was no more trouble there. But there were things that none of them knew. Jacob, the leader of the twelve, had decided to stay in the Holy City; and so Simeon bar Jonas had elected to remain there too. The rest, and they now numbered several hundred, had taken themselves off to other parts of Judaea, and to the Galilee, Samaria, and to the cities of the Decapolis. They were no longer contained within the narrow confines of Jerusalem, but were running wild throughout the land.

Saul believed that those who had fled were no more than tattered remnants, but they had to rounded up. He went to Caiaphas, asked for and was given letters of authority that would enable him to pursue the blasphemers wherever they had gone.

Chapter 28

When Nikolaos next came to the house he was visibly distressed. They sat him down and gave him wine (he did not even think to produce his own cup), and asked him what was troubling him. "Philippos has done a terrible thing."

"Which Philippos is that?" Mordra wanted to know. "I know of two. One is a member of the twelve, the other is one of the seven; and no doubt there are lots more."

"The Greek, not the Hebrew." Nikolaos replied, "the one who sat with me among the seven."

"What has he done?"

Nikolaos began to relate that this Philippos was going down to Gaza. He had covered about half of the distance, and was approaching Betogabri when he saw a magnificent carriage and escort halted upon the road. As he drew near he could hear someone reading inside the carriage.

Mordra and Lucius were aware that it was the Jewish way to read aloud.

Philippos had immediately recognised the words that were being read, it was from Didymos Judah's record of the sayings of Joshua. Philippos went up to the carriage and knocked on the wood. An embroidered curtain was drawn back and a fat man, richly dressed, looked out. "Do you understand what you are reading?" Philippos asked.

"How can I," he said, "unless someone explains it to me?" So, he invited Philippos to come up and sit with him as they journeyed to the south. The man was a most important official, the Treasurer of the Candace.

Branwen interrupted to ask whom the Candace was.

Nikolaos explained that it was one of the many titles of the Queen of Ethiopia. Then he went on to relate how Philippos, according to his own account, had told the Ethiopian the good news that Joshua had risen from the dead and would lead his people to the Kingdom of the Lord. The man pointed to a passage: 'If the flesh has come into existence because of the spirit, it is a marvel, but if the spirit has come into existence because of the body, it is a marvel of marvels.'

"I do not understand this passage. I do not understand what marvels this Joshua has brought about."

Philippos said: "This is what Isaiah son of Amoz saw concerning Judaea, and Jerusalem, and Joshua:

'In the last days
the mountain of the Lord's Temple will be established
as chief among mountains;
it will be raised above the hills,
and all nations will stream to it.'"

The man still could not understand. Philippos told him: "This same Isaiah said:

'He was led like a sheep to the slaughter,
and as a lamb before the shearer is silent,
so he did not open his mouth.
In his humiliation he was deprived of justice.
Who can speak for his descendants?
For his life was taken from the earth.'"

The man said: "Tell me, please, who was the prophet talking about, himself or someone else?"

Mordra knew that Isaiah had lived a long time ago. The Book of Isaiah was obviously written by several men because it covered a period of some two and a half centuries, ending more than five hundred years ago. He could not, as some of the zealots seemed to be claiming, have been talking about a man who had only died in the last few months. He kept this knowledge to himself.

Nikolaos went on to tell how Philippos had reported that he had continued to tell of Joshua, and of his followers, as they had travelled the desert road. When they arrived in Betogabri it was almost the time for evening prayer and Philippos went straight to

338

the Bet Knesset, the man followed him. Philippos had entered the mikveh for his purification, and the man had been behind him.

Nikolaos was choked with emotion. He could not go on. Branwen poured more wine and the young man gulped it down. He looked at the other three. "The mikveh will have to be dismantled, it has been profaned beyond all hope. I don't know what will become of the synagogue itself."

He hosts could not understand why these extreme measures might be considered necessary. Mordra had visited Bets Knesset and synagogues many times, although he had more sense than to try to bathe in a mikveh. "I know that it is wrong for a Gentile to enter a mikveh, but surely you have your purification rituals. And why should the Bet Knesset be threatened?"

Nikolaos wondered if he had been wasting his time in explaining all of this. "As I told you, the man was not only a Gentile, he was a high official in the court of the Queen of Ethiopia."

Lucius's eyes widened. "You mean...?"

"Yes, Marcus Lucius. The man was a eunuch! He has bathed his mangled flesh in the purifying water of a holy mikveh. It is written in the twenty-third chapter of the Book of Deuteronomy: 'No-one who has been emasculated by crushing or cutting may enter the Assembly of the Lord.'"

Mordra was familiar with this passage, and he had never been able to reconcile it with the fact that all Jews were circumcised. Although that rite could not be compared with castration, it was still an alteration of what was natural. "Didn't Isaiah have something to say about eunuchs, something a little more charitable?"

"He did, Mordra, in the fifty-sixth chapter he says: 'Let no foreigner who has bound himself to the Lord say: "The Lord will surely exclude me from his people." And let not the eunuch complain: "I am only a dry tree." For this is what the Lord says: "To the eunuchs who keep my Sabbaths, who choose what pleases me and hold fast to my covenant – to them I will give within my temple and its walls a memorial and a name better than sons or daughters. I will give them an everlasting name that will not be cut off."

Lucius and Mordra exchanged amused glances at this

reference to being cut off.

Branwen rose and silently left the room.

Nikolaos continued. "I know that a eunuch is not responsible for his fate; he was cut before he was old enough to have a say. I accept that there can be righteous eunuchs, most righteous, and selfless, if they follow the ways of the Lord because they know that they can never approach the Lord. Isaiah says that their names may be commemorated; he does not say that they can enter the temple. They cannot see their names even in the Court of the Gentiles."

Lucius still thought that it was a lot of fuss about nothing. "I can see that this Philippos has offended against your religion; but surely your brotherhood can deal with him."

"No, Marcus Lucius. The brotherhood is horrified that a eunuch has entered a mikveh, but there are those, among my own party, who have no objection to a Gentile purifying himself in that way as a means of demonstrating that he has accepted the Way of the Lord and of Joshua."

"I can see why some Greek Jews are saying that, they are influenced by Hellenism." Lucius said. "It's a variation on the Greek custom of *baptein,* dipping in water, such as they practise as part of their Orphic and Eleusinian mysteries. Other peoples have dipped initiates into the Nile, or the Euphrates. The followers of Mithras are immersed into a bath of bulls' blood."

"They are not Jews." Nikolaos was surly.

"But surely," said Mordra, "if you want to bring Gentiles to your god and to your laws, then you must grant them access to your holy places."

Nikolaos felt that he had reached the end of a long and difficult road. "I wanted to take *knowledge* of the Lord and of Holy Law out to the Gentiles, not to make them into Jews. Only a Jew can live the life of a Jew. Only a Jew can approach the Sanctuary of the Lord in his sacred temple. Only a Jew can be one of the ten, the *minyan,* needed for communal prayer in a synagogue.

"I have been wrong. Saul is right. Joshua was a great man, a great prophet, but Joshua is dead. Those who claim to be following Joshua are now taking the wrong road. I will go from here and tell the brotherhood that I am going home to Tarsus, far away from the upheavals of this land, and there I will live my life as a Jew."

Without another word, he rose and left the house. Lucius poured two more cups of wine. "I think that he is unwise to take his resignation to the brotherhood. He'd be better off just getting out of Judaea."

Mordra agreed. "He could be the next one to be stoned."

Lucius rose, and stretched. "Roll on spring. This country's getting too much for me. I'm all for debate, I think the three of us thrive on it, but I've had enough of Jewish debate – it never gets anywhere. And the way the zealots conduct themselves can only have one end. You know," he laughed, "the problem is that they take religion far too seriously. I tend to agree with the philosopher who said: 'I find it difficult to be dogmatic about the existence of gods, partly because of the obscurity of the subject matter, and partly because of the brevity of human life.'"

Mordra smiled. "It isn't only on Rhodos that they read Protagaros. I've always agreed with his view that man is the measure of all things. I don't share Branwen's belief in the gods."

Mention of his wife's name gave Mordra the reason to excuse himself from Lucius's presence. He wondered why she had left so suddenly. He found her sitting on the roof of the house, looking west towards the dying sun, her hands in her lap, a look of infinite sadness upon her lovely face. She looked up as her husband approached, and attempted a small smile. "I suppose you're wondering why I left so abruptly."

"Yes."

"I care nothing for the laws of these people, and who can and cannot do this or that, go here or there." She spoke with a quiet savagery. "I certainly care nothing about the fate of a eunuch." She suddenly burst into a fit of wracking sobs. The tears flooded from her eyes. Mordra put his arms around her and held her close.

For a long time she clung to the strong man. When it seemed that she could have no more tears to shed, she looked up into the loving, concerned, eyes that gazed down on her. "Do you remember when Aulus Plautius bought me from that brute in Massilia?"

"I should do, it took me all day to persuade him."

"Why did you do it?"

Mordra smiled. "At the time I thought that it was only because your were Prydeinig, and because you were being brutalised by that animal, I wanted to rescue you. But I soon realised that there was another, much deeper, reason. I have loved you from the first moment that I saw you."

"I know you have. I've never known how you could. You knew how I was living, you soon learned what had happened to me, and how I had rid my body of the filth that the Roman had put there. I couldn't even bring you my virginity. You knew that I was the whore of a dirty legionary."

"No!" Mordra was angry. "You were not a whore, you never could be; it was not your choice. You were a victim, the innocent victim of a foul regime and its army."

Branwen was silent for several minutes, then, in a low voice she said: "I killed him."

"I know. When you said that you had to go back to his lodgings for your possessions, I knew what you were going to do. I wanted to come with you and do it for you but I knew that, as a Silurian, it was for you and you alone to avenge the great wrong. I did have confidence in a Silurian over a Roman. And, anyway, you had few enough possessions."

"I took his head."

"I would expect you to. Do you want to tell me the rest?"

"How do you know that there's more?"

"I know you."

"When I got back he was drunk, as usual. He had Aulus's money. He tried to take me one last time, ripping my clothing away, I fought him. He turned his back upon me to find a rod to beat me." She gave a sad smile. "That's where he made his mistake. I have found before that being left-handed can have its advantages; it can confuse an opponent. They are not sure where the blow is coming from. I picked up his sword and, as he was turning back towards me, I swung at his neck. His head was half-severed by that one stroke. I hacked it off. I kicked it across the room."

Mordra remained silent. Branwen took a deep breath. "With his own dagger I cut his genitals away."

342

Now Mordra could see why she had reacted so to mention of a eunuch.

"It was the weapon with which he had abused me so many times. I stuffed it in his mouth. If his head had still been attached to his body it would have choked him. I wanted him to choke until I had rid the world of him for ever. I dragged his body out and rolled it into a stinking ditch. I took his head to the river and gave it to the goddess. Then I bathed in the river, washing the last of him away from me. I returned to the room, dressed, and came to meet you."

Her husband held her very close. "You were right; he had no place on earth, or in the Otherworld."

She pulled away. "Was it justice, or revenge?"

"Justice."

"Did I have the right to make the judgement?"

Mordra thought for a while. "What would you have done if another woman, a Silurian woman, had come to you with the story that was yours? What would your judgement be if it had all happened to someone else, a complete stranger, exactly as it happened to you?"

She shook her head.

"It *did* happen to me, and so I cannot make a rational judgement in the case of your hypothetical woman."

"I'm sorry," Mordra said, "but I must present you with another hypothesis. I never want you to see a crucifixion. You can imagine, from what you've heard, that it is the worst death that I have ever seen. It is far worse than your worst imaginings can envision. The first three to be crucified in the present troubles were men who were fighting to rid their land of Rome, as my grandfather had fought for Gaul. Since then, Aulus has crucified many more, including old women, young girls – after being ravaged by his soldiers, children, household servants whose only crime was to be employed by the wrong people. How do you judge the men who did these deeds?"

Branwen thought for a long time. "Their deeds were foul, but they were done in accordance with their law. They need not have gone so far, killed so many. The soldiers who carried out the executions were ordered to do so. They are of a disciplined force and had they refused those orders they would have died.

343

Even Aulus Plautius and Pontius Pilate, being members of an hierarchical system, were only obeying orders."

"So what would your judgement be?"

"I think that I would behead Aulus and Pilate for an excess of killing and, under our laws, for unfair killing. Many of those who died were patently not guilty of anything. But I'd re-unite them with their heads in death and hope that they would learn some humanity in the Otherworld."

"And the soldiers who hammered in the nails?"

"I would do nothing to them."

Tenderly, Mordra kissed his wife. "The soldiers who raped you in Gaul, the legionary who claimed you, they were not obeying orders. They did what they did out of their animal lust, and out of their disregard for a fellow human being. They were not fit to live. They had no right to enter Afallon. They must not be allowed to return to this life."

The sun had long descended below the horizon. Branwen looked up at the brilliant stars in the clear sky.

Her heart swelling in her breast, she turned to Mordra. "It is a new day!"

Chapter 29

It was fine for soldiers such as Aulus to risk the perils of the winter sea, but the four in what Lucius still referred to as the 'British Academy' had decided to delay their departure until the spring. Lucius had worried on the journey to Judaea about Paulina's seasickness, and he wanted the smoothest possible passage home. They were to go first to Samnium, then on to Gaul and Lutetia where Mordra could be re-united with his family and introduce his wife to them. It would probably be another spring before they would journey across the narrow sea to Ynys Prydain, and to Siluria.

The two men spent their time following and recording the break-up of the followers of Joshua. They had come to agree with Nikolaos's assessment that the brotherhood was finished. They knew that Jacob and Simeon, remained in Jerusalem. Galba knew it too, but they all knew that the threat was over. The Hebrews had divided into two camps, each following one of the two one-time disciples. Both men craved the leadership but, as time went on there were fewer and fewer to lead. The tribune was satisfied that his idea of letting them pull themselves apart was working. In his occasional discussions with the High Priests, Galba had less and less to report; and although the Sanhedrin continued to watch, to warn, and to flog a few, it was all dying down and soon no one would even remember Joshua of Nazareth.

There were still pockets of trouble elsewhere. Galba had struck up a friendship with the Centurion Cornelius. From time to time his duties took him to Caesarea where he was given the bigger picture throughout the province, and in the Galilee where Herod Antipas had chopped a few more heads off. Marius enjoyed Galba's visits to the provincial capital, and his own visits to Jerusalem. The two officers had much in common; not only had they both risen from the ranks, but they shared a sense of humour. Marius would sometimes read aloud extracts from his wife's letters, and Galba took to joining in the compilation of riddles.

Nikolaos had remained in Judaea, at some personal risk. Mordra and Lucius were of the opinion that he was a young man in search of a cause because, having abandoned the brotherhood, he had now allied himself to his countryman Saul. Together, with a detachment of the temple guard, they had rampaged around Samaria, gone south to Joppa, and on to Gaza – a perennially troublesome place ever since the heyday of the Philistines and the exploits of Samson whose deeds were recorded in the Book of Judges.

Wherever the two went they sought out the followers of Joshua, mainly Greeks, and had them arrested and flogged.

Branwen joined the other two scholars whenever she could. She was concentrating on Lucius's language lessons and expressed herself well satisfied with his progress. He could now converse with confidence in the British tongue. None of them could use Branwen's language in the presence of Paulina, and they saw this as something of a handicap. Branwen made a real effort to make a friend of Lucius's wife, but it could not be done. The Silurian could accept Paulina's haughtiness, her snobbery, her limited range of interests – these were not her fault, she was a product of her upbringing. But how could Lucius have married anyone so stupid? Not only did Paulina not know anything, she did not want to know. She could read, just, but never picked up a book. She could write, badly, but only ever picked up a wax tablet to leave simple instructions for Scylla, instructions that the efficient governess did not need.

It was only in Marcus that the two women could find a common interest. The sturdy boy was now running around and set upon exploring his surroundings, much to Paulina's dismay. She was terrified that he would fall down stairs, into fires, down wells, be abducted by zealots even. "She probably worries that he'll be eaten by lions as well." Branwen had said to Mordra one night as they lay in bed and Mordra was trying to sleep. "Why can't she let the boy enjoy himself and learn about the world he lives in? You'll never guess what happened today."

"What?" her husband yawned.

"He wanted me to tell him a story, you know what children are like. Well, I was telling him a tale that my mother used to tell to me…"

"Don't tell me," said Mordra, "she didn't want him to hear Silurian tales."

"No, no. It wasn't that. I doubt that she realised that it wasn't a Roman tale. No, Marcus was trying to say the names of some of the characters, simple names like Math and Bran. So, I had what I thought was a bright idea. I picked up a tablet and wrote the names down, in the Greek alphabet of course. Well, Paulina snatched the tablet away from me; she said that it would be soon enough for him to learn that nonsense when he had to go to school. Nonsense!"

Don't forget," Mordra mumbled sleepily, "that she has to put up with a scholar husband. She's not like you." He turned over, breathed deeply, and slept.

For the thousandth time, and more, Branwen knew how fortunate she was in being married to a man with whom she could share much more than just a bed. She turned towards him. Gently she tweaked his moustache. Mordra twitched, growled, and started to snore.

For herself, Branwen was not sorry that Paulina was finding all kinds of excuses not to accompany them to Gaul and Siluria. She would miss Marcus, but definitely not his mother. She felt sorry for Lucius. He would miss his wife and child, and would be forced to return periodically to Samnium, so interrupting his studies. At first she had only wanted to use Lucius as a means of getting back to her home. Now she was looking forward to introducing him to her people, showing him the wonders of Nudd.

One evening, at dinner, they had been discussing the best route from Gaul to Siluria. They had decided that they would sail down the River Sequana from Lutetia, and then across to the land of the Cantiaci. From there they would take ship, or a series of ships, along the south coast of Prydain and either cut across the land of the Durotriges and then take a ferry across the channel to Siluria, or sail around the peninsula of Cernyw, the land of the Dumnonii. Paulina was soon bored with this, and left them.

Mordra asked his wife when they would first see her land if they went that way. She recalled voyages that she had taken on ships bearing ironware. A faraway look came into her eyes. "We will cross the channel at its widest point, near the mouth, and first see Dyfed, the land of the Demetae. The hills will appear out of the sea mist, and we will pass high cliffs with the wild waters breaking at their foot. Then there is a massive bay, many miles in length; there are miles and miles of golden sands, then the estuary of three rivers. Oh, Lucius, wait till you see our rivers! Then a great spit of rock juts out into the sea. They say that it is a dragon that was overcome by the gods and turned to stone. This is the beginning of the peninsula of Gwyr, it is Siluria. Next there is another broad bay with two rivers flowing into it. The second of these rivers is named for the father god Nudd. As we turn up this river, we will see the first of our forts, a powerful structure guarding the river crossing and the port. As we sail into the port we will be able to see straight up the valley to the dark mountains so far beyond. To the right we will see the smoke of the furnaces, making the iron upon which we depend. To the left will be the lighter smoke of the largest of our hundred settlements – the Cantref of Nudd." Her eyes were shining with the vision, and with the tears of hiraeth. "When you see it, Lucius, you will know why we are the people of our land, and why our land is us – we are the Cymreig!"

Mordra was caught up in his wife's talk of her land.

"Remember the old saying, 'As the light lengthens, so the cold strengthens'?"

His wife smiled at him, he took her hand. "Imbolc is the most wonderful season of all."

He turned to Lucius. "In temperate Europe we have more of a sense of the turning year. At first the stark coldness seems winter-locked until we see the emerging tips of snowdrops to herald the return of the sun. As the lengthening shafts of sunlight pierce the earth, all growing things put forth shoots, buds begin to open, and flowers bloom. In the season of Imbolc, the sprouting season of new growth, we will finally emerge from our long exile, and move towards fresh hope." He gently stoked his wife's face. "In Imbolc we will leave this land for ever."

Now the time was upon them. Passover was approaching. It was the mid-point of the season of Imbolc, the mid-point between the sun's least and strongest appearance. It was the day to leave Jerusalem.

When Lucius had first come to the city, his baggage, which had followed him later, was mostly his books. When he had come the second time, with Paulina and Marcus, it had taken a caravan of two carriages and six camels. When Mordra and Branwen had first come to this city, they carried nothing that was their own. Now their caravan comprised three carriages and eleven heavily laden camels. It would take them all of three days to travel the 65 miles to Caesarea. Paulina fretted about their safety on the journey. Her husband reminded her that the zealots were a spent force. He said nothing about hill bandits, but they had never recovered from the slaughter of the uprising almost a year ago. He also knew that Mordra carried a sword, and that he knew how to use it, and that Branwen still had the sicar that she had taken from Judah. Mordra often wondered what had happened to that tormented man. He had heard various rumours; that he had hanged himself, that he had been disembowelled. Both seemed possible, either he had killed himself or one of his one-time friends had taken a curved knife to him.

The caravan paused at the Joppa Gate as the Roman guard cast an obligatory but cursory glance over the stacks of goods. Lucius and Mordra stood together and looked back upon the Holy City of Jerusalem. Neither was sorry to leave. "It will be a relief," said Lucius, "to be able to forget about invisible and unforgiving gods, Holy Laws, zealots, and Messiahs."

Mordra put an arm around his friend's shoulder. "From now on we can enjoy our scholarship, knowing that if we ever hear about this lot again, it will be from far away and have nothing to do with us."

They rejoined their wives in the carriages and, with the day's young sun behind them, rode out of Jerusalem.

At the same time another party was assembling at the Damascus Gate to depart from the other side of the city. Nikolaos and Saul of Tarsus, with four men of the temple guard, were eager to ride towards the ever rising sun. Saul was still breathing murderous threats against the followers of Joshua. He had gone to the Sanhedrin and asked for letters to the synagogues of the cities of the Decapolis, so that if he found any there that had been led astray, whether men or women, he might take them prisoners to Jerusalem.

It was on the morning of the day of the spring equinox that Saul of Tarsus, with the fire of righteousness in his heart, rode out on the road to Damascus.